The Bone Ships

"They are rabble! Nothing! We are Fleet! We are Hundred Isles!" And all around Joron glances were exchanged, small smiles crept on to tanned and scarred faces and her words were repeated, becoming loud and strong as the arrows rained down. He thought her a madwoman, but it seemed Meas's words were true as not one arrow found flesh . . . Women and men around them were shouting now. "We are Fleet! We are Hundred Isles!" Were they all mad, was this what battle did to women and men? Meas straightened, held her sword held aloft as she stared out over the rail. Arrows fell about her, bounced off the deck, stuck in the bonerail, left her untouched.

"Come to me!" she shouted to those on the sea. "Come and die at the hand of Lucky Meas and her crew!"

By RJ Barker

The Bone Ships

RJ Barker

www.orbitbooks.net

ORBIT

First published in Great Britain in 2019 by Orbit

A CIP catalogue record for this book is available from the British Library.

ISBN 978-0-356-51183-2

Typeset in Apollo MT by Palimpsest Book Production Limited,
Falkirk, Stirlingshire
Printed and bound by Clays Ltd, Elcograf S.p.A.

MIX
Paper from
responsible sources
FSC® C104740

Papers used by Orbit are from well-managed
forests and other responsible sources.

Orbit
An imprint of
Little, Brown Book Group
Carmelite House
50 Victoria Embankment
London EC4Y 0DZ

An Hachette UK Company
www.hachette.co.uk

www.orbitbooks.net

Contents

SHIP SHULME

Bernshulme

Keyshanblood Bay

Arkannis Island

Flensechannel

SKEARITH'S SPINE

Two hundred boats of leaf and line,
Five thousand held aboard.
Spear in hand and Cassia rode
Foremost of the horde.

A spray of ships upon the brine
To hunt the beast below.
For Maiden, for Mother to the Hag's embrace
The many now would go.

But oh what feast
And oh what riches
And oh what fame does beckon.
Five hundred ships,
Ten thousand crew
To hunt the arakeesian.

Traditional

1
The Castaway

"**G**ive me your hat."

They are not the sort of words that you expect to start a legend, but they were the first words he ever heard her say.

She said them to him, of course.

It was early. The scent of fish filled his nose and worked its way into his stomach, awakening the burgeoning nausea. His head ached and his hands trembled in a way that would only be stilled by the first cup of shipwine. Then the pain in his mind would fade as the thick liquid slithered down his gullet, warming his throat and guts. After the first cup would come the second, and with that would come the numbness that told him he was on the way to deadening his mind the way his body was dead, or waiting to be. Then there would be a third cup and then a fourth and then a fifth, and the day would be over and he would slip into darkness.

But the black ship in the quiet harbour would still sit at its rope. Its bones would creak as they pulled against the tide. The crew would moan and creak as they drank on its decks, and he would fall into unconsciousness in this old flenser's hut. Here he was, shipwife in name only. Commander in word only. Failure.

Voices from outside, because even here, in the long-abandoned and ghost-haunted flensing yards there was no real escape from others. Not even the memory of Keyshan's Rot, the disease of the boneyards, could keep people from cutting through.

"The *Shattered Stone* came in this morran, said they saw an archeyex over Sleightholme. Said their windtalker fell mad and it nearly wrecked 'em. Had to kill the creature to stop it bringing a wind to throw 'em across a lee shore."

"Aren't been an archeyex seen for nigh on my lifetime. It brings nothing good – paint that on a rock for the Sea Hag." And the voices faded, lost in the hiss of the waves on the beach, eaten up by the sea as everything was destined to be, while he thought on what they said – "brings nothing good". May as well as say that Skearith's Eye will rise on the morran, for this is the Hundred Isles – when did good things ever happen here?

The next voice he heard was the challenge. Delivered while he kept his eyes closed against the tides of nausea ebbing and flowing in hot, acidic waves from his stomach.

"Give me your hat." A voice thick with the sea, a bird-shriek croak of command. The sort of voice you ran to obey, had you scurrying up the rigging to spread the wings of your ship. Maybe, just maybe, on any other day or after a single cup of shipwine, maybe he would have done what she said and handed over his two-tailed shipwife's hat, which, along with the bright dye in his hair, marked him out as a commander – though an undeserving one.

But in the restless night his sleep had been troubled by thoughts of his father and thoughts of another life, not a better one, not an easier one, but a sober one, one without shame. One in which he did not feel the pull of the Sea Hag's slimy hands trying to drag him down to his end. One of long days at the wing of a flukeboat, singing of the sea and pulling on the ropes as his father glowed with pride at how well his little fisher boy worked the winds. Of long days before his father's strong and powerful body was broken as easily as a thin varisk vine, ground to meat between the side of his boat and the pitiless hull of a boneship. His hand reaching up from black water, a bearded face, mouth open as if to call to his boy in his final agonising second. Such strength, and it had meant nothing.

So maybe he had, for once, woken with the idea of how wonderful it would be to have a little pride. And if there had been a day for him to give up the two-tailed hat of shipwife, then it was not this day.

"No," he said. He had to scrape the words out of his mind, and that was exactly how it felt, like he drew the curve of a curnow blade down the inside of his skull; words falling from his mouth slack as midtide. "I am shipwife of the *Tide Child* and this is my symbol of command." He touched the rim of the black two-tailed cap. "I am shipwife, and you will have to take this hat from me."

How strange it felt to say those words, those fleet words that he knew more from his father's stories of service than from any real experience. They were good words though, strong words with a history, and they felt right in his mouth. If he were to die then they were not bad final words for his father to hear from his place, deep below the sea, standing warm and welcome at the Hag's eternal bonefire.

He squinted at the figure before him. Thoughts fought in his aching head: which one of them had come for him? Since he'd become shipwife he knew a challenge must come. He commanded angry women and men, bad women and men, cruel women and men – and it had only ever been a matter of time before one of his crew wanted the hat and the colours. Was it Barlay who stood in the door hole of the bothy? She was a hard one, violent. But no, too small for her and the silhouette of this figure wore its hair long, not cut to the skull. Kanvey then? He was a man jealous of everything and everyone, and quick with his knife. But no, the silhouette appeared female, undoubtably so. No straight lines to her under the tight fishskin and feather. Cwell then? She would make a move, and she could swim so would have been able to get off the ship.

He levered himself up, feeling the still unfamiliar tug of the curnow at his hip.

"We fight then," said the figure and she turned, walking out into the sun. Her hair worn long, grey and streaked in the colours of command: bright reds and blues. The sun scattered off the fishskin of her clothing, tightly wound about her muscled body and held in place with straps. Hanging from the straps were knives, small crossbows and a twisting shining jingling assortment of good-luck trinkets that spoke of a life-time of service and violence. Around her shoulders hung a precious feathered cloak, and where the fishskin scattered the sunlight the feather cloak hoarded it, twinkling and sparkling, passing motes of light from plume to plume so each and every colour shone and shouted out its hue.

I am going to die, he thought.

She idled away from the slanted bothy he had slept in, away from the small and stinking abandoned dock, and he followed. No one was around. He had chosen this place for its relative solitude, amazed at how easily that could be found; even on an isle as busy as Shipshulme people tended to flock together, to find each other, and of course they shunned such Hag-haunted places as this, where the keyshan's curse still slept.

Along the shingle beach they walked: her striding, looking for a place, and him following like a lost kuwai, one of the flightless birds they bred for meat, looking for a flock to join. Though of course there was no flock for a man like him, only the surety of the death he walked towards.

She stood with her back to him as though he were not worth her attention. She tested the beach beneath her feet, pushing at the shingle with the toes of her high boots, as if searching for something under the stones that may rear up and bite her. He was reminded of himself as a child, checking the sand for jullwyrms before playing alone with a group of imaginary friends. Ever the outsider. Ach, he should have known it would come to this.

When she turned, he recognised her, knew her. Not socially, not through any action he had fought as he had fought none. But he knew her face – the pointed nose, the sharp cheekbones, the weathered skin, the black patterns drawn around her eyes and the scintillating golds and greens on her cheeks that marked her as someone of note. He recognised her, had seen her walking before prisoners. Seen her walking before children won from raids on the Gaunt Islands, children to be made ready for the Thirteenbern's priest's thirsty blades, children to be sent to the Hag or to ride the bones of a ship as corpselights – merry colours that told of the ship's health. Seen her standing on the prow of her ship, *Arakeesian Dread*, named for the sea dragons that provided the bones for the ships and had once been cut apart on the warm beach below them. Named for the sea dragons that no longer came. Named for the sea dragons that were sinking into myth the way a body would eventually sink to the sea floor.

But oh that ship!

He'd seen that too.

Last of the great five-ribbers he was, *Arakeesian Dread*. Eighteen bright corpselights dancing above him, a huge long-beaked arakeesian skull as long as a two-ribber crowned his prow, blank eyeholes staring out, his beak covered in metal to use as a ram. Twenty huge gallowbows on each side of the maindeck and many more standard bows below in the under-deck. A crew of over four hundred that polished and shone every bone that made his frame, so he was blinding white against the sea.

He'd seen her training her crew, and he'd seen her fight. At a dock, over a matter of honour when someone mentioned the circumstances of her birth. It was not a long fight, and when asked for mercy, well, she showed none, and he did not think it was in her for she was Hundred Isles and fleet to the core. Cruel and hard.

What light there was in the sky darkened as if Skearith the godbird closed its eye to his fate, the fierce heat of the air fleeing as did that small amount of hope that had been in his breast – that single fluttering possibility that he could survive. He was about to fight Meas Gilbryn, "Lucky" Meas, the most decorated, the bravest, the fiercest shipwife the Hundred Isles had ever seen.

He was going to die.

But why would Lucky Meas want his hat? Even as he prepared himself for death he could not stop his mind working. She could have any command she wanted. The only reason she would want his would be if . . .

And that was unthinkable.

Impossible.

Meas Gilbryn condemned to the black ships? Condemned to die? Sooner see an island get up and walk than that happen.

Had she been sent to kill him?

Maybe. There were those to whom his continued living was an insult. Maybe they had become bored with waiting?

"What is your name?" She croaked the words, like something hungry for carrion.

He tried to speak, found his mouth dry and not merely from last night's drink. Fear. Though he had walked with it as a companion for six months it made it no less palatable.

He swallowed, licked his lips. "My name is Joron. Joron Twiner."

"Don't know it," she said, dismissive, uninterested. "Not seen it written in the rolls of honour, not heard it in any reports of action."

"I never served before I was sent to the black ships," he said. She drew her straightsword. "I was a fisher once." Did he see a flash in her eyes, and if he did what could it mean? Annoyance, boredom?

"And?" she said, taking a practice swing with her heavy blade, contemptuous of him, barely even watching him. "How does a fisher get condemned to a ship of the dead? Never mind become a shipwife." Another practice slash at the innocent air before her.

"I killed a man."

She stared at him.

"In combat," he added, and he had to swallow again, forcing a hard ball of cold-stone fear down his neck.

"So you can fight." Her blade came up to ready. Light flashed down its length. Something was inscribed on it, no cheap slag-iron curnow like his own.

"He was drunk and I was lucky," he said.

"Well, Joron Twiner, I am neither, despite my name," she said, eyes grey and cold. "Let's get this over with, ey?"

He drew his curnow and went straight into a lunge. No warning, no niceties. He was not a fool and he was not soft. You did not live long in the Hundred Isles if you were soft. His only chance of beating Lucky Meas lay in surprising her. His blade leaped out, a single straight thrust for the gut. A simple, concise move he had practised so many times in his life — for every woman and man of the Hundred Isles dreams of being in the fleet and using his sword to protect the islands' children. It was a perfect move he made, untouched by his exhaustion and unsullied by a body palsied with lack of drink.

She knocked his blade aside with a a small movement of her wrist, and the weighted end of the curving curnow blade dragged his sword outward, past her side. He stumbled forward, suddenly off balance. Her free hand came round, and he caught the shine of a stone ring on her knuckles, knew she wore a rockfist in the moment before it made contact with his temple.

He was on the ground. Looking up into the canopy of the wide and bright blue sky wondering where the clouds had gone. Waiting for the thrust that would finish him.

Her sword tip appeared in his line of sight.

Touched the skin of his forehead.

Raked a painful line up to his hair and pushed the hat from his head and she used the tip of her sword to flick his hat into the air and caught it, putting it on. She did not smile, showed no sense of triumph, only stared at him while the blood ran down his face and he waited for the end.

"Never lunge with a curnow, Joron Twiner," she said quietly. "Did they teach you nothing? You slash with it. It is all it is fit for."

"What poor final words for me," he said. "To die with another's advice in my ear." Did something cross her face at that, some deeply buried remembrance of what it was to laugh? Or did she simply pity him?

"Why did they make you shipwife?" she said. "You plain did not win rank in a fight."

"I—" he began.

"There are two types of ship of the dead." She leaned forward, the tip of her sword dancing before his face. "There is the type the crew run, with a weak shipwife who lets them drink themselves to death at the staystone. And there is the type a strong shipwife runs that raises his wings for trouble and lets his women and men die well." He could not take his eyes from the tip of the blade, Lucky Meas a blur behind the weapon. "It seems to me the *Tide Child* has been the first, but now you will lead me to him and he will try what it is to be the second."

Joron opened his mouth to tell her she was wrong about him and his ship, but he did not, because she was not.

"Get up, Joron Twiner," she said. "You'll not die today on this hot and long-blooded shingle. You'll live to spend your blood in service to the Hundred Isles along with every other on that ship. Now come, we have work to do." She turned, sheathing her sword, as sure he would do as she asked as she was Skearith's Eye would rise in the morning and set at night.

The shingle moved beneath him as he rose, and something stirred within him. Anger at this woman who had taken his command from him. Who had called him weak and treated him with such contempt. She was just like every other who was lucky enough to be born whole of body and of the strong.

Sure of their place, blessed by the Sea Hag, the Maiden and the Mother and ready to trample any other before them to get what they wanted. The criminal crew of *Tide Child*, he understood them at least. They were rough, fierce and had lived with no choice but to watch out for themselves. But her and her kind? They trampled others for joy.

She had taken his hat of command from him, and though he had never wanted it before, it had suddenly come to mean something. Her theft had awoken something in him.

He intended to get it back.

The tide it ran for miles,
Left ship and crew a-dry.
Don't sacrifice the babe,
The sea put out the cry.
But the hagpriests didn't listen,
Said, "The babe must surely die."

Anon., "The Song of Lucky Meas"

2

Child of a Pitiless Sea

From the hill above Keyshanblood Bay Joron could see his ship – *her* ship – *Tide Child*. The ship lay held by the staystone and, as befitting a ship of the dead, his bones had been painted black and no corpselights danced above him. His wings, which had been clumsily furled atop the wingspines jutting from the grey slate of the decks, were also black. Every inch of the ship should have been black, but the ship's crew and his shipwife – *and he* – had been slack in their care and it looked as if a gentle rain of ash had fallen over the ship, dotting him with specks of white where the bone showed through. His prow was the slanted and the smooth hipbones of a small arakeesian, a long-dead sea dragon, angled to cut through the water. At the waterline the beak of the keyshan skull poked out from the hipbones, and curving back from it were the ribs, four long bones that ran the length of the ship and helped him slide through the water. Above the ribs were the bones of the ship that made his sides, and these were sharp and serrated, a riot of odd angles and spiked bone meant to repel borders, the shearing edges and prongs making him hard to climb.

Tide Child's colour showed he was a last-chance ship, the

crew condemned to death. The only chance anyone had for a return to life was through some heroic act, something so undeniably great that the acclaim of the people would see their crimes expunged and their life restored to them. Such hope made desperate deckchilder, and desperate deckchilder were fierce. Though if any forgiveness had ever been offered to the dead it had not been in Joron's lifetime, nor in his father's lifetime before him.

He should have been a terror, cutting his way through the seas of the Scattered Archipelago, but instead of roaring through the grey seas *Tide Child* sat at the staystone, weed waving lazily around him from where it had grown on the slip bones of his underside, the water about the black ship greasy with human filth: sewage, rotting food and the other hundreds of bits of flotsam a ship constantly generated. Across the spars of the wingspines sat skeers, lean white birds no more than dots from this distance, but he knew their red eyes and razored bills, always hungry.

"Mark of a lax ship," whispered Meas from beside him.

"What?"

"The skeers. If a deckchild falls asleep they'll have out an eye or a tongue – seen it more than once. Should have someone with a sling out there. Mind you, you don't have to see the birds to know that ship's not loved as it should be; you can smell it."

He sniffed at the air. Even up here on the hill he could smell his ship, like a fish dock at the slack of Skearith's Eye when the heat burned down from above and there was no shadow, no shelter, no release.

"*Tide Child*," he said.

"A weak name," she replied and strode off, vanishing into the foliage which grew strong and thick away from the old flensing yard. Her dark body disappeared among the riot of bright purple gion leaves, thick spreading fans providing respite from the slowly climbing eye of Skearith. Twined around them was bright pink varisk, vines as thick and strong as a woman's thighs, leaves almost as big as the gion, fighting it for the light.

Resentment was his companion through the forest, not just because she made him struggle through the foliage, rather than taking the longer, clearer path kept by the villagers. It was also for the ship, for his command. In the six months since he had been condemned the ship had filled his life; thoughts of riding it to glory or escaping it completely had trapped him in a current of indecision. The ship may not have been much, but it had been his, and when she insulted it she insulted him. *Hag's curse on you, Lucky Meas.* He had no doubt she would turn out to be anything but lucky for him, for the ship or for those aboard, though in truth he cared far less about them, keyshans take them. He stumbled after her, mouth dry, body aching for the gourd at his hip, shaking for it, but the one time he paused to unlimber it and take a drink she had stopped and turned.

"We'll find water in the gion forest," she said, "or we'll tap a varisk stalk. My officers aren't soaks."

Her officers? What did she mean by that? And he added another item to a growing list of resentments in his head.

The huge gion and varisk plants were at their height now; any paths there may have been through this part of the forest had been quickly overgrown by bright creepers, and their sickly colours made his head ache even more. The plants fell easily to his curnow and a creeping sense of claustrophobia grew within him, a feeling of being trapped that joined the crew of his discomforts as he felt the path behind them close up, overtaken by the relentless growth of vines and stalk and leaf. The forest birds raised a cacophony at the clack of blade on stalk, some calling warnings, some singing out threats, and his knuckles whitened on the hilt of his swinging blade. This was the time of year when most were lost to firash, the giant birds darting out in ambush, opening guts with their claws and dragging their dying prey away to eat alive. He wondered if Lucky Meas would fall to one. But no, somewhere inside he knew Lucky Meas was not destined to die in a forest at the claws of a great bird.

Joron was so lost in his thoughts he barely heard Meas when next she spoke.

"Is your crew on board?"

He stumbled over a thick root pulsing with blue sap.

"All except the windtalker."

She stopped, turned and stared at him. "Black ships do not have windtalkers."

"Ours does, but the crew won't have it aboard when the ship is still – say it's bad luck."

She looked at him as if wanting more, but he could not think why – surely everyone knew this? Just the thought of the gullaime made his flesh creep over and above the shaking and nausea wracking him for want of drink.

"Where is it then?"

"Where?"

"I'll not ask again. Are you so cracked in the head by drink that you cannot answer a simple question?"

He could not meet her eye.

"On the bell buoy off the bay entrance. We cast it there."

"And the last time it touched land? The last time it was brought to a windspire?"

"I . . ." His head refused to clear; the world swam before him in a thousand bright colours that twisted like his aching guts.

"Northstorm's whispered curses, man, have the drink you long for and pray to the Sea Hag it brings you sense if not sobriety. I'll ask the windtalker myself when it comes on board." And she turned away, stalking through the bright forest. He brought the flask to his mouth, taking a gulp of the thick soupy alcohol. Something hidden by the gion and varisk around him screamed out its last moment as nature played out the endless game of prey and predator.

The nearer they came to the beach the stronger the smell of the ship became. He had never noticed it on his return before, never thought about it, but today it was nauseating. It was not the smell of death that drifted across the bay from the black ship, but the stink of life – carefree, chaotic and unconcerned. They had found this quiet bay where orders were unlikely to reach them a month ago and tied up the ship. The fisher village in the bay wanted nothing to do with the crew so Joron had felt it safe to leave. The very few among *Tide Child*'s crew who could swim were not enough to be a threat to the hard women and men there. His tumbledown bothy was far enough away that the deformed land hid the ship from him, and he wondered what it said about him that he had chosen somewhere where he could not even see his command?

Nothing good.

The flukeboat lay where he had left it, askew on the pale pink beach. The sand looked attractive, relaxing, but each grain was a lie as it was a beach of trussick shells. Most were smashed but in among them were plenty of whole ones that would shatter under a foot and cut the sole open, so as they walked over the beach he had to pick his way carefully forward while Meas, booted Lucky Meas, strode confidently on.

The flukeboat resembled a cocoon. Built from gion leaves which had been dried and treated until they became soft and pliable like birdleather, then wrapped around a skeleton of fire-hardened varisk stalks and the whole thing baked in the sun until it was bone hard. Flukeboats were brown to start with, until their owners painted them in lurid colours: symbols of the Sea Hag, Maiden or Mother, eyes of the storms or the whispers of the four winds. This flukeboat was little more than a rowboat, big enough for ten but light enough for one to row if they must. Flukeboats ranged as large as to hold twenty and sometimes thirty and more crew, with large gion leaves, dried and treated to act as wings, catching the wind above and powering the boats through the sea.

Vessels for the foolishly brave, most said, as they were brittle, not like the hard-hulled boneships. A flukeboat could be wrecked by one good gallowbow shot. But Joron knew they had advantages too, those brittle boats; he had grown up helping his father on one, just the two of them against the sea in a boat bright blue and named the *Sighing East*, for the storm that loved a deckchild. It had been fast, able to outrun almost anything, even the crisk and the vareen, and when those great beasts of the sea raised their heads looking for prey they had never caught the *Sighing East*. The little boat had run with the wind, salt spray stiffening Joron's hair as he stood in the prow, laughing at the danger, sure in the knowledge his father would steer them safe. He always steered them safe, always found the fish, always protected his singing boy. Until the last day, and then he could not. Sometimes it was hard to believe that had been Joron's life, that just months ago he had been that scarless, careless, laughing boy in the prow of a flukeboat.

How had it come to this?

How had he ended here?

Nineteen years on the sea and condemned to die. The world pulsed, the blue sky darkening at the edges.

He knew these thoughts as offspring of the drink, the melancholy it brought he had only ever been able to drink through, running toward oblivion to escape himself. But he could not drink now. Not in front of her. He would keep going even if just to spite her. If she put him to cleaning filth from the bilges he would do it, biding his time, waiting for his moment.

Meas reached the flukeboat, pulling it upright so the thin keel cut into the sand and she could slide it into the lapping water. No happy colours for this boat; it was unnamed, painted black and given only the one eye on its beak to guide it through the sea. She went to the front, one foot in the hull, one raised on the beak, looking every inch the shipwife. She did not look back, did not speak, did not need to. He knew what was required.

He was crew now.

She stood where he should have, though never had; no

member of *Tide Child*'s crew would ever have rowed him anywhere, would have laughed if he had asked. By the time he had picked his way across the sharp beach the boat had drifted out into the still bay and he had to wade out to it, the salt water stinging a hundred tiny cuts on the bottoms of his feet. He pulled himself, dripping, into the boat, feeling the wetness as humiliation while the growing heat burned the moisture from his clothes. He picked up the two oars and set them in their notches.

"Foolish to leave the boat here," she said.

"Who would steal a boat fit only for the dead?"

"The dead," she said and pointed at *Tide Child*, far ahead of them and thick in the water. The ship was not dipping or moving with the motion of the sea, it looked as steady and immovable as a rock, a rock to wreck a soul upon.

"I brought it to the shore so they could not have it." He said the words, though he wanted to shout at her. Could she really not know the crew would use the boat to run if he left it with them?

"Well, unless they are an uncommon lot, I reckon at least a few of 'em can swim?" She did not look round to see if he acknowledged what she said, did not need to as they both knew she was right. The only reason the boat was still there was probably because the crew of *Tide Child* were so drunk they had not thought it through any more than he had. Again the damp clothes against his skin felt like shame. "And it may have passed your notice" – she pointed at *Tide Child* – "but they already have a ship." He stared at her, feeling like the fool he was. "Row then," she said, impatient, not looking back. "I would see what poor sort of crew a poor man like you is shipwife to."

Warm, damp clothes against his skin.

3

In the Shadow of the Black Ship

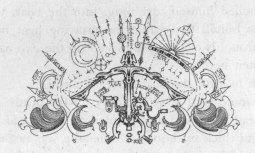

Black water, they called it, that greasy area where the detritus of a ship held the water that little tighter to it, a disturbance that caused a circular calm about the vessel. And this water was black in more than name. The reflected hull of *Tide Child* made rowing into the black water to approach an abyssal hole, like the places where the floor of the sea fell away beneath a ship and a deckchild heard the Sea Hag's call to join her in the depths. One moment Joron rowed through limpid green sea where the pink sand gently shoaled away beneath them, and then they were in the cold shadow of the ship, rowing through darkness towards darkness: life into death.

There were rules in the Hundred Isles navy for a shipwife's approach: calls to be made, horns to be blown, clothes to be worn and salutes to be offered. Lucky Meas – perched on the beak of the flukeboat – received none of this; not even the careless courtesy of a ladder thrown over the ship's side greeted her. And though she said nothing, Joron could feel the affront radiating from every taut muscle of her body. When the flukeboat was within a span of *Tide Child* she leaped from the beak of the boat, the sudden change in weight as she jumped pushing it down into the black water, buoyancy pushing it back up in a fountain of white foam that tried, and failed, to follow Meas Gilbryn up the side of the ship. Where the water fell back, disturbing the bits of food and rotting rubbish, sending them bobbing away from the smooth black ribs of the hull, Meas seemed to defy gravity. She needed no ladder; the ship became her steps, each spike and sharp edge, each piece of the vessel that made him nervous — he knew they existed to take life, to ruin flesh, to end women and men, *to grind them against the hull* — she swung between them, booted feet finding purchase between the blades of the ship, hands knowing instinctively where to grasp without being cut. All this despite never having seen *Tide Child* before, never climbing his sheer sides, never inspecting the hull for rot or learning the curves and undulations of him. It did not matter to her. Joron's father had talked of those who were "born to the sea" and he had never really understood. Not until he saw her.

In a moment she was over the rail and on the deck. Joron heard the thud of boots on the slate as he tied the flukeboat on. Then he heard the thud of a boot meeting a body. He climbed the ship quickly, but so much more carefully than she had. He heard the sound of voices, surprised voices, angry voices, and something in him trembled at it. He knew this crew, this seventy-two that rode *Tide Child*. Some had been there for years, some only for months, and there was not a one he would turn his back on without worrying they would draw a curnow on him, but she was fearless, her shrike-voice barking out.

"Up! Up! I'll have no slate-layers on this ship now. Twiner may have afeared himself of you but I know no such thing. Last woman or man lying on the deck" — a boot against a body — "will feel the bite of the cord." A shout, something indeterminate. "I care nothing that your skins were burned as you slept drunkenly under Skearith's Eye, you deserve those blisters. I'll give you worse if you do not obey."

Joron came over the rail to find the crew — *his* crew — standing around, bewildered, as if they had been caught in the curse of the Southstorm, the sudden squalls that come out of nowhere and wreck ships on the unseen rocks and reefs of the Lairo Islands. And he shared that feeling. She was like a storm, a fury, like the Mother had come among them to wreak her havoc and demand her justice. Meas strode to the rump of the ship, the slightly raised area at the rear where tradition-ally only the officers and the oarturner would stand. As she moved between poorly coiled mounds and tangles of rope and past the huge slack gallowbows – jumping a badly stacked pile of wingshot – she kicked out at those she passed.

"Up, up!" Always shouting. "Off my deck! Off the rump unless you think yourself up to facing me!" A kick, a punch, a whirlwind of noise and fury and bright colours amid the drab, hungover, eyeburned crew of *Tide Child*, who now stood, slack and bleak as their fates, watching this woman who wore the two-tailed hat.

He wondered if any one of them gave a thought to him. If they wondered where he was or even if he lived.

He thought it unlikely, and as he watched, standing by the rail between two great gallowbows, a little blood from a stinging cut on his foot stained the water at his feet. A slowly branching pattern of dark red against the grey slate of the deck.

They had no interest in him, the crew. They had sometimes regarded him with interest when he'd returned to have the purseholder dole out the meagre amount of coin due to him as shipwife. Heads had sometimes turned, cold eyes had some-times followed him as he went below to the shipwife's great cabin.

In the great cabin was his chest, holding what meagre posses-sions he had – even more meagre than when he had come aboard as what money he got was never enough to buy what he needed from the fisher village. Each time he left *Tide Child* he had been worried about that chest, though he could not take it with him as that would be to finally abdicate all authority, to say he had run from the black ship. But when he returned he was almost frightened to approach it, in case he saw the hasp broken, as that would mean that his authority was gone — *what authority?* In the claustrophobic heat of long nights in his decrepit bothy he had dreamed of that moment: the shattered lock, the quick knife to the kidneys and the blood upon the white boneboard in the great cabin. The light finally fading as *Tide Child* claimed its due, passing his weary soul into the hands of the Sea Hag, who waited for all.

But the moment had never come, and each time he had seen that lock still in one piece he had felt sure, somehow, deep inside, that his small authority was intact. Only now, watching the reddened backs of what had been his crew, did he realise how wrong and foolish he had been. Sea chests were sacred to the deckchilder, and to meddle with one was one of many small superstitions, like throwing paint in a dock or on the spinebase, that was never to be broken.

They paid him no mind as he stood and gently bled, but they could not take their eyes from her as she paced back and forth like a caged firash. There was that unmistakable fury to her, something internal, a roaring fire that was not seen, only sensed — sensed through the strict movements of her legs, of her arms, the glare of her eye as she surveyed the state of the deck, kicking at loose bottles and old rope. Her mouth moving as she paced. Rehearsing the words she would cast at the crew? The feathers in her grey and blue and red hair glinting like lightning in a far-off storm.

As she paced he realised that, apart from the few he considered an obvious threat, he had lied to himself about this crew. He did not know them. He did not recognise them from their eyeburned backs. They were not his and never had been. When he looked at them, at the myriad different-coloured skins and shapes of the Hundred Isles, he had no clue what names those skins clothed. Even those whose faces he saw as they emerged, blinking and confused from belowdeck, he could not name as they squinted and wondered about the sudden and tempestuous change in the winds that had blown into their lives. He did not know them at all. Where she invited their gaze upon the stage of the rump, he had avoided it. Where he had quailed and hunched and scurried past disinterested eyes, she demanded they look upon her – and they did. They could do nothing else.

He could do nothing else.

Joron started to count them, gave up and guessed the entire crew must be present. He saw the courser slinking around at the edge of the group in their grubby, patched and holed robe – damn him he should at least know their name. He had known it, what was it? Alerry, Alerrit? Aelerin. That was it, Aelerin. But the courser was one of the othered, and made him uncomfortable; they were neither woman nor man and he regarded them with the same sort of superstitious dread that came upon him when he thought about the gullaime, the windtalker, stranded far out on the bell buoy.

"You stink," said Meas quietly. "You hear that? You stink and it shames you. From the lowest fisher in a flukeboat to the crew of the mighty *Arakeesian Dread*, the sailors of the Hundred Isles are clean. We're no raiders. No Gaunt Islanders to wallow in our own filth and fly ships that can be smelled before they breach the horizon. We have pride." Her eyes pricked at the crowd, making feet shuffle, heads bow. "And yet, you stink."

"Who are you to tell us this?" The speaker was hidden in the crowd, but at least that was a voice he knew. Old Briaret. The woman was as taut as rope and had been condemned in youth. Hardly knowing any other life than *Tide Child*, so she knew little of the world outside it. Only to her could the identity of the woman on the rump be a mystery.

"They call me Lucky Meas."

"Not that lucky then," said Briaret, "if you're sent here to join the dead."

Meas seemed to grow, to straighten, as if what should be shame was a mark of pride.

"I am Meas Gilbryn. I broke the Gaunt Islands fleet at Keelhulme Sounding. I took the four-ribber *Bern's Woe* with only a handful of flukeboats. I am firstborn of Thirteenbern Gilbryn, who leads us all."

He heard the whisper at that, like the hiss of wave on shingle – "Firstborn cursed born, firstborn cursed born . . ." – and so did she.

"I hold no curse for I am chosen of the sea and it washed me ashore as a babe when raiders wrecked around me. I hear the whispers of all storms, North, South, East and West, and I am favoured by the goddess of the young, the goddess of the people and the dark goddess of the depths. Maiden, Mother and Hag listen when I talk." She stopped then, royal, regal, ruler of the ship, and she dared any to say otherwise. When she spoke next she sent her words into a stillness as profound and full as any becalming. "You will find, and I believe, that the Hag sends me where I am needed." She looked around the ship – at the filth, at the resentful faces and lastly at him, at Joron Twiner. "And Hag knows I am needed here. Sorely needed."

There was a moment then when Joron waited for the challenge. He felt like someone should turn the glass at the rump so the sand could pour and time could be seen to pass, but none did and no challenge came. He picked out the ones most likely: Barlay, a woman as huge as any and flanked by two of her cronies; Cwell leaning on a rail, looking alone as always, and as thin, lithe and dangerous as any longthresh, but she had her followers too; then there was Kanvey, surrounded by his boys, standing on the other side, and it was him that Joron feared most, for he was a predatory man and more than once he had found Kanvey's eye travelling up the curve of his calf, and the man's open lust scared him. But for now they were stilled, shocked by the onslaught of Lucky Meas's contempt.

"Clean this deck," she said, "coil the ropes, stack the shot and tie down the gallowbows. Get *Tide Child* ready to fly and fight, for that is what we will be doing, make no mistake about it. And I know you are a rough lot, so when the time comes" – her eyes roved around, settled on Kanvey, settled on Cwel, settled on Barlay — "that you feel the need to test me. Then do it like deckchilder, do it to my face." She rested her hand on the hilt of her sword. "Because the Bern sought to give me to the ships as a light when I was a babe, even after the sea returned me. And in the ceremony the Mother came upon them, and she said I would not die then as sacrifice and I would not die in treachery, you hear? She said I'd die fighting. So unless you question the will of the Maiden or the Mother or the Hag, you'll pull your blade to my face, ey?" Again her roving eye, her fierce, bird-of-prey features waiting for a reply that never came. Only silence faced her. "Well, to it then! Move!" And they did, and inside Joron something twisted, and he learned — in a moment of shock and revelation — how much he desired what she had, that easy command, the way she barely seemed to feel the weight of the two-tailed hat on her head. "Twiner" — she spat on the deck — "come with me to the great cabin."

"No." This from Barlay. The woman stepped forward, flakes of skin had caught in the blue dye of her short hair. Her cheeks pale as ice and her eyes almost hidden within the round of her face. From a pocket in her deck trews she took out a crumpled black object and held it up. "Order us to clean the ship . . . well, you wear the two tails and few are more worthy, so it is your right. But you'll not take that" — she pointed at Joron — "to the great cabin like he is your second." She unfolded a black rag, the onetail, the hat of the deckkeeper, second in command on the deck of a boneship, and she placed it on her head. It barely fitted, just perched on the crown looking ridiculous, and only waiting for a stiff wind to snatch it away. "He wants my place, he must take it."

A shiver of fear down him, like cold sea making its way inside a heavy stinker coat, freezing him all the way to his bones.

"I want your place," said Meas, stepping down from the rump, "and I want it for him for my own reasons and I do not need to share them." A circle began to grow about the two women. "So I will take the hat from you, for my own reasons and I do not need to share them either." Barlay's hand went to the curnow at her side and Meas shook her head. "No no, my lass. A strong girl like yourself has no need of a sword. I am a slip of a thing and sure you could squeeze the life from me without too much trouble, ey?"

Barlay eyed her, suspicious but unable to disagree, and she nodded.

"But think this, lass. You won that hat through strength, ey? But your accent says you are from Glenhulme, where they breed for strength and naught else. So, lass, how are your numbers, ey?" Meas crouched by the rumpspine, dipped her hand for luck into the pot of red paint at the bottom, finding it almost dry. Then she spattered what paint she found on the deck to join the lines and dots already there and stood, touching her fingers to her face, leaving red dots on her cheeks and stepping forward. "How is your hand for holding a quill and taking my notes, ey?" Meas stepped forward again and what Joron saw seemed impossible: Barlay – huge, frightening Barlay – took a step back. It was as if each of Meas's words was a lash of the whip.

"Strength is what is needed for a ship, naught else," said Barlay. Now she stepped forward, pulled herself up so she towered over Meas.

The shipwife did not waver.

"How do you calculate the quickest course between islands, ey lass? How do you understand the courser's notes? How do you steer when you cannot see Skearith's Eye? How do you read the map and know the reefs? How close can you travel to Skearith's Spine without losing the wind?" Each word a fist that battered Barlay back once more, but Joron could feel the woman's building anger the same way he felt a storm on his skin, could see it in the red of her face, usually as pale as his was dark. "How do you—"

Barlay moved, running forward with a scream of rage, great meaty fists swinging. Meas ducked, sidestepped and kicked out, sending the bigger woman sprawling on the deck. From there she was on her, straddling her back, using her slight weight to twist a massive arm back and push it against the joint until Barlay was silenced, her anger reduced to grunts of agony. Meas leaned over, her hiss loud enough for all to hear. "I see in you, Barlay, a strength I will sore need at the steering oar, you hear? I see a place by me on the rump, you hear? But I do not see you wearing that hat, ey?"

"Hag take you!" screeched Barlay. "Hag take you, Meas Gilbryn! You take the storm-cursed hat then."

And Meas did. Picking it from where it had fallen on the deck and standing, walking away without looking back as if she were not worried that the bigger woman might attack again.

As she passed him she threw him the hat.

"The great cabin, Joron, and be quick, or" – Meas pointed at the hat, limp in his hand – "she may want that back."

4

To Find a Place to Fit

He followed Lucky Meas down the steep stairs, through the hatch and steadying himself on the rail – one hand for the ship one hand for himself. As the deck blocked the sun he descended to darkness. The bowpeeks on the side of *Tide Child* were tied open, but they let in little light and did little to cool the ship. The heat down here was of a different set: more oppressive, more solid. It had substance. Where the heat above was dry and stark, this was moist and enveloping; it sucked you in, stole your breath.

The smell of confined humans was almost unbearable.

They were forced to walk bent over, heads bowed to avoid the overbones, staring at the deck below, stripes of light from the bowpeeks showing the scuffed and variegated floor – black to grey to white to grey to black – where the crew had run and scratched and pulled objects over it. These were the stripes of his shame as much as any scars left on a deckchilder's back by the cord, showing how he had neglected *Tide Child*, and every step he took, past poorly stowed hammocks and through the stink of rubbish, made him feel smaller. Somewhere, water had got in and been left to pool – when had he last worked the pumps? – and started the arakeesian bones of the ship rotting. That smell was always there, always somewhere on a ship, but now, too late, he realised it was too strong; the not-quite-unbearable stink of rotting bone filled the underdeck, a greasy grey stink to rotting flesh's purple stench.

In the great cabin sat his chest.

He wondered, once again, if the lock would still be in place.

Meas opened the door. It creaked. One of the panes of glass in the door was broken, a serrated crack running across it, prints from greasy hands around it. Meas paused for a moment, running a long slender finger along the crack. When she took her hand away there was a smear of blood left on the glass, like a promise of violence.

The great cabin was *Tide Child* in negative, the only place on the ship that had been left bone-white. The boneboards of the floor, cut from the wide bones of what must have been an enormous arakeesian, were scuffed and smudged with dirt. Still, the whiteness of the place was shocking – the intent of course, meant to dazzle any crew entering the domain of the shipwife. Meas strode across it, manifestly undazzled. The desk of cured varisk and gion and the chair that married it had been pushed to the side, away from the windows at the rear which let light stream in. She grabbed the desk, pulled it so it sat in front of the windows, gave it small shoves and pushes until it found its place – a rut that it had worn into the bone over the many years of its existence until it had become comfortable there. An imperceptible place on the deck where it had always sat and a place she knew would be there, had not even had to think about being there. This was her world, it was what she knew, what she was.

When she sat behind the desk she took a moment, looked around. Stopped. Became still. A breeze from somewhere pushed a strand of coloured hair across her face, set a feather a-twisting and charms a-tinkling on her tight deep-blue uniform jacket.

The silence oppressed him, forced him to speak because she

clearly had no need to, not yet. As he opened his mouth he realised he stood at attention, not at ease, not slouching. The tautening of his muscles had crept upon him as quietly as a sea fret creeps up on the land.

"Why?" he said.

"Why?" She let it hang. It was not a question she asked of him, maybe it was a question she asked of herself because she did not yet fully understand her reasons. "Why?" she said again. Above, the stamp of feet, the growl and hiss of brushes pushing water across the deck, the thump of objects being stowed and the shouts of women and men up and down the rigging of *Tide Child*'s spines and wings.

"Why give me this?" He held out the crumpled one-tailed hat. "Why fight to give it to me?"

"A shipwife needs to show a crew she is strong, and it gave me the opportunity to do that. It will cow them, for a while, ey?" She nodded to herself, ran her hands across the desk, stretching her arms out to either side. "And I did not lie, either. I need my second to understand numbers, so tell me I have not chosen badly, Joron Twiner. You know numbers, right? And you read?"

He nodded.

"How did you know?"

"Joron Twiner is a fisher's name, so I presume you are a fisher's son?"

He nodded.

"I have never met a fisher who did not plan for their child to be more, though the Sea Hag knows our world may be a better one with more fishers and less fighters." She mumbled that last, running her hands over the desk, along the cured leaves which had been bound to it to create a flat writing surface, and back in front of her. She looked up. "Where are your charts?"

A shock upon him, a paralysis that made him long to take a pull at the flask on his hip, for the charts lay in the hands of the pilot who had guided his ship here, into Keyshanblood

Bay. He had traded them for knowledge and coin, spending the money on drink and food to take to the tumbledown bothy that had let him hide from his fate.

Hide. A joke of course. The Hag sees all and never forgets.

"Charts? I . . ." He had no answer, no honourable way to finish the sentence.

"Sold 'em for drink, ey?" He started to make an excuse, expecting condemnation as she stood. "Listen to me, Joron Twiner." She stepped around the desk and towards him, keeping her voice low. "A ship is a world, you understand? And this ship is mine now, my world, my rules. My word here is law to all who fly with us. What happened before *Tide Child* felt the weight of my heels on the deck? Well, that is between you and the Hag and I care nothing for it. We will deal with it as we have to." She stared up at the overbones, listening to the rasp of brushes on the slate deck. "Hear that? We make the decks clean so we may begin our work, and I have much work for us to do. So truth is what I need at this moment, for I have a purpose and little time to get about it." He waited a moment, expecting some trick from this sudden gentleness, but she said nothing, leaving only space in the air for his words.

"There are no charts."

"Very well. We will pick some up when we return to Bernshulme, together with supplies and wages for the crew to send to their families, if they have them. For now, go to the hold, make sure we have at least four days' food and water in, and send me the courser and tell them to bring charcoal. We shall write our charts upon the deck in here, and you shall check the numbers for me."

"But the courser is—"

"Very likely better at that than both of us, ey, but I do not know that, not yet. Until I do you and I shall also check what they say. You understand?" He nodded. "Be gone now, Joron Twiner." He turned but as he reached the door she spoke again. "I forget, one other thing." His fingers twitched for want of the door handle in them, to be out of this place, to be out of her presence.

"Yes?"

"You address me as Shipwife, Deckkeeper." The hardness back.

"Yes, Shipwife."

"Before they condemned you, Joron Twiner, how long did you say had you been in the Hundred Isles fleet?"

"I had not, Shipwife."

"Not even for a day?"

"No. Shipwife, not even for a day."

He could almost hear her confusion, her wondering what strange circumstance had led to him being here, shipwife of a black ship at nineteen years old, and not lain in the sea with his veins open, hoping he bled out before the creatures of the deep found him. But she did not ask, and when she said no more he took his leave, out of the light of the great cabin and into the darkness of the underdeck. All along the deck glowed wanelights, the skulls of kively birds filled with skyfish oil, which let out a dim light, glowing through bone.

Shipwife, deckkeeper, deckholder, courser and windtalker, all had their own cabins next to each other in the rear of the ship, though he had only ever seen the inside of the great cabin. The courser and the windtalker made him uneasy in different ways and he found it best to avoid them, and the deckkeeper's cabin had belonged to Barlay, who frightened him with her size and potential for violence. He knocked on the courser's door, then silently cursed himself to the Northstorm for it. A deckkeeper had no need to knock; he was the shipwife's hand and could go where he wanted.

"Enter." Their voice soft. He entered, finding the courser sitting on their bed, dirty white robes pooled around them and the cabin filled with a sweet-smelling incense that failed to keep the general stink of the ship at bay.

"The shipwife wishes to see you in her cabin," he said. Joron could not see their face under the hood of their robe.

He wondered at the sudden curiosity that filled him, the desire to pull the hood back and find out whether they appeared male or female. Would he even be able to tell? But he did nothing, only stood, staring ahead like a new recruit desperate to avoid the eyes of an officer.

"Me?" said the courser. "But I have no charts." Was there an edge there? Blame? There should be, but he found the courser's soft voice as impossible to read as the strange whirling sigils and signs drawn on the walls of their cabin that talked of the great storms that ringed the world.

"The shipwife says bring charcoal and draw on the floor."

"Well," said the courser, "if the shipwife wants, I shall obey." The courser levered themselves off the bed and carefully put out the incense burner – fire was always a worry. Bone may not burn easily but the glue used to fuse boneships together was flammable. The slight figure brushed past Joron, and he wondered what someone so unassuming could possibly have done to have found themselves among the condemned. He touched the birdfoot he kept strung around his neck, taking a little solace from the rough scales and sharp talons while whispering a few syllables to the Sea Hag, in hope of redemption when he stood in front of the bonepyre deep below the water.

He left the cabin and closed the door. On the way down into the belly of the ship he passed Cwell, as small as the courser but far more dangerous. She watched him with bright eyes from under her mop of stringy grey hair.

"You made a mistake, letting Meas on board, boy," she said. "We'll not have a moment's peace now with her on deck, mark my words. You wait, a knife'll find her despite what she says, and then it may find you."

"I am deckkeeper." He meant the words to have authority but made made them sound like a guilty secret, or an apology.

"Aye, so you seem to think." She pushed herself up on the stairs so her body was against the ceiling, like an insect, and he could pass under her. Though he did not look up he could feel her eyes burning through him as he made his way into the hold to check the supplies.

The smell of rotting bone was stronger here. *Tide Child* needed the attention of the bonewrights, but half the ships in the fleet did and a ship of the dead would always be at the back of the queue. *Tide Child* was no white and shining main-ship, corpselights burning proud above him.

Behind the smell of rotting bone was the smell of human urine; no doubt some had relieved themselves here in drunken stupors. He tried not to think about what his bare feet were treading on, wading through, concentrating instead on counting the water pots, huge and square, checking the beads on them to see their levels. Enough water for a few days, but not much more. Less food, but fish could always be fought for their flesh if they were desperate. Any decent-sized ship attracted beakwyrm, and one of them would feed a crew, though they took some killing – and killed in turn if given the chance. Further on were pots of hagspit, distilled and mixed with powders by the bonemasters, a viscous oil that could be launched in the wingbolts. It burned hot enough to melt bone and flesh and could not be put out by water. They did not have much of it, but he did not imagine they would need it. Besides, he did not trust the crew not to spill it. That would be more dangerous to *Tide Child* than any enemy so he dragged two of the huge water pots over to hide the hagspit vats. Satisfied with this, he decided that what they had here would do for them, and he was glad, because he had no doubt that they would be getting under way quickly. Meas had a shine in her eye, a purpose, and he wondered how he could tell her that if it was fighting she was after it was too soon. That if she intended action she did not have the crew for it. They were cliquey, little groups all holding their own resent-ments close, and if they were expected to work the gallowbows, well, had they ever worked the gallowbows ?

But would she listen to him? He doubted it.

5

Those Who Stand Upon the Deck

He made his way back to the great cabin through a ship full of unfamiliar industry.

With every squeak of mop on slate, rumbling of barrel across bone or voice singing out in rhythmic song as its owner pulled on a rope or turned a wheel, his resentment grew. How could she make this happen and he could not? Was it simply true that, Berncast as he was, shameful child of a weak mother, he had no authority? His mother had died in childbirth, like many women did. And though Joron was one of the lucky few, to be born without blemish or missing limb, the blood flowing from her broken body had proved his mother's line weak. Any opportunity for her son to advance and join the ranks of the Kept among the Hundred Isles powerful fled with her life.

Meas though? She was born to the most prolific of the island's leaders. Her mother had survived thirteen births and now ruled the Hundred Isles with all the hagfavour that gave her. Was it that strong blood that gave Meas some inherent power over others that he would always lack? Or was it simply that she had been brought up in the huge bothies of the fleet? Trained among the spiral stones, the vine-wrapped domes which reached up for the skies, their rounded bases covered in myriad bright paints, splashed upon the rocks to beg the favours of the Sea Hag, Mother or Maiden? Fisher boys with dead mothers never got invited to the spiral bothies; they signed on, at best to furl the wings and climb the rigging, to pull ropes and spin gallowbow wheels – and to die of course. They signed on to die. If they were very lucky they made purseholder or wingmaster or oarturner before they died, but they would never tread the rump of the ship without invite, for that was for those children of the Hag-favoured, the Bern and the Kept.

Yet he was here. And it seemed he would still be here and he would still wear the hat of a commander, though he could not for the life of him work out why. He could not be the only one aboard who knew numbers, he was sure of that.

Did he want to know why?

The desk in the great cabin had been pushed out of its comfortable rut and back against the wall. The white floor was marred with scrawled black lines and symbols that Joron knew well, though it took a moment for him to realise from where, so out of place were they. For that moment of wondering Meas ignored him, lost in the lines on the floor as the courser muttered to themselves and scrawled more symbols, added a long line with the burned end of a stick, finishing it with a flourish just as the familiarity slotted home in Joron's mind like a boneboard into a joint.

It was a chart, unfamiliar because it was so big – it covered the entire cabin floor – and because it was not on birdskin and because it was inaccurate: bays and inlets he knew well were shown as smooth spaces and many coastlines of the Hundred Isles had been allowed to peter out, plainly because they were not on the course they were to take. The symbols and numbers the courser was jotting down twisted in his head, painting another line, one that twisted across the bones of the floor but only in the eye of his mind: the route Lucky Meas intended to take *Tide Child* on, sailing through the Archipelago, between isles and through channels until it terminated at Corfynhulme, a day and a half's sailing away – if the Eaststorm was kind.

"Baffinly Channel was blocked in a landslide." Joron said it without thinking because he knew it, had heard it said in some tavern on the mainland where life was still and did not constantly rock. The courser's burned twig stopped in its track across the white floor; they raised their hidden head to Meas and the Shipwife nodded, flicked her fingers in an irritated, affirmative motion. The courser went back to their calculations, carefully rubbing out a portion, recalculating the way and adding, he estimated, another four hours to the trip.

"How sings the wind?" said Meas.

Joron did not answer, unsure whether she addressed him or the courser for a moment.

"The air is still in the bay; the storms neither bless nor curse us here," said the courser, voice not far above a whisper. "I see the clouds clip east on the horizon where the sun don't burn 'em off, Shipwife. I hear no song of great storms. I hear only the melody of kind winds."

Meas nodded.

"Ey, the ship don't rock enough for it to be anything else. Joron, put out the flukeboat and get us towed out to the bell to pick up the gullaime. It can take us the rest of the way out till we find wind enough to fill the wings."

"But it—" he began.

She had no intention of letting him finish.

"Obey orders, don't make excuses." Said without thinking, and giving him no recourse to argument. His hand touched the hilt of his curnow. She smiled, or at least her cold lips hinted at it, and that was enough for his hand to leave the hilt, and for him to turn and leave to carry out her demands on the warm light of the deck.

"I need," he began, barely raising his voice above speaking, and the words remained unheard by the deckchilder, all busy on the slate. Cough. Regroup. Start again. "I need volunteers!"

he shouted. None turned; all were suddenly busier with whatever tasks they had found themselves. "I said . . ." he shouted again. Now some turned, work slowing, unfriendly eyes focusing on him.

Barlay put down the shot she held with one hand, shot he would have struggled to hold with two, and came to him. "Twiner," she said. "Why is she here?"

"I need a group to—"

"I said, why is she here, Twiner?" Barlay's voice was full of threat, like the moment a spear sinks into a longthresh and all know the flukes of its tail are now certain to breach the water in murderous fury, but not who will die in the beast's wrath, or on its teeth.

He opened his mouth to answer her. At the same moment she took a step back and bowed her head as if in respect. For him?

No. Of course not.

He turned, knowing what he would see, must see, her: Meas, standing at the hatch.

"Barlay," she said, snaking out from the underdeck, "I am glad to see such enthusiasm from you." Barlay nodded as if that was exactly what she had been feeling, and Meas approached, pulling on one of the fishskin tethers that held her crossbows to her coat. "Pick seven you trust and take our flukeboat to the fishing village." She held out a piece of parchment. "Commandeer another boat, one big enough to take some strain, small enough to stow on deck if we need to, and with a wing if there is such a one."

"They won't like it, Shipwife," said Barlay, still looking at the deck.

"That is why I send a woman the size of you," said Meas, nodding at the parchment. "This letter promises that Bernshulme will give them the price of what we take, and as it is now the growing time they should have no trouble replacing their boat." Joron wondered if she knew she lied, that even the simplest flukeboat took at least a month to make, and a month off the water was likely to leave a fisher family starving. He wondered if she cared. "Well," said Meas, "get on then." She turned, and a deckchild scurrying past stopped in his tracks, unable to meet her eye. "You," she said, "get a catapult and start knocking the skeers off the wings of the ship. Kill a few and the rest will think twice before coming back." The man nodded and scurried off once more. "Joron, return to my cabin," she said. Her voice promised nothing good.

His heart fell to rest in his stomach, spreading a tide of sea-cold blood through his system as the skeers took off in a cloud of noise, protesting the great and mortal insult done to one of their number by a stone launched from a spinning cord.

From the light to the dark he followed her. The smell of the underdeck would not let him forget he lived among the dead, but in the bright cabin with the chart floor the light was better, even if the atmosphere was not. Meas ignored him, dragging her desk back into its rut and sitting behind it. On the desk was the onetail hat of the deckkeeper. Black material, folded up around a rounded crown, at the rear the material falling in a plaited rope to dangle down the wearer's back.

"You do not ask for volunteers," she said. "You are an officer of the fleet. You tell the deckchilder what to do and if they do not do it they are punished." He opened his mouth but she gave him no leave to talk. "And I doubt not that you think you have no authority over them for you do not, not really, and never have had, and that is your fault and no other's. But that time has passed, for now you hold my authority. So speak with it, Joron Twiner, and if I must crack a few heads for them to understand that you being weak does not mean that I am weak then I will do it. Do you understand?"

He nodded.

"Why?" That single syllable again, leaking from his mouth like water seeps into the bilges. Weak, she was right to recognise him as that.

"Because you know numbers," she said.

"As do others." These words snapped out, his confusion

forgotten in annoyance, emotions warring inside him. Who
was she to treat him this way? Who was he to let himself be
treated so? That almost-smile crossed her face again. She stood,
came around the desk and stood in front of him. Smaller than
he was, but more comfortable in her skin than he would ever
be, a fierce predator before prey.

"That crew chose you as shipwife, Joron Twiner, not just
because they believe you weak — and that is a hard course you
have set that you must, in time, find your own route through
— but because you have no loyalty to any other and you gave
no clique an advantage. I have seen such decisions before."
Her tone was almost jovial, and he relaxed, if only a little.
Then, as if remembering herself, who she was, what she was,
where she was, the storm came upon her and she picked up
the deckkeeper's hat from the desk and took a step closer to
him. "They do not respect you, but no one owns you and you
owe no one. They have played you like a fish on a line, Joron
Twiner, but I have made you deckkeeper so you owe me now,
you hear?" She lifted the hat, showed it to him and then placed
it on his head. "You owe me, not them. I chose to let you live,
and you owe me. You belong to Lucky Meas, and you'll learn
to work a ship and those aboard or they'll scrag you one night
and your sentence is then earned and carried out, Sea Hag
have you. But I own you now, you hear?" He nodded. "I own
you. Speak it."

He did not want to but saw no way out.

"You own me."

She stared into his face, examining the lines and ridges,
staring into his eyes as if searching for something.

"I hoped there was a little fight in you, but maybe not.
Now check these numbers on the floor. The courser seemed to
know their way, but I would have the numbers checked again."
And she turned away, sitting at the desk and taking a small
book from her pocket, leafing through it and staring at each
page as if it held all the world's secrets. And maybe it did.

Joron wondered what they were.

With the numbers checked he returned to the deck as Barlay brought in the boats. The new one she had crewed with her people, and they rowed it hard, wing hanging loosely from the spine, towing their own boat behind.

"Get up front," he shouted, then pointed to the two deck-childer nearest to him and spoke with Meas's voice. "You and you, up to the beak, tie on the boats and then put together enough childer to pull the oars of them both." They sneered at him and skulked away, but did as he asked and for a moment he felt almost like he was a real officer on a real ship. Past those he ordered, Cwell stood on the deck, looking at him. A pyramid of wingshot had collapsed and spilled across the deck, the nearest shot by his feet, and it was all he could do not to kneel and start to stack it again, stack it correctly as his father had taught him to do. But he could not do that, because that was not an officer's job. When he glanced around there was no one near enough to call on to do it except Cwell, who stared so balefully at him. He turned away, starting to stoop as Lucky Meas appeared on deck, striding towards the rump and barely sparing him a glance, caught as he was between kneeling and standing. Though he had no doubt she noticed, no doubt at all.

6

Onwards, Ever Onwards

The beak of a ship was always reaching for the future. The curling spines of bone along the rail and above the ribs of the ship pointed forward. Below the rail the skull of the long-dead arakeesian, eyeholes filled with green sea glass and boneglue, stared sightlessly forward. Below the eyes the beak, clad in metal, built to ram its way into other ships and through the waves, to cut a curling path of spray and foam, pointed out the ship's course.

Today it barely moved. Weed waved lazily around the beak of *Tide Child*, and fish, skin scintillating with light, darted in and out of the safety of the plants, vanishing into the depths in a sparkling cloud as noisy women and men ran ropes through the hipbones of the prow and back to the flukeboats – one old, one newly acquired.

Joron knew towing the ship out of the bay should be a simple operation, and yet it was not. Voices were raised; no one quite knew what was expected of them, and when Joron intervened he was met with sneers by those who listened and the deaf ears of those who did not. And though there was plenty of noise and industry at the beak of *Tide Child*, the job remained undone, and the disapproval of Meas at the rump of the ship began to loom over him like stormclouds at the rim of the world. But eventually, as the eye beat on his back and when it felt like the storm must break over him, the job was suddenly over, messily, untidily and in the least fleet-like way possible, the flukeboats were attached to *Tide Child*, and the women and men of the crew were scurrying back to them along the ropes like insects returning to a nest. He wondered at the casual bravery they showed. Few of *Tide Child*'s crew, including him, could swim, and to fall into the sea? He heard his father's voice – *In't water is only death, boy*. Knew it for true. If it wasn't the choking death of drowning then it was to be met with tooth or stinger or tentacle from the denizens of the water, creatures that brooked no trespass in their medium, for they hated anything of the land as much as they seemed to hate each other. *Nothing as fierce as the seas, son.*

Around him, as women and men worked, he tried to find his voice, to give orders, but it felt like drowning. *I am out of my depth*. For a moment he considered taking the short walk, not far to go, only three, maybe four steps, and the vicious sea would swallow him up; his sentence would be served and the Sea Hag sated.

That feeling did not last long.

He did not, had never, have it in him to take his own life.

He was Hundred Isles born and bred, and they did not raise you to give up in the Hundred Isles, for life was hard on the rock and sand. They bred you to see the world through a veil of anger and vengeance, and it was this stubborn sullen anger that had kept the war with the Gaunt Islanders going for so many generations – so many ships lost, souls lost, territory lost and regained, the causes of the war and number of years it had raged long lost to anything but night tales for children: *They take our healthy men, they murder for joy, they eat our childer, especially those like you, that will not sleep*. Behind him he heard Meas's voice: "Row! Row or I'll take a finger from each of you!" The voice of the Bern, the casual threat of cruelty. No, he would not take the sea walk. The anger in him had a target, though he did not know if he would ever get the chance to loose at it.

"Row!" he shouted, adding his voice to hers. "Row hard or the Sea Hag'll have you." But the women and men in the flukeboats were not rowing, not yet, though he let himself believe they hurried a little in settling themselves down on the benches, in taking the strain and readying themselves.

He hoped they would not show him up; knew they would.

The oars, when they moved, did not move in unison, some barely even scratched the water, and he saw a man – *What was his name? He did not know.* – fall backwards when his oar did not meet the expected resistance. Barlay slapped the man with a meaty hand, moving among the small crew, shouting at them in a way he felt only jealousy for. She knew each and every one. Of course she did; they were chosen from her clique, loyal to her.

Meas appeared by his side, roaring at the other boat. "Look, fools! Look at them! Are you stonebound?" She pointed over the rail. "Will you let Barlay's crew out row ye?" A man in the smaller boat – one-eyed, a hand missing two fingers – stood and started to shout at those in his boat, forcing them into rhythm with harsh barks. "Who is he?" asked Meas.

"I do not know," Joron said.

"You should." She walked away. "You two," she said to two women crouched on the deck, "I'll have no slatelayers on my ship. Raise the staystone. We'll have our ship in the true sea soon enough but not with the stone a-laying. So raise the staystone stone and sing me a song!"

Women and men rushed to the central windlass, a huge wheel made from a slice of vertebra. At first it did not move and it was as if *Tide Child* fought them. As if he had become comfortable here, away from the threat of war. Joron wondered if he had left the ship here too long, if weed and floorcakers had cemented the giant round stone to the seabed.

As women and men strained a song started.

Bring the babe a-world.
Push, hey a-push hey!
Bring it out in blood.
Push, hey a-push hey!
Bring the babe a-world.
Push, hey a-push hey!
Be Bern girl and be good.
Push, hey a-push hey!

And as more and more of the crew put their weight and voice to it the windlass began to move. Joron felt the song in his throat, remembered the old joy of a tune but could not sing, not as an officer, and not since he had lost his father. The bone creaked against the slate of the deck. Joron felt the ship list slightly to landward as the weight of the staystone moved from the sea floor to the ship. Bone complained, moaned, shuddered, and then he felt it, felt the same thing as everyone aboard, and he knew it because the air filled with excitement. In some almost imperceptible way it felt as if the ship beneath his feet woke from a deathlike slumber, as though he came alive.

"Stone comes up!" came the cry from the rump of the ship. Deckchilder guided the great stone into place against the side of the hull and bound it there. Then feet beat the deck as women and men ran for the great central spines, climbing the ropes and ladders, moving across the spars to put themselves among the ship's wings, ready for the wind. Ready for flight across the sea.

At the beak the rowers rowed hard, but though the ship quivered he did not move, not yet. It was as if the rowers fought against a great current and their muscles and sweat challenged the heavy dead bones of *Tide Child*. Then, with a sigh of water along his sides, the ship moved, gave in to the pull of the oars, and a shout went up. Even Joron, sullen, resentful Joron, felt some degree of satisfaction in this small victory of intelligence and muscle over inert matter and cruel water. At the rump Meas took the great oar that would steer

Tide Child, and from the beak Joron shouted direction to the rowers as they pulled the great ship towards the bellcage that tolled mournfully at the entrance to the bay.

The cage was a set of twisted metal arches built around a floating platform to protect the bell within, and on it he could see the silhouette of *Tide Child*'s final crew member, the gullaime windtalker. A shudder passed through him. There was nothing anyone in their right mind wanted to do with a gullaime, but in turn there was so much they needed. The creature could, to a degree, control the thing most important to any deckchild – the wind.

It sat atop the bell cage, stick-like body hunched over so its alien form was hidden beneath the ragged robes falling about the cage. The clothes, despite their length, were far too thin to muffle the sound of clapper against bell as the buoy rocked on the waves where the currents of the sea met the still waters of the bay. The gullaime crouched, unmoving, unreal in its lack of movement, but that same lack of movement pulled the eye towards it, made it impossible to ignore. The cage moved but the windtalker did not so much as rock, making it seem to hover above its perch. The closer *Tide Child* came to the creature, the more of it he could make out: the filth of its once-white robes, the bright colours of the leaf mask that covered the pits where its eyes had once been, the sharp and predatory curve of its beak. Underneath the robes was an inhuman body, three-toed feet with sharp claws, puckered pink skin tented against brittle bones and punctuated by the white quills of broken feathers. He did not know why the gullaime lost their feathers, only that they did, and he guessed it was due to the filth they chose to live in. The source of all lice and biting creatures on any ship was the windtalker, as any deckchild knew.

The creature's head moved, a short and sharp movement almost too quick to follow. One moment the head was almost hidden, hunched up in the hollow between its shoulders, the next it was focused on the ship, on Joron, as if by thinking of it he had called its attention upon him. Each oar stroke brought them closer, and its unseeing gaze never wavered. The eyes painted on its mask, meant to represent Skearith the Stormbird, god of all creation, never left him, and he felt them as an accusation: *You put me here. You left me on this thing. You gave no comfort.*

It was true, though he told himself he did it to protect the creature, that if he had not removed it from the ship the crew would have tormented it.

No, he had removed the creature from the ship for the same reason he did so many things, because he was scared. The crew mostly took the gullaime for granted, ignoring it completely as if it did not exist. But Joron was not Fleet and had only seem them from afar, in the pens of the lamyard or being led to their ships. A ship the size of *Tide Child* would usually have more than one of the windmages, and he thanked the Sea Hag for the small mercy that it did not. The thought of them talking to each other in their high-pitched, whistling language, of having to hear that eerie and strangely beautiful chorus of communication made his skin itch.

Tide Child slowed, not at his order, simply because those rowing knew where they headed. The great ship came to a halt within an arm's reach of the bell cage. The gullaime inverted its head, twisting it round all the way on its flexible neck, keeping its painted eyes on him all the time. Then, upside down, it opened its filthy yellow beak and screeched at him, showing the serrated teeth and tongue within that marked it as a predator. Its annoyance made known, the creature leaped from the bell cage — from still to movement without warning — and crashed into the side of the ship. The robes around it spread; the claws on the elbows of the naked wings beneath gripped bone, the beak doing the same, and the powerful hind legs found purchase on spine and blade. From there it clambered up the side of the ship, moving strangely, inhumanely, before finding the hatch that led into its underdeck quarters and slithering through into the pit it called a home.

"What do they call it?"

"What?" He turned to find Meas at his elbow again. She moved through the ship as if it were part of her already, as if *Tide Child* conspired to keep her movements secret from him.

"The windtalker, what do they call it? Crews always name them even if the creatures will not name themselves."

"It has no name, Shipwife. They did not name it. They do not like it."

"Never met a crew that did like them, Skearith's beasts frighten any sensible woman or man, but to control it you must have named it."

"I have never controlled it." The words made him feel like a fool, and from her expression she thought the same.

"Never, why?"

"It will not come, will not help. Will not even speak to me, Shipwife."

She nodded as if a question had been answered.

"I thought it unusual a black ship had a windtalker, but if it will not help maybe that explains it. Anyway, it will speak to me." She leaned over the rail to shout for'ard at the fluke-boats. "Barlay, row us out of the bay, and call me when we have enough wind to let loose the wings."

"Will, Shipwife," she called back.

Meas turned to Joron."You, come with me. We will explain to our gullaime its duties."

"It will not talk to you. It will not . . ." He was filled with a strange panic at the thought of going near the windtalker. The beast was unnatural. Important, yes. Needed, yes. But that did nothing to make him comfortable with it. "It will talk to no one," he said.

She turned away, and he felt himself drawn in her wake, as if she were north and he a compass needle. "It will talk to me, Deckkeeper Twiner, it will talk to me."

Compelled, he followed her into the underdeck.

The great cabin sat directly beneath the rump of the ship, four times as big as any other. To the seaward sat the deck-keeper's cabin, still to become his, and next to that the courser's cabin. On the landward was the deckholder's cabin, though the ship had no one to fill the position of third in command, and then the nest of the windtalker. It was a place that seldom saw visitors, for most deckchilder were just as superstitious and scared of the gullaime as Joron. The beasts were governed by many rules, as were the interactions of those who must deal with them: never remove the mask, never pronounce it free and never kill a gullaime on pain of your own death – unless the ship itself is about to founder. The gullaime were creatures of the Mother, born of the last egg of Skearith the Stormbird, who created all things, and this made them precious, made them creatures who must be protected. The fact that the gullaime controlled the winds, well that was rarely talked of; instead all things to do with the gullaime were done in the name of their safety and in the name of Skearith and the Mother.

"Gullaime," said Meas, pushing the door open before she finished the word, "I enter in the name of your safety and in honour of the Mother and Skearith the Stormbird, who—" The crash of shattering glass sent Meas staggering back.

After the glass came the screeching voice of the gullaime.

"Out! Out! Not your place! Not your place!" The door slammed shut, and Meas stood, shocked, almost as if she was unable to understand that anything may defy a shipwife on her ship. Behind the door something heavy moved, then something else clumped and glumped across the deck. Then, after much squawking and crashing and smashing, there was quiet.

"This is not how gullaime act," Meas shouted through the door. Her hands held at her side clenching as if kneading some unseen oar handle.

"This one does," said Joron.

"And you let it?" She put a hand on the handle of the door. "It is here to serve the will of the Mother and Skearith, and that is done through the shipwife." She pushed against the door, it refused to move. Something else smashed against it. Around them, crew gathered at the noise.

"Away go! Away go!" screamed from inside.

"It will not come out," said Joron. "It has never come out."

The look Meas gave him would have withered a vine. She turned to the nearest deckchild.

"Bring axes," she said. "We will break the door down if we have to." The woman stood unmoving, staring at Meas. "Bring axes or feel the cord!" she shouted, and the woman ran to obey, vanishing down the underdeck towards the armoury.

"They will not break the door down," Joron said, and saw the words she was about to say, *maybe not for you*, forming in her mind before she realised it was not the case. Of course they would not break the door down. Deckchilder were the most superstitious of all women and men; they would not intrude upon the gullaime's nest. As Meas thought, her mouth moving slightly, the woman returned with an axe. The deck-child made no move towards the cabin door, only holding out the axe towards Meas while the shipwife weighed up the damage this could do to her. What was worse? To let the windtalker defy her or to go against the geas and smash down the door of its nest? The shipwife took the axe, hefted it, getting a feel for it, and then stopped, considered the bone of the door and dropped the axe on the black-painted floor.

"Let the creature have its space. We will have to hope the storms bless us with good winds, and when we return to Bernshulme we will maybe find ourselves a gullaime better able to understand what the Mother and the Stormbird wish of it. This one will go to wherever those of its kind without use are sent." She raised her voice, "You hear, beast?" She banged on the door. "You hear that?" She turned away, striding towards the ladder that led up to the slate and the rump of the ship, where she could stand and fume.

But Joron found himself silently thanking the windtalker, for it had shown him Meas Gilbryn was not unassailable after all, shown him that she could be beaten. And he tucked away this fact like a child tucks a hopeful feather against their heart when their parents go to sea.

He was a ship of blood
And fifty beakwyrms chased him.
His crew were not withstood
And fifty beakwyrms chased him.
The Sea Hag well rewarded
And fifty beakwyrms chased him,
Lost women and men aboard.

Aboard ho! Aboard!
Bows to shore and sea.
Riches ho! Aboard!
Bows to shore and sea.
Aboard ho! Aboard!
Bows to shore and sea.
And all the beakwyrms chasing.

Traditional winding song

7

Bone of Old Gods

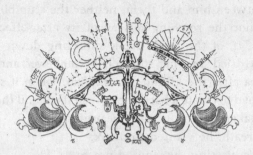

As they left the bay the Eaststorm gifted them a whisper, and the crew of *Tide Child* jumped into action. Women and men scaled the rope ladders of the ship's spines and let loose the wings; others stowed and made secure the oars and sails of the flukeboats, and stacked and tied them safely in the centre of the deck. Water laughed along the sides of the ship and curled away from its smooth bones in a white line of froth and bubbles to slowly fade behind them. It should have amazed Joron that this crew of the broken and the bad could pull together efficiently enough to fly the ship across the sea, but it did not. He had seen them do this before, seen them when he first took command, if that had ever been the word for his place among them.

These were the people of the Scattered Archipelago. Hundred Islander or Gaunt Islander, all in these waters flew their ships across the sea; it was a part of them as much as breathing or walking or fighting.

And yet . . .

And yet did he sense something more? Was there a difference here? Did Barlay at the steering oar hold herself a little taller than usual? Did Kanvey watch the men he gathered around himself with a little more pride and a little less lust than was usual? Did Cwell watch the crew around her with more suspicion and resentment than was usual? Were the eyes she turned to him crueller than they had been before Meas came aboard?

Or was it simply that he watched the crew this day without alcohol between him and them, neither the stumbling fuzz of drinking nor the retching misery of its after-effects. At the thought of it, of the thick drink slithering down his throat, his mouth dried and his stomach became wet and noisome, like the sea after the killing of a skyfish, when it seemed the water wished to create a barrier between itself and the creatures who had taken one of its most beautiful lives.

Hag's breath, he wanted to drink.

Maiden's blessing, he wanted not to.

He felt a need to pace the deck but was afraid of the way the crew would look at him as he moved among them. Afraid that what he would see in their eyes was not what he was starting to see in their eyes when they looked at her. Not respect, not yet, and it was not fear, not that yet either. But there was some worth they found in her that they knew was lacking in him.

So he stayed where he was, by the for'ard gallowbow, and made a show of examining the weapon.

Tide Child carried four great gallowbows to seaward and four to landward on the maindeck as well as ten smaller bows a side on the underdeck. There were four in a gallowbow crew if you included the bowsell, who was there to aim and give orders, but in reality it only took three to loose the great bows or the lesser ones below. One to loose and two to spin the winch that pulled back the launching cord between the outspread bone arms and to load the bow with the huge bolts that could smash through the sides of a ship as easily as they smashed through a body, or the stone bolas designed to cut rigging – or the most feared of the gallowbows weapons, wingbolts: giant carved stones, thick in the middle and tapering out into wings. He had heard stories that a skilled shipwife and windtalker could keep one aloft over a distance further than a person could run in a day, though Joron did not believe it. But he knew the wreckage a well-aimed wingbolt could cause, especially when the centre was filled with hagspit oil. As a child he had suffered nightmares of burning to death, locked in the hold of a ship as it melted in the fierce heat of bonefire, and only his father's strong arms had ever been able to banish that fear. *An arm reaching from the bloodied sea.*

A good crew could loose two shots from a gallowbow in under a minute – spinning, loading, aiming, firing – but Joron had no idea how quickly his crew could loose. A shipwife was meant to exercise the bows once a week at least, but Joron had never dared to ask his crew to untruss them. Never dared to begin the rituals of practice in case no one followed his lead. So whether this crew were as adept with the bows as they were at getting the ship under way he had no idea. He suspected that they had no great skill. He did not know what Meas expected of them, but even if she expected very little, he felt she was sure to be disappointed.

He should tell her. He did not know where they headed, but from her urgency it must be to action. She stood at the rump of the ship, staring forward past the spines, past the huge billowing wings of the ship that scooped up the air and dragged *Tide Child* through the water, past the sharp beak of the ship and into the distance, beyond the islands that dotted the sea around them.

But what end did she see that he did not?

She spoke, said something he could not hear as it was torn away by the breeze, and behind her Barlay leaned into the steering oar. Above Joron the weave of the wings creaked and cracked as more of the Eaststorm's whisper was gathered into them. He felt a pang. Jealousy?

No.

Annoyance that Barlay was where he should be, on the rump, and that she still had the blues of command painted on her scalp, although he wore the one-tailed hat. Had Meas told her to keep them, just to make sure he was aware of how precarious his position was? Or had the colours simply not run from her skin and hair yet?

"Beakwyrms, Shipwife!" The call came from the front – male – but he did not see who called. Five or six crew were leaning over the for'ard rail.

He did not know their names.

"Good," shouted Meas from the rump. There was a merry breeze now, trying to catch her voice and tumble it away, but it fought a losing battle. That hoarse cry had fought against the worst the Northstorm had to give. "We have some speed then. If I thought Deckkeeper Twiner could find it, I would ask him to throw the rock and see how fast we move." Laughter around the ship, and he felt himself colour like it was his first laying night. "Twiner, count the beakwyrms for me. Let me know how dangerous they think my ship is." He could feel the approval of the crew at this nod to the Sea Hag's ways as he made his way to the beak. Those on the rail did not move for him, and knowing Meas watched he grabbed the smallest body and hauled them away so he could lean over.

Vertigo.

The sudden reeling feeling that the ship and the sea stayed still while he rushed forward. Panic clawed at him, for forward was into the sea and, if lucky, to be crushed by the beak of the ship. If unlucky, to be food for the wyrms below.

"Numbers, Deckkeeper Twiner!"

Was it a trick, to be sent forward? He expected to feel sudden hard hands, gnarled and rutted with years of hauling on ropes, grab his feet and push him up and over. It did not happen, and the rail was sturdy in his too-tight grip, his knuckles bone-white against dark skin.

"We count five, D'keeper." This from a girl, young but terribly scarred, half her face smashed by something or someone, skin tight with old burns, the flesh around one eye drooping as she tried to smile at him.

"Only cos you can't count no higher, Farys," said another

deckchild. Laughter, but he clung to that unexpected bit of friendliness as tightly as he clung to the rail.

"You shut your trap, Hilan," she said.

"Five is it?" said Joron. "Then let us count twice for it pays well to double-check all a ship's numbers." He'd heard his father say that, and from the way Farys and the old man behind her nodded it was clearly something they approved of.

"Ey," said the old man, Hilan, as weathered and scarred as Farys but by time not violence. One ear was missing, a deformity that marked him as Berncast, his bloodline weak and he as a man who could never rise in the Hundred Isles. "Sea Hag's arms open for them as don't double-check every knot and number, and all know that to be true." Again that little murmur of agreement, but behind them one of Cwell's clique caught Joron's eye and spat over the side of the ship. Joron turned away from her.

The sea was full of ugly creatures but beakwyrms were famously among the worst. They looked like the intestine of a kively when it was cut from the bird to make sausage: pink, glistening and shot through with blood. The creatures surfed the waves of foam that the boneships kicked up. Each was as thick as a big woman or man and about ten or fifteen paces long, not as big as he had seen but big enough. The wyrms ended bluntly, like fingers, and they had no eyes or nose or any way Joron could see for them to sense the world around them, but Hag knew they had teeth. When attacking, the whole end of a beakwyrm would draw back and reveal it was little more than mouth, row upon row of serrated teeth right back into the darkness of its throat, teeth that could chew through flesh and bone and so noisy to work few. Iridescent frills spiralled around the wyrms' sickly pallid-pink flesh, propelling them forward in a twisting, shimmering dance through water and wave before the ship. They spun around one another as if they were lovers dancing.

"Five wyrms, Shipwife," he shouted. "We trail five wyrms at the beak."

"Five," she said, and she made no attempt to hide her disappointment, though it was five more than had ridden with them when Joron brought *Tide Child* up to Keyshanblood Bay. "Five only, ey? Well, the wyrms are drawn to blood, so you can be sure we'll ride many more when we make our way back to Bernshulme." She nodded, but to herself, and though she spoke out loud he did not get the feeling she addressed the crew.

He had heard of deckchilder cheering the thought of action loudly and long as if they wished for nothing more than to put their bodies in harm's way in the name of the Hundred Isles, but on *Tide Child* her words were met with sullen silence. Meas turned away from them, leaving Joron feeling as if he had disappointed her somehow, and angry with himself that somewhere, deep within, it bothered him.

Later, as Skearith's Eye started to dip beneath the far islands and *Tide Child* made his way through the greying sea, Joron went to the deckkeeper's — his — cabin. It had a bed, thin, barely wide enough for him to fit his body on, and he was by no means a well-built man, but Joron had grown up on a fisher boat sleeping in a hammock. He was accustomed to the way the hammock moved with the ship and communicated the sea to him. In a bed he was haunted by nightmares of stone, of land that shook beneath him and cracked and broke, swallowing him up, dragging him down to be entombed in the dark earth, whereas in the hammock he dreamed of soaring above the sea like a bird. So, in a cabin still full of Barlay's possessions, he slung his hammock and tried to sleep.

He woke at the night bell to take his turn at the watch. Out the squeaking door of his cabin, head slightly bowed to avoid the overbones. Wanelights glowed, skyfish oil burning slowly and meekly within kivelly skulls. Most of the crew slept, and the air was thick with the bitter scent of sweat and bodies. Hammocks rocked and Joron moved between them, careful not to knock into any sleeper and wake their wrath.

No sign of Meas on deck; barely anyone there at all. A figure at the steering oar that he did not recognise and a few others cast about the deck like stones for fortune telling. He said nothing to them, only took his place on the rump of the ship, his bare feet cold against the slate. The breeze ruffled his hair, bringing a curse to his lips. He had left his hat in the cabin. What was worse, to stay where he was or to go back to his cabin through the dark ship? He did not know, remained there unmoving and undecided, appearing steady when he was anything but. The thick tangles of his tightly curled hair caught the wind, the sweat on his scalp gifting him some relief from the night's heat.

Against the black of night Skearith's Bones shone above, the final blessing of the vast bird that had created the land for them to live on when she needed a place to lay her eggs. Though Hassith the spear thrower had killed her with Myulverd, the spear made by his sither, she had given them her bones as a final gift, to light the night. Even when her Blind Eye closed and vanished from the night sky, her bones remained, tiny dots of bright white, smudges of colour smeared across the black like giftpaint on a doorway. Skearith's Bones changed with the season, revolving through their thirteen forms, but Skearith's Gift, the three brightest stars that made up the point of her beak, always pointed directly at the Northstorm. Though the rest of her bones moved with the coming of the cold days, the gift always pointed the way for a deckchild, and Joron found himself talking to Skearith. As a people they rarely prayed to the storm bird – through guilt for Hassith's wrong? Possibly. They gave their prayers to the more apparent goddesses, the ones that felt more real and present, the ones that inhabited the world around them: the Sea Hag, cold and cruel; the Maiden, capricious and full of curiosity; and the Mother, who welcomed all in need of succour but was strict and unforgiving to those who disobeyed her. But this night, as they quietly cut through a calm ocean on the whisper of the Eaststorm, he found himself silently asking Skearith, "Show me the way, Stormbird, show me the way."

But, of course, Skearith was long dead and no answer was forthcoming.

"Where is your hat?" Meas, out of nowhere, like the Sea Hag come to claim her due.

"In my cabin, it is a fine night, and I—"

"I care not for what the night it is; you wear the hat rain or shine, heat or cold. It is who you are. I will fix you up boots too, from Hoppity Lane when we return to Bernshulme. A barefoot deckkeeper, whoever heard of such a thing?" He did not answer, and did not think she wanted an answer. "Haime," she said, and he felt the man at the oar stiffen at his name, "steer us a mite more seaward. We approach Frana's Isle and though no one lives on it there are a fair few hidden reefs around it."

".Where are we going, Shipwife?" said Joron.

She glanced at him, her face all angles and points, grey and unhealthy-looking in the pale light of Skearith's Blind Eye, a creature of shadows. Only the gleam of her eyes gave a clue to how fierce and alive she was.

"North," she said. "We go north, ever north, and as for what we do there, well, I will tell you with the rest on the morran. For now, Joron Twiner, go get your hat."

8

To Put Together on a Menday

Skearith's Eye was barely above the horizon, a bloodshot smear seeping into the morning's clouds, when Meas gathered her crew before the rump of *Tide Child*. It was Menday, when traditionally the people of the Archipelago rested from work, although that rest generally took the form of fixing ropes, darning clothes, checking hulls and spines for damage.

Joron was faintly surprised to find that it was Menday – he had lost track of the days and never regained it – and that familiar cycle: Madenday, Toilday, Mareday, Clensday, Hagsday, Menday, had been denied him ever since. He had felt that to ask such a simple question as "What day is it?" would have been to admit just how lost he had become since his condemnation. It had not occurred to him, until this moment, how that lack of order had subtly affected him in other ways. Knowing what day it was again felt like being bound to the sea a little more, as if the deck beneath his feet took on a little more solidity, as if the bones of *Tide Child* somehow pulled themselves a little more watertight, and his position on the chart of his life became a little clearer. He knew what would come next today, knew it from every fleet story he had heard on his father's knee – Meas would read the Bernlaw.

And every Menday, boy, the shipwife reads the Bernlaw so the crew will know their duty. And you will listen and you will obey and one day you may be oarturner or purseholder. Imagine that! The boy I raised on the rump of a fleet ship, ey? Corpselights dancing for joy above your head as you sing and work.

The feel of his father's hand on his head, ruffling his hair. Strong fingers,

Warm hands.

There were seventy-two crew assembled. None slept when the Bernlaw was read and even the ship's pumps were left unattended. There were three missing, two lying in the hagbower below the underdeck where wounds taken in fights on board slowly festered and they could die out of sight, and the gullaime, which still refused to leave its cabin. Them aside, all stood before Meas. Not enough, not really, not a big enough crew for a ship this size; a hundred and fifty was the minimum complement, one hundred and thirty sailors and twenty soldiers. Two hundred to really run the ship. Joron had never thought about it before, how woeful his ship was, how little he had in common with the actual fleet of the Hundred Isles. Maybe he had been the shipwife the ship deserved, but now *Tide Child* had Meas Gilbryn, Lucky Meas, the witch of Keelhulme Sounding. Fierce, gifted, storied Lucky Meas.

What had she done to deserve this?

What had any of them done? Himself apart, he did not know.

He should have known.

"Stand upon the slate, my children." All here but him were of the fleet, and it was as if the ritual of the words was burned into them. Their reaction, the turning to the rump and the woman stood upon it, was involuntary and inescapable. Not one could resist the draw of it, even those who had their own power. Barlay, Cwell and Kanvey were drawn to her. Oh, with distrustful, calculating eyes, and maybe she saw the same calculating gleam in him when she talked, but still they listened, as if they could do nothing else.

She read the Bernlaw in a harsh staccato voice, the list of rules that must be obeyed, and at the end of every line she paused and barked out, "To go against this is punishable by death." And this was met with a solemn nod of the head by every woman and man among them. Even though those deaths were already certain.

"Shall keep themselves in good health. To go against this is punishable by death."

And it did not matter.

"Shall obey those the Bern put above them. To go against this is punishable by death."

And none found humour.

"Shall pay true honour to the Maiden, Mother and Hag. To go against this is punishable by death."

And none made light.

"And woman may lay with woman and man may lay with man, but woman may not lay with man and risk a child aboard ship. To go against this is punishable by death."

In that death was always the intended destination for this crew and this ship.

Only at the very end did Meas's voice waver. At the end of the Bernlaw the last words were always the same: "May the Maiden play no tricks, may the Mother hold us close and may the Hag look away. So says the Bernlaw. So say us all." And the crew repeated the words back.

But aboard *Tide Child* the words were changed to reflect their condemnation, and though Meas read loudly, "May the Maiden play no tricks," her voice quietened at, "may the Mother hold us close," and did she almost falter at the last? Did something almost crack in her voice as she read the words unique to those condemned to a black ship? "And may the Hag welcome and forgive us."

Did it?

He was sure it did, just a little. And if he noticed he knew every other aboard the ship would have too. But the crack was papered over quickly; the weakness did not last, and when she read the final words, "So says the Bernlaw. So say us all!" she was as strong and fierce as ever, glaring at them as they returned the words to her. Then she walked from the rump commanding the first watch to break their fast below and the second to take their places on the ropes and the spines and the deck.

"Clean my slate! For I'll not have it run with filth!" she shouted. "Barlay, what stand you there for?" she bellowed at the huge woman. "Can you not see the oarturner is practically asleep on his feet? Take your place and steer us straight." Barlay nodded and made for the rump. Meas turned as she passed Joron. "Deckkeeper, to my cabin, and I will speak with you of where we go and what is expected. Bring me the masters of your bowteams – I'll know the bowsells afore we fight." She stopped, feeling his hesitation. "You do have bowsells assigned?" He did not, had never given such a thing as much as a thought, but already he felt Meas's wrath and knew her well enough to not chance an answer she did not want to hear. At the same time he did not wish to tell a lie she would easily see through.

"Not full teams, Shipwife," he said, "only two."

She sniffed at him, unimpressed. "And their names?"

Names? He had none to give to her, then, with a rush he realised he did know two names, though nothing of the men in question. He hoped they would serve him well.

"Farys and Hilan."

"Well, Deckkeeper Twiner, let us hope they know their craft. I will pick some others once we have spoken."

He joined her soon enough, after a quick whispered conversation with Hilan and Farys, eyes widening as he told what he had said of them; eyes narrowing, smiles appearing at this little shared subterfuge.

"Shot me a gallowbow aboard the *High Riding Wyrm*, I did," said Hilan. "Never aimed the team but I know enough." He nodded to himself. "Oh I know enough."

"And I loaded on two ships," said Farys, "before . . ." And her voice faded away at the memory of her disfigurement.

"Well, you are my aimers now. Lead your teams and we will

do as best we can for Meas, right?" They nodded. "Stand firm, my crew," he said, and they rewarded him with smiles.

In the great cabin the smiles were gone. Meas sat at her desk, the courser to one side, head bowed, hands behind their back while Meas stared at her book, open on the desk before her. She gave them just long enough for the nerves to build before she spoke.

"So you are Joron's bowsells, ey?" Farys and Hilan nodded, voices stolen by the presence of a woman such as Meas Gilbryn. "Your names?"

"Hilan, Shipwife."

"Farys, Shipwife."

Meas nodded.

"I wanted to see you, to know you before we fight today." A shock went through Joron at that, though he had known it was coming, must be coming. If the same shock went through Hilan or Farys he could not tell. "And we will fight today, so tell your crews to ready themselves. And if you know others who can work a gallowbow then pick two more teams and do it in the deckkeeper's name, right?" They nodded. "Very well. Go to your work."

They bowed their heads and quickly left the cabin, Joron almost feeling their relief at them doing so. Meas let silence fall in the cabin, left him standing there until he cleared his throat.

"You did not say where, or why, we fight," he said.

"You are not of the fleet, Deckkeeper" – she did not look up from her book – "so you will not know that I do not need to. Deckchilder are there to fight, why and where only concerns them if it will affect their tactics. Otherwise I point them, they loose bolts, they stab and kill. That is their place aboard a ship – to do and to die. Especially aboard a ship like this."

"And a deckkeeper's place?" he said. It felt almost a brave thing, to question her. She looked up from her book.

"Well, you must know a little more, so I will tell you where and why. And then point you to loose or stab or kill, and do or die, ey?" He did not speak, had no reply and could not stop a rush of fear, for if he were to loose or stab or kill and do or die, then others would be coming to do the same to him. She sat back in her chair. Raised her hands above her head and stretched out some ache, then shrugged her shoulders and relaxed. "Each year at the hot bonetide the isle of Corfynhulme has a festival of the children. It is a dull thing meant for the stonebound, for farmers and fishers." Did he bristle a little at having his father's profession lumped in with those of the land? "They parade their children around the isle and dance and feast and do the things the stonebound do." She stared at him as if waiting for a challenge and when none came carried on. "It used to be that the festival was raided regularly, not by the Gaunt Islanders – Corfynhulme is too close to Bernshulme for them to risk a ship on that – but by raiders, the dregs of the sea. For nigh on a decade now the festival has been safe, but the Hundred Isles has seen reverses – our fleet has had losses and we do not patrol as often as we once did."

Something went cold in him at that. He had, ever since his youth, taken it for granted that the inner isles were safe – the great fleet kept it so – and to hear that this was no longer the case felt almost like Meas spoke treason. But she did not look shocked or like she imparted some great and terrible secret. If anything, she simply looked tired.

"At the moment the majority of our fleet is drawn south. The Gaunt Islanders have been massing on their side of Skearith's Spine, and the Bern and Kept are sure they plan action of some kind. And, though you may not know it if you have not been paying attention to Skearith's Bones, today is the hot bonetide. The water will rise; Skearith's Eye will burn, and the children of Corfynhulme will walk their island. But it has come to me that they will not be safe this year. Raiders have been growing in strength in the warm seas of the western isles, and they are finally strong enough to attack. Corfynhulme is an easy target. They have no walls, no gallowbows to guard their harbour and few soldiers. From what I hear their barracks are on the point of falling down."

Another shock. Joron's picture of the Hundred Isles came from his father's stories. They were a string of island fortresses, walled and armed against the rapacious appetites of the Gaunt Islanders, a people whose whole culture was that of the raider, a people who had forced the Hundred Isles to become hard. "So Joron, we fly fast, and when those raiders, so brave in the face of the defenceless, turn up they will find themselves facing *Tide Child*."

He wanted to tell her that *Tide Child* was not ready, to expose the lie of his gallowbow teams, to tell her this was foolhardy, but when he spoke those were not the words that fell from his mouth. "I have never been in a battle," he said.

She stood.

"And you may not be today. If we arrive in good time, then it is likely the sight of a fleet ship, even a black one" – she paused, sighed – "especially a black one, will be enough to make them think twice."

"And if we are not in good time?"

"If we arrive after the raid has started we will fight. There is only one way in and out of the harbour bay, so the raiders will have to come through us to leave." She smiled at him but there was little happiness there. "They will be in flukeboats. A few decent gallowbow shots will finish them. It will be no great battle." He should have said it then – that they would be lucky to get even one decent gallowbow shot from *Tide Child*. He did not. "If we arrive too late, Joron Twiner, the raiders will have the children, and they will sell them and get rich. The Gaunt Islanders will buy them and sacrifice our children for corpselights instead of their own, and they will get stronger and the Hundred Isles will get weaker. So it is important we are not late." He nodded. "So rig the ship, make us fly, Joron Twiner. Make *Tide Child* fly, and then sharpen that curnow on your hip." As he turned she spoke again. "If it comes to a fight, Twiner," she said softly, "it is a chaotic thing to fight on a ship. Stay by me and keep your own crew at your back."

"And that is all there is to it?" he said.

She laughed.

"No, that is more complicated than it really is. Kill the enemy and stay alive is the crux of it. That will be the only thought in your mind in your first battle."

"I thought you were a tactician, Shipwife Meas," he said.

She nodded.

"Oh, I am, Deckkeeper, I very much am. But that is because I have seen many battles, too many maybe."

"My father made battles sound like glorious things."

"That is for stories," she said quietly. "We fight in the hope that others will not have to, and we fight to keep those we have come to care about safe. We fight even for those who do not deserve it. There is no honour or greatness in what we do, except among fools. I fight, in the end, because I have no other choice" – she held his gaze with hers – "and neither do you. So remember this, if you hear tales of bravery and greatness, they are nearly always told by people who have only watched battle from afar. Those of us who have suffered through it know such stories as a skin over the horror of what is true. No sane woman or man wishes for war, and those that do never would if they thought it would leave paint on their doorsteps." He was shocked by how bitter she sounded, and what she said cheapened the memory of his father, made something dark rise within him.

"My father fought. And he wanted me to go into the fleet. He was no fool."

"No, I do not say he was. But he was poor, Joron Twiner, and what other route do the poor have to any riches in the Hundred Isles, ey? They fight or they are nothing. Now go. Ready my ship for me." And she returned to her desk, sat and stared at her book, leaving him wondering who she was, this warrior who spoke like she hated war.

Was that why she was here?

He did not know, and he dared not ask.

9

The Breaking of *Tide Child*

The winds treated them kindly if not keenly. *Tide Child* danced across a sea that barely swelled and the beakwyrms twirled and danced before them. Meas Gilbryn paced the rump of the boneship, twice sending Joron with some crew into the hold of the ship to re-stow the supplies in the hope of altering the balance of the black ship and squeezing a little more speed out of him. But no matter how much they sweated and swore as they dragged the stores about in the dark heat of the hold, it seemed to make little difference. The ship had found a speed he was comfortable with, and the deckchilder, though competent, were never quite efficient enough to wring the last drops of speed from the wind.

So Meas paced, and Joron felt like he was somehow letting her down and stewed in his own anger – at her for making him feel this way and at himself for caring about it.

As Skearith's blazing Eye rose to its midpoint, chasing away what little cloud there had been and turning the sea into a hundred thousand mirrored shards, bright enough to hurt the eye, a cry went up from the top of the mainspine.

"Islands rising to landward!"

Half the crew ran to the landward side of the ship, and Joron felt it list as Meas's voice bit through the hot air.

"Back to work! You'll see these isles soon enough! What business is it of yours what is seen by the topboys, ey?" Meas left the rump and hoisted herself up on to the rail, one hand on a rope, the other holding her nearglass to an eye, long grey hair shot through with red and blue streaming behind her as the women and men returned to their work like guilty children. "Calferries Mount. We steer to landward of it, into the channel," she shouted so Barlay at the oar could hear. "From here 'tis no more than eight turns of the sand or so to Corfynhulme." She glanced back. "Deckkeeper, break out curnows and pikes from the armoury and arm every woman and man. Then a tot of anhir for all. Have the gallowbow teams ready! My crew, my crew," she shouted, her eyes wild, "ready yourself, for today we fight," and she punched the air with the hand holding her nearglass. She received a cheer in return, and Joron found himself wondering, *If you hate battle so much, Meas, why do you look so full of joy at the thought of it?*

Barlay leaned into the oar, and Joron felt the ship alter course and had an inkling of what *Tide Child* could be if he had a crew that worked him correctly – something light over the waves, able to dance over the sea and around his enemies. But he was not that, not yet, and might never be. How could he?

The beak of the ship came to point to landward of Calferries Mount, which rose from the sea, its grey spine ringed with green vegetation and surrounded by flocks of skeers, always crying out to the wind with their keening calls. His father had told him that they were the spirits of sailors who had been marooned and starved to death on barren rocks just like Calferries Mount.

Past Calferries, a line of islands, gradually growing in size and clothed in the familiar pinks, blues and purples of gion and varisk, rose out of the sea like broken teeth in a jaw. A wheel of birds turned above the island they headed for, marking it for miles around as a place to find food. Joron wondered if there was more food than usual, if they were too late and it was now a place of carrion strewn with the dead. Part of him, a small part he did not like but could not deny, hoped they were too late; the thought of those who wanted to kill him and having to kill in return filled him with fear like he had never known. But another part, the one raised on the tales and stories of his father, hoped they were in time, thought of how he would be a hero, flying in on a black ship to save the children of Corfynhulme. It was the sort of thing women and men sang about. Certainly the mood on the ship was a good one, and it was not just due to the barrel of anhir that had come up and was being ladled out into waiting cups.

Strangely, Joron found he had no wish to drink.

When the armoury was opened and the weapons brought out, the crew brightened further; it was as if the curnows and shields and spears and gaffhooks brought not only the ability to take life but also some sense of worth to the owner – a thing Joron did not understand. To him a blade was a tool, and the thought of the cutting and grinding made him think of his father's strong body ripped apart by the spines of the bone-ship's hull.

Not so for the crew; there had been haggling for favoured weapons, women and men making practice swipes at the air, hefting and weighing curnows and then swapping them, even coming close to blows over certain weapons that Joron guessed must carry some favour or story. He had thought about taking out the blade he wore at his own hip, taking some practice swings and seeing if he could discern some special quality to the weapon. But he did not. He felt it was not seemly for a deckkeeper to walk around swinging his curnow, and besides, apart from the standard fighting skills his father had taught him, which all learned, he had little experience of blades and did not think he would know a bad one from a good one. He even feared finding out too much about his sword. He had been given the curnow when he boarded the ship for the first time. "For the shipwife," they had said, and he had been foolish and innocent enough to think they did him some honour.

He doubted they had.

"Untruss the bows," shouted Meas, and Joron watched as Farys and Hilan, each with three deckchilder, and Cwell and Kanvey with crews of their own, started to loose the ropes that immobilised the bows and stopped them swinging free in bad weather. Freeing the great gallowbows caused the excitement to notch up another level on *Tide Child*, and when Cwell opened the box at the base of her bow that held the cords and kept them dry he expected a shout of joy. But instead, there was only anger from the shipwife.

"Hold there, woman! We do not string them and set them till battle is sure." Joron wondered if Meas saw the evil look Cwell gave her for reprimanding her before the entire crew – a promise of revenge later. If she did she ignored it and turned her back, staring out over the rail.

Joron could make out Corfynhulme now, the last of this run of islands and the largest, at the head a huge stack of stone. From there the island curved away from them like a woman laying down to sleep in the cold, but unlike a woman the island had no curves, only a long straight taper lost to a riot of gion and varisk sweeping down to meet the sea. As they approached he fancied he heard the calls of the birds wheeling above. Only when they got nearer, and he could make out the small dots of those rowing flukeboats did he realise it was the screams of people, not birds, he heard.

On the rump of the ship Meas leaned forward, as if she could lend the ship a little more speed by doing so.

"Ready the bows," she said, but she paid little attention to the action on deck, her focus on where they were heading. "And wet your hands in paint, spatter it on the spines for the Hag."

As they came around the headland the boats of the attackers became clearer, and the wind dropped slightly in the lee of the land.

"Furl topwings," she shouted. "We need all the wind we can catch, but I don't want to run aground either."

There were many more raiders than Joron had expected. There must have been thirty flukeboats, mostly small, but there were at least four double-sailed boats, brightly coloured, painted with silhouettes of the Sea Hag's fearsome skull. The women and men who crewed the boats had stripped and painted themselves red and white to resemble meat marbled with fat, as if the skin had been flayed from their bodies.

"Hag's breath!" shouted Meas. "I said string those bows!"

Joron turned. Farys and Hilan were doing a reasonable job of running the cord between the bow arms and the firing mechanism, but they were doing it slowly. Cwell had managed to get her cord hopelessly tangled in the mechanism of the bow and was shouting at one of the women working with her. The final bowteam under Kanvey were all looking dumbly at the cord, as if it were an entirely new thing to them.

There was a good chance it was.

"Maiden save us." Meas ran across, took one look at Cwell's bow and shook her head. "Tie it down and go join the fighting teams." Cwell shot her a look of pure hatred and her crew started to secure the bow. Meas ignored them and leaped across to the next bow, taking the cord and threading it in an easy practised motion that had it in place in moments. She glanced across at Farys and Hilan, who now had their bows strung, and then looked forward. "Deckkeeper!" she shouted. "Are you just standing there like a fool? Take in more wing or we'll run aground!"

A shudder ran through Joron. It was true. He had been so transfixed by the mess at the gallowbows and the sheer number of boats they faced that he had stopped concentrating, and *Tide Child* was carrying far too much wing.

"Bring down forewings and mainwings," he shouted. "Leave only topwings. Steer us seaward, Barlay!" he shouted, then Meas was striding past him.

"Quiet that order, Oarturner. Steer landward so we can bring the bows to bear."

"But Shipwife—" began Joron.

"No buts, Deckkeeper. I already have topwings furled. What is wrong with you? We steer landward – we are here to fight." She turned away. "Spin the bows!"

The three remaining bowteams frantically started to wind the pulleys that tensioned the arms that tightened the cord. In the curving harbour many of the smaller boats were heading away, the appearance of a fleet ship enough to ward them off, but the four bigger flukeboats were near land and clearly had no intention of stopping. *Tide Child* began to turn and Joron opened his mouth. He knew this harbour, had been here with his father: there was a reef on one side, and if the ship did not head seaward before bringing its bows to bear it would not have enough room to turn. He looked for the courser, to ask them what they thought, but the courser would be below during a fight, too precious to risk. He was about to raise his voice, to tell Meas, but the words died in his mouth. She was Meas Gilbryn; who was he to gainsay her word? What if she knew something he didn't? What a fool he would look then.

"Spin!" shouted Meas, "Spin the bows for the Mother's wish!" A woman struggled past Joron, holding three long bolts of varisk stalk dried and tied together and tipped with a pointed head of shaped stone. She gave one to each of the bowteams' loaders. Joron heard the click of each cord coming to rest behind the firing hook. The bolts were placed. Bolts loaded, each team steadied the huge bone crossbow on the greased ball socket that allowed it to turn.

"Sitting targets!" shouted Meas. "Look at those flukeboats. They barely even move, they are too close to the shore. Hurry, before they get their oars out. Loose as we come to bear." She sounded thrilled, full of triumph.

It was not to be.

The three bows fired at the same time. The first, crewed by Farys, let out a deep thrum but the cord miscaught the bolt, which made it shoot almost straight up into the air, sending the bowteam scurrying away in panic to avoid the falling bolt, which smashed against the side of the ship, cracking the rail and then falling into the sea. The second and third bows fared a little better, at least getting their bolts off. One flew far over the flukeboats in the bay, and the other did little to worry its target. Meas glared at the bowteams, and if the look on a face could have sunk a ship, *Tide Child* would have been bound for the Hag's embrace there and then. But it could not and he did not, though Joron half wished he had.

"Hag's tits," hissed Meas, then she was striding forward. "What did you people do before I came aboard? Spin!" she shouted. "Spin the bows, Hag take you all. Bring more bolts! Bring them!"

The bowteams obeyed while the rest of the crew stood looking lost, like they did not know what to do with themselves, though some at least had the Maiden's grace to look ashamed and certainly Joron was one of them. The big fluke-boats had their oars out and were turning their beaks to face *Tide Child* – a face-on ship was a much smaller target than a side on one, and the shipwives of these boats knew one hit from a great bow would doom them. "Spin! Hag take you!" shouted Meas.

A scream. The cord on the first bow had been overtightened by the panicked team under Hilan and snapped, the cord whipping back and cutting Hilan almost in two. A wave of blood ran across the deck. Meas ignored the death, ran to the next bow as the loader, staring in horror at the dead man, dropped his bolt and backed away from the great weapon. Farys, small and damaged Farys, spattered with her dead friend's blood, stepped in. She lifted the bolt, grunting as she put all her strength into placing it.

Meas sighted along the bow. "Wait, wait," she said, more to herself than anyone else, and then she pulled the trigger rope. The bolt scudded out, skipping over the surface of the sea and smashing into the beak of a flukeboat, ripping the hull apart and scattering the crew into the water. A roar went up from *Tide Child*. Then Meas was back at Hilan's bow, rethreading it. Shouting for it to be spun and the body to be put over the side, she grabbed Farys, dragged her over and pushed her against the aimer's lean, loading the bow herself and standing behind the girl. "Watch," she said. "You watch. See when the boat is in the notch?" Calm, as if *Tide Child* flew through a fine day, then Meas raised her voice: "Launch!" Another bolt streaked out, cutting through a second flukeboat, and another roar went up from the crew. Meas stood straight. "See!" she said. "That is how it is done. Now we finish the—"

Joron was thrown, bodily, from his feet together with every other member of the crew, including Meas, and a terrible sound came from the ship – a screaming and groaning and cracking of the ship's bones as they were put under terrible stress. Another crack and, almost in slow motion, the mainspine of the ship toppled, bringing wings and rigging with it, its stately fall only stopped by the ensnaring web of rope, leaving it leaning at a crazy angle over the deck.

Joron's world swam and tilted, changed, took on strange colours. He tried to stand but could not. He thought of standing, but the thought was becalmed and did not move from his mind to reach his legs or his hands. Then he was being pulled up by a large shape he could hardly make out. *Barlay?* Then a voice: "Bare your sword, Deckkeeper." And he was stumbling forward, tangled in rigging, fighting his way out, the ropes and the world becoming clearer, little by little. His face was wet. He touched it, licked his finger. Blood. Had he cracked his head?. A moment of fear. *How bad was it? Father's skull bursting like overripe fruit.* Then moving. On the deck before him a woman lay unmoving. Dead. Further on, a man whimpering in pain, his leg shattered, shards of grey-white bone showing through red flesh, like Meas's hair in reverse. But he was drawn on by a voice demanding his service. Her voice.

"Deckkeeper, to me! All of you! To me!" The ship, how badly damaged was it? Did that even matter at this moment? No.

His thoughts started to come together. *They were stricken.*

Had hit the shallows just as he had thought they would. What would the raiders do?

Run?

No.

Attack.

Of course they would. A few children to sell to the Gaunt Islanders was nothing compared to the profit to be had in a boneship, even a black one, even a wrecked one. With the arakeesians long gone boneships were a dwindling resource and the fewer of them there were the more their parts were worth. Oh, you could make a ship from gion and varisk, fair enough, but they were brittle and delicate things compared to keyshan bone, no good for war, no good for fighting and easily broken by a strong sea, by a shallow reef. All knew that the Hag favoured ships of bone upon her dark waters.

He made it to the side of the ship, felt the deck sloping away behind him. Meas was shouting. Like him she was bloodied. She held her left arm awkwardly, as though hurt. Behind her the sea was alive. The two largest flukeboats were rowing for *Tide Child* with all the speed they had and pulling who they could from a sea already red with blood and thrashed to foam by hungry longthresh, feeding on the stricken. The fleeing smaller boats had turned and were making for *Tide Child*.

"All of you," she said, "pick up your blades and get ready to repel boarders." If Joron had been quicker, braver, maybe he would have taken that moment to defy her. To shout her down. The raiders would like nothing more than to be presented with a boneship without a fight and would probably welcome him among them. But in the back of his mind was his father's voice and a hundred stories of the glorious fleet, and he couldn't bring himself to betray them.

Betray her? Yes. But his father? Never.

"Did you not hear the shipwife?" shouted Barlay from behind him. "She said prepare to repel borders."

There was a pause then, as if *Tide Child*, balanced on the

reef, and could have fallen either way, stayed marooned in the bright light of Skearith's Eye or fallen to sink into darkness.

Then Meas jumped on to the ship's rail. Arrows were flying from the approaching flukeboats but she acted as if they were nothing.

"Well?" she shouted. "Are you fleet? Or are you scum?" She raised her sword. "For I am fleet!"

As *Tide Child* tipped, a lone voice called out. Joron did not know whose voice it was, but it was clear enough in the moment.

"Ey! We are fleet!"

And with that it was decided. All those around him picked up weapons. Joron glanced at the approaching boats, those aboard bare-chested, shaking spears and brandishing their bows.

"You are hurt," he said to Meas.

She looked at him like he was a fool and tried to raise her left arm, grimaced.

"Ey." She walked to the stump of the mainspine. "A dislocation, nothing more." And with that she drove herself into the wildly canted spine, pushing her shoulder joint back into place, and though she did not scream her knees almost buckled at the pain. The crew watched her, as if her actions gave them some sort of power. "It is better now," she said. "It takes more than a little pain to stop a deckchild, ey?" This she said to the nearest woman, who grinned back at her, showing teeth black from chewing harsi gum. "Bring the wings down. We'll bunch them up and use them as a shield against arrows. One along this rail, one back on the rump. Get to it." The woman nodded and ran. Others scaled the rigging, and he heard the sound of axes cutting rigging, bringing the mainwing down to be swiftly repositioned along the front of the rumpdeck.

And the boats came, and they came.

Another wing was pushed against the rail on the side of the ship.

And the boats came, and they came.

Arrows started to hit the sides of *Tide Child*.

Joron stared at the women and men on the flukeboats; there were so many. The two big boats were overflowing with raiders furious for blood, their bodies red with paint. The rowing boats – he counted eight of them – held at least six raiders in each, and he found himself mesmerised by what he was sure was his approaching death.

Meas pulled him down as a shower of arrows fell across the decks of *Tide Child*.

"Do we have bows aboard, Deckkeeper?" He did not know, looked at her blankly. "Never matter. I've sent crew to close the bowpeeks on the lower decks so they won't be getting in there. All may not be over, Twiner." She was smiling, and her breath was coming quickly. He couldn't understand why she was smiling when they were all about to die. When everything had gone so terribly wrong. "There are no children in those boats, we got here in time."

"Or they were on the boats we shot out of the water."

"They were heading towards land when we came. We have interrupted them, and now we must crush them against our ship, broken as he is."

"There are so many."

"They are rabble, Deckkeeper. And we are fleet." She turned to the man crouching next to her, scar-faced and gap-toothed. "Did you hear that, what are we?"

"Fleet," he said. But too quietly for Meas.

"Then show some pride in it, man. Shout it." She stood, oblivious to the arrows coming in, the light glinting from the feathers in her hair and the fishskin on her tunic. "They are rabble! Nothing! We are fleet! We are Hundred Isles and they cannot touch us!"

And all around Joron glances were exchanged; small smiles crept on to tanned and scarred faces, and her words were repeated, becoming louder and stronger as the arrows rained down. He thought her mad, but it seemed Meas's words were true as not one arrow found flesh.

She leaned over, her mouth close to his ear. "We fight here to start, when they come over the rail. When it gets too much we lead the crew back to the rump."

All around the shouting.

"We are fleet! We are Hundred Isles!"

Were they all mad, was this what battle did to women and men?

Meas straightened, held her sword aloft. Arrows fell about her, bounced off the deck, stuck in the rail, left her untouched.

"Come to me!" she shouted at the incoming boats. "Come and die at the hand of Lucky Meas and her crew!" Joron heard the bump of a flukeboat hitting the side of the ship – *his father ground between the hulls* – and a roar. A hand appeared on the rail. Meas lunged and there was a scream. When she held her sword aloft again blood ran from it. More swarmed up the ship, faces in the gaps between rumpled black wing and the ornate uprights of the rail. Some were bloody already, cut by *Tide Child's* spiked hull.

Joron found he was standing close to the rail, had no memory of moving. He turned. Old Briaret. She pushed a spear into his hand.

"Better for this work, D'keeper," she said. A face appeared between the uprights, hands scrabbling to find purchase on the rail, leaving wet, dark smears of blood where *Tide Child* had claimed his price. Joron jabbed his spear at the man's face, feeling it jar his hands as it cut through flesh and found bone. The man fell back with a cry, hands to his gaping wound.

And that was how it was. Shouting, stabbing, screaming, confusion.

If a face came at him from the direction of the rail then he jabbed at it. He jabbed at hands, he jabbed at bodies. He jabbed at legs and was surprised by how easy it was. How being on the slate of *Tide Child* gave him such an advantage over the raiders scaling the ship. He began to believe it would end here and end quickly.

A scream from down the deck.

He turned.

A group of raiders had managed to get aboard at the beak of the ship and were cutting into the end of the line of defenders. Meas took a step back from the rail, pulled one of the small crossbows that hung on her blue coat from its cord and calmly loosed a bolt down the deck. Tossing the crossbow aside before the bolt took a woman in the throat, her next crossbow already in her hand.

"Look to the beak!" she shouted. Better-trained deckchilder may have reacted more quickly, rushed to counter the attack, but this crew were not drilled; they were lost in their violence. Another bolt sang down the deck, but now raiders were swarming over the beak of the ship. Screaming in their triumph. "Twiner," shouted Meas. "Pull them back to the rump. Come, do it!"

Joron grabbed Old Briaret, shouting, "Retreat!" in her face. The woman was grinning, covered in blood, eyes alight with joy. In her fury she looked years younger. "Back," he shouted. "Back!"

Old Briaret turned and hurled her spear down the deck at the raiders and took up the call. "You'll need your curnow now, D'keeper," she said, and grabbed Farys, dragging her away from the rail. Joron threw his own spear, taking a man in the stomach. Hearing the calls to retreat, the attackers surged forward, as fierce and strong as a riptide. Cutting down those in their path. All around, the crew of Tide Child were fleeing down the ship, those crew at the rail peeling away. As they did, more raiders came over the rail like a froth of boiling water coming over the edge of a pan.

Not all the deckchilder ran; some were lost in fighting and killing, unable to hear anything but the roar of blood in their ears, and the raiders hacked them apart. Some tripped on loose tangles of rigging, slipped on blood or were simply not quick enough and were caught by the furious mob of woman and men rushing up the deck. Blood spilled over the slate and into the sea, and the longthresh churned furiously in the water below. Joron ran, feeling guilty that he was thankful some had fought and fallen or been slow, that their deaths bought him time to escape.

On the rump of the deck stood Meas; by her stood Barlay. A hasty barricade of broken spars and wingcloth had been built, and Joron realised that, while he had been thinking about keeping raiders off the rail and staying alive, Meas had sent Barlay to make this barrier. The big woman was holding a spar up so crew could run underneath. Joron ducked through, wingcloth rasping against his back, and as soon as the last of the crew were through Barlay dropped the spar. Scattered across the rump of the ship were bows. Joron was shamed by them. They were in poor condition, and he had had not even known they were aboard.

"If you know how to shoot a bow," shouted Meas, "get up the rumpspine" – she motioned behind her – "and take down their archers first." She pointed at the raiders climbing the for'ard spine, and then her own crew were climbing, bows held in their teeth and arrows in their hands. Meas pushed a fishskin beaker of water into Joron's hand. Another thing he had not even thought about: an open water barrel stood at the bottom of the paint-spattered rumpspine.

"Drink now. You'll be thirsty though you may not feel it."

He drank, suddenly aware how much his body needed water, and he gulped the whole beaker down, like it was the best anhir he had ever tasted.

"Pass it on," said Meas.

Joron dipped it into the barrel and pushed the full beaker into Old Briaret's hand, but the old woman passed it over to Farys and ran to get her own water as the raiders finished off those who had not made the barricade in time and massed for their assault.

"They come!" shouted Meas.

It was grim work under the heat of Skearith's Eye. Curnows were slashing weapons, the weighted ends helping them bite through flesh. They required little skill but made the muscles in Joron's arm burn. Around him deckchilder died; in front of him raiders lost their lives, and he had no sense of who was winning. He only knew the burn in his arms, the ache in his lungs as he fought against panic to breathe, the desperate need to survive.

Meas fought with barely disguised fury. Barlay's strength took life after life, and further away fought Cwell, her movements precise and lethal. Some remembrance of fleet discipline lurked in Meas's line, and it held against the onslaught. She stood in the centre, not that tall, but fearless. Her straightsword a silver line, rising and falling, trailing streamers of blood as it did. Her voice a clarion call. When Joron's arms burned, his lungs rasped and he started to feel the pain of the many cuts and bruises on his body. When he began to feel like he could go on no longer, she shouted, "One more push!" and from somewhere he found more energy. Not much, but enough – enough to kill, enough to roar at his enemy.

And, at the moment he thought he could give no more, something changed. The raiders were leaving, streaming over the side as if the Sea Hag herself had come for them. He turned to Old Briaret, but the woman lay on the deck, her bleeding head in Farys's lap, eyes vacant and a terrible wound in her skull.

"Took it in the first attack, D'keeper," Farys said quietly. "Looked after me, she did. Her and Hilan. Who will do that now, ey? Who will watch for poor Farys now?"

And Joron knew the answer he should give but did not have the energy to speak, so he only watched as a scarred girl cried over the still body of a criminal.

10

The Return

There was little sense of triumph once the raiders had been beaten back. Joron did not know what he had expected – some congratulation from the people of Corfynhulme, maybe? Even help from them would have been something. It was rare that those upon the sea did not to help one another when it was needed. But, though the women and men of Corfynhulme came out in a small flotilla, they did not come to *Tide Child*'s assistance. Instead they took the raiders' boats and rowed them back to shore. Joron watched them painting the raiders' boats in their own colours, a happy riot of greens and yellows.

The atmosphere aboard the black ship was sullen.

To Joron's thinking, and to most of the crew's, they had a won a victory here.

Not to Meas.

She walked the slate like a most terrible insult had been offered to her person, shouting at anyone who got in her way, demanding an already tired crew work even harder to get the ship back into some sort of shape.

Already teams were cutting away rigging and broken spars, and for the first time Joron got to examine the spines of the ship. He had thought them bone and was surprised they were not, not totally. The main rises, the thick round bottom parts, were arakeesian bone, but the higher uprights and the cross spines were made of gion stalks, dried and bound in bunches then tightly tied to give them extra strength, the whole lot painted black to match the ship. The centre part of the main-spine of the ship was similar, but of Gion trunks, also dried, bound and fitted with collars of bone, and it amazed him that he had never known these simple things about the ship, that he had never taken the time to look.

"Will you gawp all day, Twiner," said Meas, "or will you deliver me the Hag's cost for this debacle?"

"Shipwife?"

"How many died, Deckkeeper? How many crew have I got left to try and get this wreck floating again?" There was a barely hidden fury in her.

"I tried to—"

"No!" She threw the word at him, and Joron felt the eyes of the entire crew turn on him, a heat, in its own way more intense than that of Skearith's Eye. "You let us run aground. No stonethrowers at the front to warn us, none of the safe-guards a ship should have. And you knew about that reef?" She was talking quietly, but still Joron was sure all aboard could hear her. "If the deckkeeper knows a thing, it is their job to make sure the shipwife also knows. This mess is on you, Twiner, and if you were not already among the dead I would see you there for it." She turned and walked away. "Bring me someone who can swim." She hacked out the words. "I need to know how fast the keel is in the seabed."

A deckchild grinned at Joron's discomfort, and Meas snapped as she passed, "You! Why do you sit there like a fool? Get together a crew for the flukeboat and ready it for towing. There'll be some hard muscle needed to get this hulk moving." From there she vanished belowdeck, no doubt to sit in her cabin while others worked, he thought.

Joron went off to carry out her orders, only to find the

bodies of the fallen had already been lined up on the deck; the dead raiders had simply been thrown over the side.

He counted twenty-two corpses in cured varisk leaves with rocks sewn in to carry them down to the Hag. Farys sat at the end of the line carefully wrapping a body. Joron felt like he should say something but had no words, so he walked away, up towards the rump of the ship, where he thought he could be alone, out of sight of the crew. But the rump had been the place of their stand and he found no peace: deckchilder were busy clearing away the barricade that had saved them. Barlay stood among them, lending her strength.

"Do you swim, Oarturner?" Joron said, and he knew the moment the words had left his lips he sounded hesitant. She glanced at him, then took the two steps needed to be just that little too close.

"No, Deckkeeper," she said, "I do not, but Karring there" – she pointed at a man who looked more bone than flesh – "he swims like he was born in the water."

"Thank you, Oarturner," he said. Barlay nodded, and was it his imagination or was there a little less hatred in the woman's fleshy face? "Barlay, there is a girl, a friend of Old Briaret."

"Farys, aye. I know of her."

"Well, it seems Old Briaret and Hilan were her only friends, and now they are gone. She could sore do with a friend, I think."

"Do you order it?" said Barlay, her words as still as slacktide. Joron wondered what to do. He should order it – to not do so was to give away some of his authority, and Meas had warned him he spoke for her.

But she had also told him he must navigate these waters himself.

"No," he said, "I do not believe a friendship can be forced." Barlay stared at him then took a step back.

"I have the rump of the ship to clear," she said.

"Of course," replied Joron, feeling he had somehow failed again.

Then Barlay glanced back him.

"I'll look to the girl," she said. "But Briaret may yet survive. She's a tough one."

"She lives?"

Barlay nodded, some faint condemnation there that he did not know this?

"Ey, she is in the hagbower with the hagshand. He says she may live."

He nodded, as if he knew.

"Thank you, Oarturner." He approached Karring. "Barlay says you can swim like you were born to the sea."

"Ey, D'keeper." The man did not look at him. He wore only loose trousers and a scarf wrapped around his head which hid his hair. The skin of his body was as dark as Joron's own.

"From the Broom Isles, are you?"

"Ey D'keeper." The man still did not look at him.

Joron wondered why but did not pursue it.

"Well, they breed good swimmers there, I have heard. The shipwife wants to know how fast we are held. Could you look for her?"

"Ey," said the man, but the look of terror that crossed his face gave Joron pause.

"You do not wish to do this?"

"I will swim happily, fer the shipwife, D'keeper, happy as the Maiden's lovers, but 'tis the beakwyrms, see. They hang about a ship and there's longthresh too." At the mention of the predators he swallowed, looked away. "With all these corpses about, see. They will be down there."

Joron took a step back, the thought of being under a ship, in the dark and unable to breathe while being attacked by beakwyrms or longthresh, filled him with terror. Could he send a man to do something he would never do?

"D'keeper."

He turned. Another deckchild, a woman he did not know.

"Yes?"

"On Shellhulme we gather shells for decoration, and they fetch a good price."

He stared at the woman, unsure of why she told him this. "And?"

"Well, D'keeper, the beakwyrms and longthresh often gather where the best diving is, see."

"So you have to deal with them?"

"Aye."

"And how is this done on Shellhulme?"

"We kill one, D'keeper, or wound it badly. The others fall upon it and you will have time to send down your swimmer."

"Well, gather some spears then," he said, "and some deck-childer. We have a beakwyrm to kill."

"We may not need to go that far, D'keeper," said another deckchild, "with all the bodies in the water. If we chop up a few away from the ship, the blood will bring the beakwyrms."

He turned back to the woman from Shellhulme. "Will that work?"

"Should, I reckon. A beakwyrm don't care what it eats as long as it eats."

"Like you, eh, Torfy?"

Joron ignored the speaker and the laughter that followed. "We should bring aboard any bodies near *Tide Child*, and leave the ones further out floating; it would be good to damage them a little more though."

"Ey, the more blood the better, we will still need the spears, ey? Get 'em good and bleeding?"

He gathered a small group and handed out spears for them, and it seemed to Joron that puncturing the corpses of the raiders brought a disproportionately large amount of joy to his crew. It was not long before the beakwyrms appeared from under the ship, spinning through the water toward the blood, and following them came longthresh, sinister white shapes swimming away from the shadow of the ship.

He turned to Karring." Right, over the other side. Quick as you will." As the man climbed the rail Joron stopped him, holding him by the top of his arm. "Get as much information as you can. The shipwife is not one for a job half done, but all know that, right?" He heard a chorus of "ey" from around him. "But if you see the wyrms or the thresh, forget it and come back up with what you have. The Hag has had enough of us today. Understand, Karring? I have no wish to annoy her by crowding her pyre any further."

The man nodded, gave him a brief grin and went over the side. Joron turned back to the group of spear throwers feeling like he had done well and saw Meas at the other end of the ship, watching him, unsmiling.

He made his way up the ship towards her, any joy within him withering as he walked.

"We lost twenty-two, Shipwife," he said. "I have sent a man over the side to check the keel and see how hard fast we are."

"It's too many," she replied. "We can't crew a ship this size with only fifty, and the boneglue is cracked right across the hull. We'll need to work the pumps day and night if we're to make it back to Bernshulme."

"We go to the capital then?"

"Where else would we go? This ship will need work to make him seaworthy and crew to make him fly. Bernshulme has the best of both."

"Shipwife," he said, wondering how she could not have realised the truth of her position, "we are a ship of the dead. Maybe in a quiet port with little work we may get some repairs, but Bernshulme? The whole fleet will stand in line before us."

Her eyes were as grey as a sky before rain.

"I still have some friends, Deckkeeper."

"But . . ." He did not finish because her eyes would not let him. The fury that he had felt burning within her, contained by her muscular frame, was ready to leap from her. He did not want to be the one that was scalded.

"Of course, Shipwife."

She nodded.

"Joron Twiner, is there some reason you have no wish to return to Bernshulme?"

"No, Shipwife." And bitter words slid from his mouth: "You own me. You command the ship, and I go where you say."

"Good," she said. "Good." And then she turned away from him.

Of course, he had very good reasons for never wanting to set foot in Bernshulme again, and he could not shake the feeling she knew exactly why. He wondered what she would do with such knowledge. What she would do with him.

Karring returned, soaking and with a bloody rip along his arm.

"What happened down there, Karring?"

"Keel is caught in rocks, D'keeper. I tried to shift them and scratched myself. Is no great thing."

"Well, see the hagshand. I do not want to see your wound festering. How bad is the damage?"

"Bad, D'Keeper. The keel has a crack right across it." The man must have seen the dismay in Joron's face. "He'll fly, D'Keeper, he will. But if the Northstorm spies us out we won't last a strong blow."

"Is there any good news?"

"Aye, the current is turning. I reckon the tide's as low as it gets now and it is coming in. It should lift us enough to get loose. We'll not be trapped come higher water."

"Right then," Joron said, then raised his voice. "Rig for towing! We'll not stay stuck on these rocks any longer than we have to." He was amazed that the crew jumped to his orders. Most amazed that Kanvey, who was a minor power among the deckchilder, was first to lead a group of about twenty into the bigger of their two flukeboats. Then his amazement turned to dismay. As the crew of the smaller boat started tying on ropes and making things secure, he saw that Kanvey's flukeboat was rowing for the open sea. Kanvey himself raised the wing on the flukeboat, before turning to shout some obscenity at *Tide Child*.

Meas ran to the side of the ship.

"You man!" She threw her words at the retreating boat like gallowbow bolts. "Get back here now!" But Kanvey only laughed. Then he knelt, grabbed something from the bottom of the boat and stood. He held a spear. He hefted it, leaning back, altering his grip on the shaft once, twice, until he found a balance in the weapon that pleased him, and then put all his weight into a throw.

Joron ducked. Meas did not. She did not move at all, only raised her head to watch the flight of the spear, which arced through the air. It landed with a heavy thud and stuck in the side of *Tide Child* just below Meas. She did not even flinch. Only remained there, like a statue, watching the fleeing boat.

11

Homeward and Bound

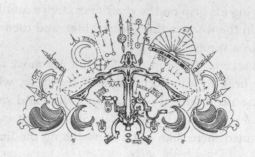

It was a ship of bleak thoughts that limped his way back to Shipshulme Island. Limped through thick mist and with little assistance from the wind to Bernshulme, the capital of the Hundred Isles, there to beg for help and succour. Bleak because of the fell mood that had fallen on Meas Gilbryn, who glowered from the rump of the deck. Bleak because Joron Twiner could see no way he could have done anything more than what he had for the ship, and yet he knew he had failed. Bleak because the ship was holed and the pumps worked day and night, so hard to work they left those pumping exhausted and so noisy to work few could sleep. Bleak because twenty and more died fighting raiders and seven more died of their wounds on the way back – and they did not even have the good grace to die quietly. The cries of the dying haunted the ship as he stole through the mist, and it became easy to believe that they truly were lost to the dead and drifted, haunted, through the Sea Hag's watery darkness.

The misery of those aboard should have fled when they finally arrived at Bernshulme – an end to the constant work at the pumps belowdeck and to the constant patching and mending above it. Some respite for Joron from the baleful glare of Meas Gilbryn, who seemed, as far as he could tell, to hold him responsible for all the ship's ills.

Of all the Hundred Isles Shipshulme was the largest, and Bernshulme the biggest harbour and the biggest town. The island shared the slowly rising crescent shape of most of the isles – a flick of pen on parchment – only on a much larger scale, and was a riot of primary colours when the varisk and gion jungles came to life. Two long causeways curved out from the island, constructed when the bones of arakeesians were taken for granted. They could still be seen, sticking out from the rocks piled around them to make barriers against the sea, which, though it only gently lapped against the moles, and showed none of its fury, could, and often did, swell and crash over them, even though those walls of bone and grey slate were almost as tall as the spines rising from *Tide Child*'s decks.

The black ship's approach was observed by armed women and men on the light towers that sprouted like jutting teeth from the end of each stone pier. Joron watched as two figures on the light tower to landward of them leaned in close to one another, evidently discussing them, and then a red flag was waved, telling them to stop.

"Shipwife," shouted Joron, though he felt his voice waver, still nervous of her obvious anger. "They wish us to halt."

Meas stomped down the slate of the deck and stared up at the woman waving the flag. Then glared at the pier and narrowed her eyes against Skearith's Eye – just starting to touch the top of the mountain that crowned the island.

"Ignore them. We are no danger to shipping and we are sore in need of a dock."

Joron was about to open his mouth, tell her that to ignore a warning flag was punishable by death, for all knew it to be so. But she grinned at him – no, she more gritted her teeth, for there was only the bleakest humour there at how a sentence of death was wasted on this crew. Bleak humour for a bleak ship.

Tide Child came about, his spines creaking, the pumps rumbling and the whole ship wallowing as no matter how they pumped they could not keep up with the leaks. The boneship had spent the entire journey on the point of sinking. Joron now got his first view into the harbour since he had left here, too grief-stricken to look about him.

Bernshulme was packed with ships: two-ribbers, threes, fours, even a five-ribber – all rising bone-white and beautiful from the slack water. From one ship a flukeboat was casting off, oars sticking out from its sides, a moment of confusion when they pointed in all directions before a shout brought them into unison, smoothly stroking the water and powering the boat forward. On the prow was a figure in a two-tail hat, bright colours across its chest. The harbour keeper no doubt. The boat made straight for *Tide Child*. Behind the harbour keeper stood three lackeys, all waving red flags at the black ship.

"All stop! All stop on that ship, in the Thirteenbern's name!" The man invoked the name of Meas's mother as if that alone was enough to halt a ship; he had the trilling voice of the Kept, the men who served the Bern. "All stop, that black ship. You have no permission to come into Bernshulme and shall not be given it. Come further and the harbour gallowbows will be turned on you."

Joron glanced over at the huge bows on the ends of the moles. They were many times bigger than those on a ship and capable of ripping through even a four-ribber like *Tide Child*. They had already been spun up and loaded with wingshot, fires burning where the hagspit had been lit, making sure the threat of the harbour keeper's words was not ignored. Meas leaned over the rail, looking down on the flukeboat.

"Harbour Keeper," she shouted, "my ship has taken fell damage defending the children of Corfynhulme from raiders."

"That is not the problem of Bernshulme," returned the man. "You must—"

"There is no other port we could reach," Meas yelled over

him, though she sounded perfectly calm and reasonable. "This ship is taking on water faster than a purseholder can drink anhir. Now, if you wish to be the man responsible for five thousand jointweight of arakeesian bone sinking to the sea floor then, by all means, I will turn this ship about and we will sink." She paused as if calmly considering her ship's fate. "We may sink away from the harbour mouth so it is not entirely blocked, though in truth I doubt it we will get so far." Joron saw fear start to cloud the harbour keeper's eyes; his duty was to keep the docks safe and in use. "But, Harbour Keeper, you say the word and we will turn *Tide Child* around and see how far we get before the Sea Hag claims us." Then she leaned further over the rail and let menace enter her voice. "But call this wrong, and you may find you bring my mother's wrath down upon you, and you will end your days wearing a black armband and on my crew while your family go bankrupt paying the loss cost of this ship."

"But if you sink in the harbour—"

"That would be expensive for you also." The keeper looked alarmed, but also lost in the face of Meas's self-assurance. "What I suggest is that you have a land cradle made ready for us." She pointed past his boat at the distant shore, past the ships at their staystones to where the huge ship cranes could just be made out through the mist. "I see an empty cradle. I think we can make it if I keep the pumps running." The harbour keeper turned from her and had a swift whispered conversation with two ostentatious dandily and scantily dressed Kept who accompanied him. Then he turned back.

"Very well. We will send out pilot boats to bring you in. Your crew will not leave the ship. We will have soldiers meet you and, when we are ready, will have your crew moved to a hulk outside the harbour until you leave. If you try to deviate from the path the pilot boats take you on then the gallowbows will sink you no matter the loss. Do you understand?"

"Perfectly," she said. "And I would expect nothing less." She turned away from the man as if he had never been, and as she walked past Joron he heard her whisper to herself. "Jumped-up purseholder – never even seen the storms."

Tide Child's crew were standing around like lost children. Meas snapped, "Get ropes, ready the ship for towing and double the speed on those pumps. I've been embarrassed enough; I won't have this ship sink in the harbour under me." Then there was at least a pretence of order aboard the ship. Women and men ran around, stowing spars and shot, getting ropes tied on to the ship's beak ready for the pilot boats. When the boats arrived there was no communication with Tide Child; the ropes from the black ship were attached in silence. Meas had already changed the teams on the pumps and told those going off duty to get some rest. Then she called for Joron to join her on the rump of the ship.

"Twiner, we pass through the harbour now, you and I. We will stand here, and we will say nothing. We will look at no one and we will feel no shame at the colour and state of our ship. Do you understand?"

"I—"

"You need only say, 'Yes, Shipwife.'"

He swallowed, nodded.

"Yes, Shipwife."

"Good."

And they stood, feeling the strange motion of the ship moving, seemingly of his own volition as the pilot boats towed him through the harbour. All about them rose the boneships of the Hundred Isles fleet, white and whole and shining. Each one named and loved by his crew, polished until he shone in the dipping light of Skearith's Eye, corpse-lights dancing merrily above them to show that, unlike Tide Child, these ships lived. As a young man Joron had enjoyed sitting with his father, watching the ships come in – enjoyed the drama of it and the joy. The way a ship would come back, flying flags of victory or, even better, towing a prize and with his crew looking forward to the coin they knew it would bring. And his favourite moment had been when the crews of the ships in the harbour would line the rails and spars of their own ships and cheer the new arrival into the harbour.

But there was to be no cheering in for *Tide Child*.

The women and men of the Hundred Isles lined the rails and spars of their ships, right enough, and above them glowing corpselights gently spun around the spars, but as *Tide Child* drew near they turned away. Turned their back on the black ship. Joron knew it was no honour to be on the crew of a ship of the dead, but he had never seen this before, never even heard of such a mass rejection of a fleet ship. But gradually, as each crew turned away from them, he realised it was not his shame they refused to look upon, nor the sorry state of the ship – it was Meas they repudiated.

She showed no emotion, not even when they passed the ship that had been hers, the five-ribber *Arakeesian Dread*, and the crew that had once served her turned away. Still she stared forward, as if *Tide Child* was the only ship in the harbour and the only thing that interested her. But as they rounded *Arakeesian Dread* he saw the first crack in her armour.

Another five-ribber, newer, much smaller, had been hidden behind the *Dread*. Joron did not know this ship, had not heard of him before. Across his beak was the name *Hag's Hunter*, and above him floated seven corpselights, one shy of a ship's full complement and all the blue of firstlight – to show the ship undamaged. Blood still stained the ship from sacrifices, lines of bright red down pristine white sides. He was not a truly new ship – could not be, must have been taken from the Gaunt Islanders. But it was not the ship that made Meas clench her hands, fight back a look of such sudden and complete fury that Joron took a step away from her. It was the woman on the rail, the shipwife of *Hag's Hunter*. Only she, among the thousands of women and men on the many ships in the harbour, did not turn away. Instead she watched *Tide Child* as he was gently towed past. Like Meas she wore the two-tailed hat, but where Meas looked fit to kill, she watched with something akin to amusement and never took her eyes from *Tide Child's* shipwife.

So, thought Joron, *who are you, ey? And what do you hold over Lucky Meas?* But there was no clue from Meas. She did not look again at the shipwife of *Hag's Hunter* and she did not look at Joron, only stared ahead at the town of Bernshulme as it began to appear from the mist.

To take his mind from the rows of backs on each ship Joron concentrated on Bernshulme too. It was a town of curves. A single curving path wound up the steep side of the mountain and along the path were the spiral bothies, the houses of the Bern and the buildings of Bernshulme's government and fleet. Small ones at the bottom and around the old harbour, little more than the height of a tall woman standing on another's shoulders, each the shape of half an eggshell, and growing larger and larger as they climbed the hill until it reached the Spiral Bothies. These were enormous beehives of flat stones placed carefully and artfully so that each stone locked together and held up the building no matter what the storms might throw at them.

As the ship approached the cranes, Joron began to pick out colours around the bases of the bothies, where women and men had thrown bright paint for luck or blessings. At the very top of Bernshulme, about a third of the way up the hill, was the greatest bothy of them all, the Grand Bothy, the palace of Thirteenbern Gilbryn, its stone alternating between dark and light so twin spirals ran right the way up it, ten, eleven, maybe twelve times the height of a tall man. And this was not a simple beehive shape; it was more like the upturned hull of a ship, the top floors a latticework of stone and plates of cured and bleached clear gion. Joron had heard it also went back into the mountain, hiding multiple floors and rooms within the rock, though a fisher boy would never gain entry to such a place.

On the lower floors judgements were handed out and ceremonies took place; higher were the small rooms where the women of the isles went to bear their children. Any woman strong enough to live through childbirth and who had children unmarred by the Hag's curse lost their first child to the ships, though they would join the Bern and rise in power for it.

Joron's mother had died birthing him in those rooms, and his father had taken his tiny bloodied body from the bothy. Miserable at the loss of his wife, but glad his son would live. Weak stock for weak stock, the hagpriests would say of those found wanting, and they would not take him for the boneships, his soul to inhabit the living structure and glow above it as a corpselight.

It was not lost on Joron that the Thirteenbern's firstborn, a child who should have gone to the ships, had somehow survived to attend the spiral bothies and be trained as fleet. He did not believe all the talk of miracles around Lucky Meas Gilbryn's survival. The Gilbryns were an old Bern family and those raised among the Berncast in the wharves and sea caves knew the truth. Nothing was fair in the Hundred Isles. Only strength was respected, and few were stronger than the old Bern families.

Tide Child slowed and Joron glanced at Meas. He followed her gaze until he found himself looking at the ochre block on the harbour side that commanded her attention. Three steps that went nowhere, built from the white limestone only found in the sea stacks along Skearith's Spine that were as likely to wreck the ships of those coming to quarry them as give up stone. But the stone was white no longer; it had been stained ochre by the blood of the firstborn, sacrificed to float as light above the boneships.

"Get *Tide Child* ready for the cradle," said Meas quietly. "I want everything that can come loose tied down and then tell the crew to put on their shackles. I'll give no seaguard an excuse to wet their spear on my crew." Joron nodded and set to work, though there was little to do. Everything not essential had been thrown overboard on the journey to lighten the ship and keep him afloat. And the women and men of the crew were so tired they had no energy to argue with Joron when he ordered they be shackled like gullaime leaving the lamyards; they simply put out their hands to be cuffed by their fellows, Barlay and Cwell. Then the two women came to Joron, who secured them in turn, Barlay resigned to the fact of her bondage and Cwell staring at him as he tightened the hasps around her wrists, mocking him without ever speaking. By the time *Tide Child* came to rest in the cradle, the shore workers sweating and grunting as they took up the slack in the ropes and lifted *Tide Child* just out of the water, the entire crew was shackled.

Seaguard surrounded the ship, stone-tipped spears held aloft and armour of silver-painted leather shining. Behind them the women of the lamyards waited to take the gullaime. Meas climbed down the side of the ship and went to the seaguard commander and nodded at something he said. The crew were formally given into the care of the seaguard, gangplanks were then placed against the side of *Tide Child,* and the commander led his troops on to the ship. The crew, meek as children, marched off the ship and along the harbour front watched by townspeople who jeered and spat at the condemned.

"Come," said Meas. "Even dead officers get their own quarters in Bernshulme, though given where the seaguard commander told me they're located, I dread to think what state they're in."

12

To All Who Serve, Comes A-Calling

They were billeted in Fishmarket. No place in Bernshulme stank like Fishmarket. The beehive-shaped bothies that surrounded market square had been tunnelled through to allow access in and out of the market squares. Bit by bit a mixture of neglect and utility had turned these tunnels into passages, so each bothy was cut in half. The work had been done poorly. The roofs regularly collapsed, and the stone – always valuable – rather than being used to rebuild the bothies was simply spirited away and the roofs patched with varisk and gion leaves, badly cured ones, as was proved by the leak above Joron's bed. It was not a large leak, but large enough to leave the bed he slept on – dreaming of high seas and engulfing waves – as damp as any bed aboard ship.

But he was tired, and neither the wind creeping in through the holes, nor the overpowering stink of rotting fish from the market, nor Meas's obvious contempt was enough to stop him sinking straight into sleep in the dark room atop the half-bothy in Fishmarket.

But he did not sleep for long.

"Twiner." A whispered word, heard from a long way off in the pitch darkness of the room. "Joron Twiner." Harsher words.

Was he drunk again? Was that why he felt so cold, so shivery? "Wake, Deckkeeper." Then he was awake. Eyes wide though there was no light to fill them. He felt her near him, the movement of air as she moved.

"Meas?"

"Ey, and it is 'Shipwife' to you, on land or sea. Cover your eyes." He did, heard the spark of flint on metal and and then gradually uncovered his eyes to the warm glow of the wanelight she held in her hands.

"What is—"

She covered his mouth with her free hand.

"Shh." She glanced at the flimsy door. "Someone comes — more than one — and from the sound they are armed." It felt as if icy seawater ran down his back. "Pick up your curnow." She took her hand from his mouth and pulled one of the small crossbows from its cord on her coat. "Take this. Do not loose unless I do."

"Have they come for me?" he said.

She smiled, a slit in her face.

"Possibly, Twiner, but I have many enemies too." The smile widened. "More than you, I imagine." And he felt foolish. "Now listen, Twiner. Stand ready by me, hold your sword like you know what it is for, right?" He nodded, listening to the faint sound of feet making their way up the steps of the bothy from below. "I reckon you have time to put on some trousers too, if you hurry." He nodded, struggling into damp clothes, the comfortable feel of old fishskin around his legs, the illusion the cured material would give some protection.

By the time he was dressed and standing ready behind Meas, the sounds moving up the bothy's tight staircase were louder. "You out there," shouted Meas, "if you come to rob us then know we are awake and we are armed before you come through that door."

There was only silence.

Then.

"We do not come to rob you," came a woman's voice, "and

for the Hag's sake, Shipwife Meas, keep your voice down." Meas lowered her sword, its tip coming to rest pointing at the floor as if disappointed to be denied action.

"So, she cannot leave me alone, even here." He heard her say those words and was sure he was not meant to; they were little more than a sadness breathed out. "Put up your weapons, Joron Twiner, and accompany me. If I am to die tonight then you are the nearest I have to a friend just now."

"So you will take me to die with you?" he said. He had seen little that made him believe they had any sort of friendship, but this seemed little thanks for it.

"They would only kill you here otherwise." She sheathed her sword, raised her voice. "Enter then, and take me where you will." The door opened to reveal two of the Grand Bothy's guard, a man and a woman, decked out in their finery: glittering fishskin and feathers, chestplates of shining metal — a fortune's worth just there — and helmets of hard birdleather sculpted to look like vicious sea creatures.

"You are to come with us, Meas Gilbryn," said the man. They were armed only with the daggers at their sides.

"Very well," she said, straightening up. "Come, Twiner. We will let these fellows escort us and keep us safe from bandits."

"Nothing was said about bringing him." The man pointed at Joron.

"Were you told not to bring him?" said Meas.

"No, but—"

"He is my deckkeeper, and a shipwife goes nowhere without a deckkeeper." She took a step towards the guards. "Of course, you are not fleet, so you may well not know such things." If the man recognised this as the insult it was he did not show it. "But no doubt the person who sent you did and would have said were I not to bring my deckkeeper." The man looked over his shoulder at the woman behind him, who shrugged.

"Very well," he said. "Bring him if you must."

They followed the two soldiers down the tightly winding stone stairs. The walls touched his shoulders and, to Joron, used to wide seas and the wind in his hair, there was something of the coffin about these houses of the stonebound. A ship, even his father's small fishing boat, was always moving, creaking, speaking, *breathing*. Not these houses, and he was glad to get out on to the narrow, too hot, streets. At first they had swayed and moved beneath him as his legs became used to land once more, but now the ground felt too solid and still. Strange, unnatural.

The guards picked up the spears they had left with two more of their number at the door and then the four marched Meas and Joron through the streets. The few Berncast, scurrying and suspicious, out in Fishmarket this late vanished before the soldiers. Meas did not seem worried by what was happening, at least not yet. Even though she had said they might be going to their deaths, she did not act like it. So Joron, in the way learned from his father, borrowed no trouble from a good wind.

Strange though, that Meas acted almost like she had expected this to happen, as if it were normal.

They threaded their way out of Fishmarket and through Narrowtown along Hoppity Lane, where the one-legged made shoes and boots, then joined the Serpent Road, which led up through Bernshulme, eventually, to the spiral bothies. It was only when they turned off the Serpent Road and down towards Fishdock that Meas changed. Her easy, predatory lope tightened a little, became more of a bird-like strut. Her head turned like a kively looking for a predator, and she moved a little nearer to him. Then in that almost-but-not-quite-speaking voice:

"Keep your hand near your curnow."

"What?"

She shot him a look of irritation as he made no attempt to keep his own voice down, but the guards paid no attention to him and she whispered back:

"I thought they came from my mother. It is not unusual for her to demand my presence, though I thought it finished once she condemned me."

"But?" This time he whispered.

"We do not head towards the spiral bothies, so I do not know where we go."

"I wish you had not told me."

"If wishes were fish then the starving would bloat," said Meas.

They walked further into Fishdock. Newer than the rest of Bernshulme, in Fishdock the buildings were tall and square, stone for two levels and then cured gion and varisk above. Many of them rose five or six storeys and they teemed with people: single men with weakblood children, the deformed, the imperfect, those too debilitated by keyshan's rot to continue working the shipyards and the docks. Here also was the engine that powered the Hundred Isles, providing them with those strong enough to be sailors and soldiers, servants and workers, all eager for a way out of the poverty and misery of the tenements. Always more women than men here too, as male children were often given up to the sea. The only hope most had was for a fertile girlchild. If she was strong enough to make it through childbirth and lucky enough to have perfect children she may even become one of the Bern. Some said Meas Gilbryn had been raised in these houses. Joron doubted it. These were the places of the Berncast, where Joron had grown up, and few ever rose from here.

The guards stopped under a flaming torch outside one of the many tenements.

"Go up," said the guard. Joron looked at the man, looking for some hint that he would walk out of the door again, but the guard remained stone-faced. Meas ignored him and led Joron through the door, straight up a tight staircase. Again that feeling of claustrophobia. It took him a moment to realise the tenement was not like the one he had known. There was no smell of damp, and the constant noise of the people who lived in such buildings, sometimes as many as six or seven people to a room, was absent. And when they climbed from the stone storeys to the varisk and gion levels he noticed a quality to the construction work generally lacking in Fishdock. The variskwork shone as if polished; gion stalks had been intricately scrimshawed with scenes of the sea.

"This is not a tenement," said Joron.

"No," said Meas, "it is not." She sounded tired. At the top of the stairs there was an intricately carved door showing Skearith the Stormbird being killed by Hassith the spear thrower, the man who had brought misery to the world. Joron expected Meas to knock but she did no such thing, instead giving the handle of the door a vicious twist and walking straight in. The room that met them was panelled with starched gion leaves that had been left to mature to a very dark brown, mottled with streaks of deep red. They were also carved with scenes of the founding of the Archipelago. Here Cyulverd and Myulverd lay down to sleep until the sea smashed them and they became the islands. There Skearith sang the storms into being to protect her eggs. On another wall her spirit gave the gift of the gullaime to the Mother after banishing the Hag and the Maiden to the sea and the air. Usually, Joron would have been fascinated by such beauty, but instead he was frozen in place. Held still by the scene before him.

A desk and four chairs. A man.

There is a feeling to being tricked, and it is like no other. Especially when that trick is an unpleasant trick and it is played on you by one you trust. Joron realised, when that feeling overcame him – a heaviness in his stomach, a catch in his throat and an anger he had to bite back that showed only in the tightening of his hands into fists – that somewhere, deep within, he had, at some point, decided to trust Meas. Though not to like her, never that. But at some point he must have started to think that her stern demeanour counted for something. That she would be hard but fair.

No longer.

Oh no, no longer.

Behind the desk sat Kept Indyl Karrad, one of the most powerful men in the Hundred Isles. Beautiful, as was the way of the Kept, his face painted and burnished in silvers and bronzes along the line of his cheek. His skin clean shaven but for the hair that grew under his chin, which had been twisted into a long plait woven with colourful reeds. He wore little more than straps over his torso, the better to show off the oiled and finely sculpted muscles of his chest and arms. Under the desk Joron knew he wore tight trousers which showed off the muscles of his legs and were covered in embroidery to exaggerate the groin and advertise his fertility. Below that, long boots. Joron remembered those boots. Remembered being led out of the Berncourt, condemned, head bowed in shame he should not have felt, and noting that Indyl Karrad did not wear his clothes merely to advertise his station but also out of vanity as the boots were subtly heeled to give him a little extra height.

Power and vanity are a bad combination, lad – the voice of his father. He could not bear to hear it, not here, not in front of this man, though there was possibly no place he was more likely to hear it than in the presence of Kept Indyl Karrad.

Once there had been a young man called Rion, shipwife on a boneship, who had offered Joron five iron pieces in compensation for grinding Joron's father into mush against the hull of his warship. *It is a good price, fisher boy – more than any fisher is worth.*

Joron had stood speechless, furious that this man – barely older than he was himself – could take all his father was and meant, could break him simply because he was too drunk and proud to give way and follow harbour rules. Then, with his blood still darkening the water, to value his father's life as worth no more than a few bits of coin. It was more than Joron could stand, and he had challenged Rion to a duel. He fully expected to die, but at that moment he had not wanted to live either, and what better way to join his father at the Hag's fire than to die trying to avenge him? But Rion, in either overconfidence or stupidity, had robbed him of his chance to be reunited. He had spent the day of the duel drinking with his friends and when it came to the moment, Joron, with what even he knew was a lucky blow, had killed the man with a single thrust.

And that should have been it. Justice is swift and harsh in the Hundred Isles – "A life for a life is a fair price." But Rion's father, the man he stood before now, was powerful. So Joron found himself called a murderer, accused of drugging the boy and called before the court of the Bern. Not that he had cared – he was ready to be sentenced, to go into the sea with his veins open and wait for the Hag to claim him – but Indyl Karrad must have seen that Joron wished for death. Joron could still see the moment the man had understood that the man who had killed his son did not fear for death – the cruel smile that crossed his face as he requested the Bern send Joron to the black ship, to a place where he was neither dead nor alive. Caught in limbo, snared by grief.

"Karrad," said Meas. She almost spat the name.

"Meas." He was little more welcoming. "You bring the murderer of my son to me?" He had a nightroom voice, warm and soothing despite the venom in it. Joron remembered that voice – sweet and thick as gion syrup – from the court of the Bern as it argued for him to be cast to away to a ship of the dead. "Send the flotsam away, Meas" – Karrad nodded at Joron – "and then I must speak with you."

"He is my deckkeeper, Karrad, and I bring him so what is said by you is witnessed by another officer of the fleet."

"Deckkeeper," said Karrad quietly to himself, tapping a quill on the desk in front of him. "Well, how you have risen, eh, Joron Twiner." His eyes flicked up to Joron's and then back to his desk. "You are a joke which seems to have backfired on me somewhat?" He shook his head and laughed quietly to himself. "Still, I imagine a few days under Meas's command will see you so far out of your depth you drown and the Hag will take you. I shall look forward to hearing of this flotsam becoming jetsam."

Joron was about to speak but Meas stepped forward, physically cutting him off from Karrad.

"I thought I was rid of you when they sent me to the black ships," she said. "I thought we were done. What use am I to you now?"

"What you did was stupid," said Karrad. Joron almost held his breath. *What was it she had done?* He waited for Karrad to say, but he was to be disappointed. "You make a mistake though, if you think foolishness frees you from your obligations, Meas. If anything, a black ship gives you free rein in a way a fleet ship never could."

"In what way?"

"You are outside the order of command, expected to cruise, looking for trouble. You are able, nay, required, to take orders that may not come through the usual channels, and though I am fleetwife, my lack of service on a ship gives me less access than I would like to our ships. But a black ship? You I can have." *Did he leer?* "And you can go to places I could never send a fleet ship."

"So, you intend to use me as a glorified messenger, is that it?" Meas shook her head. "I think we have spoken enough, Karrad. I think will take my chances with fleet orders."

"Well," said Karrad, "that is up to you, but how well has that gone, eh, Meas?" Before she could reply he stood. "And how will you get that old ship fixed, eh? Fleet orders for you will be to rot in Bernshulme while they break up your ship. Maybe a two-ribber will no longer hold the corpselights in its bones and take the black, if you are lucky." He left a silence, interrupted only by the chirping of the night insects. "Besides," he said more quietly, "that is not what I want you for. To have you delivering letters to spies is beneath you, and I know it." Was there a warmth there? Something beneath the timbre of his voice? "And a black ship is hardly unlikely to draw no attention, is it? No. I have something much more in keeping with your talents in mind. I know you, Meas." He came around the desk to stand nearer to her and Joron felt like an interloper, a voyeur watching an intensely private moment. "I know what you want," he whispered. "I know what you will enjoy."

Meas seemed to collapse in on herself. It was not overt, only a collection of minute changes in posture, as if all the cockiness and surety fled from her and left her stranded, out of her element.

"I am sick of this, Indyl."

"Have you forgotten the dream, Meas?"

"That is all it is to you."

"It can be so much more."

"I am not sure I believe anything you say."

"You believed in the dream at Harrit Bay, Meas."

"And look what it has got me." She held out her hands. Inside, Joron was jumping from foot to foot. *What was all this about?* "Where were you, Indyl? Where were you when they shamed me and stripped me? You did not come. Your word would have saved me."

"I could not have saved you. Everything I . . ." Karrad took a deep breath. Picked up a small ornament from the edge of his desk and then put it down again. "Everything we have worked for would have been lost. They would have condemned us both."

Meas raised a hand, almost touched his cheek, and it felt to Joron as if the air were harder to breathe, or maybe it was that he became a ghost to these two people. That to them he no longer existed.

"Indyl," she said, "when I hear you speak" — that voice so soft — "I understand your actions." Karrad smiled. Then something changed in his eyes — a warmth entered them. Then Meas's hand came away from his cheek. "I think you even believe what you say when you say it." She shook her head; the gentle sound of hair moving over leather. "But words mean nothing without action."

"You were too overt, Meas." He tried to grab her wrist, but she was too quick for him. He took a step back, putting space between them. "The rule of the Bern cannot be fought head on, Meas. It is not the way."

And Joron did not want to know what they spoke of. He wished he was not here, that she had not brought him. He went cold from foot to fingertip.

Treason.

They talked of treason. Meas Gilbryn, the greatest shipwife of them all, was a traitor. He was about to say something, to ask to leave, when she turned to him.

"This is not what you think, Twiner," she said. "This is Hundred Isles politics, so don't get ideas about running to the Grand Bothy with tall tales and expecting to win your life back. You will not know who to speak to, and you are as likely to get a knife in the gut as you are to be rewarded. And remember who owns you – remember that – and if you think you have any honour, look to that before you act."

"Honour." Karrad laughed. "Sooner expect a kivelly to fight a sankrey than to find honour in one such as him."

Again the silence, hot and suffocating, filled with the trilling of insects.

"He does for me, Indyl," she said. "For now."

"I heard he ran your ship into a reef."

"I did that," she said, and it shocked Joron that she did not hesitate, did not dissemble or blame him as she had done on *Tide Child*. "I was shipwife. I was responsible."

"Not the way I heard it."

"It is the way it happened." She shrugged. "I suppose I should not be surprised to know you have spies on my ship."

"I have spies everywhere. He'll be the death of you, Meas," said Karrad with a nod towards Joron. Then he returned to his place behind his desk. "But your command is your choice. Now, do you wish to hear what I have to say or not?"

"Speak," she said. "I will listen, as will Twiner. And we will sit, not stand like we owe you some allegiance or meet you in honour."

Karrad shrugged. "By all means take the weight from your feet. Twiner's feet are particularly filthy and you do me a favour to remove them from my floor."

Everything that was Joron tensed, but he showed none of it. For in that moment of Meas taking the blame for *Tide Child*'s grounding the ebbing tide of loyalty he had been feeling towards her rose once more. He did not know why, or understand it; maybe it was that she was the nearest he had to a safe port in this room and that was all. But it did not make it any less true or real in the moment.

Joron sat opposite the man who had made sure he was condemned to a ship of the dead, and, in so doing, he heard of the miracle that would make him part of a legend.

Thirteenbern called out,
Give the child to the ships!
And the sea came to her rescue
As word left the Bern's cruel lips.

Anon., "The Song of Lucky Meas"

13

Here Be Dragons

"There is an arakeesian coming," said Karrad.

It was as if all the air was stolen from the stuffy little room. Oh, the wanelights still burned and they could still breathe, but for a moment Joron was light-headed. *An arakeesian? A sea dragon?* Their bones were the building blocks of fleets, but no keyshans had been seen for over three generations.

"Is this a joke?" said Meas. Though Joron could tell she felt it too, the excitement, the wonder, the awe at even the possibility of it.

"No," said Karrad. "I wish it was."

"Why have I heard nothing?" she said.

"A number of reasons, Meas," he began. "Chiefly because you are now shipwife of a black ship and no one wants to speak to you." They locked eyes and Karrad was first to look away. "But there are other reasons. My spy network is still the best – I get the news first. At the moment all the people who know of this beast are in this room."

"How sure of this are you?"

"As sure as I can be."

"What of your spy?

"She had an accident."

"A poor reward."

"Some secrets are too precious to risk on one life, Meas. My spy rests comfortably by the Hag's fire and her children are not too Berncast — no missing limbs or such, only a few marks on their skin. They will find themselves invited to attend the schools of the spiral bothies. She would think it a good trade."

"Did you ask her?" said Meas. "A military school makes a poor mother, as I well know."

"You always have had a mouth on you, Meas." He saw the true Karrad then — vicious, unpleasant, cruel — but it was gone as quickly as smoke in a storm. "Because we know of the arakeesian first, we can get to it first. Before the Gaunt Islanders or the Hundred Islanders."

"What?" The word escaped Joron's lips involuntarily.

"Quiet, Joron," said Meas, but he could not have said any more if had he wanted to. He was out of his depth and drowning here. *Who were these people?* What he thought Meas was changed and twisted in front of him. First he had met the loyal and respected shipwife, then had come the political plotter, and now, despite what they had said to him, it seemed she really was an outright traitor. But if she was not loyal to the Hundred Isles, who did she fight for?

Why did she fight?

What else was there?

"How sure are you of this keyshan, Indyl? You know how deckchilder talk."

"Absolutely sure." He opened a drawer in his chest and took out a rolled chart, spreading it across the desk. "In the old days they called the first arakeesian of the season the wakewyrm, so I have named it that."

"You think there will be more?" said Joron. Karrad looked up at him, becoming utterly still for a moment before answering.

"I hope not."

This made no sense. More arakeesians meant more ships, and the fleet sore needed them.

"It has been spotted here" — Karrad pointed at the map —

"coming in near Soris Isle in the far south where it is too cold for anyone to live."

"This is how no one knows?"

"Aye," he said. "And it is small, for an arakeesian, I am told, but it is still many magnitudes bigger than anything else in the sea."

"And you need us for this why?" said Meas.

"There are old charts in the Grand Bothy, long forgotten. I have dug many out and hidden them, but I cannot be sure I got them all." Karrad looked worried. "The arakeesians always followed the same routes, which is what made them easy to hunt, though they were hard to kill, of course."

"Yes, yes, that is why the black ships were instituted," said Meas. "This is not news."

"Well, exactly," said Karrad. "Though when you read the old accounts, most of the killing was done from towers over-looking narrow straits. The black ships were mainly a punishment." He gave her a small, unpleasant smile. "Now, follow the red line on the map. That is the course the keyshan should take, mostly past deserted isles – there are few places it will be seen. They always keep to the deep channels."

"So," said Joron, "you want us to go back to what the black ships were intended for and hunt you an arakeesian?"

Karrad stared at him as if he were a fool.

"Of course not," he said. "I want you to keep it alive."

"Alive? But we need its bones." He stared at Karrad then added, "For our ships," because the man did not seem to understand this most basic need of the Hundred Isles. "And we need ships to fight the Gaunt Islanders. They are massing in the south – everyone knows this. They will attack soon."

"You have told him nothing of what we do, Meas?" Karrad said this with a sneer on his beautiful face.

"I did not know how much you would reveal of us and our cause, or how much I should. Or even if he could be trusted." Her words like a knife in him, even though he was not sure in this moment that he could be trusted either. "But as it seems you are happy to share everything, you may as well fill him in."

"Very well." Karrad nodded at her. "How long have we fought the Gaunt Islanders, Twiner?"

"For ever."

"And why?"

"Why?" He had no answer. It was what Hundred Islanders did. What they had always done. Eventually he said, "They steal our children."

"Why?"

"To sacrifice to their ships."

"Why?"

"To light the corpselights and give them good fortune in the fight against us."

"And, in turn, we steal their children for the same, and when neither side can steal children we sacrifice our own. And all for what?"

"I . . ." Joron found himself lost. Karrad was talking as if everything he knew, had been raised with, was somehow wrong. "It is what we do," he said.

"We steal children to keep fighting each other so we may steal more children. In turn we attack them and they attack us to avenge the children taken. And so it goes — round and round and round. But what if there is no need to steal children? Eh, Joron Twiner? What if killing each other is not the only way?"

"But without the fleet what would we do?"

"We do not know," said Meas quietly. "But maybe it would be good if we could find out."

"The Gaunt Islanders will never accept peace," said Joron. "They hate us and love war."

"And they say the same of us," said Meas quietly. "But they love their children also. Such things bind us all together."

"You work with them? They are our enemy, and—"

"Many of them are our enemy, yes," said Meas, "but not all. There are those who feel as Indyl and I do. That war is futile, a waste of what we have. Not a lot of them, and there are not a lot of us. But those who think that war must end grow."

"An arakeesian though," said Karrad. "That will put a stop to any chance of peace. The war will start again, worse then ever."

"Why?"

"We have less and less bone for ships every season, Joron," said Meas. "Fewer ships, smaller ships. And as people begin to realise what a waste it is to throw our people at the sea for war they come to us."

"But the Sea Hag," said Joron. "She demands war. She—"

"Have you ever met the Sea Hag, Twiner?" said Karrad.

"I hope not to."

"No one has," said Karrad, "though I would be glad to send you on your way to her if you are truly curious. It is women and men that decide what the Sea Hag says. The hagpriests speak *for* her, but I have never heard of one who speaks *to* her. It has always been so. And Thirteenbern Gilbryn is tied to war and tradition – give her the bones of an arakeesian and she will build warships. The same is true of the Gaunt Islands' rulers. It is all they know, all they want. Fear is how they stay in power."

"But if the Hundred Isles gets the arakeesian bones," said Joron, "then our advantage will be overwhelming."

"It does not work like that, Joron," said Meas, sitting back in her chair. "It never has. Bones are stolen and smuggled and sold by the greedy. Raids are made. Traitors betray ships to the other side for money. One arakeesian will fuel war for a generation, if not longer."

"So," said Karrad, "the beast must be protected until it reaches the Northstorm."

"That is a long distance. You expect us to fight all the way?" said Meas.

"You are a ship of the dead," snapped Karrad. "It is your duty."

"Duty is good, but to give us an impossible task helps no one."

Karrad paused, as if gathering himself for a last charge. "The timing of this is good for us, Meas." He leaned forward. "The tension in the south has drawn many of the ships of both sides. Even now, out there, our greatest ships get ready for a show of strength in the south. Trade has slowed as the brownbones and their shipwives are wary of sending their cargoes across the sea with such tension, and the lack of boneships makes raiders braver. The keyshan has already passed where the ships mass and it seems no one saw it. The main routes south go nowhere near where the keyshan should swim. You will not face too great a challenge."

"Even if we succeed," said Meas, "what of next year, when it returns?"

"I do not intend to let that happen."

"How?" said Joron.

"At the edge of the Northstorm, where the currents are fast and strong, you will kill it. No one will be able to salvage the corpse; the storm is too fierce."

"One ship against a sea dragon?" said Meas, incredulous. "You are not the only one who has read the old accounts, Indyl. It is impossible."

"It is not impossible," said Karrad. "I have been reading deep on hunting arakeesians. They can be killed with one shot." Meas snorted. "You would be surprised what we have forgotten." Karrad leaned over his map. "The arakeesian's route is mostly deep water. From here" – he pointed at where it had been spotted – "to here" – he pointed at an area far to the west of it – "the keyshan is safe, and the waters empty for fear of ice, so no one will see it. There are only really three or four places where it can be hunted. Though I suspect every island it passes will send out flukeboats to try their luck, they can mostly be ignored or they will run when they see a fleet ship. To hurt the keyshan only big gallowbows will work, the type mounted on the harbour moles or a ship's maindeck. It is almost conceivable that you can travel the whole route without ever being seen or having to fight."

"Almost?" said Meas.

"Few of the old keyshan towers remain; stone is valuable, also many have been dismantled. But here" – he tapped the map where a thin line of blue ran between an island and the basalt slabs of Skearith's Spine, the mountain range that divided the Archipelago – "this is Arkannis Isle. There are still towers either side of the channel. One on the island, one on the spine itself. They have long been held by raiders who take a toll for passage – it has never been worth our while fighting them. And the towers have giant gallowbows, big enough to damage the keyshan, maybe even kill it if they are quick with their loosing, though who knows how many bolts it takes. Anyway, you must take those towers."

"You make it sound so simple, Indyl," said Meas.

He ignored her.

"Then there is Berringhulme Sound in the far north. It is deep enough for a big ship to come in, shallow enough to retrieve the corpse. If news reaches Bernshulme quickly, they could get a ship up there." He talked as if the prospect of another ship was a slight thing. "But as you see, Meas, you need not fight all the way, just accompany the creature. One fight, maybe two at the most. It is not an impossible task I set you."

"Not impossible in the unlikely event it goes perfectly," said Meas.

"I have arranged help too. You will be joined in the south by some of our friends. Keep the beast safe until the Northstorm and then finish it. That is imperative if we wish to ever end our wars."

"How do we finish it, Indyl? Arakeesians used to rip apart five-ribbers with ease. *Tide Child* is only four, and small for it."

"I have three hiylbolts," said Karrad.

"But they are a myth," Meas protested.

"Well, I have three, so plainly they are not."

"What are they?" said Joron.

"Hiyl was a poison that could kill a keyshan within minutes if you hit the beast in the eye, Joron," said Meas. "But I have only ever heard of it in tales. How do you know it is real, Indyl?"

"It was hidden away. I found talk of the hiylbolts in papers and tracked down where they should be, found only an empty room. But I had seen mention, somewhere, about a room used to hide treasures in case Bernshulme itself was raided. These papers were ancient, Meas," he said, tapping a finger on the desk. "But I found the room and the bolts, behind a collapsed wall in a dark corner of the Grand Bothy, with some other papers and unimportant objects. I have no reason to doubt the bolts are what I believe. The room had been undisturbed for generations."

"How do we know this poison works?" said Joron.

"Well" – a wry smile crossed Karrad's face – "there is only one way to find that out."

"Do you seek to send me to my death, Indyl?" said Meas.

He shook his head.

"No. Never." And strangely, Joron believed that. "I have the bolts. We have them. They will kill the beast with one hit."

"You hope," said Meas.

"I am sure," said Karrad. "You only need to get your ship out of the way once the bolt has been loosed in case its thrashing smashes your ship." Meas and Karrad stared at each other over the desk, as intent as lovers. Then she gave a small nod. "Good," said Karrad. "Good! Load them on to *Tide Child* just before you leave. I will put them in my warehouse."

"Why not now?" said Joron.

"Because," said Meas, "he cannot be sure no one else knows of them."

Karrad nodded.

"No one has ever died from being too careful."

"That," said Meas, "may be the most truthful thing you have ever said." She tapped the desk as Karrad relaxed back into his chair. "How many of these 'friends' will there be?"

"A pair of Gaunt Islands two-ribbers will join you. Black ships like your own."

"There are other things I will need, Indyl, or I will fail before I even start."

Karrad nodded, his oiled chest shining in the weak light, a smile on his face.

"Tell me, and if I can help I will."

"*Tide Child*'s keel is cracked. It must be fixed and the mainspine rebuilt before I can fly the sea."

"The ship is already out of the water and with the bonewrights. They work on him as we speak."

"And no slapdash job simply because he is a ship of the dead. I know what they think of black ships."

"I have taken steps to ensure the ship will be well cared for."

"I need provisioning for at least four months."

"It is unlikely to take so long, two months at most."

"The provisions are also for ballast. *Tide Child* could be a fast ship if he is weighted right."

"Very well."

"I need bolts, shot, wingbolts, cutters and hagspit oil. And decent weapons for my crew."

"Not a problem. Weapons we have."

"I need more crew too, not only deckchilder. A ship should have seaguard, and if we must fight on land, as you say, we will need them."

"I have access to criminals only; the seaguard answer to Thirteenbern Gilbryn and she says they harbour only the best of us so, of course, the seaguard commit no crimes."

Meas let out a snort.

"Even those seaguard that brought us here?"

"They risk a lot for me, Meas. Do not mock them."

She looked away from him.

"Very well. Give me more crew than I need, and I will train twenty as soldiers. I'll need arms and armour for them."

"Is that is all?"

"No. I need a gullaime."

"I have heard you have one."

"Not one that is any use. It will not obey."

"How else do you think a gullaime ends up on a ship of the dead, Meas? You are lucky to have one at all."

Meas leaned forward, her lips peeling away from her teeth like those of a furious animal.

"What use is the creature if it will not obey, Indyl? It is like no other gullaime I have met, it does not know its place. What if it simply decides to wreck us?"

"Look upon it as part of the ballast you require."

Meas made to stand.

"Keyshan's rot take you and your mission, Indyl Karrad. I need a gullaime or—"

"A long time ago, Meas," he said softly, and she paused, "you told me you were the best, and I said surely it was your crew that made you the best. Do you remember what your answer was?"

She did not look away, was not in the least cowed, and no one would have believed that this was a meeting of one of the most powerful men of the Hundred Isles and a condemned criminal.

"Yes," she said through gritted teeth.

"You told me a shipwife makes their crew, not the other way around. So, Shipwife, make your crew."

"I did not talk of a crew of criminals and a mad windtalker."

"You will have to work with what you have," he said to her. "And now I think we are done." He glanced at Joron. "Kindly get that murderer out of my rooms."

Meas did not reply, only stood and turned her back on him.

"Come, Joron."

He followed her out of the carved door and down through

the building. She stopped before the street door as if she wanted to speak to him, but before she spoke, he did.

"You knew."

"Knew what?" She did not turn, did not give him the courtesy of her full attention.

"What I did. Why they put me on the black ship. You knew I killed his son."

"It never hurts to have your enemy wrong-footed."

"I thought he was your friend."

She laughed then.

"Oh my deckkeeper, you have so much to learn. I am Lucky Meas, greatest shipwife the Hundred Isles has ever known." Now she turned, little visible of her in the dim light but the gleam of her eyes. "People like me, Joron Twiner, we have no friends."

14

A Gathering of Cold Souls

On their way back to their stinking room in Fishmarket Meas had them stop off at a cobbler on Hoppity Lane, where, by tradition, those born with a leg or foot missing carried on the trade of shoe making. From there they went to Handy Alley, where by tradition those with an arm or hand missing carried on the tailoring trade. As they walked through, the left-armed catcalled the right-armed and vice versa, but Meas ignored them all in favour of a tailor she knew well. Then they went to claim what sleep they could before morning, which, as Meas warned him, was when the real work would begin.

But sleep would not come to Joron. He was angry. Meas's use of his history as a tool to try and manipulate Indyl Karrad filled him with a fury he barely understood. She had treated the memory of his father as carelessly as Jion Karrad had treated his life. And twisted up within that anger was worry. The cobbler had measured him for boots, good ones, and the tailor for a fine jacket and trews, but he had no way of paying for either. All his iron had gone down his throat long ago. How would he tell her that when the time came?

Beneath it all another feeling struggled through the tide of resentment and apprehension: excitement. An arakeesian. No one in living memory had seen a living keyshan, and that he may be be one of the few that did filled him with awe. Oh, he had no doubts about the danger of their mission, none at all. But if a man was to die then what a thing to die for. A sea dragon.

And if somehow he could bring its bones back to Bernshulme? If anything could win him freedom from the black ship then it would be that. Maybe. Karrad and Meas had spoken of the long war ending, and maybe such a thing was a worthy, a grand dream, even. But it *was* a dream, and if life in the Hundred Isles taught you anything it was that dreams did not come true. The Hundred Islanders warred to defend themselves, and the Gaunt Islanders murdered for the joy of it. To even think that there could be peace with them was the sort of capricious trick the Maiden played on the unworldly.

Where did he stand here?

Where were his loyalties?

Imagine – to turn over two traitors and the body of a keyshan? Revenge on Indyl Karrad, and he would be respected. Be someone. Of course Meas would be finished but why should he care?

It's not about respect, boy; it's about loyalty.

His father's voice.

Whatever happened, he would see an arakeesian.

What he would have given to share such a sight with his father.

He tossed and turned in the damp bed in the high room of the Fishmarket half-bothy, impatient for the moment when Skearith's Eye would peer in and Meas would start the day. So when it came – a shaft of blinding light, golden dust suspended within – he was not rested but he was filled with adrenalin. As Meas washed herself in a bowl of dirty water he paced backwards and forwards, the gion boards beneath his feet creaking in complaint.

"If you must walk, go to our door and find what is left outside it."

He stopped, screwed up his brow.

"What?"

"Just do as I say."

He opened the door. To one side he found a pair of boots – he had no idea how they had got there; maybe they had been there all night. How had he not heard them be delivered?

"My boots?"

"Did I not say a deckkeeper needed boots?"

"Yes, but I regret to say—"

"Payment is dealt with." She waved a hand at him then lifted it, washing under her arm with her cloth. "Put them on then. They will hurt at first as you are not used to them. Your feet will blister, you must work through that. No need for you to wash today," she added, "as your clothes will still stink no matter how clean the skin beneath, but more fitting clothes will arrive before we leave. Then you will stay clean, even if I have to throw you in the sea each day to ensure it. You are an officer now, you understand?"

He nodded, bewildered once more by this woman.

"Put them on then," she said again, "then find us food. There should be a coin hidden beneath the turn-up of the boot, for that was what I agreed."

Bernshulme was busy and it was not hard to find food. Though Skearith's Eye had barely woken, vendors were already out, and the stink of rotten fish from the market mingled with baking bread and cooking flesh. If the food did not smell appetising, then at least it did not smell as bad as Fishmarket at night. Joron bought two helpings of fish in pastry from the cleanest-looking stallholder, a woman with a malformed jaw, and made his way back to the half-bothy. Meas emerged as he approached the door with his mouth full of pasty which, if mostly bone, was at least hot.

"Thank you, Deckkeeper," she said, taking her pasty from him, and he nodded. "We'll go straight to the fleet dock, see how they treat *Tide Child* and make sure he is well cared for. From there we go to the hulks in the harbour to find out who our new crew are to be." She paused in the act of lifting the pasty to her mouth. "Although perhaps we shall run some other errands first." She turned, walking away and chewing.

A busy day ahead, he said to himself and followed, quickly finding himself limping as the boots, just as promised, were pinching his toes and rubbing at his heels.

"I think we must find ourselves charts," said Meas.

"I have no coin."

"You do not need to keep reminding me of your penury," she said without looking at him. "I have plenty of money and little use for it."

"They did not confiscate your goods when you were condemned?"

"Only what they could find," she said. "Charts we will get from the Grand Bothy, whether they want us to or not."

"Are you welcome at the . . ." His voice petered out as he realised what he had been about to say would have been unwelcome, but it was too late. Meas's tone, almost conversational up to this point, became storm dark as she turned to him.

"You saw how welcome I was when we brought in *Tide Child*. I imagine it will be similar at the Grand Bothy. Thirteenbern Gilbryn may call us to her if I am seen; you will have to prepare yourself for that possibility." Before he could reply she was off and he followed, his feet complaining at every step they took over the cobbles.

The fleet dock was the biggest harbour facility in Bernshulme, taking up a whole side of the island's inner crescent. Joron counted thirty ships at their staystones and four in dry docks, held up on scaffolds of rock and bone. Only one ship was the black of shame. *Tide Child*, shunned like a dead chick in a thriving colony, space around him as if he made the other ships uncomfortable. Even those who worked on *Tide Child* seemed to do so at a slower pace, and with less enthusiasm, than those clustered around the white ships. Where the white ships glistened in the sun and rang with working songs, *Tide Child* absorbed the light, squatting in silence in his cradle.

"I thought Karrad said he would make sure they did a good job? They barely seem to be working," said Joron.

A roar came from *Tide Child*.

"Get on, you slatelayers! Lazy grabarses! So the ship's cursed? It does not mean you are. You'll work these bones as well as any other or I'll have you skinned." From behind a lean-to of gion leaves came a man almost as wide as he was tall. Dressed in a leather apron and little else, he strode about the base of *Tide Child* giving orders as Skearith's Eye rose and the heat of the day began to beat down upon the bones of the ship. Around his shoulders, arms and thighs were wrapped dirty bandages, stained with blood from the sores of keyshan's rot, a disease that came to all in the boneyards eventually.

"Bonemaster?" said Meas as they approached. The man turned and Joron saw the black band of the condemned on his arm.

"You must be the shipwife who treated this poor beast" – he pointed at *Tide Child* – "with such contempt he has ended up in my loving care."

"And by the band on your arm that makes me your shipwife, so some respect is in order, is it not?" The man did not answer, nor did he bring his forearm to his chest in salute nor show any of the respect that was her due. "How did you earn the band?" asked Meas.

"A bonemaster takes a little for himself, here and there." He puffed himself up like a bird in a fighting pit the moment before its handlers let it go. "It is normal." His voice rose and fell, as if to head off any thought she may have that he had done anything wrong in stealing from the shipyard.

"So says every bonemaster sent to a black ship, ey?" said Meas.

The man squinted at her.

"There are many here take far more than me."

"Then why do they not wear the band?"

"Because, Shipwife" – there was a lusty lack of respect in the way he said her title – "they have better friends than poor

Bonemaster Coxward, and so they may carry on stealing the Hundred Isles' wealth, where I will go bleed for it."

"Well, it was promised the bonemaster would do a good job on my ship," said Meas, "and now I see why it was said with such confidence, since you are to fly him with me."

"It will be a month before we do," said Coxward. "Ey, at least a month."

"We have a week, and we must also load supplies. So you have four days to get him ready for sea."

"Four?" The bonemaster's teeth almost leaped from his mouth in horror. "Sooner break a keyshan's heart than let him out in four."

"It is what the fleet calls for."

He stared at her then shrugged.

"The fleet often calls for the impossible from us poor souls, hagspit upon them who give out orders not knowing what they mean." He put his hands on ample hips and turned to look at *Tide Child*. His voice dropped a tone, became flatter, more serious, the voice of a professional considering his charge. "The mainspine I can fix. The hull also. Much of the rest of the damage is superficial, the rails and such." He waved towards the ship. "That can be fixed at sea if you give me a few hands to do it. But the keel, see, that is a different matter." He turned back and a spark of mischief glistened in his eye. "A ship was never meant to go on the land, you know, Shipwife."

"I am aware of that."

"Well, we can set it, we can glue it. But the glue needs to dry, and that takes time. It cannot be hurried. If we fly to your timetable—"

"Which we must."

"Well then, Shipwife" — again, such obvious discourtesy but Meas did not seem bothered — "the keel will be weak, and there is little we can do about it. You must command your ship with that knowledge and nurse it as much as you can, otherwise the keel will break and our dark fellow will capsize. Then the Hag will have her due from poor Coxward."

"Thank you, Bonemaster," she said. "I know I ask a lot."

"Not as much as I shall ask of these." He raised his voice and pointed at the bonewrights around the ship. "Slate-laying wyrms! Get on with you." He walked back to the ship, ignoring Meas and Joron.

"Why do you let him be rude to you?" said Joron.

"Because he is a skilled man and good at what he does. He will be a credit to the ship, and his skills will keep us afloat. Bonewrights are often eccentric; the glue does strange things to their minds, and he has the signs of keyshan's rot. It sends those afflicted mad eventually, so I allow such people some slack. Only a little, mind."

"And what of the keel?"

"Oh, he is entirely right in what he says: the keel will be brittle. We will treat *Tide Child* as kindly as events allow and hope he treats us well in return."

These were not words that filled Joron with confidence.

From the fleet dock they made their way up the Serpent Road to the spiral bothies. At each turn of the road there were fewer common people and more seaguard, the clothes of the people became finer, the fishskin that hugged their bodies better cured, the feathers that decorated them longer, the paint on their faces more elaborate and colourful, their bodies more whole and less Berncast, their ignoring of Meas Gilbryn more ostentatious.

"There are many places in the town that sell charts, Shipwife," said Joron, not for her benefit, but because the increasing richness around them made him uncomfortable.

"Oh indeed, Joron. But if I go somewhere other than the Grand Bothy my mother will hear of it and will think I avoid the spiral bothies because of her, because I am ashamed. Before I was condemned I would have demanded charts from the Grand Bothy. I will not let her think she can force shame on me."

At the arch that marked the entrance to the Grand Bothy the guards let them through but turned away as Meas bent to dip her fingers in the red and blue paint. She flicked the paint over the stones, adding to the thick riot of stringy colour built up over generations. Inside no one approached or spoke to her. She walked through the welcome hall, cleaning her hand on a cloth she took from her pouch, and although she was not acknowledged it would not be true to say she was ignored. The women and men of the bothy, almost without fault, stopped to stare, to whisper, to point.

Joron felt their interest like a weight, and if he felt it that way he wondered how much heavier the attention weighed on her. Meas showed no sign it concerned her. She strode through the bothy, her boots clicking on the slate floor and echoing from the stacked stones of the walls. There was nothing soft in the place to absorb the sound, and the whispering of gossips whirled around them – a malicious zephyr. Meas walked on, taking a landward path down into the tunnels that ran from the bothy into the mountain. Like all the main isles Shipshulme was given to earthquakes, so the tunnels were shallow, skirting the base of the mountain. Down here were all manner of small rooms: armouries, smithies, stores and the chart rooms.

And it was to the chart room that Meas took Joron. Down a dark tunnel, barely lit with wanelights, to a room that to Joron first seemed pitch-black. It took a moment for his eyes to adjust as the sole light was down to the dregs of its oil, no one having seen fit to refill it. The chart room's single occupant sat amid a riot of gion shelving on a stool of varisk and slate, his long white hair falling around his face, his clothes old and careworn and his eyes white with blindness.

"Meas," he said, his voice quiet as an early-morning breeze. "They said you would never come back. I knew you would." Nearer, Joron could see the smooth skin of old burns across the old man's face, and where his nose should have been was only a gnarled lump of flesh.

"I will always come back, Shipwife," she said and reached out, gently taking the man's hand. He had only two complete fingers, the rest stumps.

"Do not call me that, Meas. I am not a shipwife any longer and have not been that for many years. Just Yirrid the chart keeper now."

"Always Shipwife to me."

He smiled at her words.

"Too loyal and too stubborn. You always were. I shouldn't be surprised you ended up on a black ship." He shook his head but his voice was full of warmth. "Now, why are you here?"

"Charts," she said, "I need a full set. The ship I was on lost them."

"Sold for drink by some fool who did not know their worth, no doubt," said the blind man, and Joron felt himself blush. "But charts we have plenty of. I am meant to palm off old ones on the black ships" – he slipped from his stool – "but half the shipwives who come through here would not know a good chart from a bad one, so I will give you my best." He walked, trailing his two fingers along the shelves, feeling at the pegs stuck in below each shelf that told him what he would find there. "Here." He stopped. "The newest ones from the coursers, by Clenas, who is an artist with a chart, I am told. They certainly sound like they know their business when they visit." He took out a sheaf of rolled charts. "These were meant for the *Dread*. Hastin has it now."

"I cannot grudge him it. He is a good shipwife, if an unimaginative one."

"Your sither, Kyrie, has the new five-ribber *Hag's Hunter*. No doubt her reward for helping to put you on the black ship." He passed over the charts, and as she took them he reached out, grabbing her wrist. "Be careful, Meas. You play a dangerous game."

"I know."

"Be as careful of your allies as you are of your enemies." Yirrid sounded resigned, saddened.

"I know that too."

"Yes," he said, letting go of her hand, "I imagine you do."

"I will return to see you again, Shipwife."

"I hope you will." Yirrid turned away, going back to sit on his stool and staring into nothing as Meas led Joron out of the room.

Outside stood two seaguard. They came to attention, spears cracking on the stone in unison, making Joron jump at the unexpected noise.

The taller of the two took a step forward.

"Shipwife Meas Gilbryn, I come in the name of Thirteenbern Gilbryn, ruler of the Hundred Isles, protector of the Berncast, grandmother of the fleet, scion of the seaguard, high priest of Mother, Maiden and Hag, and wellspring of our fertility."

"I know who my mother is," said Meas softly, but the guard gave no sign he heard her.

"I am to bring you before the mother of all." The thought of being brought before the ruler of the Hundred Isles almost unmanned Joron. He felt his knees weaken, his stomach flutter.

"I am grateful for the invite but I am afraid have a ship to prepare and the tide waits for none." Meas made to walk past him, but the guard stepped forward, using his spear to bar the way. Unlike most seaguard he wore no armour; his clothing was more akin to that worn by Kept Indyl Karrad, an arrangement of leather straps designed to show off his oiled muscles. "You are a toy, not a soldier, Tassar," said Meas to the man. "Do not obstruct me. I have business."

"I think you will find I am both toy and soldier, Meas. Now, follow me." He turned.

Meas watched him for a moment as he made his way up the gloomy tunnel, light burnishing his bronze skin. She waited, for long enough to make it seem like she made up her own mind to follow, though in Bernshulme no one turned down the invite of the Thirteenbern, not even her daughter.

To ascend the Grand Bothy was to enter the light. The higher you went, the more elaborately the bothy was constructed. On the lower levels the walls were patterned with specially chosen stone, the colours within making glittering gold, green and red spirals that ran around the building. Joron and Meas ascended the ramps that ran around the outside, up and up and up, walking behind the two seaguard. Further up, the bothy became more delicate. The Gaunt Islanders made their buildings from blocks of stone fixed together with a mixture of sand and chemicals that the Hundred Isles regarded as ugly and utilitarian. The Hundred Islanders built their bothies from small stones, each fitted together by the stonewrights without recourse to any form of glue, the weight of the buildings keeping them up. The spiral bothies were the finest exemplars of the stonewrights' art and the Grand Bothy the greatest of them all. By the time they reached the highest level, the sixth, the bothy was a spider's web of artfully constructed stone ribs with gion — bleached, treated and thinned until it was hard as iron and as clear as the air on a fine day — stretched between them.

Beneath this web, bathed in light, sat Thirteenbern Gilbryn, proud of what she was. Her hair was grey now, and she wore no colour in it — a break with tradition, but she was a woman who did not feel the need to advertise her authority. She wore a skirt, and her flat breasts hung down to her navel, almost covering the stretch marks across her belly, which had been painted in bright colours, the scars of her battles there for all to see: the marks of her power. There was no denying the strength in the Thirteenbern's body, and that was why she showed it. She flaunted her fertility. This woman was the bringer of thirteen perfect children to the isles and claimed title as mother of all. Her skirts were of iron, laced together with birdgut and enamelled with stylised fish which danced across her lap. Like Meas she wore long boots. Unlike Meas, who stood upon a ship of shame, she sat upon on the throne of tears, a seat of polished and bonded varisk carved into the semblance of firstborn children, each child weeping as they held up the weight of the Thirteenbern and through her carried the weight of the entire Hundred Isles.

Gilbryn shared a face with Meas: imperious, eyes that could

silence with a look, mouth thin, though it looked to Joron as though she longed to laugh. Maybe she did; maybe he only thought this so he felt less uncomfortable before her. Tassar walked to the seaward side of the Thirteenbern. Apart from him and those before her throne, the well-lit room was empty. There was nothing here: no tools, no papers, nothing. Thirteenbern Gilbryn had no need of possessions, because she owned everything in the Hundred Isles and all answered to her.

"What is he doing here?" Gilbryn pointed at Joron, and he wished he could vanish into the grey slate of the floor.

"Twiner is my deckkeeper."

"Uh," she said. An amused sound. "You raise up a simple Berncast fisher boy, have the weak-blooded share your deck." Joron could feel his face burning with embarrassment, but Meas did not so much as look at him. "I thought, maybe, the certainty of death would make you less likely to stack the odds against yourself. It seems not."

"It is not I who stacks the odds against me," said Meas. Something crossed her face, a salt spray smile. "Is it, Mother?" she added.

The amusement on the the Thirteenbern's face vanished and she was standing. From relaxed to fury in one movement, face contorted with anger.

"You do not get to call me that." Cold words like an ice floe.

"It is what you are," Meas replied.

"You are my curse. Every day I ask why the Hag took nine of my children in war but never so much as touched you." She glared at Meas, letting silence settle like sediment in shipwine. Then she sat once more. "Tassar, take her plaything down a level; I would speak to my *daughter.*" She made the confirmation of their relationship into something mocking. "And I shall speak to her alone."

The Kept stepped forward and motioned to Joron to follow him, which he did. They walked down the ramp to the level below, and behind them was only silence; Gilbryn had no wish to share her words with such as him.

Tassar openly stared at him. "It is unusual," he said, "to see an officer who is neither Kept nor Bern brought through the spiral bothies, but I suppose Meas has little quality material to choose from among the dead." Tassar's eyes wandered down Joron's body until they came to rest on the blade at his hip. "Do you even know how to use that?" He stepped a little closer to Joron. "Would you like me to give you some lessons?" He put his hand to his mouth. Touched his lip. "I could teach you how a man uses a sword."

"No." Joron swallowed, looked away. "I have already killed with this blade – I am quite comfortable with it."

Before Joron could stop him Tassar leaned in and yanked the curnow from the hook on his belt.

"Not a real sword," he said, hefting the weapon. "Swordcraft isn't just about waggling it around. It takes skill. You'd be surprised what a real man can do" – he left a long pause – "with his sword."

"May I have that back?" said Joron. The Kept did not look as though he had heard him and Joron pointed at the elaborate scabbard on Tassar's hip. "Or are you proposing we swap?"

Tassar laughed.

"A wit! What a wit. Maybe you could have ended up one of the Kept had you been born stronger. But I hear your mother was weak." He did not offer Joron the sword.

"You know nothing of me or my mother." The words whipped out of his mouth, fast as a rope snapped taut by the wind.

"I know all about you, Twiner. I know you've been to see Karrad; no doubt he seeks to win the Thirteenbern's favour. How would he do that, eh? If you knew, I could reward you." He smiled, holding Joron's sword loosely in his hand. For a moment Joron considered telling him everything, but only a moment. For all he hated Karrad he at least understood him, but this man was something different. He sensed some need beneath the innuendo, but it was not a deckchild's fleshly pleasure he sought, not the company of a shipfriend. Besides,

Meas's warning still rang in his ears. He knew nothing of the world in the bothies, had no idea who could be trusted. He believed what he knew of Karrad was valuable, to the right person. But he did not think Tassar was the right person to tell, not at all.

"I was not privy to what Karrad and my shipwife discussed."

"*Your* shipwife?" The eyebrow raised in amusement caused the glittering turquoise paint around his eye to flake away. "Well then, I suppose you are Kept, in your own way. You've been given Meas's favour at least, eh? Though I reckon you spend your seed in vain there. If she were to be Bern she would be by now. Hag knows she's tried hard enough. Still, better to seed a field in hope than hate, eh?" He leaned closer, grinning. "Though sometimes it adds a little spice if it is both."

"I am sure the Thirteenbern would love to hear you say that," said Joron. Tassar's broad, blocky face hardened, and Joron wondered if the Kept would draw on him, but instead he flicked the curnow into the air so the blade landed in his hand. Then he stared hard at Joron, grasping the blade tight enough to make the muscles in his arm ripple and for the blade to draw blood from his hand. Then he offered Joron the hilt.

"Do not joke about such things." He took a step closer. "Do not think to repeat any of my words to the Thirteenbern." He stepped even closer. Joron took one step back on the ramp and had a moment of vertigo, realising how close he was to the edge, how far he had to fall. "Be very careful how you tread. Many people have slipped and fallen on their way down the spiral bothy, Deckkeeper Twiner. It is often a fatal fall."

"Meas would be upset if I fell."

The yawning void behind him.

"You are presuming Meas will ever leave the room above," he whispered. "I am afraid that sometimes a mother's love is not all it should be."

"She will leave."

"And how do you know that, Deckkeeper?" He did not know. But not knowing did not make him any less sure. When he did not immediately reply a smile spread across Tassar's face.

"She will leave because she is Lucky Meas, Seaguard," said Joron, and the smile swiftly vanished.

"My title is Kept, Twiner, and I am Kept of the Thirteenbern. You should remember that. And if after what Meas did, you still believe she will come back? Maybe you are simple." Joron must have betrayed something, made some tiny movement of his face that Tassar, schooled in the ways of deceit and politicking among the Bern and the Kept, picked up. "Oh . . ." He drawled out the soft exclamation. "You do not know, do you? Of course, stuck away on that black ship, you do not hear the news. Do not know what sort of creature you serve. And she is unlikely to tell one as lowly as you. Well, I do not think I shall tell you either; I shall leave you to wonder."

Before Joron could say anything else Meas appeared on the ramp. She had something of a air of a fighting bird that had, if not lost its contest, definitely not come off best from it. Though maybe it had done enough to keep its pride and stay out of the pot, for now.

"Come, Twiner."

Tassar gave Joron a smile and nodded his head at Meas as she passed.

"Go then, Joron," he said, "and remember, my offer to teach you the sword remains open."

Joron ignored him. He caught up with Meas who, as they walked away whispered to him,

"Tell me that Tassar did not bait you into a duel."

"He did not, though if I am honest I more thought he was trying to get me into his bed."

Meas laughed — a real laugh, a bright sound.

"Oh, I did not think on how little you knew of their ways. No ship's rules for the Kept, Twiner. Their lives depend on the strength of their seed, and they strut and preen like cock birds to gain the favour of the Bern. To be accused of loving men is a mortal insult among them. But you did not know that, and all his work to goad you into insulting him was for naught."

"I know no one who cares of such things."

"That is because you are fleet, ey?"

"But I am not fleet," he said, confused, and he could not keep the sadness out of his voice. "I have never been fleet. I am just a simple fisher boy."

"The Thirteenbern mocked you," said Meas, coming to a halt, and when she spoke she was fierce, but that fierceness was not aimed at him. "Do not let that affect you. Do not worry about not being fleet, for I will teach you all you need to know. My mother's words were loosed to hurt me, not you. And if Tassar mocked you it was for the same reason. This does not mean you cannot be angry – be angry, be angry by all means. But believe me in this, Joron. The greatest revenge is not that taken with a blade, it is that done by taking your enemy's taunts and throwing them back in their face." She stared at him, her tongue moving in her mouth. "You will be fleet by the time I am finished with you, Joron Twiner. I promise you that."

"Or dead," he said.

"There is that. But I would not dwell on it, for there is far less opportunity for revenge in death."

15

A Reunion

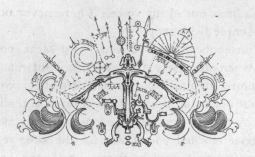

There were few things sadder in the Scattered Archipelago than the prison hulks, ships so badly damaged they were no longer salvageable, not even to become a black ship to carry a crew to glorious death or a brownbone hauling cargo in short hops from island to island. Instead they lay sluggish on the surface of the greasy water outside the harbour and rotted. Skeleton crews of seaguard garrisoned them. No one wanted the duty, so it fell to the worst of them to guard those who, through crime or poor luck, had been judged unworthy of the land and locked below. They barely lived on whatever slop was served up and were forced to prey upon one another to survive, begging the Sea Hag that their sentences be served out before the hulk's bones finally gave way and the old ships went to the bottom. For if you were imprisoned on a hulk when it sank, surely your death was the Hag's wish?

No wonder the hulkbound flocked to the call when the black ships recruited.

It was to the largest of the hulks that Joron rowed Meas. They were neither white nor black, but the awful brown of rotting bone. And as every bit of keyshan bone that could be salvaged became more and more precious, the hulks became as much gion and varisk as they were old bone. And the gion and varisk were kept up no better.

They stank.

Joron had believed *Tide Child*, sad and neglected in Keyshanblood Bay, was the worst thing he had ever smelled, but that was only because he had never been near a hulk before. First the stink of rotting bone, wet and organic. Then the stink of human filth. The hulks were little more than open sewers, and in the high heat the reek was almost unbearable. Joron found himself retching as he pulled on the oars; Meas, as ever, seemed unaffected. And behind the louder scents that insulted Joron's nose there was another – more subtle, almost undefinable but in its own way far worse – misery. The stink of women and men who were at their last, the desperate and the lost.

Meas dipped her hand into her pouch and brought out a posy of bright flowers, holding it to her nose to ward off the stink as Joron, choking on the malodour, rowed them further into the miasma. At the side of the hulk a seaguard let down a rope ladder, done with no ceremony or care. Meas ignored the insult; she seemed to have skin thicker than a keyshan. The shipwife grabbed the ladder, shimmying up in a couple of easy leaps while Joron tied the boat on to the side of the hulk and then struggled his way up the rungs as they swayed left and right with his weight.

When he crested the rail of the hulk, the once-ornate bone splintering in his grip, leaving brown smears and shards sticking into his his palm, he was met by a long line of prisoners waiting for Meas to cast her eye over them. Around them stood seaguard, and if women and men as different from those who guarded the spiral bothies could have been found, Joron could not imagine a better collection than those gathered here. Where they bothered to wear more than the birdskin leather hat of the seaguard, their uniforms were dirty, and their faces were pinched and mean.

They had no respect for Meas. Mostly they ignored her and

instead spent their time walking up and down the line, occasionally lashing out with small clubs for some infraction that Joron could neither see nor understand. The prisoners appeared completely cowed and subservient.

A seaguard raised his club, about to bring it down on the head of the old man before him.

Meas grabbed the man's arm before the club fell.

"No."

"No? This flotsam looked at me like I were nothing. He deserves a beating."

"This flotsam," said Meas, "may become part of my crew, and if he is to be punished I will see it done. Put down your club."

"Make me," said the seaguard. By the time he had finished that last word he was on the deck and his club in Meas's hand.

"If you can take this back," said Meas, brandishing the club, "you can beat who you wish."

But the seaguard, mouth bleeding from a blow he never saw coming, made no attempt to reclaim his weapon.

"Keep it," he said, pulling himself to his feet and wiping blood from his lip. "There's plenty more of 'em on this ship." And he walked away.

She watched him vanish into the bowels of the hulk and shook her head, dropping the club on the slate and glancing around at the other seaguard, who if they did not respect her at least watched her warily. The convicts, on the other hand, began to stand a little straighter.

"Twiner," she said, "join me while I pick a crew. Some I want for the ship, some I will use as soldiers. You will help me decide who goes where." He stepped in close to her. His new boots bit into his feet, the barely cured fishskin of the clothes they had picked up on the way felt too tight around his arms, rubbed the tops of his legs where his skin was still damp from the bathhouse, but he did not let his pain show.

"Yes, Shipwife."

"Now." Her whisper was a warmth in his ear. "We need a

deckmother to keep the crew in check and provide discipline. A purseholder, for I do not trust the man *Tide Child* has. Oarturner we have. I will not turn out Barlay — she proved herself at Corfynhulme. A bowsell of the maindeck to run the gallowbow teams, and some who at least have something about them to be bowsells alongside her. Bonewright we have also. I will forego a hatkeep for my clothing but I need a seakeep who knows boneships, and the same for a wingwright. Now, I do not say the women and men we find here will be trained, or used to those positions, but we may be lucky. However, if they know what I want they will all claim they have the experience I look for, and no one lies like a deckchild. So we walk the line, we talk to these women and men and we choose ones we like, ones we think we can use and ones with a bit of spark in 'em. And we want violent women and men too, the kind that are trouble, for I will make them our own seaguard if Karrad will not give me any. You understand?" He nodded. "Very well, then let us inspect our livestock. You speak to 'em; it is better if I appear distant."

Joron approached the first in the line, a woman he guessed was at least thrice his years. Long white hair, matted and caked with filth, reached down her back.

"What is your name?"

"Caller," she said, but her eyes were far away and he did not feel that she was naming herself. Nevertheless, he took her answer for want of any other.

"An odd name, for an old woman."

She stepped in close to him. A gnarled finger reached up and hooked around his collar, pulling him down to her.

"Do you sing?" she said.

"What? No, not since . . ." He stopped. He had no need to explain his songs had stopped with his father's death. Not to this old woman.

"We'll be all right," she said. "You sing boy and we'll be all right. The Hag is coming, you'll see. She'll take us all to—"

He was pulled away by Meas. "Not this one; her mind is

gone." She turned to a seaguard. "You can take her below. Move on, Twiner." She leaned in close to him once more. "Don't waste your time on the lame birds. Look for strength and intelligence – you can see it in their eyes." She glanced down the line of ragged figures. "Though I suspect we might end up taking them all no matter what, as half will die before we get over the horizon. Find me my crew, Joron. Find me the ones who will make my ship fly."

He wondered why she was letting him choose. Was it really so she could appear aloof? Or was it a trap of some sort? Not that it mattered as he could not refuse. If it was a trap he must walk into it.

Joron moved along the line, and if there were sorrier and weaker women and men in the Hundred Isles he could not imagine where they would be. Occasionally he would stop in front of one, considering that if they were fed up to full health then maybe . . . but Meas would shake her head and he would move on. The first lot were rejected completely, Meas looking downcast at the sight of them trooping below as the next batch were brought up.

He walked over to her as the second lot organised themselves into line.

"Not a one among them, Shipwife? Are you sure?"

She nodded.

"They have been here too long – would cost us food and then they'd probably die. I'd take a tailor or a cobbler over them, missing limb or no." And so it was with the next and the next. And Skearith's Eye moved over the spines and more were brought up.

Another dismal lot.

The only hopeful one was the last of them, a huge man though he stood stooped, staring at the deck, and his face was almost lost in ragged black beard and hair.

"You," he said, "what is your name?"

"Muffaz, Deckkeeper," he said. His voice was barely above a whisper. Joron almost moved on, thinking Meas would judge the man weak as he looked utterly beaten, but there was something about him he could not put his finger on, and it was not just his size. "What was your crime, Muffaz?"

"I am Maiden-cursed, D'keeper."

Joron's heart sank.

"Unfortunate," he said, as all he knew it was ill luck to take a man who had murdered a woman aboard ship.

"Who did you kill?" said Meas.

"I murdered my lover, Shipwife. Six month with child she were." He coughed, choking back a sob. "I should take the short walk and feed the longthresh, but cannot do it. Drink, it were. Anhir and the temper it brings. Never touched her before in anger, but one moment and all is ruin. I have sworn never to touch another drop of the drink as long as I live, may the Hag make my life short."

"What position did you hold before you were condemned?" said Meas.

"I was oarturner, Shipwife. On a four-ribber, see. Worked it ten years." Joron looked him up and down again, a bad feeling in his gut about having his sort on the ship. Then glanced at Meas.

"We are a ship of the dead, Twiner," she said. "Cursed all, and a strong back is always useful." Was there a light in the man's eyes at that? A sudden flare of hope?

"Go and stand over there, Muffaz," said Joron. The man nodded and Joron moved on to find himself inspecting such a collection of ne'er-do-wells and ragged lasses that he could barely believe any of them had ever flown the sea. These people were as far from the image of fleet deckchilder given to him by his father as it was possible to be.

In the next three lots they found one woman – Hasrin – nearly as tall as him and one of the few to look him in the eye. She had been a deckkeeper herself, and when he asked her crime she was cagey, dancing round the subject and refusing to meet his gaze. He was going to pass over her, but Meas was standing behind the line, scrutinising the prisoners from the rear, and she gave him a nod. So, despite him feeling it was a mistake, Hasrin joined the crew.

The heat built up, his new boots and clothes rubbed, the quality of the prisoners got no better. Joron started to long for the drink he had denied himself. But a glance behind him at the bowed, guilt-broken, Hag-cursed form of Muffaz helped stop him reaching for the flask at his side. Meas had given up, gone to the rail to stare over the sea and no doubt fret about how she would complete her mission, any mission, without crew. All seemed lost before it had begun.

The next in line was a small man, and unlike the rest looked barely broken at all by his experience of the hulk. He had a huge smile, and if the eyeburn on his bald scalp bothered him he did not show it.

"And what is your crime?"

"I punched my officer, D'keeper." He seemed inordinately pleased about it. Before Joron could ask any more he heard Meas's boots on the deck as she strode over and spun the man around.

"Mevans?"

"Ey, Shipwife."

"What are you doing here?"

"As I said to the deckkeeper" – he grinned, showing a full set of teeth – "I punched my shipwife."

"I told you to serve well."

"Ey, you did. And when I heard you were moved to a ship of the dead, well, seemed obvious that where you go, I should."

"Mevans," she said, "I should have you corded for disobeying me. You will die, that is all that awaits anyone on my ship."

"Hag comes for us all, Shipwife," he replied, his jollity not even touched by the reminder of mortality. "Besides, for what she did, Shipwife Kyrie needed a punch."

"You're a fool."

"Oh aye, and not the only one. Cosst, Mebal, Tarnt – they're all here too. Fair queueing up to punch your sither, they were."

"Fools!" But Meas could not hide the smile on her face. She stood straighter and shouted, "Those here who were once my crew, stop hiding yourselves and step forward." About fifteen women and men stepped out of the line further down, which made Joron wonder again what type of woman Meas was that so many would walk into certain death just to be with her.

"Well," she said, a harshness coming back into her voice, "you may join my crew, but consider each and every one of you demoted to deckchild for such stupidity." They walked over to join the small group bound for *Tide Child*, and if they felt sore about being demoted they managed to smile through it. Only Mevans stayed where he was, bobbing his head and grinning. "Is there a reason you remain here, Deckchild Mevans?" said Meas. "Do you disobey because you have changed your mind? For it strikes me as a bit late to do that."

"No Shipwife, never. Where you go I go. 'Tis only . . ." His voice tailed off.

"Only?"

"The old woman, you must have seen her earlier. Seems a little strange. She has been here a long time."

"It has broken her mind."

"No, Shipwife, she has the Hag's spirit in her."

"You have adopted another broken soul, Mevans. A fleet ship is not the place for—"

"She is lucky, Shipwife, she is. Her name is Garriya and she is lucky."

Meas shook her head before turning to one of the seaguard. "Bring back the old woman," she said then turned back to Mevans. "At least tell me she can sew."

"I do not believe so, Shipwife." chuckled Mevans. "She's no use for nothing. But she is lucky."

Meas stared at him for what felt like a long time, then shook her head. "As well as the usual, Mevans, I need women and men for seaguard. Violent men and women, but ones with discipline."

"Plenty of violence but little discipline on this ship."

"You know those aboard this hulk well?"

Mevans nodded.

"Ey. I reckoned were only time till you turned up. Some of those you have turned down I reckon could be worked up. I have a list of their skills. Most are a bad lot, little more than stonebound, but there are those who will measure up."

"Well, in that case you can free up Joron and I." She leaned in and spoke quietly. "We need good crew, Mevans, and as many as you can get."

"I shall find them for you," he said.

Meas nodded but Mevans held her gaze.

"What?"

"There is one other thing."

"Only one?"

"Well, 'tis one for us, by which I am meaning your crew. But come to think of it, it may also help you."

"And what is it?"

"Black Orris."

"Three women's tits," said Meas. "Black Orris? Really?"

"We cannot fly without Black Orris."

"And where is Orris?"

"In the hands of Mulvan Cahanny. But, and this is the thing. I happen to know that Cahanny wishes to move some freight and he wishes it to be secret."

"How can you know such a thing from aboard a hulk?"

"It is where they bring criminals, Shipwife, and some of my family may have passed through."

"I am still a fleet shipwife, Mevans, not one of your criminal cousins here to help smugglers."

"Ey, I know that. Only a ship of the dead . . . Different rules, that, ain't it, Shipwife?"

"I am not a pirate."

"'Tis just that Cahanny would send his people with this shipment, for I heard it is fair valuable, and his people, well, they are both violent and disciplined, which is what you are wishing for."

"But they would not answer to me, Mevans."

"Well, no, they would answer to Cahanny. But if he puts 'em under your command then they would be yours and you could ask for Black Orris in return. As payment, like."

"If Orris's mouth has not got him killed already."

"Orris won't be killed," said Mevans, flashing a smile. "He's lucky, see. Like you are."

Meas took a step back.

"Seaguard," she said. "This man, Mevans, now holds the rank of hatkeep. Obey him as you would obey me in his choice of crew." She turned away. "Joron, we must go ashore."

He nodded and stepped close. "Who is this Cahanny?"

"If a bone is stolen from the boneyard, or goods are smuggled in, or a body ends up in floating face down in the harbour, well, Cahanny is the man most likely behind it."

16

If the Boot Fits

After the miasma that surrounded the hulks it was almost a relief to be back in the stink of Fishmarket. The streets were busy, but Meas threaded her way through the throng as though the people were barely there. She had a natural grace, was always aware of her place and that of others in the world around her — part of what made her a good shipwife. In a sea fret or a heavy fog to have a constant idea where the enemy would be was an invaluable skill, like being able to hear the shoalsongs of the fish had made his father a successful fisher.

Can you hear the song, boy? Can you hear it?

In the centre of Fishmarket, in a square surrounded by stalls loaded with the bounty of the sea, hagpriests were conducting a ceremony under a statue of the Maiden made from varisk stalks. They stood on the raised base of the statue, and behind them were three Kept, skin oiled and bodies strapped tight. The priest's faces were covered by masks painted in bright reds, greens and blues. They were Bern, as all priests were, dressed as the Women of the Sea: Maiden, Mother and Hag. Kneeling before them was a girl holding a baby. A crowd had gathered to watch the committing of mother and child, but when Joron glanced at Meas he caught an expression on her face hovering somewhere between revulsion and fear.

"We should get out of here," she said, "before they start." But it was too late. The seaguard had blocked every exit from the market square and the priest in the long mask and ragged robe of the Hag was raising her voice.

"Listen all! Stop all! Stand and watch this soul committed!" The crowd, already standing, staring, became silent.

"Listen all! Stop all!" shouted the priest in the short robes and ruddy-faced mask of the Maiden. "This girl attended the laying week. And found many who would ask her favour. And she gave her favour. And the Maiden smiled and favour bloomed within her."

"Listen all! Stop all!" shouted the priest in the long robe and mask of the Mother, drawn and serious. "This girl brought her bloom to pass. Her belly swelled, and when the Mother tested her strength she was not found wanting. And she gave birth to a healthy and strong child. Hail the firstborn!"

The crowd returned the shout: "Hail the firstborn!" And when the shout died away the only sound left was the crying of the child's mother.

"Hold up the child, lass," said the Hag. The girl did, peeling the baby from her breast. It screamed as she took it in both hands, holding it above her head.

"As the waves are monuments to the power of the Hundred Isles, so the fruit of the laying is our strength," said the hagpriest. "I pronounce you firstborn and cursed born. But fear not, child."

The Maiden and Mother echoed, "Fear not, child," as the Hag took the babe from its mother. "A ship rides in the harbour, built from the bones of our wrecks; keyshans fall in your name and you will ride the bones as a corpselight. So your body dies, but your soul lives in the ship." The Mother priest stepped forward, removing her mask and taking the girl's elbow, helping her stand.

"My baby," said the girl, bereft, forlorn.

"Your baby serves the three now," said the Mother. "And

you I will call sither and Bern. And you shall join us at the spiral bothies and have your pick of the Kept and rise in power through the magic of your fertility and strength. For you are no longer of the Berncast."

The Maiden priest stepped forward, also removing her mask.

"And I will also call you sither. And I will dress you and teach you the ways of the court and the ways of men." She stared out into the crowd. "Now tell truth, sither. Do you know the father of your babe?" The girl shook her head, but she glanced into the crowd and her eyes alighted on a boy whose stare back was so intent Joron had no doubt he was the child's father. Joron was not the only one who noticed the glance; both the Maiden and the Kept behind her saw. "So you lay with many?"

"Many," said the girl, her head bowed.

"Then I congratulate you for following our customs as the Women of the Sea desire." The Maiden squatted and dipped a feather into a pot of blue paint. "For the Northstorm," she said and flicked the feather. A line of paint appeared on the girl's face. Then she repeated her actions for south, east and west, criss-crossing the girl's face with blue before turning to the crowd. "Now, good people," she shouted, "let us go to the harbour and the committing block and send this child upon its great journey, for it will be fleet!"

The Mother kept a tight hold on the sobbing girl's elbow.

"And while you celebrate the renewal of light above our glorious boneships, I will take this girl to become Bern!"

A huge shout of approval rose from the crowd, though when Joron looked at Meas behind him he saw she was clenching her fists so tightly her hands looked bloodless and her face bent with fury.

Of course.

That child had been her once.

Everyone knew the story. As a babe Meas had been taken to the committing block, to ride *Arakeesian Dread* as a corpse-light, but it was no fine day like this. It was a dark day full of ill omens. The ground had moved in the days prior, and strange lights had been seen in the sky. As Meas was taken up to the block and the rites were said, the link between block and ship made, the sea had vanished, running out of the bay, stranding the ships, leaving the sea floor exposed and all its toothed and clawed horrors flipping and gasping. And when the hagpriests had tried to continue with the rite, the sea had returned, as if in fury that none had understood its warning. A great wave had come in, wrecking ships and town alike. As far up as the second bend of the Serpent Road had been awash. The priests who had brought Meas to the block had died, but the babe, miraculously, had been found washed ashore, safe and squalling, and none dared touch her with the knife then.

Though none had wanted her either.

The crowd started to stream towards the committing block in the harbour and Joron looked to Meas once more. She was staring at the statues in the centre of the market square where the ceremony had taken place and the girl's family and well-wishers were shaking her hand and wishing her good fortune at the spiral bothies. Most were Berncast, missing arms, legs, fingers, faces twisted, eyes gone, bodies palsied.

"They think she goes to glory," said Meas, "but she will never be much more than a servant."

Behind them the Bern who had played the Maiden was talking to one of the Kept, who then went across to one of the seaguard. There was no mistaking what was happening. The Kept subtly pointed out the boy, who stood stock still, staring at the girl and ignoring everything but her. In turn, she could not keep her eyes from him. Where she was unmarred, he had a blood birthmark, livid red across his cheek.

"Twiner," said Meas. "That boy."

"Yes?"

"He comes to our ship."

"But he has done nothing to be condemned."

"Go to him." Meas was staring at the seaguard. "Do it now."

And Joron was moving, pushing against the current of the

crowd like a fish fighting a river to get home to spawn. When he reached the boy, who could not have been more than fifteen, he took him by the arm and the boy tried to fight him off.

"Child, my shipwife wishes to speak to you, so you will come with me." Mention of a shipwife was enough to cow most in the Hundred Isles and the boy stopped resisting, let himself be led back to where Meas stood watching the seaguard, who had set their own course for the boy.

"Shipwife," said the boy and bowed his head. "How may I help you?"

"What is your name?"

"Gavith," he said.

"Well, Gavith, I take my ship to fly the waves soon, and I will need a cabin boy."

"I am honoured, Shipwife," said the boy. He still could not look at her, such authority plainly frightened him. "But I must stay here, for I am to join the Kept." Then he looked up, a happy glint in his eye. Meas attempted to contort her face into an expression of kindness, though she could not quite manage it. "You are the father of the child just taken?"

"Aye, and when Bassa is in her bothy she will tell the Thirteenbern I am the father and choose me as her Kept."

Meas put a hand on his shoulder.

"I have a harsh truth for you, Gavith, and one that will be hard to hear. Someone at the bothy will tell Bassa when she arrives never to ask for you or mention you again, and that she must choose her Kept from those who are already there, already favoured."

"She will not," he said. "We have loved each other since we were—"

"Look up there." Meas pointed at the statue. The three Kept were still there and were staring at Meas, Joron and the boy. "They have no wish for competition. The Bern advance through bearing children. And the Kept seek the favour of those women who breed well and navigate the court with ease. Now, Bassa is only firstbern. She has no importance yet and the court will be a stormy sea for her, as long as she lives. But if her strength holds and she makes fourthbern? Or fifthbern? Every man among the Kept will want to be with her. And they know the ways of the court, they know about power."

"I will learn."

"You will never get the opportunity," she said, harsh now. "You have seen your face in the water. You are Berncast."

"It is only a mark. It will fade. My mother says it will—"

"You will never be Kept, boy."

"Not if I go to sea with you." He tried to escape her grip.

"They will kill you," she said.

As he was about to reply – indignant, furious – they were interrupted.

"The boy is to come with me." The seaguard was a big man, armoured and threatening. One hand rested on his curnow. "I am to take him to his woman." Gavith looked at the seaguard and Joron could see the war on his face. He wanted what the seaguard said to be true, but Meas had sown a seed of doubt.

Kept Tassar appeared from the crowd.

"Shipwife Meas," he said, "and my friend Joron, how good it is to meet you both again." He sketched a small bow with his head. "I am afraid I must take this boy with me." Now Gavith's face changed, for there was no hiding the threat radiating from Tassar. It was as if the man could not control what he was, the darkness emanating from him. "I wish to teach this boy the ways of the Kept. I wish him to know – the sort of things a man needs to do to survive in the spiral bothies."

"I am afraid this boy has signed on with my crew," said Meas. "He is mine now." The boy was like a kivelly locked by the glare of a predatory sankrey, unable to talk or move.

"Well," said Tassar, "in that case I will not stand in your way. The outcome will be the same for him either way, eh?" He turned and walked away. "Saffin, come," he shouted, and the seaguard followed him.

"What did he mean," said Gavith, "the outcome will be the same?"

"I am shipwife of a black ship," said Meas simply.

The boy's face fell as the truth of his situation came home.

"He was going to kill me."

"Ey," said Meas.

"And now you will do it instead."

"Maybe," she said, "but I do not intend to die, and you should not either. Take what life you have and enjoy it. Now, you must come with us. I do not trust Tassar — he rose far and quickly, which means he is ruthless. He may still decide to make sure of you. He has always been a thorough man, if an unpleasant one."

They walked through the back alleys of Fishmarket until they arrived at a drinking den named Boneship's Rest. A sign above the door showed a boneship wrecked on rocks. A huge woman and man stood before the door, both all muscle and with long black hair that had been elaborately braided.

"I wish to see Cahanny," said Meas.

"And I wish to grow wings, fly and escape my fate as much as any gullaime," said the woman. "Don't mean it will happen."

"I am Meas Gilbryn."

"Fancy names sink nothing here, Lucky Meas," said the man.

"I have a ship," she said, "and I understand Cahanny needs a ship. So there may be a deal to be done."

"Toth," said the woman, "go see what he thinks."

They waited in uncomfortable silence in the alley, Joron pretending an interest in the various bones and fish heads that littered the ground.

The man returned. "He'll see you," he said, holding the door open. "Not the boy." He nodded at young Gavith. "He waits here."

"You will protect him?"

"Aye," said Toth, "and if you don't come out we'll find a use for him. Have fun in there, Lucky Meas." Joron did not think he meant it.

Inside the Boneship's Rest Joron could not tell if the place was dim because it was badly lit or dim because it was full of smoke from the gossle burners in the corners. Smoke leaked from the braziers, curling up into the air like the long graceful necks of courting laybirds, twisting and dancing around one another in delicate spirals as they filled the room with pungent, narcotic fumes. He found himself transfixed.

Meas nudged him.

"Try not to breathe in too much gossle, Twiner. It can be disorientating, at first anyway, and it is known to make people foolish. We will need our wits about us."

Cahanny, and Joron had no doubt it was him from the way he held himself — he strutted like a fighting bird — came forward. A small man dressed in tight fishskin and with his right arm missing below the elbow, Joron wondered whether he was born so or if he had lost the limb in a fight. He had a face like an eating root, that fat round kind that sometimes came out of the ground looking like a wizened human head. Joron wondered how old he was. Cahanny brought up his one hand and tugged on his left ear, an ear that stuck out nearly as much as the right one, and then coughed.

"Lucky Meas." A voice like a hinge creaking, and now he was nearer Joron could see he had the tight shiny skin of someone who had been badly burned. Two of the fingers on his left hand were also fused together. "I never thought I would see Lucky Meas walk into my drinking hole."

"Well" — Meas shrugged — "then we are as surprised as one another, ey?"

Cahanny laughed, but there was little humour there. His eyes roved over Meas, appraising her, but not as a woman or man appraised another, more as a trader appraises goods before making an offer.

"So then, Lucky Meas" — Joron wondered if everyone in the Hundred Isles now made her name sound like a joke — "how can Mulvan Cahanny help you?"

"I think it's how I can help you, Mulvan Cahanny."

He took a step towards the bar, a plank balanced on two

barrels in front of a stack of eight, shaking his head as he did.

"Oh no," he said and picked up a beaker from the gion-stalk plank, taking a sip from it. "Sooner see a keyshan breach in Bernshulme Bay than expect Lucky Meas to help a man like me. You must be wanting something, unless you've come to close me down." He put his cup down. "But I reckon you've come a little short-handed for that."

"I have heard you have a cargo that you wish transported," she said. He said nothing, only stared. "And as I now command a black ship, I have a little more autonomy than most shipwives."

"Oh, you do, do you?" He grinned. "See, you – shipwives and Bern and Kept – you all think you're better than us Berncast. But now you have fallen, you see what you really are – the same as everyone else, only with the right amount of fingers and toes. You're just another criminal now, despite your storied name, Meas Gilbryn." He took another sip of his drink.

"Do you want your cargo moved or not?"

"Who's your man?" He used his cup to gesture at Joron, who felt a tremor run through him.

"He is my deckkeeper."

"I generally make people fight, to prove themselves to me." Another sip and now he did not even do them the courtesy of looking at them; instead he stared at the stacked barrels of anhir. "No point dealing with anyone who can't look after themselves, or who doesn't want my trade enough to fight for it."

"Who do you want me to fight?" said Meas.

"Oh, not you, Meas," said Cahanny, turning from where he leaned on the bar. "I do not doubt you can fight. But what about him?" He pointed with his damaged fingers at Joron, who could not hide an involuntary swallow – a movement that gave away his fear. Cahanny grinned again.

"My deckkeeper," said Meas, "wears new boots and as such is in no fit state to duel anyone for your pleasure."

"Then we have no deal to make, Lucky Meas," said Cahanny and turned back to studying his barrels.

"Very well," said Meas. "We are done here, Twiner," she said, making for the door.

But before they were had gone two steps Cahanny called out:

"Wait!" He was smiling again. "What do you want in trade, Meas Gilbryn? Let me know that before you leave."

"Nothing you would not want yourself anyway."

He tapped his beaker on the plank.

"And what do you mean by that?"

"This cargo is valuable?" Cahanny nodded and she continued. "So you would wish to send guards with it?"

"Not generally. Those I deal with usually know better than to betray me."

"I run a ship full of criminals condemned to death."

"Could be said of any fleet ship," said Cahanny.

Meas allowed herself a smile at that.

"Possibly, though let us say my criminals are a little more, well, committed, than most."

"These guards of mine, if I felt the need to send them," he said, "they would be under your command while on your ship, I take it?"

"Ey."

"And how many of these guards do you think I should send?"

"Twenty," she replied.

Cahanny laughed.

"Not a chance. Five."

"Fifteen. I can do with no less."

"Ten," he said.

"Very well, I can accept that. Send them to the fleet dock. They must bring their own weapons."

"Agreed." The two stared at one another until, eventually, Cahanny broke the silence. "You have not asked what you transport or where it goes."

"I care not what it is, and where it goes must wait upon my schedule."

"What if I have a timetable?"

"You do not," she said. "You are too relaxed."

Cahanny shrugged. Then laughed.

"I like you, Lucky Meas. I think we can do business, you and I."

"Yes." She headed for the door. Stopped. Turned. "Oh, while I remember . . . Black Orris. I heard you have him and I am sure he can bring you no joy. I will do you a favour and take him with me."

Cahanny let out a chuckle.

"Oh, Black Orris brings me no joy at all, but you do not fool me. You want him, and I give nothing away for free. So what can you offer me now, Lucky Meas? As our first deal is done, we must have another."

Meas knew what Joron knew: that they had little else to offer Cahanny.

"I have money," said Meas.

"As do I," said Cahanny. "I like having things people want, that people value, Lucky Meas. I find it very useful."

A silence. An impasse.

"I'll fight for him," said Joron. He almost brought his hand to his mouth upon saying it, he was so shocked by his own words. But after the shock came a wave of self-belief. He could do this. "You did want me to fight, right?"

"Joron," said Meas, "you need not."

"He has offered now," said Cahanny. "And I thought a fleet officer never went back on their word."

"Ey, I have offered," said Joron. He felt giddy, like when he took the first hit of anhir on a morning when he had not touched any for days. "We get Black Orris whether I win or not, right?"

"Aye," said Cahanny. "Just prove to me you want him."

"I forbid this," said Meas.

"We are not on your deck now," said Cahanny, and he seeded his next words with spite. "Are we, Shipwife?"

"It is not like we fight to the death, is it?" said Joron. He felt himself grin, but the grin fell away and the feeling of self-belief went with it at the looks on the faces of those around him. Hard, unforgiving, feral.

"What other type of fight is there?" said Cahanny. "Anzir, come forward." From behind Cahanny came a woman far bigger than Joron. Her shoulders bulged with as much muscle as any Kept, and Joron felt himself become light-headed once more. It was as if since meeting Meas he had been led from one near-death situation to another, but this time he had jumped in himself — feet, in his fancy new boots, first.

Anzir had a short sword at her side and a small round shield on one arm. Everyone in the drinking hole moved back to create a rough circle. Fear burned through Joron. Anzir's strength was obvious. He imagined the damage she could do, the way her sword would cut through him. *The flensing of flesh from bone, the parting of his guts, the smashing of his skull, the grinding between hulls.*

Anzir flexed her muscles, cut the air with her sword. A killer. Joron knew enough to know a killer when he saw one. Hag's curse, he was no duellist.

Think.

He needed a leveller. He coughed. Spat.

"You want entertainment, right?" His voice felt thin, small. But it was heard.

"Aye," said Cahanny.

"Well, Meas mentioned I have new boots, and the fight will not last a turn of the glass if I wear them."

"I doubt it will last even a quarter-turn," said Cahanny. "It is the blood that I like to see, if I tell the truth."

"But would you not like it to take a little longer? For the loser to bleed a little more?"

"Take your boots off then, if you wish a moment more of life," said Cahanny. "It is not a hard puzzle to solve."

"But my feet are still sore hurt, and your woman is in rude health. It will still not be even near a fair fight."

"It was never going to be that." Cahanny and his men laughed.

Meas gazed at him, her tongue exploring her upper teeth in thought. Was there amusement in her eyes? Did she laugh at the prospect of his death?

"Do you have some proposal, Deckkeeper?" she said.

"Ey. I do, Shipwife. Make her wear my boots," said Joron. He knelt and started taking them off.

"Wear your . . ." Cahanny looked at him, then at Anzir. A smile crossed his face. "Well, let it not be said Mulvan Cahanny organises an unfair fight or passes over a chance for real amusement. Anzir, put on his boots."

"They are too small," she said.

"Do I need to cut off your toes then, so you know to obey my orders?"

She shook her head, hooked her sword on to her belt and took the boots from Joron. He watched as she sat down and forced her feet into them – it was plain they were a poor fit. He felt Meas behind him.

She whispered into his ear.

"I have always taught that if you cannot fight well, fight clever. This is cleverly done, Joron, but she will still be dangerous, so do not be overconfident. Force her to move a lot and when she falls, that is your moment." He nodded. "One more thing." He looked round at her and she slapped him hard across the face. "A little pain is good for clearing gossle from the system, Twiner, and you are plainly under its influence. Now, go to it. Fight well."

Anzir stood and took a couple of steps, her balance off. Everything in Joron screamed at him to attack her straight away, the way he had with Meas when they first met. But she had not even drawn her sword yet, and he was sure that to attack before she was ready would mean neither him nor Meas ever left Boneship's Rest.

"Unhook your blades," said Cahanny. They obeyed, Joron's arm feeling like something alien to him as it took on the weight of the curnow.

Opposite him Anzir unhooked her blade but did not move, only planted herself and waited, short blade in one hand, small shield on her other arm. He was tempted to test her, but Meas had moved around the circle so she stood behind Anzir, and as he took a step forward she shook her head. So Joron took a step back and waited. It was not a long wait. The expectant silence of the spectators changed to something else. First catcalls, then jeers as the two combatants stood, unmoving.

"Hag's tits, Anzir," came the shout from a woman in the crowd. "Finish him. It's plain he barely knows one end of a sword from the other." Anzir did not move, she simply watched him from deep blue eyes. Her hair was shorn close to the skull apart from three braids falling from the top of her head. The crowd started to chant her name.

Cahanny looked bored.

"Kill him, Anzir," he said. "We do not have all day." Anzir swallowed, and Joron knew she did not want to move, that she felt unsafe in the unfamiliar boots. But she had been given an order and, like any good soldier, she obeyed.

The woman went for a straight attack, reckoning on Joron's lack of skill to let her in close to finish him. And she would have been right to do so — usually, but fear inhabited Joron, it set his nerves jangling and his legs and arms felt like they would jump from his body while at the same time he could not move. He was rooted to the spot, not by the woman's advance — and she came on as death, deadly as the Hag's judgement — but by Meas's gaze.

Anzir's sword came up.

Joron felt the Hag's breath on the back of his neck.

The noise of the room rushing in his ears.

Meas's mouth opened, and the command "Move!" danced in the air, a song between them.

That word gave permission to his frozen body to do what he wanted, as if it were the wind that made him fly. He leaped to the side. Anzir's sword punched through the space in the air he had left, and she staggered forward, trying to right herself only to be betrayed by the boots. She could not keep her balance. Joron, with the speed fear lent him, was on her, bringing his curnow down on the back of her neck, but, at the very last, he pulled the stroke and used the flat of the blade rather than its edge. The impact knocked Anzir to the floor, and then his blade rested on her neck. The crowd's screams for blood faded as Mulvan Cahanny started to clap – slow, single handclaps.

"Well, finish her then, Deckkeeper."

"There is no need," said Joron. "I have won. My father once told me a senseless death will follow you right to the bottom of the ocean for the Hag to see. So I will not cause one."

"I will have a crowd with me when I meet the Hag then," said Cahanny. "But this is your victory. Take it how you will."

"I will have my boots," he said to the woman on the floor. She rolled over, looked up at him and nodded. Joron turned to Mulvan Cahanny. "And now you will bring Black Orris to my shipwife. As you promised."

"Aye." Cahanny smiled. "Bring Black Orris then," he said.

A man vanished into a back room and when he returned there was a large black bird on his arm.

"What is that?" said Joron.

"Black Orris," said Meas.

"Hag's tits!" squawked the bird.

17

A Pledging

They left Boneship's Rest and made their way back to Fishmarket, Black Orris perched on Meas's shoulder.

"I risked my life for a bird," said Joron, an anger simmering within him as he pushed past the women and men of Bernshulme, eager and impatient to be about their business.

"Not just any bird, Twiner. Black Orris. Mevans would tell you he is lucky."

"Arses," said Black Orris.

"A foul-mouthed bird."

"Your arses," said Black Orris.

"Oh indeed," said Meas. "None more foul-mouthed. He is a corpsebird, from the far northern isles. We picked him up when the *Arakeesian Dread* stopped there. Mevans taught him to talk, and the entire crew considered Black Orris a symbol of their ship."

"It is just a bird," said Joron.

"Arses."

"Never, Joron Twiner, underestimate what morale can do for a crew. You look at *Tide Child*'s crew and you fear them. Rightly, I may add." Meas threaded her way through the crowds. "They had no respect for you, still mostly don't. But Black Orris will make those who believe a bird can be lucky – and many do – fight all the better. And among those of my old crew, though they may not be many now, when they find out you fought to bring Black Orris to them, well, they will feel much kindness towards you."

"And how will they know?" said Joron. "I cannot tell them. It would be like I boasted, and all deckchilder hate a boaster."

"Have you forgotten that we trail a new crew member?"

Joron glanced over his shoulder. He had indeed forgotten about Gavith; the boy barely spoke.

"He was outside."

"No, he was not. The two on the door had no wish to miss a fight and brought him in with them. I am sure the boy will not be slow to tell the story of how he came aboard the ship, and of the fierce battle his deckkeeper fought to save Black Orris. How, despite most would think him outmatched, he fought anyway and won through his wits." Meas stopped and turned to the boy. "Ey, Gavith? Will you do that?" The boy swallowed and nodded. "You do understand what I mean?"

"Yes, Shipwife. I am not to tell but I am to tell."

"That is it," she said. Then leaned in closer to him. "But if you ever speak of things you hear around the great cabin without my permission, I will have the skin corded from your back. You understand that too?"

The boy's eyes widened. "Aye, Shipwife."

"On a ship we say. Ey. Boy. Aye is a stonebound term, right?"

"Aye, I mean ey."

"Good, now make your way to the fleet dock, find the bone-wrights and ask for Bonemaster Coxward, tell him you are my cabin boy and ask what work he has for you. If you have any family they need to know your situation, so ask him to send a messenger. Tell him any cost will come out of my purse." The boy stared blankly at her. "Well? Go! And stop for nothing and no one." And he went, vanishing into the crowd.

"Do you think we will ever see him again?" said Joron.

"We are not far from the fleet dock. It is unlikely Tassar will intercept him between here and there."

"I mean he may choose simply to run."

She shrugged.

"Then in that case I will not mourn him. He is unlikely to last the night without us, and I value intelligence in my crew, even in the least of them." She glanced at him and he felt his resentment rise like a winter tide. "Now come. I think we are followed, and I would find out by who. It will be quieter nearer the docks, make them easier to see."

"How do you know we are followed?" said Joron. Meas stared over his shoulder into the crowd.

"You get a feel for such things, Twiner."

"Arses," said Black Orris.

They turned for the docks. The first sign they approached the deep-water harbour where the bigger ships docked was the sight of their spines rising above the blocky tenements that fronted the harbour. Then came a noticeable thinning of the crowds. The people they did meet were nearly all heading away from the docks, no doubt having attended the sacrifice of the child Joron had seen earlier. Many had the bloody fingerprint on their forehead where the hagpriests had blessed them. Women and men chattered excitedly as they passed, but Meas gave them no attention, keeping her head down.

"A fool's custom," she hissed under her breath and pushed a passing juggler out of the way.

"But it keeps our ships safe," said Joron.

Meas stopped. Turned to him.

"Does it? Or are they just pretty lights that people like?"

"No," said Joron, "they are the health of a ship. At lastlight, the yellow, we know a ship is dying and must be appeased with another life. The lights are his soul. That is why the black ships are dead: they cannot hold corpselights."

"And yet, Joron, they still fly and they still fight, do they not?" She did not wait for an answer, only walked away.

He watched her go. The corpselights above a ship had always been something merry to him, something to be celebrated. Those given to the ships were the chosen of the Sea Hag, guaranteed a place by the pyre and passage beyond the storms that circled the world, and yet Meas had no respect for the lights. *Maybe because of what had happened to her as a child? Maybe she was bitter at being denied the Sea Hag's favour?*

They rounded a corner and found themselves on the docks. Directly in front of them and strewn with flowers – though they could not hide the blood – was the committing block where the child he had seen earlier would have been sacrificed. Behind the block rose the scrap-built five-ribber *Hag's Hunter*, its sides rising like white cliffs. The crew could be heard, singing as they worked. They were drunk, no doubt. A committal day was always one of celebration, and when Joron looked up into the web of ropes and varisk and gion spars he counted eight blue corpselights dancing above the ship. On its pristine white side was a long streak of crimson blood.

A face appeared over the rail and just as quickly vanished. A moment later the shipwife of *Hag's Hunter* appeared, standing on the rail and holding on to a rope with one hand to keep her balance. If Joron had thought Meas's clothes fine, they were nothing to this woman's. She was festooned with shimmering feathers.

"Meas!" she shouted, her voice ruddy with false bonhomie. "I am glad to see my sither on this celebrated day." Meas cursed under her breath but did not look up.

"Arse," said Black Orris.

"I seem to remember, Meas" – as they walked along the dock the woman above followed them, balancing on the rail – "that you said I would never make shipwife. But here I am!" They reached the end of the ship, Meas pointedly ignoring the woman, who nevertheless continued to harangue her. "So what do you say now, Meas! Ey? What do you say now that you are shipwife to the dead and I am married to this fine beast, ey?" She stamped her foot on the rail of the ship.

Meas stopped and looked up at her.

"I never said you would not make shipwife, Kyrie; I said that would you never make shipwife through skill." She let her eyes run down the length of the *Hag's Hunter*. "And I was right, was I not?" She turned her back on the other woman and walked away. Joron followed and behind them the Shipwife Kyrie Gilbryn shouted after them.

"I only told Mother the truth, Meas! I only told the truth!" There was a note of desperation in her voice but Meas did not turn. "It seems we both go a-hunting Meas. Let us see who brings home the prize. Do not doubt I am a better shipwife than you. We shall see who really deserves Mother's favour!"

When Joron caught up with Meas there was no mistaking the smile on her face.

"Kyrie thinks, Deckkeeper," said Meas quietly, "that being shipwife is all about the enemy ships you bring back or sink. But she is too impulsive and too desperate to prove herself, it will get her in trouble."

"Arse," said Black Orris, and Meas reached up, stroking the bird's chest and making him coo with pleasure.

They walked further along the docks, seeing fewer and fewer people. Meas led them up a filthy alley, empty apart from rubbish and the thick smell of rotten fish. Without warning – and Joron had no idea how she knew her moment – Meas whirled around. Joron did the same but saw no one. The alleyway was empty. Completely empty.

"You can come out," said Meas. "I know you are there."

"Who is there?" said Joron.

"That I don't know, but an alley like this should be full of skeers looking for food, and none have flown in behind us." She raised her voice. "So come out. Do not make me come and find you."

Out of a doorway stepped Anzir, and if Joron had held anything at that moment he was sure he would have dropped it.

"If you have come to avenge your defeat," said Meas, "then you will have to face us both, and I am a little more skilled then Joron with a blade, and a lot less merciful."

Anzir looked confused.

"He beat me," she said.

"She sounds surprised," said Joron.

"Can you blame her?" said Meas. "Even wearing your shoes I thought she would kill you."

"Thank you, my Shipwife."

"I have come to offer him my service," said Anzir.

"What does Cahanny think of that?" said Meas.

Again Anzir looked confused. "He only pays me; this man bested me. I am his now."

"I don't want you," said Joron. It sounded far more harsh than he meant it to, but the woman did not appear offended.

"You send me away then?"

"I—"

"Wait." Meas's hand flashed up.

"You may need a protector. You are no great bladesman and it is no shame to have a shadow to protect you."

"You have no protector," snapped Joron.

"I do not need one, but you are wrong in that also. It is only my protector has not returned to me yet, but she will. It would do you no harm to have someone you trust at your back in a fight."

"I do not want to be responsible for another life," said Joron.

"And yet you are." She turned to Anzir. "Where are you from?"

"Clavill Isle, in the north."

Meas nodded at that.

"Joron," she said, "it is your decision whether to take Anzir on board or not. I will not press anyone unwanted upon you as you cannot force a trust nor a friendship. But you should know that to turn Anzir down is to shame her. And it is the custom of the Clavill Isle that the shamed take their own lives."

Joron looked from Meas to the hugely muscled woman down the alley and back again.

"I don't have to marry her, do I?"

"I doubt she would offer to serve you if that were the case, Deckkeeper."

"Arse," said Black Orris.

18

To Sea, Once More to Sea

In the week preceding the relaunch of *Tide Child* Joron worked harder than he had ever done in his life. Hands that had become hardened in youth from years of pulling on the ropes of a fisher boat were bloodied and ripped. Feet torn by unfamiliar boots added an unfamiliar ache, and when not working, he seemed to fall straight into sleep, being woken rudely and far too early to begin one of the thousands of tasks Meas had lined up for him before *Tide Child* could be relaunched.

It was not all grim work. Joron found a strange solace in being around Coxward, the bonemaster. The man was odd, as Meas had said, opinionated and often short-tempered, but he clearly loved his craft, and his way with the bones of the ship was a joy to watch. And Joron warmed to Mevans and those members of the crew of Meas's old ship who had found their way, through many and varied misdemeanours, to *Tide Child*'s decks. To those she trusted Meas had added Aelerin the courser, Barlay and Farys from the original crew, and a few others, but Joron did not know their names, not, not yet – though he would learn them. Joyfully, he recognised Old Briaret, who had survived her wound and was back on deck. And as he worked, what Meas had promised came to pass. Her old crew, though suspicious at first, quickly warmed to him as the tale spread of his fight to bring the foul-mouthed bird, Black Orris, back to them. His word was never questioned, and the tasks he ordered to be carried out were done quickly and efficiently and in a way that made him realise just how very poor the crew of *Tide Child* had been compared to what Meas was used to. Mevans had quickly taken Muffaz, the Maiden-cursed giant who Joron had renamed Solemn Muffaz, into his work crew, and his sheer size and melancholy demeanour had a way of making sure Joron's orders were carried out without the man even having to speak.

Anzir had worried him at first. She was his silent and looming shadow. When he needed to pick up anything heavy and required help, she was there. When he was tying a knot and needed a hand to hold the rope in place, she was there. When some harbour bonewright spat upon him, or questioned his orders as he was from a black ship and nothing to them, she was there, and whatever he wanted done was quickly done. And though he could not prove it, from the way the deckchilder acted around her, he felt sure that, in the underdecks, Anzir had twisted more than one arm and blackened more than one eye in his cause.

In the end he had asked her to be a little less present, realising that he could not function as an officer if his authority was based mainly on fear of her. When he had explained this to Anzir she had accepted calmly, and Joron had turned to find Meas, making one of her rare appearances on the deck, appraising him.

This apart, Meas he barely saw. It could not be claimed that she let her crew work and did nothing herself – she was never there when he fell into his cot to sleep, and her bed was empty when he woke, though there were definite signs it had been slept in: food left by the bed, the covers arranged slightly differently, dirty clothes left there one morning and gone the next. He found lists of tasks written in her perfect, curling handwriting on his pillow each morning.

One day Joron saw a woman sitting on a wall near *Tide Child* — small, dark-skinned with dark hair and keeping her head bowed, as if she did not wish her face to be seen. He stopped Mevans as the man passed, balancing a spar on his shoulders.

"Who is that, Mevans? Should they be here?"

"That is Narza, D'keeper. I'm surprised she did not appear sooner. She is the shipwife's shadow."

"I should speak to her," said Joron and started towards the woman, but Mevans grabbed his arm.

"No," he said, then let go of the dark blue material of his coat. "Apologies, D'keeper, but Narza does not take kindly to strangers. I would let the shipwife introduce you first."

He stared at Mevans, then gave him a short nod.

"Very well."

Occasionally he would see Meas, now shadowed by Narza, and he got the feeling that if Anzir was dangerous then Narza was doubly so. Joron had never seen anyone like her before. She never raised her head to meet the gaze of another; in fact he was not entirely sure Narza even saw other people. In some he would have taken this as shyness, an attempt to escape the inquisitive gaze of those wanting to pry into her life, but he got no sense of that from Narza. It was more that she seemed not to find anyone else interesting or worthwhile enough to raise her head and look at them. At one point he had seen Meas stride across the shipyard followed by Narza and found himself pausing in his task of shifting crates to the dockside to watch them.

"What do you think she did?" said Mevans from by his side.

"Punched an officer, like you, Mevans."

Mevans was shaking his head.

"Nish on that, we of the *Dread* planned what we did together, Narza joins herself with no woman or man but the shipwife, nor cares for them." He glanced at her just as Narza vanished around a corner after Meas.

"Murder then," said Joron. "She has the air of it about her."
Mevans grinned.

"Something funny in that, Hatkeep?"

"Only that you imply it in the singular, D'keeper. From what I hear she left a trail of bodies."

"Why?"

"Why?" He lifted a spar of wrapped varisk stalks. "You'd have to ask her, but if you do you're a braver man than I." He walked away with the spar over his shoulder whistling happily.

The entire week was one of little more than hard physical work. Rough hands became rougher, tired bodies became tireder, minds dulled by monotony became duller. The tedium of the work was broken only twice. First when *Hag's Hunter* left dock. This was done with all the pomp and ceremony the Hundred Isles could muster. Every bonewright in the yards downed tools and streamed over to the deep-water dock. As did every woman and man of the town – except the crew of *Tide Child*, who were pointedly not invited, so they worked and listened as everyone else celebrated for the day. While every deckchild from the *Hunter* found a partner to share a bed with, they worked. While people danced and sang to the drums, they worked. While the Bern and the hagpriests shouted blessings over *Hag's Hunter* and sang of the spirits of those sacrificed for the ship, they worked. While bright paint was spattered over the bricks of the docks, they worked. Only when Skearith's Eye began to close, darkness enveloped the docks, and a great shout went up from the town did they pause. Joron stopped what he was doing, as did everyone else, experiencing a peculiar sensation. His ears felt blocked, like someone held pillows either side of his head, and above the roofs of the buildings a bright blue glow momentarily appeared.

"It is the gullaime, D'keeper," said Mevans from by him. He grinned but it was not at the look of puzzlement on Joron's face, it was simply Mevan's ever-present expression. "The feeling in your ears is the gullaime changing the air. The crew will want to watch *Hunter* leave."

"Ey," said Joron. "Well, they have worked hard; we should reward them."

Every woman and man Meas had trusted to work on *Tide Child* came with him. They streamed from the ship on to the dockside to watch *Hag's Hunter*, huge and graceful, turning in the entrance to the harbour, a tower of billowing white. Joron caught the sound of gullaime calling as they pulled the air currents around to push the ship's beak towards the open sea, a song both mournful and inhuman but also familiar, like it had a meaning just beyond his reach. When *Hag's Hunter* faced the open sea, the gullaime's calls changed, became something that sounded to Joron more ancient and more sad.

For a moment he thought the earth beneath his feet shuddered, but no other seemed to feel it. Then there was a lull, his ears stopped hurting, and all noise ceased before the ache in his ears returned, bringing with it a fist of air that filled *Hag's Hunter's* wings and powered him out of the harbour on a tower of tight varisk weave. If Joron had not known it was the magic of the gullaime filling the ship's wings he would have found it easy to believe it was the cheers of the town that powered him away. Or the shouts of the crews of the other ships as they lined the rails of their pristine white boneships and watched *Hag's Hunter*, trailing eight blue corpselights, glide out of the bay before slowing to a stop and dropping its staystone outside the harbour.

"I thought it was to go north," said Mevans.

"North? But I thought the trouble was in the south?"

"Ey, as did we all. But the word of those I know aboard is that Meas's sither goes north. Empty seas and easy duty that way, so it would not surprise me."

"Ey," said Joron. But he was not so sure and wondered if all was what it seemed, for he knew *Tide Child's* mission would eventually bring him north. There was no love lost between Meas and her sither, and all knew the Hag loved a reckoning.

The other change to their routine happened on the very last

day of dry dock. Of all the days it was the longest and the hardest as *Tide Child* was lifted from his cradle and gently lowered into the water – a task done professionally and quickly by the bonewrights, under the watchful eye of Bonemaster Coxward. In his youth Joron had seen the launch of a new boneship, the last to be built from the stock of bones kept under the spiral bothies, and he still remembered the joy of that day. The giant ship *Bowwyrm*, so white it seemed impossible, his sides streaked with red where blood ran down from the sacrifices that had provided the eight corpselights floating above.

Joron remembered thinking it was all so beautiful – not the deaths, but to be the keyshan price and to live on as part of the ship, as part of the fleet his father always spoke of. It was an honour he could only dream of. As the ship moved down the slipway, gathering speed until it hit the water and caused a huge wave that soaked the wildly cheering crowd in briny water, he had shouted as loud as he ever had. Later, his father had bought him a bit of meat on a stick and told him stories of the fleet and said he hoped that, one day, Joron would be part of it. His father had never imagined Joron would serve on a black ship. What parent would ever wish to see their child drowning in dishonour? But sometimes he could still taste that meat, savoury and wonderful in a way only a memory can be: a flavour lost to his tongue for ever the way the warm feeling of his father's arms around him had become a cold place deep inside.

The relaunch of *Tide Child* was nothing like the launching of *Bowwyrm* or *Hag's Hunter*; if anything, it was placed in the water almost apologetically. The ship looked better than he ever had under Joron's care – black as night from beak to rump – and smelled better – of sea and the eye-watering vapour of still-drying and extremely flammable boneglue. But there was a sadness to the launch, a lack of ritual. Women and men simply stood around watching as the huge crane lowered *Tide Child*, lacking spines and spars still, into the water. Placing him there with barely a splash, as though slipping him secretly into the sea and hoping it would not notice.

"Well" — Joron turned on hearing a familiar voice; Meas was walking down the dock, Narza trailing behind her — "don't just stand there. There are spines to go up, rigging to web, and those of you not up to such tasks can start carrying aboard our cargo and setting it in the hold." She glanced around. "Solemn Muffaz! You are strong; you can lead the stowing. *Tide Child* pulls to seaward so load with that in mind, and show Gavith how and why you do it."

"May just have been loaded badly before, Shipwife," said the huge man.

"Ey, well, we'll find that out when we fly. For now load as if he pulls." She turned but Solemn Muffaz did not leave; he was almost hopping from one foot to the other in a slow and nervous way, and the cabin boy, Gavith, stood behind him. "You have something else to ask, Solemn Muffaz?"

"Aye, Shipwife," he said, staring at the floor. "Only, on my last ship I were oarturner, and you have Barlay on this ship."

"And you wonder on your place?"

"Ey, Shipwife."

"Your place is in my crew, Muffaz," she said not unkindly. In the background Joron noticed Barlay had drifted nearer, looking equally nervous. "I have given Barlay that place, and as long as she serves well in it I will not go back on that, for it is not my way. Any who have served with me will tell you my word is good."

Solemn Muffaz nodded and behind him Barlay seemed to straighten slightly, as if freed from a weight she had not known sat upon her shoulders. "I need a deckmother, Muffaz, someone to enforce my discipline," she said. "You have been around boneships a long time, from what I hear, and I know it is not a popular task, but I will need someone strong for it."

He nodded.

"Then I will do this thing for you, Shipwife."

"Good, and though Barlay is strong she does not yet truly

know the task of oarturner, so I would also put you to helping her understand her duties."

Muffaz nodded again. "We have already spoken of her task and how to approach it, Shipwife."

"We are reborn on this ship, Solemn Muffaz, understand that. We leave our crimes behind on land. Keep that in mind." She turned and shouted, "Mevans! To me." The little man did not run to her, as most would, but walked quickly enough not to seem as though he disobeyed. He had a strange gait, bobbing his body as he moved as if avoiding the overbones of an invisible underdeck. "Mevans, I shall need a seakeep to keep *Tide Child* in good order and make sure everything aboard runs as it should."

"Fogle, she's be good for that, knows a ship backwards does Fogle," he said.

"I was talking of you," said Meas.

"I'm a hatkeep, Shipwife," he said. "I mean, I will do whatever you say, only that I think there are those better suited."

Meas looked hard at him for a moment. "Very well then. You can tell Fogle she is seakeep, but if I find her drunk, even once, she is back to deckchild."

Mevans nodded.

"She won't let you down."

"I hope not. But, and you will not turn this next task down. The purseholder on *Tide Child*, Sprackin, is as corrupt as they come. You will take his place and there is no argument about this."

Mevans shrugged.

"Well, I am a man skilled in the keeping of your valuables, so to keep the whole ship's is not much of a stretch. I cannot fault your choice." He smiled, but the smile fell away as he noticed something behind Meas. She turned.

Emerging on to the dock was a line of men. All were big and six were carrying boxes, two to each box. The man leading them wore his blonde hair long and strode up to Meas. He towered over her.

"You are Shipwife Meas?" Behind him the men carrying the boxes put them down. They were clearly heavy and far longer than they were wide, almost like coffins.

"You are from Mulvan Cahanny?"

"That we are," he said. "The boxes need to be stacked safe in your hold, somewhere they will not get wet or damaged."

"What is in them?"

"That is not your business,"

"He is my ship," she said.

"What is in the boxes is Mulvan Cahanny's business." As he spoke Joron counted the men with him: fifteen strong bodies in all when Cahanny had only promised ten.

"I must know the contents of these boxes do not endanger my ship in any way."

"They do not, or I would not go aboard with them. I am Cahanny's second." Meas stared at him, then gave a small nod.

"What is your name?"

"Coughlin."

"For now, Coughlin, I must find a safe place for your cargo on—"

"Cahanny said to put it on your ship."

"Do not interrupt me." Her words cut him dead. "Cahanny has placed you under my command."

"In battle," said Coughlin, and he stared off towards *Tide Child*. "Otherwise we are here to guard the cargo and nothing else."

"That was not my agreement," said Meas.

Coughlin shrugged. "That is not my concern. I do as Cahanny tells me. Now, Shipwife," he said, turning away, "get my cargo aboard."

Meas's hand shot out, iron-hard fingers grabbing the man's massive arm. He turned back, trying to look as if this was a mere inconvenience, but he was plainly surprised by the strength of her grip.

"I am going to presume you have never been on a fleet ship before because I know you are a man of the rock." If Coughlin was offended by this, he did not show it, though it was possible he did not know the disservice Meas did him. "So I shall let the insult you have just offered me go this once. I am shipwife. My word is law. What I decide rules your life from the moment you board *Tide Child*. You respect me and do as I say, or you die. It is that simple." She let go of his arm. "Now, when the time comes, I shall have my crew load your boxes. When the time comes, and my crew because loading a ship is a skill in itself and one I doubt you or any of your men have. But from now on, you will do as I say, you understand?"

He nodded.

"I hear what you say," he said. It did not escape Joron's ears that Coughlin was not agreeing with her or admitting she commanded him. "But the time to load them is now."

"I am not well liked, Coughlin, and there are those who would love nothing more than to see my veins opened to the sea. So I imagine my ship will be searched before we leave. I have no wish to die for Mulvan Cahanny's cargo, and I am sure Mulvan will be displeased if it is impounded." She turned to Mevans and leaned in close, pointing at the boxes before turning back to Coughlin. "Mevans will see your cargo hidden, and before we leave I will have my crew load it for you."

"As you wish." He walked away, joining the rest of his men, glancing back at Meas with eyes as deep and cold as the sea in the north, where great islands of ice float through the night, waiting to wreck the unwary.

"Mevans," said Meas quietly, "I am not sure I have made my best decision in bringing Cahanny's men aboard my ship. If ever a gift struck me as poisonous it is this one."

"Don't you worry, Shipwife," said Mevans. "They're all men of the rock for sure. The minute they get on the sea they'll be too busy suffering the Hag's curse and throwing up over the side to cause trouble. You'll see."

Joron watched the men as the crew went back to their business and could not help doubting Mevans' words. They did not look like they would be brought low so easily. And Meas was clearly not sure about them either.

"Are you sure about Muffaz, Meas," he said as Mevans left to arrange the hiding of Cahanny's cargo. "The crew will have a hard time accepting a wife killer."

She nodded.

"You are right. But deckmother is a lonely position. It is the best place for him, and did you see the look in his eye when we said he could be crew?"

"Ey, Shipwife."

"Gratitude, Deckkeeper. He is a man who wishes to make amends for something that can never be forgiven. I have taken him on board and given him a place. He will die before he disobeys me, mark me at that." Joron watched as she walked away, realising she could see things that he could not, and was prepared to use people in ways that would never occur to him.

The next surprise turned up as *Tide Child*'s wings were being hauled into position on the newly lifted spars: a small man with a slight limp, though he was wide and well muscled and had a pleasing face. The brightly coloured stripes of command ran through his hair, and he dragged a heavy sea chest behind him. Meas called Joron to her and they went to meet the newcomer.

"Can I help you?" Meas asked.

"Ey. My name is Dinyl Kiveth, and I am sent by Kept Indyl Karrad to be your deckkeeper."

Joron was shocked, although he should not have been. Karrad was vindictive, and as all Joron had was his place on Meas's ship that was what the Kept had decided to take from him.

"You have been through the spiral bothies?" said Meas.

"Ey, and served on the *Mother's Wish* and the *Welcome Breast*."

"Then you well know, Dinyl Kiveth, that if you join *Tide Child* and put on the black armband, you may never take it off." Joron though, on the edge of despair at the thought of losing the slowly growing pride within him, saw a mirror of that despair in Dinyl's face.

"I am beholden to Kept Karrad," he said. "His money put

me through the bothies, and now he sends me to this ship to do his work. Give me the armband" – he put out a hand – "and I will wear it."

"You should know I have a deckkeeper, Dinyl Kiveth, and I will not have him usurped," she said. "If you come on to *Tide Child* you come on as deckholder, no more." Joron did not think it was possible for the man to look more miserable, but he found a way at this demotion.

"What choice do I have?" he said, a picture of despair. "I cannot go back to Karrad having disobeyed his orders. I am fleet."

Meas nodded and from a pocket produced a length of black material which she wrapped around Kiveth's bicep.

"Let the Hag know, you are now beholden to me." Dinyl stared sadly at the rag around his arm. "For what it is worth, Dinyl," she said quietly, "I am sorry. Now take your chest and load it on to *Tide Child*. Find Solemn Muffaz, our deckmother, and he will tell you how I wish the ship's stores stacked in the hold." Dinyl nodded and walked away. As he left, Coughlin and the rest of Cahanny's men watched from where they lounged on the dock in front of the ship. "First I take on pirates, and now a spy," said Meas quietly.

"At least we know who the spy is," said Joron.

"That one at least," Meas replied. "But I suspect he is a distraction. Karrad will have others on board, and my mother will have those loyal to her too."

"Your mother, I understand," said Joron, "but I thought you and Karrad were allies."

"We share a common cause, Joron," said Meas. "But I see freedom in it, where Karrad sees power. So I am not sure we share that much at all."

19

All at Sea

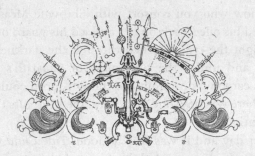

It took them two further days to balance the spines, tie in the spars and web the rigging, and all the time Meas was like a woman possessed, glancing up at Skearith's Eye as if its progress across the sky was a personal insult. Always she was there – "Work faster, work harder, work better' – and the crew knew no respite. Joron continued a twilight existence, falling into bed and waking, barely rested, to more labour. He mostly managed to avoid Dinyl Kiveth but could not help pangs of jealousy when he saw the easy and knowledgeable way the man had with the ship and the crew.

As Meas had suspected, the ship was searched. The evening before they were due to set out seaguard came aboard. All the good work done in stowing the cargo was undone. Crates were thrown over, water barrels smashed, and all the chaos that could be caused was caused. As they wrecked, Meas followed the seaguard and Kept Tassar, who headed them, keeping up polite conversation.

When they were done, hot and angry at finding nothing, Meas was all apologies.

"Such hard work, Tassar. Generally I would have Gavith, my cabin boy, bring you water or anhir, but sadly my barrels seem to have been damaged in your search. Tell me, were you looking for anything specific?"

"We will be watching you, Meas," said Tassar.

"Shipwife Meas," she corrected, "when you are on my ship. I am sure you would not wish to break the Bernlaw."

"We know who you consort with, Shipwife Meas," he said, then turned his oiled back on her and led his guard off the ship.

That night the crew worked through the darkness to right the mess, and under the wan glow of Skearith's Blind Eye Cahanny's cargo was brought on, though Joron could not help noticing there was now one box extra, the hiylbolts that Karrad had spoken of.

Another day and it was finally done. *Tide Child* was towed out into the harbour and they dropped the staystone while the remaining crew were brought from the hulks. Meas retreated to the great cabin with the courser and left Joron and Dinyl to assign posts to those brought aboard.

It was a dull job and Joron had little to do. He and Dinyl stood behind Mevans and Solemn Muffaz, who sat at a desk on the deck, rating each woman and man by experience: deckchild for those with plenty, bowsell for those they thought may have talent with the ship's weapons, right down to stonebound for those who knew nothing of the sea, though only the boy Gavith and old Garriya were ranked so low. Joron could not meet the old woman's eye – something about the frailty of her mind made him uncomfortable – though she was keen to meet his, grinning at him while Mevans took down her details, her experience and any family she had.

Joron turned away, pretending to study the harbour and the horizon. They had an almost clear view now as *Hag's Hunter* had left.

"Clench the muscles in your legs," whispered Dinyl to him.

"What?"

"It is an old trick to ease the ache of standing still for long periods, Deckkeeper. Wiggle your toes, clench the muscles in your calves, then your thighs. None can tell, and you will not look like you are fidgeting."

Joron did this, often, in the long hours of rating more than a hundred men and women.

"Thank you, Dinyl," he whispered as the line came near to its end.

Only when the gullaime was brought aboard did Meas appear. The creature was brought to the ship on a top-heavy ungainly-looking flukeboat by a crew from the lamyards. The gullaime's cage was suspended from a crane above the boat, and the beast screamed and shouted its displeasure, both in the language of the Archipelago and in its own atonal squawks.

The commander of the ship called over as they approached, "This is yours?"

"Ey," shouted Meas, leaning over the rail. "Why is it caged?"

"Almost killed one of my women trying to escape."

"Kill all!" screamed the gullaime.

"Maybe you should take it back with you then, get us a different one," shouted Meas.

"Hag's tits no. It's your problem now." The crane swung, bringing the cage over *Tide Child*'s deck, and then, none too gently, unspooled the cord that held it so it crashed on to the slate, making the gullaime renew its squawking with even more fury. Black Orris deserted his perch and flew up into the rigging, swearing all the way.

"Kill you all!" shouted the gullaime. "Drive you on rocks. Smash you with wind."

Joron stared at the creature. He had never before thought of gullaime as dangerous. They were a gift to the people of the Archipelago from Skearith. He was used to seeing and thinking of them in that way, watching them pass in their filthy robes, blind heads bowed as their handlers took them to the ships, or seeing them from afar, standing on decks in small groups as they controlled the wind and sang their songs. But as this gullaime threw itself against the bars of its bell-shaped cage, he saw the curved claws that sprang from the elbows of the wings hidden within its robe. Saw the much larger, scythe-like claws on the creature's feet. And how could he never have noticed before that their beaks were those of a predator, curved and sharp and shaped for tearing at flesh?

Meas stepped nearer the cage and took one of the small crossbows that dangled from her clothes, loaded it and pointed it at the gullaime.

"No one wishes to be on this ship, Windtalker," she said. "But you are the only one aboard who could wreck us if you wished it. So give me one reason not to kill you here and now." Joron heard the whole crew gasp at her words; to even threaten such a thing was unheard of.

"Ill luck," squawked the gullaime. "Ill luck to kill gullaime!" It climbed up the inside of its cage, wingclaws and feet scraping at the bars. Joron fancied he could smell its dry and dusty stink, one that stuck in your nose and refused to leave. "Ill luck!" it squawked again.

Meas shrugged.

"I'd rather have ill luck than a creature that will summon the wind to run us on to a lee shore, or drive us on to rocks. Much rather have ill luck than that." She raised the crossbow, aiming it at the bird's blind head. From the rigging came Black Orris, fluttering down to land on Joron's shoulder, where he started to preen his feathers. The gullaime's blind head flicked round as though sensing the corpsebird. Its beak opened and closed slowly, its body language changed.

"Would not do that thing." It almost purred the words.

"Why should I believe you?" said Meas.

"Gullaime cannot swim. Cannot fly."

"Well, Gullaime," she said. "Then you must be crew. And if you are to be crew you must be useful. So, tell me, can you be useful? For if not I will send you back to the lamyards, whether they want you or not." The creature hissed at her, its beak opening to reveal the cave of sharp spines and the long thin tongue within.

Joron found himself stepping forward, Black Orris fluttering at his ear as words came into his mouth, springing into being without volition or question.

"What do you want?" he said.

The crew, gathered to watch the spectacle, held their breaths, not only because he had interrupted the shipwife, but because the gullaime was now orientated on him, opening and closing its beak as if confused.

Or interested.

"Want?" it said eventually.

Joron nodded. "These women and men of the crew, they get food, they get drink, they get paid even though this is a ship of the dead. The money is sent to their families. That is why they serve." Joron felt his throat and mouth drying as he realised everyone was staring at him. "What do you want? What would make you serve?"

The gullaime's head recoiled on its long thin neck, as if to better take in a world that had abruptly changed in a way it found most surprising. Though of course there were no eyes behind the brightly painted leaf mask to take in the sparkling water, the bright eye of Skearith above, the shocked deckchilder gathered on the slate or the calculating gaze of Meas Gilbryn as she watched her deckkeeper. The beast's eyes would have been removed soon after it hatched, for if that was not done the creatures wandered and hurt themselves.

It was a kindness, really.

"Want?" it said again, quietly. Then it softly opened and closed its beak and climbed down from where it hung on the bars of the cage. "What does gullaime want?"

Meas stepped up to Joron. He waited for the reprimand, but she turned from him to the gullaime.

"I would be interested to know this too, Windtalker."

"Great shipwife," spat the birdmage, "asks what gullaime want?" It seemed to shrink down into itself. "But gullaime serve, all know gullaime serve." And was it bitterness in that otherworldly voice, spoken without lip or true tongue? Could Joron really know what the inflections such a creature gave its voice meant?

"Maybe gullaime do serve, and that is the way of it on most

ships." Meas left a pause, a long one. "But as Joron has reminded me, this is not a normal ship. So maybe things on *Tide Child* will not be done the normal way." Something inside Joron glowed a little at the faint praise contained in Meas's words. "So, Gullaime, what is it you want?"

It squawked quietly and thoughtfully, more to itself than to Meas or any of the watching crew, and as if in reply Black Orris squawked back at it from his perch on Joron's shoulders:

"Arse!"

Silence.

"String," said the gullaime, the word slow from its mouth. "Want string." Then it tipped its head to seaward and thought a little more, before adding, "And dust." Another pause. "A lot of dust." A squawk of excitement. "And cloth and needles and dust . . ." Then it was reeling off a list of things, strange and seemingly pointless things, some everyday, some extremely rare, and for the life of him Joron could not work out what the beast could want with any of it. But Meas listened and nodded, and when the creature took a breath, for it showed no sign of stopping, she interrupted.

"String, dust, cloth and needles, these things I can do; some of the other things are harder to find. But trust blows both ways. You must prove yourself to me."

"How?" It tipped its head on one side. Opened its beak and snapped it shut.

"While we have been speaking, my crew have raised the staystone. All that holds us here is lack of wind."

"You want wind?"

"Ey," she said. "I understand you have not visited a windspire for a long time. We will take you ashore to the spire above Bernshulme and allow you to breathe it and—"

"No need!" squawked the gullaime and it raised its featherless wings inside the cage. Heat washed over the ship, and Joron felt like someone had clapped hands over his ears, so quick was the change in air pressure. The black sails of *Tide Child* cracked and shuddered in the sudden gusts. For a moment

Meas was shocked at the power the beast conjured up. Then she was reacting.

"Oarturner!" she shouted. "Oarturner! To the rump of the ship!" They were moving already, *Tide Child* listing and creaking as the wind brought by the gullaime hit, and the ship began to move smoothly and swiftly forward, without thought to direction. Meas was running for the oar as was Barlay. "Steer us landward. Aim for the harbour entrance," she shouted. Now the wind was howling around the ship, and Joron knew there was danger, but the look on his shipwife's face contained nothing but exhilaration as she threw herself against the oar, laughing, bringing *Tide Child* round to point his beak at the open sea. They flew out of Bernshulme harbour like a thief leaving the scene of a crime, and not one deckchild in the harbour or woman or man of the rock cheered their passage.

Though you would not have known it from the shouts of of joy from those aboard.

It seemed to Joron the ship was somehow lighter. He did not understand why – it carried more crew, more cargo, more weight than ever before – but the black ship skipped across the waves, and not only when the gullaime brought the wind. The birdmage's magic lasted only until they were out of the harbour, and then the gullaime turned its head to Meas and gave her an emphatic nod, as if to say, *Well, there you go. Doubt no more.* Then it sat down in its cage amid the straw and filth, and the breeze coming off Bernshulme picked up where the creature left off.

Meas wandered over to the beast.

"When was the last time you were at a windspire to charge the strength within you, Windtalker?"

"Six times the cold eye of night opens and closes," it said quietly.

"Six months?" She put a hand on the bars. "Six months and you still conjure a wind to bring us out of the harbour? Most of your kind would not last a week."

It stood then, raising itself from sitting without needing to steady itself with elbow or beak. Standing, it was of a similar height to Meas.

'Hurts,' said the gullaime and stroked its chest with a wing-claw, "but I am not most. Not most."

Meas stood back.

"We shall find you land and windspire the first chance we get," she said. "And the other things you ask for, I shall have Deckkeeper Twiner find them." The creature's head shot round, unerringly finding Joron even though it was blind. Then Meas opened the door of the cage and stood to one side. It scuttled out, across the slate on all fours and down the stairs to the underdeck, watched by all.

The sight made Joron shudder, but the rest of the crew seemed inured to the gullaime; to them it was just a part of the furniture, as much a fixture of the ship as the turning oar, spines or spars. But to him it was something dark, unnatural. As a child he had dreamed he heard the storms talking to him, and his father had told him to put such thoughts aside, that nothing good could come of them and that if he spoke of them he was likely to find himself floating blue above a ship as a corpselight.

And then what would I do, Joron? Left all alone without my boy? But how could he not be reminded of such things when a creature that could control the winds with just its thoughts walked the same slate as he did?

They flew across the sea and Skearith's Eye closed on them. The lights of the town were slowly absorbed by the night, going from many to a few to a single fuzzy glow that Joron supposed, at least to some of the crew, must be sad to see vanish, though he was not one of them. Then Skearith's cold bones lit the sky, a myriad glowing messages for the courser and the shipwife who huddled below, charting *Tide Child*'s course. How had he found himself here? Officer on a ship of the dead, a ship of betrayal on his way to meet Gaunt Islanders.

How could that even be?

Traitors among his own kind he could almost understand

– to meet more Hundred Islanders bent on stopping war, well, that would make some sense. But Gaunt Islanders? They were little more than animals, given to eating their own children if none from the Hundred Isles were available. Masters of the underhand, reavers and murderers. But Meas had not even blinked at the idea of working with them.

How could that be?

Was that what condemned her?

And how would the crew react?

Would Meas try to hide from these rough women and men that they worked with the enemy? The people they most hated and feared would fly ships alongside them and they would have to trust them. How could they? No matter how lucky Meas may be, they surely would not follow her in this.

But without Gaunt Islanders ready to stop fighting, how could there be this peace she talked of?

Joron took a deep breath.

It was not his problem; it was hers. And maybe, if in the meantime he could learn as much as possible from her, when the time came and her treachery was unmasked, he would be able to steer the ship. He would have Mevans and some of her old crew on his side, he was sure. They seemed to like him. Then there was Anzir. She would support him. He only need prove himself and . . .

He cut those thoughts off. Why plan? He walked the slate deck of a black ship. What point in planning? There was only living. Doing and moving and being.

With that in mind he set himself to the first of his tasks, one he had decided upon himself. He would remember the names of those who served under him.

Some were easy: the bonemaster, Coxward, was a hard man to forget. As was Meas's hatkeep and purseholder, Mevans. And Solemn Muffaz – a Maiden-cursed man was not hard to recall – he would not forget the deckmother, there to keep discipline aboard and dole out what punishments were needed. Farys, the burn-scarred girl, was now bowsell of the underdeck, and he realised that there was a little bit of pride in him at this, for he had chosen her. They had a seakeep, Fogle, but Meas had warned him the woman was likely to fall into drink and asked him to watch for those who showed some skill with the ship, should the need arise for a new one.

She had chosen her underdeck officers from all over the ship, not just from her own people, knowing that to mix her own with those already here and those brought from the hulks was more likely to bond the crew like dovetail joints in bone, the crews slotting into one another and becoming one. The two wingwrights, he could not remember their names, one from the old crew, one from Meas's. What were they called? He would find out. Gavith – there was a name he knew. The heartbroken cabin boy had somehow found himself a friend in Solemn Muffaz, a man who had murdered his own wife. The same misery from different mirrors, he suspected.

As if hearing Joron think his name, Gavith appeared, eager as a chick for food, at his side.

"Mea—" he began and then stopped, frowning at himself. "I mean the shipwife wants you, D'keeper."

"Very well." He turned. "Barlay, the rump is yours until D'older Kiveth comes up. Keep us on this course."

"Ey, D'keeper." Joron listened for some hint of resentment but it did not come. Barlay only stared forward, her big hands wrapped around the steering oar as if his order came with years of experience. He made his way into the underdeck with a step that was a little bit lighter.

In the underdeck of *Tide Child* Joron ducked beneath the overbones and wove between the swinging hammocks of the crew. Many were occupied, bodies groaning and snuffling in sleep, the underdeck thick with the warm scent of too many humans crammed into a confined space. Wanelights glowed along the sides of the hull, but he stepped gingerly, avoiding those chests or packs that had yet to be stowed correctly. Meas had allowed her tired crew a little leeway, though made clear that from the moment they woke tomorrow they would work like skeer looking for carrion to deliver the type of ship she expected — an efficient fighting ship.

He knocked gently on the door of the great cabin and put his head around the door. In the gloom its floor and walls shone, almost magical in their paleness. The faces of Meas and the quiet courser Aelerin were like planets orbiting her desk, eclipsing one another, becoming one then two then one again.

"Come," said Meas gently, and he let himself in. Meas's desk was once more comfortable in its place in the floor — Joron noticed Bonemaster Coxward had done nothing to fill the indentations the desk had worn — and it was covered in charts, unrolled and held in place with all manner of things. Here a knife driven into the top of the desk, there a heavy shell of the type he knew contained a creature which shot poisonous spines. A stone, seemingly nothing odd about it but too heavy to have found its way accidentally aboard the ship. A model boneship held down another corner. The charts had been laid out so the whole of the Scattered Archipelago lay under the dim light of glowing bird skulls.

"You look struck, Joron," said Meas. "Have you never seen a chart before? It is a sight, is it not?"

"Ey, it is a sight," he said. And it was. He had never thought of his world as square. Like all who knew navigation, he knew the world was curved and they lived on half of the sphere, hemmed in by fearsome storms. What, if anything, was beyond them was unknown to woman or man — most believed the Hag's lands of the dead. But drawn on charts the world was flat, made somehow less by the pens of those who sought to control it on paper.

Running diagonally across the centre of the square was Skearith's Spine, a line of huge mountains of solid granite rising like blades from the water, far too steep to climb in most places. His father had told him they had been connected once, a solid wall between the civilised people of the Hundred Isles and the animals in human form of the Gaunt Islands, but time and sea changed all things. Now the spine was a shattered chain with great gaps between its peaks through which the ships of the Gaunt Islands came to raid, and the ships of the Hundred Isles passed to revenge.

On the landward side of the charts, taking up what Joron thought of as the top half, the better half, the Hundred Isles were scattered over the sea. He picked out the crescent of Shipshulme, roughly in the centre on the line where the seasons were most clement. He was seized by an urge to count the islands. Were there really a hundred of them? Or were there more? Or less? Some he knew, could name just by sight. Others, names written beside serrated coastlines in a delicate hand, sounded mysterious and strange, and he knew there were as many colours and shapes of people and different cultures in the Hundred Isles as there were beasts that killed in the sea. All bound together by the need to defend themselves from the Gaunt Islanders, whose lands occupied the other half of the map – the cold, uncivilised half.

Were there really fewer islands over there? Or was it only that the women and men who made the charts knew so much less about the Gaunt Islands? They were bigger than all but Shipshulme, that was definitely true, and he wondered if that was why the Gaunt Islanders were more singular in their culture, less colourful and fewer. Perhaps that was why their dark culture of raiding and murder seemed universal among them. They were a people who took the easy ways: take rather than give, using mortar rather than learning the patient art of stone laying.

And yet . . .

And yet they worshipped the same goddesses, saw Skearith's Eye in the same sky and had not been struck down by the Women of the Sea for their ways, vile though they were. Maybe those who said the Hag only wanted bodies and cared not where they came from were right.

The Gaunt Islands' capital, Sparehaven, was roughly on the same line as Bernshulme, so had similarly clement weather and calm seasons. Even the placing of their capital was stolen from the Hundred Isles, for all knew they had once kept their capital up near the Northstorm, the better to test their women and men against the fierceness of the winds and seas.

"Are you listening to me, Joron?" He was back in the room, the spinning map of his mind fading.

"I? No, Shipwife. My apologies." Once he would have lied. But not now. "I have never seen the entire world laid out so."

"Well," said Meas, "I can still remember the spell it cast on me, so I can forgive you this once. Never again though, Deckkeeper, right?"

"Yes, Shipwife."

"Good. Aelerin, you may leave now. Thank you for your help and get what sleep you can."

"Thank you, Shipwife." The courser spoke in little more than a whisper.

Meas watched them leave.

"How much have you told them?" asked Joron.

"Very little," Meas said quietly, "only the route we must take, and they go away to think on it. We head south now to rendezvous with the Gaunt Islander ships at Skeerpass here." She pointed at the map. "According to Indyl Karrad, the arakeesian should be heading up Flensechannel. Now, that's only ten hunths across. With three ships we can cover that. One of us should sight the arakeesian."

"If it exists," said Joron.

"I have known Kept Indyl Karrad be many things, Deckkeeper, not all of them pleasant, but he is rarely wrong. And as he ages and loses his looks and his strength, it becomes more important that he provides good intelligence if he is to keep his position. The Bern do not tend to suffer the Kept past their prime. The lucky vanish to some island to enjoy what money they have hidden away, the foolish die in duels they are too old to fight, and the clever find other ways to make themselves useful."

"Or become a favourite."

"That may be the riskiest course to take of them all. Bern are often fickle and cruel."

"You do not count yourself among them."

"There are no stretch marks on my belly, Joron. My body may be unmarred by Skearith's curses but I have no children to my name. What honour I have I earned on the slate of a boneship, not on a Bern's chair."

"But your mother—"

"—put me on this ship," she said, and that conversation was over, the subject clearly never to be raised again.

"If I may ask a question, Shipwife?" said Joron. "It has been bothering me." She looked hard at him, and he was sure she was weighing up the possibility of him sweeping back, tidewashed, to the subject of her mother like flotsam on a beach. Then deciding he would not. That he was either too sensible or cowardly.

"Ask."

"The black ships we go to meet . . ." He said it so quietly even he could barely hear his voice. Meas had to lean in close. She smelled of clean clothes and honest sweat. "They are Gaunt Islanders. How can we trust them?"

"Because we must, Deckkeeper, and do not believe all you have been told of the Gaunt Islanders. Remember you only hear of them from the mouths of those that want you killing them."

"Their raids are not rumours." This came out more harshly than he had expected. She paused before replying.

"No, they are not, but neither are ours on them. My advice is to judge them on who they are when you meet them, rather than on what you have heard from those to whom they are only stories."

"The stories are what worry me. I work to your order, and if there is good reason for this, well, then I will believe what you say, but the crew—"

"—will never meet them, Joron. Never. Mevans and Solemn Muffaz will row us over to the Gaunt Island ships – they can be trusted. When aboard the Gaunt Islanders' ships we will be treated as though we are of their islands. If the Gaunt Islander shipwives come aboard *Tide Child*, we will treat them as though they are from the Hundred Isles. The accents and language are not too dissimilar, our clothing barely any different. That is the great advantage of a ship of the dead, Deckkeeper: anyone may become his shipwife. The fact that no one will have heard of those who command will not be suspicious."

"We must lie to our crew."

"Ey."

"To win them a peace they do not even want."

"Does a child wish to know what it means to be born Berncast, Joron, or to grow up? Ask yourself that. Or would they rather spend their time not knowing a deformity will keep them hungry, or fearing that a babe will grow within them that will leave them dying in a pool of blood, or that a gallowbow shot will take an arm or leg and leave them begging on the streets of Bernshulme?" She waved at the chair before her table and began rolling up the charts.

Joron was surprised that the stone, the seemingly ordinary stone, she was very careful to place in her sea chest where it would be safe; the rest of her chart weights she discarded recklessly about the cabin as if they did not matter.

"Sit then," she said. He did. "Tomorrow we start to train on the gallowbows. I have bought enough shot for us to have plenty of practice. We need it. The team who does best will have the pick of the fresh eggs from the kivelly on board, which will please them, and action always cheers a crew." He nodded. "We shall train on the bows every day until we are proficient. We shall also have training in arms – in the curnow, the wyrmpike, bow and crossbow – and I will teach you how to handle a straightsword."

"But I do not—"

"You are my deckkeeper; you have no choice. You have a quick mind, and that is half the skill of swordcraft. You start late, right enough, but between me, Anzir and Narza we can make you competent if not great, and competent will be enough if you have a loyal crew around you."

"Where do I find that?"

"You are already on the way, Deckkeeper. Mevans likes you. I think Gavith feels some kinship also. The burned girl . . ."

"Farys."

"Ey, her. She is definitely loyal to you, and I hope she has skill with the gallowbow as it would be good that a deckchild who has come to you through you, not me, keeps her place." He nodded again. "The swimmer too. Kelling?"

"Karring," he said.

She smiled to herself.

"Ey, Karring. Well, on the morran we will re-stow the cargo. *Tide Child* pulls to landward still. It may be something to do with the keel. but I will have Coxward fit shot racks in the hold and the underdeck. Gallowbow shot is heavy, and racks allow us to move it about easily, to change the way the ship steers. We will be busy, you and I, but watch for crew who are struggling. You will be surprised how often an unexpected hand can win a woman or man's heart over. Apart from that, you will not be doing the physical work, only giving orders."

"Very well."

"And last, I want you to make friends with the gullaime."

"Friends?" If he had not been sitting he would have needed to. "With the beast?"

"Ey. I cannot. I am shipwife and it will see me as a figure of authority whatever I do. But, as I said before, this ship will run differently." She leaned forward, her grey eyes earnest. "Listen to me, Joron. What we have been tasked with doing – fighting ships to stop them taking an arakeesian – you and I both know it is a mind-fled task. Both the Hundred Isles and the Gaunt Islands may bring entire fleets to bear on this if – when – they learn of it. I already suspect that my mother knows something and that is why *Hag's Hunter* flew north. We will have to be aware at every moment. Every ship that could take a message telling of what we are about we must destroy if we can. Every action we undertake must be ruthless. None can escape. No mercy can be given. My greatest hope is that word reaches the fleets in the south too late for them to act, and Karrad will do all he can to make this so. Then we shall only face smaller ships." She ran her hand across the smooth top of her desk. "But even then . . ." she sat back ". . . with a ship like *Tide Child*, after two or three actions I would expect to dock and refit before carrying on, and that option is not available to us." She sat in silence for a moment. "Well, I suppose they do not call this a ship of the dead for no reason."

"You do not think we can succeed?"

She tapped the desk before her — once, twice, three times.

"I did not. Joron. Not at first. But if what that gullaime says is true, that it has not touched land for six months and yet it can bring up a wind like it did to take us out of the harbour? Then that may change our chances."

"Why?"

She stopped her tapping.

"I forget you are not fleet, and not familiar with the gullaime. What our windtalker did today, for a ship this size? That would usually take three or four gullaime, and they would scream out their pain as the magic drained from them. *Tide Child* should have eight windtalkers in that little cabin, some to use for wind when needed, some to guide home wingshot and protect the ship. But they are generally only good once before needing a windspire to recharge. Very occasionally there are more powerful ones that are good for longer and go to the biggest ships. I had one once on *Arakeesian Dread*. But what our gullaime did after so long away from a windspire? It is remarkable."

"Then why is it on our ship?"

"Because, I imagine, someone is frightened of it."

"Why not just kill it then?"

"Because, Twiner, even powerful women and men can be superstitious. Now gather the things the beast wanted. Find out what can be done for your new friend."

20

A Greased Peg Slips in Well

In the morning the calling bell rang and Joron slid from his hammock, rested for the first time in so long that he wondered what this feeling was: this lightness of head, this spring in his step, this clarity in the air.

Before dressing he took a scoop of cooking fat from the pot by his tiny desk. Barlay had noticed his uncomfortable walk and told him cooking fat would protect his skin from the rough fishskin of his new trousers. He slathered it on the tops of his thighs, then, although it had not been suggested but surely could not hurt any worse, he covered his aching feet in it before sliding on the long boots Meas had bought him.

His thighs hurt considerably less. It did not help his feet much.

On deck Skearith's Eye had already brought the godbird's heat to the air, though it was still low on the horizon. They had made good distance while he slept, and when he pulled the brim of his one-tailed hat down to shade his eyes he could see the faraway silhouette of Skearith's Spine.

"We have made good time, ey Joron?" He turned to find Meas, she seemed more alive on board the ship than she had been back in Bernshulme, her skin less grey. "The Eaststorm has been kind with winds through the night. We'll steer away-spine for the next two days and keep our course south-west, then turn south-east for our rendezvous at Skeerpass when we see the Featherspike."

"Ey, Shipwife," he said, then stared into the sky, blue and clear. "The winds should hold. Not a cloud in the sky."

"Ey, so the courser sings it. Put out the call for breakfast. We'll feed the crew, clean down the decks and strip the ship for action afterwards. Then we'll let fly the gallowbows. If there is time afterwards we'll train with blades." She gave him a smile, calculating but not cold, more amused. "You'll be on a bowteam first. I'll be mixing those who know the drill with those who don't."

"So I'll be commanded by someone else?" It felt like an affront. He had begun to feel that he was developing the veneer of the commander over the skin of the man he was, and here she was, stripping it away.

"Ey, but do not worry that it will diminish you, for I shall be bowsell to all today." She leaned in close. "And it diminishes no commander to learn from those which know more. Weak commanders dare not ask. Strong commanders know no fear of learning." She stood back. "And, just so you know, Joron, if I am in a competition I like to win, and as you are my second in command I expect you to win for me. So do not expect me to be soft on you." She turned away and went to lean over the rear rail next to where Barlay leaned into the steering oar.

Joron sidled over to the gallowbow nearest him. Tied down on the deck it looked like a bird trussed for the pot. The post that mounted the mechanism, rising to the gimbal which allowed the great bow to swivel, was carved to look like a bird's legs springing from the deck. The bone arms that propelled the bolts were currently roped back, and what would be the front of the bow, when in action, was tied to the post so it pointed at the deck. The locking mechanism was hidden from him, while the winding mechanism that drew back the firing cord was raised, its twin handles like offset feathers in a quizzical head. Something was loose on the gallowbow, and its winding handles rocked as *Tide Child* pushed through the sea. Joron, aware that such a thing was a likely target for Meas's wrath, took pity on whichever crew member was in charge of the bow and tightened the knots that held the handles in place. Then he glanced over his shoulder, almost guiltily, to see if anyone had seen him from further down the deck, but the crew were all busy.

If he had looked up the deck he would have seen Meas smile and nod to herself before turning away.

But he did not, and he did not. So that was that.

Meas had the crew eat, a meagre but filling breakfast of porridge called fossy pet made from gion pulp and dried fish. When all were fed she called them together on deck. Joron watched as Indyl Karrad's man, Dinyl, took his place opposite him on the rump. As the crew assembled, Bonemaster Coxward, together with Gavith and a few other crew, started bringing a strange assortment of flotsam, ropes, worn shipwings and odd rubbish out of the hold and on to the deck.

"Today," shouted Meas, "we will exercise the great bows. We have loosed them once before, and we did our ship no credit. Shamed him even." She stopped, glaring at the gathered crew, and even those who had not been there for the shambles at Corfynhulme looked ashamed of themselves. She raised her voice. "This will not happen again!" Meas did not move, but her stillness was the same stillness the sea had when becalmed, a surface stillness only, and below remained the depths, full of danger. "But I realise skill does not come without practice, so all who have worked a gallowbow stand to seaward."

A good half of the crew moved to the seaward side of the ship, all of Meas's old crew among them. It was easy to tell them, for her people were bright, sharp, while the rest were slovenly, meandering the short distance across the deck as if resentful of even those few steps. "Sharp to it now!" shouted Meas. The pace picked up. "Form me two lines," she said. "On seaward those who have worked a great bow, on landward who has not." The lines formed quickly. "Four it takes to fire a great bow," said Meas. She came down from the rump and walked down the deck touching every second woman or man standing to seaward on the shoulder. Some crew she changed around, some she left in position. Then she returned to the rump of the ship. "Those I touched on the shoulder will be the bowsell of a crew, and every woman and man aboard will learn to crew the gallowbows, because in the end a ship can only win a battle if it looses its bows well. This morning we will strip and set the bows; this afternoon we will loose them." She paused as if waiting for some reaction to her words, but the ship remained silent apart from the creak of the spines, the flap of the wings, the hiss of water passing along the hull and the gentle whistle of the wind. "Would you like to loose the bows?"

"Ey, Shipwife." Quiet words spoken by a man with a crooked smile on his face, as if remembering long-ago glory.

Meas shook her head.

"Mevans," she said to her hatkeep, stood at the end of the line nearest to her. "Did that sound like a crew who wishes to loose its bows?"

"It did not, Shipwife."

"If you would like to loose the bows," said Meas, louder, "then I need to hear it. Do you want to loose the bows?"

"Ey, Shipwife!" Now they all called; even resentful Cwell looked interested.

"Shout it like you mean it!"

"Ey, Shipwife!" thundered across the deck, and as they shouted they smiled, glancing and grinning at one another.

"Good. Now, Joron, you will join Dinyl, Barlay and Farys. Barlay, tie off the steering oar — we are unlikely to run into anything out here." She went among the deckchilder, choosing three other teams and sending the rest of the crew to mind the ship and keep the wings trimmed. "While you work," she shouted to those disappointed souls who were not chosen, "do your best to watch as it will be your turn later, and I will expect you to be ready."

She returned once more to the rump of the ship and addressed the six bow teams. "The bow before you is tied down – we call it trussed. You may hear a trussed bow referred to as a bird. There are three commands to untruss a bow. 'Knot!' is the first. You untie the ropes that tie the bow to the legs. We call the bow and loosing-shaft the body. Be careful, for the body is heavy, the winding mechanism and loosing triggers are not balanced and are as dangerous as any club used in anger. When I shout, 'Knot!' one of you will untruss the body. Two, and I advise the strongest two, will hold the body." She glared up into the fierce light of Skearith's Eye as if waiting for a sign, but none came and she continued. "The next command is 'Lift!' After the trigger and winder on the body you will see there is a bulge – that is the socket. Those holding the body will pull it up, bringing the winding mechanism and trigger up and over the legs. Let the weight of the body pull it down. The next-strongest member of your team should be ready to catch the heavy end and help until the socket lies over the gimbal at the top of the legs." She smacked the gimble joint that sat at about the height of her chest. "Then pull the body down so the socket locks over the gimbal. This brings down the locks around the gimbal and forces the arms out. Once the retaining pins" – she held up two varisk pins, each about as thick as two fingers – "are in, the bow is in place and balanced. You understand?"

The woman and men watching nodded.

"Good. The last command is 'String!' You run the cord from the seaward arm through the spinner, through the trigger mechanism, making sure the grippers bite, then to the landward arm. Lock the cord in the cincher and twist it tight. Generally these commands will come from your bowsell, but today we make it a race so you jump to my command. Are you ready?"

"Ey, Shipwife!"

"Then to your bows." She waited until the four teams were standing at each of the great bows on the landward side of the ship.

"Knot!"

Joron let Farys dart in while Barlay and Dinyl grabbed the main shaft of the bow. The knots came loose easily in Farys's nimble fingers, and she pulled the rope free. From the corner of his eye Joron saw the look of surprise on Dinyl's face as the body seemed to come alive in his hands, its great weight eager to crash down, but with the assistance of Barlay he held it steady.

"I had forgotten how heavy they are," said Dinyl, sweat starting on his brow.

From further down the deck Joron heard a dull thud, and as he took the rope from Farys, winding it around the keeper at the bottom of the legs, he glanced down the slate to see a woman laying supine on the deck, blood pooling round her head.

"Someone get her to the hagshand below," shouted Meas. "You will lose people in battle, so this is not a reason to stop. We carry on."

The next order came.

"Lift!"

Barlay and Dinyl pushed up the body of the bow, bringing the winding and trigger mechanisms over while Farys kept low and Joron, his stomach aching at the thought of the damage the weapon could do to him if he mistimed his actions, made a grab for the end of the bow. The handles on the spinner moved aimlessly with the body's movement, making Joron's job harder, but he managed. When the main part of the bow was almost flat, he let it slide towards him until the socket lay above the gimbal ball, but it did not click into place as Meas had promised.

Barlay glanced at Dinyl, unsure what to do.

"There is an old trick, Oarturner." Dinyl grinned. "If we pull the bow arm out a little then get in so we can put our backs to the bow and push out, it will slip on to the gimbal far more easily. But we have to do it together."

"Be quick," said Joron. "It's heavy."

They nodded, counted to three and, together, pulled the bow arms out and slid in behind, using all their strength to push the arms out until they locked behind the holding pins. Joron felt the body shudder as it fell and the locks engaged around the gimbal. Farys slipped in and fixed the retaining pins. At that moment the bow turned from something wild that could lash out and smash bones and bodies into something tame. Balanced on the gimbal it could be guided with one hand and would stay exactly where it was aimed.

"String!"

This was the command that had tripped them at Corfynhulme. But without the panic of battle and with the ship stable beneath them, it was relatively easy. Joron stepped back; Dinyl passed the cord to Farys, who quickly threaded it through the spinner and the trigger mechanism before passing it to Barlay, who slipped it through the other arm of the bow and cinched it tight so the two arms of the bow quivered, ready to loose at the enemy.

"Now," shouted Meas, "we do the same but backwards. Watch your hands as we do this. It is an easier task to put the bow to sleep, but even a sleeping beakwyrm bites."

And that was how they spent the morning. Ever-changing teams practising the routine of trussing and untrussing the gallowbows until their palms bled from the run of the cords and their shoulders ached from the weight of the firing shafts. But it felt like good work. And when it was coming up on time for them to eat, Meas set them in races against one another, and Joron was pleased to find that, although his team did not win, they came in the top six and so would be one of the first to loose in the afternoon.

Earlier he had wondered what they would loose at, but the longer Coxward and his crew of bonewrights worked with the flotsam on the deck the more obvious it became.

They were building a target.

They ate pinstew, named for the bones of the dried fish that was its main ingredient. The fish was heated over peat in a gelatinous gravy made from boiled bird bones and root vegetables, served with a piece of hard black bread as big as strong man's fist and a cup of anhir watered with the juice of the vin fruit.

Once they had eaten and the tables were stowed away, the decks were cleared as if for action. The bonewrights busied themselves in the underdeck, removing the many screens that cut it up into compartments to give some privacy to the underdeck officers; hammocks were rolled up and tied against the inner sides of the hull to provide some protection from flying bone shards; and as all of this went on the sense of excitement aboard *Tide Child* grew and grew. Grown deckchilder capered and laughed like children; friendships that had soured were remade, and by the time Meas called them together on the maindeck the ship was fairly alive with anticipation. The only sour note came from Coughlin and the rest of Cahanny's men, who sat apart from the crew and, though invited, chose to have nothing to do with the exercising of the bows.

Meas had brought *Tide Child* to a stop by the time they were ready to loose, her wingwrights running up and down the rigging until only the topwings remained unfurled to keep the ship stable. She had sent Coxward out in the smaller flukeboat, towing his target out to twenty lengths away where it sat, a crude castle of old spars and torn sails bobbing on the gentle blue waves of a kind sea. Meas watched Coxward and his mates through her nearglass.

"Well," she said into the air, "we should untruss the landward bows. You should not need me to tell you that. Bowsells, what are you lazing about for?"

They set to, Knot, Lift and String. Six bolts had been stacked by each bow, and as his team untrussed the gallowbow to Joron's orders they found that their hands had begun to move automatically. They had begun to know their places, to feel the way the bow worked. And more, that this bow, number one on the maindeck, was theirs.

"We should name it," said Joron as Barlay cinched the cord tight.

"Name it?" said Dinyl. "It is a tool."

"The Hag loves a name," said Barlay, "it is true enough."

"What do you call a bow?" said Farys.

"Hostir," said Barlay. "It were my father's name. When he were angry his hand'd be like a gallowbow shot to the arse."

"Hostir then," said Joron. "Seems as good a name as any."

"Poisonous Hostir," said Barlay.

"Why 'poisonous', Barlay?" asked Farys.

Barlay looked at the girl and grinned.

"Everything is better with poison."

Joron realised then that he did not know what crime Barlay had committed to end up on the black ships. Although he rather suspected, from the look on her face when she said her father's name, that the man no longer walked the land.

"Listen up, my crew," shouted Meas. "Coxward will free the target soon. There are four commands for a gallowbow to loose. The first is 'Spin!' When I call that the spinners take a handle each and spin like the Hag herself commanded it. When they hear the retainer hooks snap to they stop and move to the sides of the bow. Then the command 'Load!' will come. It is not hard to work out what is required of that. The next command is 'Aim!' At this the bowsell lines up the bow for the triggerboy at the aiming point. The triggerboy's field of vision is small, and the bowsell will be listening for what I want to hit. You'll need someone experienced to actually trigger the bow as it's the sort of thing you learn through feel more than anything. But today we'll take turns so everyone knows what it is like. The last command is 'Loose!'"

A spontaneous roar went up at the thought of the great gallowbows giving voice to their deep-throated *thruuum* of destruction, but Meas quietened the teams. "Now 'Loose' does not mean you should pull that cord straight away, my fine girls and boys, so don't get too excited. It only means you are free to loose when you feel you have a good chance of hitting your target. So don't fly off like a Kept with his firstbern; we wouldn't want to let our target down, now would we?" She accompanied her words with a leer and the crew grinned at each other. "Topboy!" she shouted up into the rigging. "Give Bonemaster Coxward the signal!"

Joron could not see but he knew a flag must have been waved as the line between the target and the flukeboat detached, and oars, like the legs of a water-skimming insect, sprouted from the flukeboat. It began to row away from the target, seeming to head away from *Tide Child*, but Joron knew it would come round in a huge circle, to avoid any bolts that might fly less than true.

Meas made them wait, made them watch as Coxward slowly moved away and the target drifted. She knew the thought of every woman and man on the deck, that the target would float away and their fun would end, but Meas knew better. She knew the sea and she knew how to handle a crew: how to make them want and to wish for the voice of the bows, and when it seemed they could bear it no more she gave the command.

"Stand to your bows. Dip your hands and honour the Hag."

And they did, Barlay dipping her fingers in the small paint pot at the base of her bow and splattering red on the base of the bow before grabbing the seaward winding handle; Dinyl doing the same before taking the landward; Farys between them, red-stained fingers on the trigger cord, squinting down the length of the gallowbow. Joron squeezed past Farys, dipped his fingers for the Hag and then took position behind them, leaning forward with his hands on his thighs. He stood this way as he had noticed the other bowsells standing so, but found when he did that he had a similar view of the bow to Farys, who sighted along its length. But he could also see the working of the bow and the sea beyond, where Farys's view was restricted to the aiming pin at the end of the bow shaft.

"Spin!" shouted Meas, and Barlay and Dinyl set to winding, the mechanism pulling back the cord and the tension in the great bow arms growing and growing until the bone quivered with the expectation of violence and Joron heard the click of the retaining hooks engaging.

"Load!" shouted Meas, and Barlay bobbed down, grabbed one of the bolts from the deck and slotted it into the long groove of the bowshaft. All along the deck the same action was repeated, and Joron felt the tension in his back and arms as he waited for the next command.

"Aim!" Joron shuffled forward, staring along the shaft of the bow. On the edge of his vision he could see the target. He signalled to swing the bow landward, raising his arm rather than speaking. Barlay pulled and Dinyl pushed until the ugly pyramid of spars and wings floated in front of the weapon.

"Ready, my crew, stay steady, my crew," shouted Meas. "Launch only when she comes to bear. Loose!" Further down the deck Joron heard the moan of a bow as the triggerboy let fly far too early. The bolt flew from *Tide Child*, skimming over the water until it hit the sea, splashed once, twice, three times and vanished under the waves some distance to the landward of the target. A low murmer of disappointment went up from those watching.

"Steady, Farys, steady," said Joron under his breath. The girl was nodding but not really heeding Joron's words; all her concentration was on the target. To Joron it seemed like the target was drifting out of range but he said nothing. Trust, he must trust in his crew. Then Farys jerked her arm back, pulling on the trigger cord and the whole gallowbow juddered as it expended its energy, the bone arms snapping forward. The bolt leaped from the bow, sailing through the air. Joron found himself holding his breath as he watched it, willing it towards the target. A moment later the third bow loosed, the sound of it fighting the roar of triumph from his crew as Farys's bolt punched through the wings of the target.

"Good shot, Farys," shouted Meas. The other bolt fell only just short and Meas congratulated that team too. Then the crews swapped over, and it was this all afternoon, working the bows so each crew shot two bolts at least, and from them Meas picked her main bowteams. She was about to signal a last round of firing when a shout came from above.

"Keelcatch to seaward!"

Meas was straight up on the rail, staring out over the waves past the target, now little more than a shattered mass of spars.

"What is a keelcatch, D'keeper?" said Farys.

"That," said Joron, pointing out to where a thing was rising, looking like a mass of varisk vines waving in the air as if they strove to pluck Skearith's Eye from the sky. "They foul the keels of ships, then thrash about until the ship's spine breaks. Odd to see them here though; they are beasts of the far south and deep waters."

"They hunt ships," said Dinyl.

"No," said Joron. "They have no interest in ships. They hunt other creatures by lying in wait. If they're spotted early they are no danger, but if a ship gets too near it is no less doomed."

"I did not know you were a naturalist," said Dinyl, and smiled brightly.

"I was a fisher. My father told me a lot of things. You do not live long in a small boat unless you know what may kill you."

Dinyl shrugged, staring out at the sea and the creature, which looked like a vast, wild, angry carpet.

"Is there anything in the sea that does not want to kill us, Joron?"

Joron smiled at the deckholder.

"Give the topboy an extra ration for that spot," shouted Meas. "Truss the birds and get us under way. Deckholder, the deckkeeper has a rank and I would thank you to use it when you address him. Deckkeeper, we'll have two turns of the glass rest, a cup of water and then we practise with straightsword, curnow and spear." She nodded to Joron and left the deck.

The bows were trussed and tied, and the wings of *Tide Child* unfurled, cracking in the wind as the ship headed for the Southstorm and a rendezvous with a creature from legend.

21

And All the Blackest Birds
Flock Together

On the next day the winds were not as kind. Salt spray crashed over *Tide Child*'s beak to soak the crew, but the weather was not cold enough for stinker coats, and to Joron this was nothing – simply the way of the sea. He was more bothered by the ache in his arms from practising with the curnow, wyrmpike and shield the previous day. When the crew had finished their drills he had done extra hours in Meas's cabin with a finely made curved sword. He barely noticed that his clothes were damp or that his world heaved to and fro and up and down as the ship crashed forward through the waves. For Meas it was the same, and for many of the crew it was simply a thing they took in their stride.

"Look out for black ships," shouted Meas, "for they are out there somewhere and eager to meet with us." To this she added, "Deckholder Dinyl, I shall not again remind you and those others who wish to vomit to do it with the wind, for it will make the ship much easier to clean when you have to do so later."

To some degree Joron felt for Dinyl. Though he was Karrad's man he was not a bad soul, and did his best to attend to his work despite being green-faced with the Hag's curse. When not vomiting over the side, he staggered about his duties like an animated corpse. Joron felt less pity for Coughlin and the others put aboard by Cahanny – those he was glad to see prostrate with sickness. But like most who flew the sea he had endured the curse himself once or twice, knew the misery it brought and had sympathy for those suffering, though he also knew it passed, eventually. There was no pity at all in Meas, not least because she was similarly afflicted, which shocked him. The greatest shipwife to ever fly the sea suffered the Hag's curse.

However, she had no intention of letting it beat her. And if she would not be beaten then she would suffer no weakness in those below her on the slate.

And this was how they proceeded to the south until the shout was heard from the topboys:

"Ship rising to seaward, Shipwife!"

"Deckkeeper," said Meas, "get up the mainspine and tell me what you see."

Then Joron was climbing the ropes, his hair catching in the wind and blowing around his face as he climbed up and up the spine, carefully, oh so carefully. Oh, and there was something glorious about being so high up in the rigging, despite the danger. He'd scaled the rigging of his father's boat many times but that was nothing compared to the height reached climbing the spine of a fleet ship. From here he could see the subtle curve of the water on the horizon. On *Tide Child*'s seaward side, blue pennants streaming with the wind, he saw the ships he was looking for. A pair of black ships, two-ribbers, smaller ships with two spines compared to *Tide Child*'s three. They did not carry great gallowbows, as they could not support the weight or cope with the recoil of such weapons, but they mounted four to six smaller gallowbows a side, which could be just as dangerous used correctly. Two-ribbers were fast ships, designed for hit and run attacks and to create interference while bigger ships, like *Tide Child*, slightly slower, slightly heavier, brought their greater weight of shot to bear.

"What do you see up there?"

Joron looked down. The the crew were little more than dots on the slate, and the deck looked no bigger than the sole of his boot. It appeared to move as the spine he clung to swayed. This ship, those people – such small things in the vastness of the ocean. Joron felt like he barely existed. That, if he were to fall, to have the slate smash the bones of his body and flesh of his muscles to pulp, it would make no difference to the world. Then he heard the low, familiar song of the wind, the song that had always been with him, and the moment passed. Above him the topboy looked down, waiting for Joron to speak, unsure and unsettled by her deckkeeper's hesitance, not knowing whether she should reply to the shipwife instead.

"A pair of two-ribbers, Shipwife," shouted Joron. "Travelling line astern of one another to the south of us." He squinted into the light of Skearith's Eye. "They are changing course, Shipwife. They must have seen us and are set to intercept."

"Very well, Twiner. Come down."

He made his careful way down. Harder down than up, checking for footholds and always aware how far he could fall. His hands developed a reluctance to let go of the ropes; his feet became unhappy about shifting along the spars. When his feet finally touched slate, Meas was there, and Joron had to place his hands behind his back to hide the shaking. "We are expecting friends, Deckkeeper," she said, "but it does no harm to be prepared. Have the crew be ready."

"Clear for action!" shouted Joron, and from the underdeck the crew came scurrying.

Mevens held a drum and began to beat it, and standing by him was sad-faced Solemn Muffaz, the deckmother, bellowing out Joron's order again and again:

"Clear the ship! Clear the ship for action!"

And all was movement.

From below came the hammering of the bonewrights taking down the screens. Women and men hurried up and down the rigging, setting the wings, brought bolts and shot for the great gallowbows from the underdeck. Nets were cast across the rails of the ship to catch debris from bowstrikes and to stop crew going overboard should the ship's manoeuvres take them by surprise. Sand was strewn across the slate of the deck to give extra grip for busy feet, and buckets of sand were placed at intervals along the deck in case of fire, for the only way to put out bonefire once boneglue caught was to smother it entirely.

Joron found himself on the slightly raised deck at the beak of the ship. Beneath him beakwyrms churned the water through ceaseless jaws, and the sight of their ugly, fierce bodies cheered him.

"Seven now, Shipwife," he shouted. "We are getting faster."

"Pull well now, my childer!" Joron turned to see Dinyl overseeing a group of deckchilder dragging a screen of tightly woven varisk soaked with seawater, over the main hatch that allowed access to the hold. In the spines above, only the main-wings remained to catch the wind. Farys scuttled across the deck, a cage holding squawking kivellys in each hand and though all looked like chaos, women and men running hither and thither, Lucky Meas watched the sand slip through the glass and the action on her ship with a half-smile on her face. This seeming chaos, much rehearsed over the last week at sea, was chaos with purpose, and that purpose was hers. She turned and walked to the rail, lifting her nearglass to her eye and looking out over the water.

"To your bows, my crew," she shouted. "Keep the underdeck hatches shut for now and the bows may sleep. I do not think we will need to loose them, but it does us no favours to be unprepared. Coughlin!" she shouted. Cahanny's man, his face still tinged with the green of the Hag's curse, stumbled over from his place on the rail. "Arm your men just in case." Coughlin glowered at her, but the Hag's curse had broken his will for the moment, and he turned away and had his men gather their weapons.

So it was that Meas started giving orders for the final sails to be furled and Joron began to wonder if the black ship was almost up to the standard of a fleet vessel. Oh, the drills were not as quick, not as accurate and not as fierce, not yet. Joron did not really doubt it for a second. But still he felt a thrill of pride that he had been part of this change that had come across the slate of the deck, this transformation from slovenly to shipshape, and he pulled his one-tailed hat a little tighter on his head.

The ship slowly coasted to a stop on a sea now glassy and still, as if tired now it had brought *Tide Child* to meet his new consorts. The two-ribbers stopped fifty shiplengths across from them, calm water lapping at their ebon sides. Meas oversaw *Tide Child*'s final tying-down and the dropping of the seastay. This dragged in the water and stopped the ship drifting.

She surveyed her crew and then nodded to herself.

"Mevans, put together a crew to row the flukeboat over to the larger of the two ships."

"Ey, Shipwife."

"Joron, you will accompany me. Dinyl, you remain in charge of *Tide Child*. I ask nothing more than you keep him still." Then she stepped nearer the man and whispered something, pointing down the deck at Cahanny's men, and Joron guessed she told Dinyl to make use of them if he must to keep command, for she still did not truly know this crew.

It had not escaped her any more than it had escaped Joron's notice that Cwell — pinch-faced, resentful, mean-spirited, Cwell — had become close friends with Hasrin, who had once been a deckkeeper herself, and Sprackin, who still bridled at being replaced as purseholder by Mevans. It often felt to Joron that, wherever he went on the ship, one of those three watched him, waiting for something, although he did not know what.

Dinyl nodded and Joron thought it strange that the man who had seemed so sure of himself on the docks, who had far more experience than Joron, should look so uneasy on the rump of the ship despite his fine clothes and experience.

When the flukeboat came round, Meas dropped down the

side of the ship like there were no obstacles; no hooks or spines or spikes. Joron followed, slowly and carefully, every foot placed with care, every hand also.

"Look lively, Joron, *Tide Child* won't bite those who serve him." Of course this was a lie; with his many serrations and barbs he most assuredly would. But then Joron was in the boat, thanks to a helping hand from Mevans, who then went to join his picked deckchilder at the oars. "Row for the first of the two-ribbers, the one called *Cruel Water*," said Meas quietly.

"You know these black ships?" said Joron.

"I know one of them. The first is *Cruel Water* under Shipwife Arrin, a good man. The other I do not know, but they have seen our intent and also lower a boat. We made good time to this place, Joron, better than I expected, but I would have this meeting over as quickly as possible and be on our way. The less time the three ships spend close enough for deckchilder to shout to one another, the happier I will be."

"I was surprised you brought both me and Mevans if I am honest, Shipwife. Cwell holds no love for you." She turned to him, and for a moment her eyes were full of fury and he did not understand why, but it faded as she saw the sense in his words.

"You think my crew may mutiny while we are away? It is possible, but not yet, I think. And Cahanny wants his cargo delivered, so for now we can rely on those he sent. Besides, the deckchilder have enjoyed working the bows each day. That will buy us a fair amount of goodwill no matter how Cwell and her cronies may whisper. So for today I do not worry unduly."

"Very well, Shipwife."

"There is one thing I ask of you, Deckkeeper. Mevans, I enrol you in this also."

"Trouble is it, Shipwife?" said Mevans, leaning in towards them. "You have the sound of trouble in your voice."

"Maybe. I do not know yet. I want to know what that cargo is that Cahanny brought aboard my ship."

"They guard it day and night," said Joron as the oars of the flukeboat beat the sea.

"They do," said Mevans. "They even have a man who sleeps on the damn things, down in the hold amid the stink. It does no one any good to sleep in the hold. He'll catch greenleg or blacklung, you mark my words."

"I did not ask for your words," said Meas, her voice stark. "I do not care what they do and don't do. I asked you to do a thing and I expect you to do it. Do you understand?"

"Ey, Shipwife." The two men said the words together.

"And how goes it with the gullaime, Joron?"

"I have had trouble gathering all the things it—" he began. Meas stopped him with a glare.

"Do not think I have not noticed you about the windtalker, Joron Twiner, and how it makes you nervous as a laying-night virgin. You think you are the only one who finds the beasts unnatural?" She did not let him reply. "You will never gather all it asked for, so take the windtalker what you have, first chance when we return to the ship, and find a way to make it like you."

"Like me? But—"

"I say the same to you as I said to Mevans. I do not ask what you think of a thing, I only ask that you do it."

The conversation ended as Mevans and his small crew, in perfect unison, lifted their oars so all four stuck straight up into the air, and the flukeboat coasted to a gentle stop against the side of *Cruel Water*. A rope was thrown down, and a ladder followed it to help them up the tumblehome. "Mevans, wait here. Twiner, come with me." Meas grabbed the ladder and pulled herself up. Joron followed, trying not to think about the spikes and spears of bone erupting from the side of *Cruel Water*, and though none could say he did a creditable job of scaling the ship's side he did not embarrass *Tide Child* either.

Joron did not know what he had expected of a Gaunt Islands ship – skulls and bones and rotting flesh, perhaps – but what awaited him was as far from his imagination as possible.

The shipwife, Arrin, was a tall thin man whose uniform of fishskin and birdleather was dyed a deep, deep blue. Joron had expected them to not have uniforms, to wear rags maybe, but though the cut of his coat was different and the patterns embroidered into his trousers and his two-tailed hat were silver, it would have been easy for him to mistake the shipwife for a Hundred Islander.

Apart from one thing. The man was missing half his right leg and walked upon a limb carved from varisk. Such a thing would never be allowed in the Hundred Isles – a one-legged man commanding a ship – and it was all Joron could do not to stare.

Meas stopped before him and touched her hat. Even a week ago Joron had still thought of that hat as his, but she had opened his eyes to what he should be and how much he lacked, and now he found it difficult to imagine that hat sitting comfortably on his head. Arrin's deckkeeper stood behind him – a small, squat woman wearing the same shade of blue and a one-tail hat, her hair sticking out from beneath the hat and the colours of command shining in it, freshly dyed. The crew that awaited Meas and Joron were also dressed in blue. They were not tidy – their clothes were mixed and matched and poorly dyed – but despite this they presented a strangely uniform appearance, and if they did indeed eat children, Joron thought this crew the smartest group of child eaters he had ever seen.

"Arrin," said Meas, clasping the man's forearm.

"Meas." He returned the gesture. "I fair did not believe it when I was told you commanded a black ship."

"Well, life is full of surprises, Arrin, as you well know." She turned to his deckkeeper. "Oswire," she said. "Well met."

"Well met, Shipwife," said Oswire, but there was frost in her words.

"Shipwife Brekir comes across from the *Snarltooth*." Arrin leaned in close to Meas but Joron caught his words on a tricksy zephyr of salt-rimed wind. "She knows who you are, but not what we are about, not yet. And neither do my crew outside of Oswire and a few I trust."

Meas nodded, and as she did Shipwife Brekir, a tall woman with a scarred, dark-skinned face, climbed over the rail. That surprised Joron too — to see the mirror of his own skin when he had thought all Gaunt Islanders were pale as clouds.

"Do you plan without me?" she said, her accent strange in Joron's ears, her tone morose as if she believed the world existed simply to put obstacles in her way.

"Not at all," said Arrin. "We wait for you, and now you are arrived I will have my hatkeep bring food and drink to my cabin."

The meeting was swift, the food good, though Brekir was a damp presence at the table and talked of little but what her ship and crew were lacking, and how this held her back. However, when Meas told Brekir what they searched for he saw the woman's eyes widen, and her face — which had borne an expression that seemed frozen at some particularly trying part of her life — showed some excitement.

"Well, I see why we must protect it, though I reckon every woman and man with a ship will be set against us."

"You are right in that, Brekir," said Meas. "But I can help us in that. *Tide Child* carries a gullaime of rare power, and against all but fleet ships that will give us the advantage once we have found our quarry."

"And how do we do that?" said Arrin.

"I shall show you." And then it was all charts and talking. Meas explained how she intended to find "the quarry" as they quickly decided to refer to the sea dragon. "See here." She pointed at the chart with a knife. "From where we know the quarry was first sighted it will stick to deep water where it can, for that is where its prey is: saw arms, sunfish, hullbiters and the like."

"Hag save us from hullbiters," said Arrin, "I once had one attach to *Cruel Water*, and it was half through the hull before we got it off. Killed four of my crew too."

"A hard way to die," said Brekir, "but is there any other way in the isles?"

"The only deep-water channel in this areas is here, at Flensechannel, which runs toward Skearith's Spine, and if we search, line abreast, I reckon our topboys will be able to see the ship nearest to them and cover the channel from isle to isle."

"We will have to tell our crews what we look for," said Arrin. "Otherwise they may not believe their eyes. It is not a thing we can keep secret."

Meas nodded.

"You are right, Arrin. And that excitement may stop them wondering too much about the other black ships. It could work to our advantage."

"If they believe us at all," said Brekir.

"What crew does not believe the words of its shipwife, ey?" Meas smiled at Brekir who nodded back, though with little commitment.

"Time is our enemy now," said Arrin.

"It is indeed," said Meas. "Joron, ready my flukeboat. We return to *Tide Child* and start the search here. We will sail between *Cruel Water* and *Snarltooth*. Our ship is the tallest and our topboys can cover the greatest area of sea. It'll be a day until we reach Flensechannel so that will give us time to practise flying in formation."

"And what of night?" said Brekir.

"We'll slow but all have lights and oil so we can make sure we are seen. And I reckon a keyshan is big enough to show up even at night."

"Dangerous to have fire and oil so near a ship's wings," said Brekir.

"Dangerous to be on the crew of a black ship — lethal, most would say," said Arrin.

Brekir stared at him, tapping the table.

"What if the mist comes in?"

"We must simply hope it does not, Shipwife Brekir," said

Meas, "or our mission could be over before it even starts. Now, I first heard this creature called the wakewyrm, which is as good name for it as any other."

"Wakewyrm," said Arrin, standing. He winced as he transferred his weight to the wooden leg to give Meas a salute, hand across his breast. "It is a good name." Then he turned to Joron. "You are wondering about my leg? Why I am not a tailor or stonebound?" Joron nodded at the Gaunt Islander shipwife. "We do not cast away our damaged and wounded like you do." *Was this an insult?* Joron did not know the man well enough to read him, not yet.

"Do you say you are better than us?" he asked.

Arrin smiled and shook his head.

"There are those on this ship who definitely believe so." His eyes flicked to his deckkeeper but his smile did not falter. He laughed quietly at the look Oswire gave him.

With that the meeting was over. Meas flung herself down the side of the ship with her usual abandon. Joron followed, careful with his feet and hands until he sat safe in the flukeboat and Mevans gave the signal to leave.

Four oars cut into the water, stirring the surface and sending the life beneath darting away in terror at this strange, large creature that passed over them. The crew of the flukeboat remained unaware of the fear their passage caused the tiny creatures of the brine beneath, and if they had been aware they would have been uninterested. They may not have known what was to come, but they were experienced deckchilder and knew the feel of action, knew *something* was coming, how it made the air come alive with tension. They felt that and it pleased them. Mevans glanced at the woman who rowed opposite him and they shared a smile and a nod because, though action brings its own terrors and the possibility of pain and maiming and death, it can also be addictive. It is a feast that once tasted is never forgotten, and the women and men of Meas's crew had supped at that table often. Since losing her they had been starved.

Up the tumblehome of *Tide Child*, Joron a mite more comfortable with the climb, a little more familiar, and when they stood on the slate deck there was a small contingent ready to meet them, led by Dinyl.

"Welcome back, Shipwife," said Dinyl, hand to breast and a small bow which Joron did his best to memorise, the formalities of the Bern as much a mystery to him as the bottom of the ocean. If Meas noticed the bow she gave no sign.

"Pull up the seastay," she said, striding past him to the rump. "Let out his wings." She glanced to seaward where the pair of two-ribbers were already filling their wings with wind, slowly turning, voices calling back and forth as heavy booms came over and the ships leaned into the air "Put us between those two ships. *Cruel Water* is nearest; the other is named *Snarltooth*. I want the sharpest-eyed topboys on the spinepoint, Deckholder."

"Ey, Shipwife," Dinyl said. "Hasrin says she knows *Cruel Water* from when she was deckkeeper, says it was lost to the Gaunt Islanders." He licked his lips, the warning given to Meas. "She also has been wondering about the other ship, saying she does not recognise it from her time in command."

"And you did not quieten her?" said Meas. A rebuke.

"I was—" He paused, looking for the words, and Joron stepped in.

"—waiting for facts, Shipwife. Better to give the crew facts than guess."

"Hasrin," said Mevans loudly, "has been in the hulks for a year, so she could not know that *Cruel Water* was taken back last year. *Snarltooth* was on far north station, so it's little wonder few have heard of him."

"Mevans knows his ships," said Meas, "so if there are further questions, Dinyl, you can quiet them now."

Dinyl nodded and stepped back, giving Joron a quickly mouthed "Thank you" as he turned away.

"Who has good eyes, Joron?" Meas said then.

"Farys." He said her name loudly enough for her to come

running. "You have good eyes. Who else?"

"Gulbry, D'keeper, and Karring."

"Good, find them. You'll each do two hours on and two hours off on the mainspine perch, to keep your eyes fresh. Scan the sea and watch for signals from the other two ships that they have seen something."

"Is it a ship we're looking for, D'keeper?" she said.

"No. Meas will tell us what we search for soon enough. First call the seakeep and tell her to get the wings set, then the shipwife will call us to the rump."

And so *Tide Child* unfurled his wings and caught the wind, and the ship slowly turned as the seastay came up, and all around Joron the women and men of the ship pulled on ropes and tied off wings and sang the songs of the deckchilder as the ship did their bidding. Once they had him on course, some wings were taken in, others unfurled by lines of crew standing along the spars. As *Cruel Water* flew around them towards his station they cheered the smaller ship and his crew cheered back. It filled Joron with worry that the two crews would call to one another, but the ships never came close enough for a word to be understood or an accent questioned, and they flew no flags to be recognised by. Only the blue clothing of *Cruel Water*'s deckchilder stood out, but shipwives were known for such eccentricities and few even commented on it.

Once *Tide Child* sat once more with only his top wings out, making a slow and stately white path through the water, Meas called her crew together.

"Come, come, my crew! Stand before your shipwife and hear her talk. Hear what great thing you are to be part of. A making of history, no more or less. So stand and listen quiet for you may not believe what your ears hear."

At this the shuffling and stuttering chatter that was always part of a crowd died away. Even those men sent by Cahanny, sitting indolent by the beak, sat up a little straighter. Even Cwell and her motley crew of malcontents shuffled a little nearer the rump.

"We have heard that a miracle has happened, my girls and boys, a miracle of high and strange order." She held them rapt before her for there was nothing a deckchild loved more than a tale of mystery. Even Joron moved a little closer, as if to share the way she held the crew hypnotised, as if a little of the magic in her voice may rub off on him. "We hear tell of the times of the sea dragons, when the keyshans roved the waters of the Scattered Archipelago, taking whatever beast they wished, and all feared them, ey?"

"Ey, Shipwife," came the reply.

"Well, maybe not all feared them, ey? Not the the women and men of the Hundred Isles. And maybe, they say now, we should have feared them a little more, for none remain. And because we have lost the arakeesians, no new boneships are built, no great boneships of five or six ribs break the water. We recycle what we have, building smaller and smaller, becoming less and less as the weight of bone we have ebbs with every generation." She jumped her gaze from woman to man and man to woman, making some uncomfortable, some proud, some shy, some surprised she even knew they existed. "Well, that is no more." She stood straighter on the rump. "An arakeesian has been seen." This brought gasps of disbelief, shock, and then a sudden and excited chatter.

"Are we to hunt it?" And this shout, though everybody must know the danger was great, was full of joy. Why would it not be? To be the first in generations to hunt such a beast, well, that would be to become immortal in the Hundred Isles.

Meas shook her head.

"Tell me, my girls and boys, if you had only a cock and a hen, would you kill one and still expect eggs? Would you kill one and still expect plump birds to eat when Skearith's Eye is cold, ey? Well would you?"

A chorus of "No" and "Of course not" and plenty more comments that were more ribald. The shipwife pretended not to hear them, and Joron wondered how she planned to change their minds at a later date when they had to kill the beast.

What would they think to find *Tide Child* flew the ocean to end the world they had always known?

"Exactly, my crew, exactly. But many are not as wise as you and do not think ahead. And you mark my words, they will want to hunt that lone beast, this wakewyrm."

"Wakewyrm" was whispered, moving through the crew like tide hissing through shingle.

"If one comes," she said quietly, "who is to say there may not be two? And if there are two then as surely as day follows night they'll make more, ey? An arakeesian Bern, that would be a fine thing – right, my girls and boys?"

A huge cry of affirmation in return.

"So what we are tasked with is to keep the beast alive, and doubt not, the Gaunt Islanders will come for the wakewyrm. Raiders will come for the wakewyrm. Fools from islands we pass will come for the wakewyrm. Maybe even some of our own, ignoring the orders of the Bern back home, will turn traitor and hunt the beast." Again that gaze, pinning each woman and man to the deck. "But will we let them take our future?"

"No, Shipwife." Little more than a murmur.

"I said, will we let them take our future?" Her voice rising.

"Come on, my girls and boys!" shouted Mevans

"No, Shipwife!" Louder.

"Will we let them, my deckchilder? Will we let them?"

And in reply a great cry:

"No, Shipwife!"

"Then to your places. Pull tight the topwings and keep your eyes open, for a sea dragon awaits us, and a sea dragon we shall find!"

The roar in reply hurt Joron's ears, and for the first time he truly understood, as he shouted and waved his hat in the air, carried on the current of the shipwife's words, what his father had meant by being part of the fleet.

22

Glimmers in the Night

Up Flensechannel flew three ships, though from where Joron stood on the deck the seas looked as empty as he had ever seen them, a shifting landscape of grey water cut with the lines of white breakers. Only the topboys were in contact with *Tide Child*'s consorts. They had travelled like this for two days and Skearith's Eye had dipped on the third. The sandglass was tipped every ten minutes and when it was, the shout went up: "Tell of the sea, Topboy!" A single, lonely voice in the darkness. The replies came down from the spine-points of the ship: "Ship rising to seaward, ship rising to landward." Then Joron would nod and remind himself they were not alone.

A deckchild – *Hamrish?* – he was almost sure that was the name – manned the steering oar behind him and Farys was in the tops. Meas no doubt worked below with Aelerin the courser, and dotted about the ship Joron saw others, but only as hints, impressions of movement in the inky blackness. *Tide Child* was lit of course – rump and beak held large lights – but they did not throw much light on to the decks. Wanelights marked the rails but also gave little light. It was all too easy to believe himself lost and alone, so he took comfort from those small and shadowy movements that let him know he was not, and he took comfort in the the sadly tolling bell on the slate, and and he took comfort in the hiss of water passing underneath *Tide Child*, which told him his world travelled and that he was not lost, but on a journey with purpose and destination.

Between the three ships they could scan almost ten hunths, one complete passage, from the small islands on the seaward side to the shores of the larger islands, asleep and unseen, to landward. The night was clear. Skearith's Bones shone wanly down from above and all seemed good to Joron, or as good as it could for a condemned man on a ship of the dead, standing under the light of Skearith's Blind Eye. He could see no way something as huge as an arakeesian could pass between the ships without them noticing, assuming the topboys on the other ships were as attentive as the ones on *Tide Child*, and he had no reason to believe they would not be. This was history they made.

His comfort was stolen when one of the quiet shadows resolved itself into Cwell, the pale light of the Blind Eye pasting her pale skin and sharp face with highlights, illuminating the scabbed knuckles of her hands. Joron did not want to talk to her, found her intimidating. He had noticed she had started spending time around Coughlin and his men, and this reminded him he had done nothing, so far, about the task that Meas had given him, of finding out what it was they were smuggling for the Bernshulme crime lord. He recognised that part of this was because he feared Coughlin, feared the violence in the man. He felt that same fear around Cwell.

"Is what she says true?" said Cwell.

"Her?"

"The shipwife."

"You should call her that."

Cruel eyes glinted in the wanelight. A space in the air where the waves rushed against the ship, once, twice, three times.

"Is it true what the shipwife says?" Her mouth twisted the title, making it sound somehow less than it was.

"What part of it?"

"You know what part," she said, her hand resting on the hammer she carried slung from her belt. To carry a blade on deck was forbidden to all but those who trod the rump, but her bonehammer was as good a weapon as a tool. "The arakeesian. Is it true? Does one swim through the islands?"

"If the shipwife says a thing on her ship," said Joron, "then it is a true thing."

"No ship-like talk from you – we all know you are not up to it." She took a step forward and the boom on the mainspine moved, bringing the midwing round and blocking out the gentle light of Skearith's Blind Eye, dropping Joron and Cwell into deep darkness. "Is there an arakeesian?"

"As far as we know, yes," said Joron quietly. It took all he had not to step back from the woman. "But we have not seen it with our own eyes yet."

"Turning the glass!" The call came from the rump, and Joron was glad of it. It gave him an excuse to step back from the woman, into the light, and stare up into the tops of the mainspine.

"Tell of the sea, Topboy!" he shouted.

"Ship rising to seaward, ship rising to landward, D'keeper. All else is clear." Joron hoped, as he brought his eyes back to the dark deck, that Cwell would be gone, but no, there she stood, at home in the shadow.

"Lot of money in an arakeesian," she said.

"You heard the shipwife talk."

Cwell spat on the deck.

"Ey, I did. She gambles on what might be, what may happen, and if there's another arakeesian then maybe there will be more. I only know what is. One beast could leave every woman and man on this ship set for life." She raised her voice a little as she said that. "Coughlin has the contacts to make us all rich, Twiner," she said. Did Joron imagine it or did the small amount of activity on the deck cease then? Did the women and men going about the constant tasks that kept a boneship afloat pause in what they were doing at Cwell's words? Was that Sprackin who lifted his head before going back to his work? Was that Hasrin, once a deckkeeper, now a lowly deck-child, and resentful with it, who paused in coiling a rope? Was that Coughlin, violent, angry Coughlin, who slipped back into the darkness?

"If you only deal in what is, then why talk of this, Cwell? We have seen no arakeesian. For all we know we chase rumour and fancy, and they will set up no woman or man."

"Ey," said Cwell. "You are right. But if it is a keyshan, then its jointweight makes what Coughlin has in the hold look like spoiled meat."

"So it's arakeesian bones we move for Cahanny, is it?" Cwell's eyes narrowed, realising she had said more than she should, and for a moment Joron thought she would move against him.

"Keep your nose out of my business, Twiner," she said. "Play at officer and keep out of my way."

"Deckkeeper," said Twiner. He was almost surprised that he had correcteded Cwell, a woman from whom violence rolled off the way black rainclouds rolled from a stormfront.

Cwell smiled, the ends of her mouth turning up, but it was mockery not humour Joron found there.

"I said, keep your nose out of my business, Deckkeeper. And we will get on just fine."

"Cahanny's business, those bones, surely."

"If you will," said Cwell. She turned, walked away, leaving Joron relieved twice over: once that he had one less task to mark off now he knew what Cahanny smuggled, and twice that Cwell had left him alone. But Joron could not lie to himself. He felt fear too, because he knew a threat when he saw one, and Cwell was exactly that.

"She hates you." The quiet voice came from behind Joron, and he turned to find Aelerin, the courser, face hidden beneath their cowl.

"I do not expect a criminal to like me, Coursér."

"No, but she really hates you. She will hurt you given the

chance." A shudder down Joron's back. "She hates Meas more though, and I reckon she probably hates Coughlin and the man on land who sent him too."

"Cahanny?"

"Ey," said the courser softly. "Cahanny. She is some relative, niece, I heard, but it is authority she hates. She was once part of Cahanny's gang. That is why she gets on with Coughlin. But she will not move against the crime lord or the shipwife. She is scared of Cahanny, and she is scared of Meas."

"But not me?"

"No, so she gifts you the hate she feels for Meas and her authority on the ship. I think she sees opportunity in the arakeesian and in the violent men Cahanny sent aboard. She probably thought she could scare you into helping her, but she failed, and that will make her hate you more. Be careful of her, Deckkeeper, and those she chooses to be with." Joron looked around, suddenly aware of the absence of Anzir behind him. She had struggled to come to terms with the strange timing of a ship's life, and he let her sleep through the night or she was of no use in the day.

"Do you think she seeks to prise Coughlin away from Cahanny?"

"Coughlin is probably scared of Cahanny too."

"Then surely he will obey the orders he was given."

"Cahanny isn't here, Deckkeeper. And an arakeesian is a big temptation, would make a deckchild rich enough never to be under another's authority again." The courser turned away, going to take their place by the rumpspine, to listen to the storms sing and to study the northstone in its bowl of seawater.

"Turning the glass!" came the call from the rump.

"Tell of the sea, Topboy!" shouted Joron, and he was almost surprised that his voice did not waver or fade like a sea mist on a hot day.

"Ship rising to seaward, nothing rising to landward, D'keeper."

"Say again, Topboy?"

"No ship rising to landward!"

Joron turned to Aelerin.

"You have the rump, Courser; I will go up the spine." And then he was climbing the rigging. Finding sure holds for feet and hands, feeling the rope through the soles of his boots. Making his difficult way up to the top of the ship, where the wind whistled and the wings flapped and snapped in the night breeze.

"When did it go, Topboy?" Hamrish was tall and thin and had to fold his body up to fit into the basket of the topspine. He was Berncast and the muscles on the left side of his face did not work, which made him seem permanently gloomy.

He stared into the distance.

"Not long afore you called, D'keeper. I reckon they either dipped below the horizon or their light went out." He tapped the gently swinging lantern by him. Below, the wanelights of the ship glowed, and Joron felt disorientated, like he and Hamrish floated amid Skearith's Bones rather than above the ship, and he fancied he heard the faraway, musical call of great birds. "I was waiting a turn to see if it reappeared afore I said of it."

"You did right." From his coat Joron took out Meas's nearglass, being more careful with it than he could ever recollect being with anything before. "Show me the ship to seaward, so I know what to look for."

Hamrish nodded and pointed.

"Follow the line of my arm and you'll see the light, not as cold as Skearith's Bones, but warmer, so you know it's women and men live below it." As Joron put the nearglass to his eye the world changed, jumped and grew, the light of Skearith's Bones becoming brighter than he had ever known it. "Lower, D'keeper. You'll see only sky that way," said Hamrish gently, for he knew it did not do to correct an officer.

"Thank you, Hamrish," said Joron. He lowered the lens, finding the almost imperceptible line between sea and sky in the darkness. Somewhere a skeer called. Joron scanned along the line of the horizon, occasionally opening one eye to ensure he had not passed the line Hamrish pointed out. Then he found the ship. A fuzzy glow in the night signalled the presence of *Cruel Water* and all the lives aboard it. "Got it," he said, then took the nearglass from his eye and swung around, only realising as he moved how small the space was, how low the rail around it, how precarious this perch and how far away the deck. He thought of falling. Of plummeting down through the air. He thought of what the deck would do to a body that hit it and shuddered, tightening his hand around the nearglass so as not to drop it.

A breath. Take a breath.

Lifting the lens to his eye again, he found the subtle line of the landward horizon. Letting the nearglass drift along it, he found only the cold light of Skearith's Bones and his stomach sank. One ship out of formation or worse, lost, meant a huge area with no eyes on it. More than enough sea for the beast they hunted to slip past. He found himself whispering quietly to the wind, "Come on, come on," as he stared through the nearglass. But nothing. He found himself haunted by all the terrors the ocean held and all the misfortunes that could befall a ship, but he would not borrow trouble. More likely *Snarltooth* was simply a little off course. *Surely that was it?*

"What to do, D'keeper?" asked Hamrish.

Joron took a breath. This would be his first true command decision, or the first of any import at least. He could order *Tide Child* landward, and if *Snarltooth* had simply gone off course a quick signal would bring him back. But that risked losing contact with *Cruel Water*. In the night a signal was easy to miss, as was another ship. There was no guarantee they would spot *Snarltooth*.

"We will continue to turn the glass every ten minutes and we will keep our course for the night and stay in sight of *Cruel Water*. If *Snarltooth* has lost his way he will be easier to find by day. Signals are often overlooked at night." He tried to sound surer than he felt.

Hamrish nodded, as if Joron's words were wise and spoken by a man who had commanded ships all his life.

"Ey, D'keeper."

With that Joron worked his slow and careful way back down the rigging to the slate of the deck, much happier when he felt the stone beneath his aching feet. He found Aelerin waiting for him.

"Courser, you were in the underdeck with Meas before taking your post here," he said. "Do you know if the gullaime is awake?" He hoped it would not be.

"I do not think it ever sleeps, Deckkeeper, not truly."

"Oh," said Joron. "Well, there are things it requires. I have been gathering them in my cabin and must take them to the beast. We have lost sight of *Snarltooth*, but I have decided to keep course until the Eye rises." Aelerin nodded. "You maintain command of the rump while I am below. Deckmother, Solemn Muffaz, is at the beak. Call him should you need him."

"Very well, Deckkeeper," said the courser. As Joron turned away they added, "I understand Meas wishes you to befriend it, the gullaime."

"Ey, though Hag knows how a man befriends such a creature."

"It is lonely, I think," said the courser.

"Lonely? It is an animal."

The courser shrugged, and again Joron felt the desire to lift their cowl and see who was beneath.

"It is the only one of its kind aboard the ship. No one talks to it, no one gives it any of their time unless they need it. But if you believe it cannot feel loneliness then I cannot convince you otherwise." The courser hugged themselves, wrapping their arms tightly around their midriff. "But I would say it is lonely."

Joron was unsure what to say.

"Thank you, Courser," he said eventually. "I will keep that in mind." Then he turned, raising his voice, "The courser has the rump!" and headed into the underdeck, where the heat of the air was joined by that of the bodies packed into swaying hammocks.

In his cabin he gathered together what he had managed to find of the gullaime's list of needs and stowed them in a variskweave sack. String had been no problem; all he had done was unwind some rope. Cloth was similarly easy to find on board *Tide Child*, and he had convinced one of the wingwrights to give up, grudgingly, a couple of his exquisite bone needles in exchange for extra rations of eggs from the kivelly kept on board. Dust had stumped him until he had realised it was everywhere, and he had asked Gavith to keep the sweepings he collected as he went about his duties. So now he had four great fuzzy grey balls of filth that Joron could see no use at all for, but he was not a gullaime, so why should he know how its strange and alien mind worked? The other thing he had found, and had been strangely proud of finding, from the gullaime's long list of objects it had recited, was a comb. It had some teeth missing but was a comb nonetheless. It had been lying in the darkness of the hold as if waiting for him to find it, and he had remembered the gullaime's request.

He breathed deeply before knocking to enter the creature's quarters, steeling himself for the dry smell of it, the way the atmosphere changed around the beast, became something so strange that he was sure his senses sought to reject it – like he stepped into a dream, at once familiar and strange. To be close to the windtalker was to touch the other, to take a step towards Skearith the godbird, the creator, who hatched the gullaime for the Mother, who in turn gave them to woman and man to use. Joron, like all right thinkers, was wary of the gods and the cruel games of the Maiden, Mother and Hag, and he was afraid of Skearith's ghost most of all, for men had killed her and men had most to fear.

Within the cabin all was dark. There was no sign of the creature in the barely-there light of the wanelights.

"Gullaime?"

Nothing, for a moment. Then his name was given back to him from the gloom, said as if by a creaking door.

"Jo-ron. Twi-ner."

From the seaward corner of the room the gullaime unfolded itself. He had thought it part of the mess in the room, a ball of dimly seen rags. Then the rags grew long and spindly legs ending in three-toed, powerfully clawed feet. There was a hint of wings, maybe, or was it an illusion created by the gullaime's ragged clothing? Last, a head on a thin neck that kinked halfway along. The gullaime rose in a way that look unnatural, impossible. A woman or man would have had to put a hand down to push themselves up, but the gullaime needed no such assistance to stand before him. It opened its beak and made that noise again, that rasp of saw-on-varisk noise: "Jo-ron. Twi-ner."

"I have brought the things you wanted, some of them." Joron did well not to stutter as he held out the bag. The gullaime took a step forward, the masked face tilting first to one side then to the other, the false, painted eyes regarding him as if the creature expected some trick.

"For me?"

"Yes," he said. "For you."

"For me," it said again. Then it made a strange, almost cooing sound, before shrieking, "Give!" and ripping the bag from his hand with its predatory, sharp, curved bill. To Joron's credit, or maybe simply because the movement was so swift, he did not step back or make any noise that gave away the terror he felt at that beak snapping closed so near his fingers. The gullaime dropped the bag on to the floor and, using the double elbow claws that stuck out from its robes and its feet, the birdmage swiftly untied the knot and opened the bag. "Things," it said. It sounded almost awed; then the voice changed, suddenly angry again. A furious squawk: "Lies!" Then again: "Lies! Not all things."

"I could not find everything," Joron said, words hurrying from his mouth. "Not yet. Cook is saving fishbones for you, or will when we start to fish. For now we eat only dried and the bones are soft."

"Shiny rocks?"

"We have been nowhere I can get shiny rocks. Not yet."

"Feathers?"

"There are some feathers in there."

"Not special ones."

"How do I know which are—"

"Meas has special feathers."

"Good luck getting them from her."

It froze, unnaturally still.

"The feathers are her things." The gullaime's head regarded him. If the painted eyes had been able to blink he was sure they would have. "Meas things." It dipped its head twice and then a third time, and this time its head stayed down as if inspecting the contents of the bag with its blind eyes. It placed a foot in the bag, and once again Joron wondered how he had not noticed that the gullaime's feet were crowned with claws like scythes, pulsing in and out of their sheaths in time with the creature's breath. "Needles, cloth. Good, good. What this?" It held up one of the fuzzy balls of dust with one foot, balancing effortlessly on the other.

"Dust. You asked for dust and I have had the cabin boy collect it for you."

"Not dust."

"It is dust. It is sweepings from all around the ship."

"Not good dust, not good for baths."

"Baths? You need water for baths."

"Water for drink, fool Joron Twiner. Dust no good. Take." Then it was picking up the balls of filthy dust and shoving them at Joron, who found himself with no choice but to take them. As suddenly as it had become industrious, it stopped. Became absolutely still. "Oh." And this was somehow the most human sound Joron had heard the creature make. "Oh," it said again. The blind head came down, gently picking up the comb from the bottom of the bag with its beak. It transferred the comb from beak to foot and seemed to stare at it, the eyes painted on the leaf mask fixed on the object. "Comb."

"I remembered you wanted one."

"Comb," it said again.

"I am sorry it is broken. I . . ." But the windtalker was not listening. Quick as a girret surfacing to snap at a fly, its head darted forward, snapping off the comb's teeth. Joron was about to complain about this treatment of his gift when he saw that there was a pattern to the vandalism. It was not taking all the teeth, just a few at regular intervals along the comb, creating larger spaces between the existing teeth.

"Thanking, Joron Twiner." The gullaime emitted a cooing sound. "Maybe Joron Twiner not fool."

"I am glad you are happy," he said, wrongfooted by the sudden gentleness of the creature's voice.

"Nest father had comb."

"Oh," said Joron. The gullaime took another step towards him. Joron felt a sudden sense of panic, the need to get out. He did not want it near him, did not want to hear about the gullaime's parents, or know that such a beast understood the idea of family. "I must return to the slate," he said. "We have lost contact with one of the other ships."

It nodded at his words then stepped back. As he turned for the door it spoke again, softly.

"Are you sad, Joron Twiner?"

"Sad?"

"Smell lonely. Not a good smell."

"And you would know?"

"Yes," said the gullaime, and this was the cry of faraway skeers circling over their nests, the cry that every deckchild associated with lost ships, breakers smashing on to cruelly toothed rocks. It was the sound of loss. "Yes," it said again. "I know."

23

Towards the First of the Last

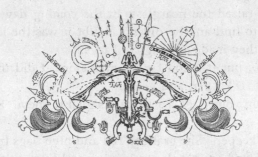

It seemed an age between each turn of the sandglass, and every time he turned it and the sand ran anew Joron hoped to hear, "Ship rising to seaward, ship rising to landward." But the ship to landward remained stubbornly unrisen.

He questioned his decision to fly on. Was it what she would have done? Not that it mattered now as it was a decision made. To go back would make him look weak in front of the crew, and his conversation with Cwell was a staystone in his mind, weighing him down with feelings of weakness he dared not acknowledge, so he said nothing. He concentrated on pushing down the feeling within that he had done the wrong thing and used up the restless energy of worry pacing the rump. Occasionally he circled the deck, checking with bonewrights, wingwrights, seakeep and topboys that all, apart from the lost ship, was as it should be.

And all was.

It was in the very early morning, when the hint of Skearith's opening Eye touched the far western horizon with a wash of pink, like newly leafed gion, that Joron's patience was finally rewarded.

"Ship rising to landward, D'keeper!"

"Can you name it, Topboy?" he shouted up to Farys.

"Not for sure, D'keeper," she returned. "Two spines, wings rigged triangle like on the fore and square on the rump like *Snarltooth*." Once again Joron made his careful way up the swaying rigging of *Tide Child* to the top of the mainspine, where he raised the nearglass. In the coming day *Snarltooth* was easy to find and he did not doubt it was the lost ship.

"Have they made any signal, Farys?"

"Maybe, but it is too far for eyes alone. I did think I saw movement, D'keeper, and colour."

"Take up your flags, Farys, and signal to them, 'Repeat last sent.'"

"Ey, D'keeper." She grabbed red and blue flags from where they were tied against the mainspine and then, without even seeming to think of the danger, climbed the final height of the spine until she stood, her feet finding impossible seeming purchase on the rope that ran twice around the bound varisk stalks. There she held out her arms and became the tallest point on the ship, flags extended, red to seaward, blue to landward, then signalled as Joron had requested. Once finished she sent again, and Joron switched his gaze from the girl and centred the nearglass on *Snarltooth*. Swiftly the signal came back: "Lost a topstay. All good now. Station resumed."

"Well," said Joron, "nothing too dramatic, ey? Keep your eyes on the water, Farys. Nothing would please me more than for one of my crew to be first to spot the wakewyrm." The girl smiled, puckering the burned skin of her face, and he wondered when he had first started to think of her, Karring and Old Briaret as "his" crew.

"It's real then, D'keeper?"

"So we are told, Farys."

She nodded and it was enough for her that he said it. His words made the thing real and she did not question them.

Joron made his careful way down the spine and Farys resumed her watch. When Joron returned to the deck it was to find his body had relaxed slightly and his mind was less weighed down. He hoped that those seeing him, as Skearith's Eye opened above and the day began to blaze, would think he had stood this way all night, sure in his command and his decisions.

Meas appeared from the underdeck, two-tailed hat and clothes as perfect as if she had just bought them. Behind her came Narza and behind her was Anzir, who took up station by Joron.

"I hear we lost a ship in the night," said Meas.

Joron felt his shoulders tighten once more.

"Ey, Shipwife," he said, handing over the nearglass.

"It would have been no trouble for you to wake me for such a thing – many would have." She tucked the nearglass inside her jacket. The wind ruffled her sash of red and blue feathers and Joron waited for a rebuke. "But you did not," she said, "and your decision was a good one." He let out the breath he had been holding. "Now get some sleep."

"Thank you, Shipwife." He leaned in close to her. "Cahanny smuggles arakeesian bone in the hold."

She nodded.

"I thought as much."

"And I am not sure Coughlin and his men can be trusted. They have some bond with Cwell, and she sees an opportunity in the wakewyrm."

Meas nodded again.

"That does not surprise me. Cwell has the tattoo of the dock families, like Cahanny. I will think on this. It may be as well to give Cwell the impression her opportunity will come. Keep quiet about this for now."

He nodded and headed belowdeck.

When Joron woke the motion of the ship had changed. *Tide Child* no longer coasted through slack seas; the ship shuddered and bucked. It was not alarming, not like the Northstorm had bared its teeth, more like when a cart moved over a rutted path. But the motion, a chill in the air and a freshness in the underdeck was enough to tell him the weather had changed in the hours he had spent unconscious, and it had not changed for the better.

On deck it was not as warm nor as clement as it had been. He emerged from the underdeck to see Cwell, followed by Hasrin and Sprackin, dragging a rope between them, heading for the mainspine. A chill ran through him as the wind attempted to rip the one-tailed hat from his head, and he had to make a swift grab for it, pulling it tighter over his wiry hair. The ship tilted as wind filled the mainwings, heeling *Tide Child* to seaward. Above the sound of the wind as it whistled through the rigging he made out a chorus of human misery, retching and moaning. The seaward rail was crowded with Cahanny's men once more.

The ocean beyond them, the ever-changing mirror of water, had taken on some of the Hag's temper. No longer the blue-green, smoothly swelling landscape that had gently chivvied *Tide Child* along, now it was grey, and its smoothness had been replaced by angular waves that bit and sniped, crossing and recrossing one another. The forespine of *Tide Child*, which stuck out well over the beak, carved spirals in the air as Joron stared along it. All this was nothing to him, for he was a fisher's boy and of the sea, and its many moods and movements were like sithers and brothers to him – he knew them intimately. Meas stood on the rump of the ship, looking out over the ashen sea towards where, far over the horizon, Skearith's Spine rose stark and black from the water.

"Good aftan, Deckkeeper," she said as he approached. She did not need to look round; she recognised him through his tread.

"Aftan, Shipwife." He followed her gaze. Though the sky above was blue, the first hint of cloud gathered in the distance.

"Cloud from the east, Twiner, and I like it not. When the Northstorm kisses the Eaststorm, its children always bring rain."

"A deckchild is often lost on a slippy deck," he said. "Seakeep!" Fogle, came running, bent at the waist due to some deformation of her spine.

"Ey, D'keeper?"

"Rain is in the offing. Bring up sand for the decks; we'll have no one slip overboard."

"Ey, D'keeper," she said, and under her breath, "As it was my intentions anyways."

Joron let the woman go, pretending he had not heard her speak. He had come to respect Meas's choice of seakeep. All aboard said that although Fogle was very odd indeed, she knew the running of a boneship like few others. There had been no sign of the drunkenness that had worried Meas either.

"You let her get away with that?" said Meas under her breath.

"What was it you said of Coxward, Shipwife? That you allow a skilled man some slack?"

"Only a little mind." He thought he heard the hint of a smile in her voice as she gazed out over the water.

"Ey, only that."

"I worry about more than losing crew overboard, Joron. A little rain will cut our visibility by a third, heavier rain by half. Any more than that, and we will have to lay up at seastay and wait it out or risk missing the wakewyrm altogether.'

"Turning the glass!" came the call from behind them.

"Tell of the sea, Topboy!" shouted Meas into the rigging.

"Ship rising to seaward, ship rising to landward, Shipwife. All else is clear."

Meas nodded.

Joron was staring up.

"Was that Farys?"

"Ey, Deckkeeper, it was."

"Has she been up there all night?"

"Says you expect her to sight the arakeesian first, and will not come down."

"I did not mean—"

"An officer must be careful about what they say to those who respect them, Joron."

He did not know how to answer that, for none had ever respected him before.

Sand slid through the glass.

"Her eyes must be tired, Shipwife. You could order her down."

"She is young. Her eyes will be good for a while yet, do not worry. And I would not order her down, for if the wakewyrm is spotted by another aboard *Tide Child* she would feel as if she let you down. Give her ten more turns of the glass, Joron, and then go up and order her to deck, gently mind. Then it is your choice and she cannot let you down."

"Yes, Shipwife." he said. Meas walked away from him to continue staring out at the grey, and greying, sky.

The glass continued to turn. The sky continued to grey. The men of the rock continued to vomit. Meas continued to become more and more worried by the sky, and rain spotted the skin of Joron's face with cold wet dots. He paced up and down the ship, finding endless small jobs for the crew. His father had always told him that keeping a ship afloat was an endless task, and that the Hag had made it so because idle deckchilder found nothing but mischief.

If Hassith the spear thrower had been set to work, then the godbird would still fly, boy, so you mend those nets and stop your complaining.

And if there were snide looks and unpleasant words said under the breath of women and men and sent in Joron's direction, they were fewer than they had been, and he thought it best to ignore them.

"Ship rising! Ship rising to the north-west!" This brought Meas from a statue on the rump to a figure of action. She was across the deck and climbing the spine.

"Say again, Topboy. I said say again!"

"Ship rising to the north-west."

"It is not the *Cruel Water*?"

"No, Shipwife."

"And not the *Snarltooth*?"

"No, Shipwife."

"How many?"

"I count four, Shipwife." Then Meas was lost among the billowing mass of black wings, no doubt staring through her nearglass, while Narza lounged at the bottom of the spine, idly picking at something in her shoe with a knife. Joron stepped nearer the mainspine to ensure he heard anything shouted down.

"Oarturner! Send us three points of shadow for'ard to the north-west. Joron, brace the ship for action!"

And Joron was turning, repeating the words.

"Oarturner, three points of shadow for'ard to the north-west. Deckholder! clear *Tide Child* for action." And Dinyl, just appearing from the underdecks passed the command to Solemn and solemn Muffaz stepped up, bellowing out the words. Behind him Gavith beat the drum.

A bevy of excited deckchilder ran for the gallowbows at the first beat of the drum.

"Not the bows, my girls and boys, not yet!" shouted Joron. In the back of his mind a little voice whispered that he had at some time taken on Meas's inflections and patterns of speech. "Not yet. Wait for the shipwife to get down so we know if we run or fight." He strode forward, raising his voice into the wind. "Clear the underdeck. Stow the hammocks. Stack bolt and shot. Tie everything down that is loose."

Meas was climbing down the rigging with all the ease of a child skipping along a path. The moment her feet hit the deck she was shouting once more.

"Four flukeboats on the horizon, Deckkeeper. Raiders from the look of them. It's time for us to put some blood on *Tide Child*. We'll need some speed, Twiner."

He nodded and turned.

"More wings," shouted Joron. "For'ard jib up, bottom wings up. Hold the flyers in reserve for now." And as if it were the most natural thing in the world, women and men were scuttling up the spines and loosing swathes of black wingcloth to flap and crack in the wind. Something in the ship let out an alarming creak, and with a shock — like cold water running down his back — Joron worried if he put too much pressure on the damaged keel. The bonemaster, Coxward, ran past without a word, and Joron felt a little calmer at that, for he knew the man was not afraid to speak his mind if he thought the ship in trouble.

Tide Child leaped forward, parting the water with new ferocity. Meas stood by Joron, staring up at the mass of black wing that caught the storm's gift and pushed the ship on. Joron realised he was grinning, feeling a fierce joy. He had done this. His words had sent the great black ship racing through the sea, and though he knew what he flew towards was sure to be danger — *his father ground between the hulls* — . He would enjoy this moment — the wind, the smell of the sea, the ship and the crew moving as one unit — and at the end? Well, he would deal with that when it came, though it filled him with a fear and excitement that he barely understood.

"He flies well, does he not, Joron?" said Meas, and she breathed deep, as if the sudden speed of the ship had outrun some terrible fate that haunted her.

"Ey, Shipwife, he does," said Joron, "he does indeed."

24

A Sight Seldom Seen

A hurried series of flags had let the other two ships know that *Tide Child* was going to break formation but that they should keep station, course and speed.

"Deckkeeper Twiner," said Meas, "let's see what your overtures towards the gullaime have bought us. Bring it up."

"Call the gullaime," shouted Joron, and from him the call went to Deckholder Dinyl and from there to Solemn Muffaz, who shouted the same to the seakeep, who relayed it down into the underdeck cabins.

Joron held his breath, waiting to see if the creature would respond. He was not the only one. As *Tide Child* raced on, it seemed the whole crew paused; even those throwing up at the rail seemed to still their aching guts. Then, as Joron was beginning to feel he must have failed, it appeared, predatory beak rising above the slate of the deck as if testing the air, head bobbing as it came up the steps, body hidden by robes that it had embellished with thread and needle, strange and beautiful patterns embroidered on the material, rips and tears fixed. Badly sewn, poorly repaired, but still fixed. The gullaime had changed. It was less messy, less unkempt, but there was more to it than that, although Joron could not quite grasp what; it was something he could not put into words.

The beak opened. The voice emerged:

"What you want, Joron Twiner?"

"We want wind, Gullaime," said Meas, striding across the deck towards the creature. "Wind to take us north-west, wind to carry us quickly. Can you . . ." And Joron saw Meas pause, not her voice, but her body. There was a stutter in her step as if some unfamiliar thought upset all she was. And when she spoke she asked, she did not command. "Will you do that for us, Gullaime? Will you bring us the wind?"

"For why, Meas, for why? So you make war in your boat?"

"For the last arakeesian, Gullaime."

The windtalker's posture changed, tightened. Its head darted forward.

"Say words again."

"The last arakeesian, Gullaime. It swims northward."

"You hunt?"

"No. I have seen raiders on the horizon armed for war, but what war waits out here? Nothing human, I reckon, Gullaime. At this moment the wakewyrm may be under attack, and we intend to protect it." The gullaime was across the deck in a flash. In front of Meas. Narza's hand went to the blades on her hip, but Meas opened a hand behind her. "No."

"Truth?" The gullaime almost stuck its beak into Meas's face.

"Truth."

Not truth, of course. A lie. Joron knew that. A lie but a necessary lie. But if the raiders were in fact hunters, then their quarry must be near.

Could that be true?

Could the creature be real?

The gullaime turned from Meas towards the north, then it shook, a small but intense shudder as if it rid itself of dust or insects. The robe lifted, exposing rope-thin legs and clawed feet, and it pointed its beak towards the north-west.

"Sea sither," it said quietly. Then raised its head to the sky and let out a cry that hurt Joron's ears — hurt everyone's ears, had people ducking as if under attack. Before they had recovered there was a hollow boom, and it was as if a great foot stamped on *Tide Child*, pushing him into the water and sending a huge circular wave roiling out from the ship. A howling wind sprang up, flattening the grey water, and then gone was the circle of water, gone was the criss-cross of waves that made the stonebound aboard so sick; instead *Tide Child* powered forward in a pocket of sea flattened by the howling wind.

"Less wind, Gullaime," screamed Meas into a gale that turned hair into whips, lashed faces, forced eyes closed against the ferocity.

"No. Save arakeesian," screamed the gullaime back.

"It's too much for the ship," shouted Meas. "You'll rip the wings from the spine, or break the keel, and we will sink." For a moment there was a strange tension, the windtalker staring at Meas with painted eyes as if it thought she lied, then it sank down slightly, its wings, open beneath the enveloping robe, closing a little. The wind lessened.

"This?" And though the wind still whistled through the rigging, it no longer howled and whipped the crew with their own hair.

"Ey," said Meas. "This is good. But drop this wind by half when the topboy tells us we are spotted."

"Get there quick," hissed the gullaime.

"Too quick and we are likely to overshoot." Meas was still shouting as if into a gale. "I shall not tell you how to conjure wind if you do not tell me how to command a ship."

The gullaime hissed at her, then shook as if ridding itself of water and let out a short chirrup.

Joron felt this was acquiescence. Meas joined him on the rump, watching the gullaime in the centre of the ship.

"Well done, Joron, it works with us now."

"Does it?" said Joron, for he was not so sure.

It did not take long for *Tide Child*, carried on the strange magic of the windtalker, which cooed to itself as it worked, for the ship's lookouts to get a clearer look at the flukeboats.

"Eight flukeboats, Shipwife," came from above. "Single sail. Some carry small gallowbows. They are shooting into the water. We are seen! Four turning to us."

"Anything else, Topboy?" shouted Meas.

"Not that I can . . ." The voice died away.

"What is it? Topboy!"

"A," — a disbelieving stutter from Farys — "a shape in the water, Shipwife, but one so vast I thought it a submerged reef."

"But?"

"It moves, Shipwife!" Then Farys shouted out an old and storied call, one not heard for generations. She shouted it so loud it seemed to rip the air, elongating the vowels and the words seemed to pull the ear and the eye upwards to hear what was screamed: "Keyshan rising!"

All aboard the ship stopped.

Farys called again: "Keyshan rising to the north-west!"

Joron could barely believe it, found himself babbling.

"It is the arakeesian, Shipwife! It is the wakewyrm! They hunt it!"

Joron did not know what he had expected to feel. Joy? Fear? Avarice? But he and every woman and man on board *Tide Child* knew they were now no longer simply the crew of a black ship; by the presence of this fabled creature, they had become part of the Scattered Archipelago's history. The name of this ship would live for ever.

"Don't just stand around," shouted Meas. "Scatter the paint! Gullaime, cut the wind but stay on deck — I may need to manoeuvre. Maindeck bowsells, crews to your bows. And be ready, Hag curse you, did you forget all we learned? Underdeck bowsells at the ready too! Coughlin, arm your men. Solemn Muffaz, break out the curnows." She clasped her hands behind her back, and Joron heard her say to herself, "Let us hunt the hunters." And for the first time since she had taken his hat on a lonely beach, he saw Meas Gilbryn's true smile.

From his place on the deck Joron saw four flukeboats, sails painted in bright yellows and greens with designs of eyefish, sawteeth and beakwyrms, coming towards *Tide Child*, oars extended and beating the sea. Behind them were four more, twins to those attacking, chasing something that could not truly be seen. Something that slid through the depths creating a moving shallow that only hinted at shape and size, something so vast that Joron's mind baulked at the the thought of it.

"Mevans, get crew in the rigging ready to put arrows on the boats when they close," shouted Meas. "Joron, ready my gallowbows!"

"Bowteams!" shouted Joron.

"Both sides, D'keeper?" said Solemn Muffaz.

"Ey, we'll crew them all," said Meas. "We'll be fighting both sides."

Joron glanced at the approaching boats; each held at least thirty well armed women and men. This felt like a repeat of Corfynhulme, and he felt panic rise like acid in his gullet. No, he would not allow himself to think that. He strode to the first bow. POISONOUS HOSTIR had been very carefully painted on it. The crew now consisted of Anzir and a man called Soffle on the winders; Gavith on the trigger – he had shown himself to have a keen eye – while Joron was bowsell for Hostir and the whole deck.

"Knot!" shouted Joron. Fingers were dipped in red paint, paint spattered on the deck. Ropes brought free. The heavy shafts of the gallowbows held and controlled.

Four boats rowed towards them with their cargos of screaming raiders.

"Lift!" shouted Joron, and the crews brought the bows over in a single, smooth motion, opening out the bow arms and locking the mechanisms on to the gimbals.

A gust of wind filled the sails of the flukeboats, boosting the efforts of the rowers. The jeers and screams increased.

"String!" shouted Joron, and as he watched his team thread

the cord he knew the same was happening up and down the ship. He heard the shout go up behind him for the gullaime.

The approaching boats gathered speed.

When his bow was set, Joron turned to the rump of the ship. Meas stood, watching the sea before them and the second set of flukeboats in the distance as they rowed against the wind in an attempt to catch the arakeesian. She saw him watching her and gave a nod.

"Spin the bows, Joron."

"Spin!"

Shout? No, he roared the word. The call was echoed all the way down the ship by the other bowsells and followed by grunts of effort and the whirr of the wheels pulling back the firing cords and tensioning the bow arms. Filling each bow with the potential to cause havoc and death and pain.

As the click of the cords being caught by the retaining triggers sounded, the next command went up.

"Load!"

The bows were loaded with viciously barbed bolts.

"Aim!"

Anzir and Soffle looked to Joron to guide them. As if in reaction, Meas shouted from the rump:

"The hulls! Aim for their hulls! Sink them before they reach us."

And Joron took up his position, lifting landward arm, the bow slowly swinging until the flukeboat was in his bow's sights.

"Aim low, Gavith. Hit it at the waterline."

The boy nodded and leaned into the bow the same way Farys had. Now they waited for the final shout. The first order to loose would come from Meas before command passed to the bowsells.

Joron heard her boots on the slate as she ran up the centre of the deck.

"Landward bows, be ready when you've loosed to wind again. I'll be swinging *Tide Child* round for the seaward bows and then back, and I hope to give you a second shot before they're on us."

Joron swallowed at that, the confirmation that they probably could not stop all four flukeboats in the time they had.

"Coughlin, be ready to repel boarders. Remember, my boys and girls, we are here to protect the arakeesian. These boats are not our real target, those are." She pointed past the approaching boats to the ones in the distance. "Now" – a huge grin crossed her face – "your bowsells have aimed you. So" – she drew her sword and held it aloft – "loose when ready!"

Part of Joron expected Gavith to loose immediately, and bow three did. The bolt went high, but a roar went up from *Tide Child* as it cut a swathe through the busy deck of the nearest flukeboat, women and men being tossed overboard, some whole, some in parts. But Joron knew it was a wasted shot.

Tide Child hit a wave, the swelling water lifting Joron's side of the ship so the bows pointed skyward. For a moment Joron stared along the shaft of the bow at clouds, then *Tide Child* rolled back down and the mast of the flukeboat came into view. Then the deck covered in furious faces. Then, at what to Joron felt like the lowest point of the ship's roll, Gavith's arm jerked back, and he heard the deep basso groan of the bow releasing. Joron's heart sank for he was sure the boy had missed, the bolt vanishing into the water with barely a splash. A moment later the final bows loosed, their bolts smashed into the hull of the same flukeboat, tearing great holes in it, but too far above the waterline to sink it.

"Spin!" shouted Joron, and the process started again.

At the same time Meas shouted, "Hold on. I'm bringing him about!" A momentary gale blasted the ship, his ears hurt, and the huge jointweight of bone that made up *Tide Child* started to swing round in the water. As he did, Joron saw that Gavith had not missed at all. He had holed the flukeboat below the water, and the boat was slowing, the front of it dipping to bring the other holes in its hull below the waterline. The boat began to list, the faces which had screamed in fury now screamed in panic. Arrows cut through the air from *Tide Child*'s rigging.

"Hold with the bows!" shouted Meas. "Those women and men are already lost."

Three boats now remained. *Tide Child* came round to bring the bows to bear on them as the landward bowteams wound and loaded.

Meas ran down the deck. "Same as the landward bows. Aim for the waterline! Sink them if you can." *Tide Child* was still leaning into his turn; Joron's bowteam stared at the water while the seaward teams stared into the sky. "Hold with the wind, Gullaime!" shouted Meas, and the Gullaime dropped to the deck. The sudden gale died away. The ship straightened on the sea as Joron turned to watch the seaward teams loose their weapons.

Thruum!

Thruum!

Thruum!

Screams but no roar of joy at a boat being sunk. Arrows flew from the rigging.

"Give me a breeze, Gullaime!" shouted Meas, and again the ship heeled round, pushing away a huge wave as the three boats closed on *Tide Child*. Joron expected the ship to come full about so he could aim his bow, but Meas stopped the wind before this. "No time for a second shot," she shouted. "Coughlin, be ready to earn your passage." Meas ran back to take her place before the rumpspike and shouted. "Bows, swing for'ard and loose when you have a target." Then she smiled and glanced up into the rigging.

Something changed.

There was a moment of stillness in the battle, as if all knew what Meas was about to say and longed to hear it.

"Full wings," she said, then raised her voice. "Get up in the spines and unfurl me the wings, you layabouts! Gullaime, give me the best speed you can!" Then she added, quite calmly but loud enough for all to hear, "Barlay, aim our beak at those approaching boats." She reached up, straightening her two-tailed hat. "Since they have seen fit to get in our way, we shall smash them out of it."

Tide Child leaped forward, and if Joron had not been grabbed by Anzir he would have sprawled on the decks — many others did. A scream echoed across the water, quickly stopped by the sickening sound of a body hitting slate as a deckchild lost their footing in the rigging and fell to their death. Then Meas was screaming at them, "Brace! Brace!" Joron grabbed the legs of the gallowbow along with Gavith. Behind them Anzir grasped the rail.

And *Tide Child* ground into the leading flukeboat. There was a huge groan as the ship's forward momentum was checked — but only momentarily — and then a terrible rending as the sharp beak and hull of the boneship ripped apart the far more fragile flukeboat.

A moment of quiet aboard.

Shock at the sudden violence.

Then bows loosed and Joron heard screams. Grapples, soaring over the rail. Two, three, four came aboard and were quickly, and professionally, pulled tight.

"Axes!" yelled Joron, and he pulled his curnow to hack at the rope attached to the grapple nearest to him.

"Coughlin, bring up your men!" shouted Meas. "All hands to repel boarders!" Arrows whistled down from the rigging as the first raiders clambered over the front rails.

"D'keeper!" shouted Gavith, "D'keeper, move to the side! D'keeper!"

Joron looked round to find the gallowbow aimed directly at him. He ducked aside as Gavith got into the firing position. Joron's mind lagged. Only at the last second did he realise what the boy meant to do. The great bow was aimed at the flukeboat that was making itself secure against *Tide Child*, its crew pushing and shoving each other to be the first to scale the boneship's spiked side. Joron had not realised how much bigger this boat was than the others, sixty aboard at least.

"I'll stop 'em!" shouted Gavith. "Hag can have 'em."

"No!" Joron dived forward, his shoulder hitting the bow and pushing it to the side just as it fired. The bolt ripped past the flukeboat and punctured only the sea, which did not care. One of the bow arms caught Joron a glancing blow on the back of the head, and he fell forward, his hip hitting the rail, and only Anzir's strong arm stopped him going over into the ever-hungry sea, or the arms of the raiders below.

"Not you too," she grunted, pulling him back, but he was dazed, unsure of what she said. So much noise, so many people shouting.

"Not me too?" he mumbled.

"Soffle went into the sea when we hit. Lost 'im," she said.

"Why did you stop me?" shouted Gavith. His eyes widened as he realised who he screamed at and he added more quietly, "D'keeper." He bowed his head. "Sorry, D'keeper, but I could have sunk 'em."

"You could," said Joron as he tried to pull himself to his feet. The world spun around him. "Sunk a ship tied to us," he said, "and maybe dragged us down with it." He screwed his eyes shut. Shook his head. Winced at the pain. Then opened his eyes and looked around.

All the action was currently at the rump. He may not have liked Coughlin, but he and his men were fighting with a rare fury while Meas and a group of deckchilder held the landward side of the ship. The attackers' numbers were of no help to them at the moment as they could not get enough of them on board. All was noise. Screaming. Shouting. Swearing.

A face peered between the uprights of the rail. Anzir shot it with a crossbow.

"They'll be coming over our rail soon," she said.

"Call Farys and the underdeck bowteams up here." His world was a little clearer now.

"You needs be with the hagshand," said Anzir. "Head wounds can be bad, D'keeper."

"No," he said and pulled himself up. He took the small

crossbow Meas had given him and loaded it, then unhooked his curnow. "I'm not that eager to die."

Joron pulled Gavith away from a grabbing arm and put a crossbow bolt into the face of its owner. She fell back in the silence of the dead, but she was only the first raider to come flooding over the rail in a wave of naked flesh painted with the Hag's face in the hope it would keep them from harm. More hands, more faces. Joron hacked at them, joined by Gavith and Anzir and the rest of the landward bowteams, but they were not enough. More raiders swarmed over the rail, forcing Joron and those around him back. Then the underdeck bowteams appeared from below with a great shout, throwing themselves into the fray, and Joron found himself part of a wall of women and men, hacking with curnows and axes, stabbing with wyrmpikes and hooking with gaffs and poleaxes.

All was noise and fury.

Joron lost himself.

He let the fear that had always been part of him take over. It erupted from him in incoherent screams. In furious blows of his sword. In a pure and burning hatred of the contorted faces before him. There was no place to escape to; he could not run. All he knew was the moment. The hoarse screaming and the rising and falling of his weighted blade. The spray of blood across his skin. There was no skill, no sense of anything but luck in who lived and who died.

It seemed to go on for ever and it seemed to go on for no time at all.

And then it was over, and there was space before him to see the bloodied deck. The raiders were retreating over the rail, and the the crew of *Tide Child* were cheering as the raiders cut the ropes to their grappling hooks and started to row away. He found himself by Meas, who was breathing hard, her face spattered with blood; her face full of joy. The strangest thing: he felt it too, that joy. Exultation at being alive. Joy as bright, and as painful, as staring into Skearith's Eye, blocking out the moments he had nearly died, the moments his blade had opened bodies and he saw what no woman or man was meant to see as guts spilled across the deck. He was alive.

"Should we sink the boat before it escapes, Shipwife?"

"No, Deckkeeper," she said. "We carry on for them." She pointed at the four boats further away, chasing the shape in the water. "Topboy!" she shouted. "Signal *Cruel Water* and *Snarltooth* to intercept that boat. Let's not deny them a part in our victory. Nothing brings a fleet together like a fight, ey?" At the word "victory" the women and men lining the rails and rigging fair jumped up and down, filling the air with excitement. "Hush your noise," yelled Meas. She leaned on her bloodied sword, breathing heavily. "Clear my deck of bodies and throw some sand down to soak up the blood. We're not finished yet."

The four flukeboats, painted in garish colours, were rowing with everything they had. Each boat bristled with raiders, and all held spears. Joron saw a spear held aloft, a length of rope trailing from its end.

"They cannot think spears will hurt something so vast," Joron turned to find the courser stood by him.

"They obviously do," said Joron.

"'Twere how it were done in the old days, Caller." This came from the old woman, Garriya, the one Mevans had insisted was brought aboard. She was hunched over, bundled up in an ill-fitting assortment of cast-offs.

"Not even you are that old," said Joron. Someone passed him a cup of water and he drank, suddenly aware how thirsty he was, how his throat was raw.

"I know of the past," she said.

"They used poison," said Joron. "Shot it into the arakeesian's eye, and it died within moments."

"And how did they make that poison, Caller?"

"They made it from the creatures," Joron said.

"Did they so?" She grinned, something mocking in it. "But one had to die first, aye?"

"Maybe they found one washed up on a beach."

"Maybe, but they needed to find out about the poison, work out how to use it, Caller."

"My name is Joron," he hissed, "and you should call me by my rank, which is deckkeeper."

She took a step closer and the scent of her — seaweed and sand, hot shells and the background reek of spoiled fish — filled his nostrils. She spoke, and her voice stopped Joron, froze him in place. Pictures filled his mind.

A sea of ships, flukeboats by the hundred. All bristling with women and men. Below them the huge shape — somehow familiar and at the same time utterly strange. He saw the shape, and he saw the islands, and the archipelago and he saw them all at the same time like he flew above them. And everything was known — the boats, the sea, the land — and everything was also wrong — the boats, the sea, the land. The boats were not the flukeboats he knew, the islands were not the islands he knew, the sea was subtly different. None of these things were as they should be and he did not know why.

Then they were gone. And the old woman was still talking.

"This is how they hunted once," she said, "though four boats is not enough. Eight boats is not enough. A hundred boats is not enough."

"Women and men in flukeboats could not . . ." began Joron, but his words faded away under the gaze of the old woman and thoughts of the scene that had played out in his head.

"Hundreds of them, Caller, filled with women and men or men and women, and they speared the beasts, tied the spears to their boats. Boat after boat after boat—"

"The keyshan would kill them."

"Aye, many died, so many, many died. But a million pinpricks will kill you eventually, and it is the same even for keyshans."

Her words revolved in his mind and the images returned, though not as strong as before; rather seen the way he had seen the stories told by his father — a shadowplay in the back of his brain.

"A determined fleet will prevail, eventually. Those who

survive become heroes. They float home the corpse and sell all those parts that can be sold. The hunters become rich, and glad they will never hunt again. And those who look on and hunger think, *If that were me* . . . And the next time a keyshan rises they are ready to throw themselves into boats. But now the boats are strengthened with bone and fewer are needed, though still many die. And when there is not a beast to hunt, they hunt each other's riches instead, and they still die and the godbird laughs at our folly."

"So we need not worry about the four boats ahead?"

"Every prick of the pin weakens the beast," said the old woman, then she turned away and scurried towards the rear hatch. And before Joron could ask any more, Meas was shouting orders.

"Be ready, for'ard bows. Gullaime, give me a breeze; I would catch those flukeboats before they catch the wakewyrm." The gullaime lifted itself from the deck not as sprightly when it raised its wings, the gusts it brought not as fierce.

But Joron had no time to think of the gullaime; he was hurrying to his gallowbow, already shouting commands and watching his team react. And then he was behind the bow, staring for'ard at the boats. Were they running from them? Or towards the arakeesian? Either way was the same to Joron, and he focused on the boat to his side of the ship – large, painted in bright blue with the sign of the Hag on its sails. It was overloaded and *Tide Child* gained rapidly.

"Bowsells," shouted Meas, "loose when you judge us in range."

Gavith leaned into the bow, staring down the shaft of the great weapon.

"When you are ready, Gavith. The blue boat." The boy nodded, and to Joron all seemed silent then – no sound of the sea passing the ship, no wind, nothing. He saw only the blue boat and the women and men aboard. Only the shortening gap between them. There was a bow mounted on the rear of the boat – not as large as theirs, but still a danger. He could not tell if the bow was wound or not.

"Down!" Meas screamed, and it seemed to Joron that the rest of the crew on the deck hit the slate; only he and his bowteam remained upright. The bolt from the flukeboat crashed into the side rail of *Tide Child*. The sound of shattering bone filled the air, and Joron felt something pluck at his side, but he paid it no mind. Instead he stayed focused on the view down the gallowbow, stayed focused on the target.

"I think I can hit their bow, D'keeper," Gavith said, as *Tide Child* caught up with the boat. Joron heard the anger in the boy's voice and was surprised by it. Had he become part of the ship so quickly? He felt that same anger, that for the raiders to hit *Tide Child* with a bolt was an insult to him, not just the ship, and he was tempted for a moment to let Gavith take out the bow. But no, his job was to stay calm, to think.

"Hole the boat below the water if you can, Gavith. Tempting to avenge their shot, I know that, but sinking the boat will kill those who fired the bow as sure as a bolt."

"Ey, D'keeper."

The blue boat rose and fell on the waves and *Tide Child* fell and rose as it came alongside. Joron could make out the bowteam on the flukeboat trying to spin the bow for another shot, but the boat was so crowded with raiders they got in each other's way. Then Poisonous Hostir spoke, the bolt flying too fast for the eye to follow but the impact apparent: a fountain of water at the rear of the blue boat. The bolt did not simply hole the flukeboat but collapsed its entire rear, spilling the bowteam into the sea, quickly followed by those around them. The boat dragged itself to a halt, its beak rising into the air, sending more and more crew into the water. Then the screaming started. Long, white, serrated backs had appeared in the water around the stricken vessel.

"Longthresh in the water!"

There cannot have been a woman or man on *Tide Child's* decks who did not shudder at that call. Of all the many ocean predators, longthresh were the most feared. Some grew as long as a boneship. Their flint-white skin encased bone plates that armoured the whole creature, and long, tapering wings propelled them through the water as fast as any ship. Those who encountered a longthresh wished only that it would kill them quickly, but they rarely did. Longthresh played with their food, biting off arms and legs before taking the body.

Below *Tide Child* huge mouths full of needle teeth opened in the sea, biting into the women and men in the water. The sheer amount of prey drove the longthresh into a frenzy, and the lucky were swallowed whole by the creatures. The beasts bit and bit and bit, chewing through whatever they came into contact with. A group attacked the boat itself, grinding through the sinking hull and the screaming crew who begged for *Tide Child* to rescue them.

But three enemy ships remained, and *Tide Child* flew on.

A bow launched, and Joron heard screams in reply over the spinning of the bow as his own team worked Poisonous Hostir.

"Down!" shouted Meas again, and Joron felt another bolt hit *Tide Child*, but further down the hull where the bone was thick. The smaller bows of the flukeboats lacked the power to do real damage to *Tide Child*'s hull. "Two points on the shadow to landward, Oarturner. Gullaime, keep the wind coming. Gallowbows, loose when ready."

"Ey, Shipwife," shouted Joron in return and stared down the deck and over the bowspine of *Tide Child* as the ship turned and the second flukeboat slowly came into view, this one painted gaudy yellow and orange.

"If we catch it and you can do what you did before, Gavith," said Joron, "you'll get my ration of eggs on the morran."

"I love an egg, D'keeper," said Gavith, and he nestled forward into the bow.

"Steady," said Joron. "Steady now." When the target was fully lined up he put his hand on Gavith's shoulder. "Loose when you are ready." And the ships moved up and down, down and up.

Gavith loosed.

"Hag's tits, too late."

The bolt had missed the hull but, more by luck than design, hit the spine of the boat. It seemed the world paused for a second, and then the spine and the gaudy wing it held came crashing down, splashing into the sea and pulling the boat around to seaward.

"Gallowbows," shouted Meas, "rake them as we pass. Loose as quick as you can!" And the world was lost to Joron in a welter of shouted commands – *Spin! Load! Loose!* – sweat and the song of the great bows as they peppered the stricken boat with bolts, leaving it sinking amid water churned white and red by more longthresh.

"Maiden bless 'em," said Anzir. "No woman or man deserves to die by the longthresh."

"But many will today," said Gavith.

Joron gave the command to spin again, and the bow was primed and loaded before Meas shouted to cease loosing.

Tide Child ploughed through the wreckage, once again ignoring all pleas for rescue. Meas had no intention of stopping.

"Gullaime, more wind, if you will." She said it so calmly it was difficult to believe she commanded a ship of war. "Gallowbows be ready."

Joron's bow swung, and he saw the final two boats. Both were well ahead of *Tide Child*, but the black ship had unfurled all its wings; even the flyers, extra wings sticking out of the side of the ship, were set. The gullaime, now bent almost double, was still conjuring a steady breeze. Before them he saw the further flukeboat heel to one side. It seemed every woman and man aboard had crowded over to seaward, and above the wind he heard their voices screaming in triumph as they cast their spears into the sea below them.

The gullaime let out an anguished screech and collapsed on the deck.

The sea below the flukeboat bowed; a curved shell of water rose, and the boat was thrown bodily from the sea by a flipper as long as *Tide Child* and crusted with white shells and coral.

As the flukeboat crashed back into the water, the flipper smashed through it, breaking the vessel in half and scattering its crew into the water.

Such a display of power – together with the ships *Tide Child* had destroyed – was clearly too much for the surviving raiders, and the last boat veered away from the huge creature below the water.

But it had also slowed, and Meas was shouting once more.

"Gallowbows, loose when we close with the boat, then we'll ram the storm-cursed thing and be done with it."

The boneship bore down on the flukeboat. Those who crewed it no longer screamed in fury or with thoughts of triumph. There was clearly panic aboard, both at the ease with which the arakeesian had smashed their comrades' boat and at the closing black ship.

"Loose!" shouted Joron, and the for'ard bows spoke, the middle bows spoke, and then the bolt from his bow's twin on the seaward side loosed and all smashed into the flukeboat. Joron was grabbing hold of the bow once more, and every deckchild aboard was finding something to hold tight to as Meas shouted, "Brace! Brace!" and *Tide Child* heeled over. It was as if the ship itself felt rage. *Tide Child* smashed into the flukeboat amidships, shuddering and screeching as it broke the craft in two.

Then there was only sea before them.

The sea and the leviathan.

And on the deck of *Tide Child* lay a frail and broken avian body that had given all it had.

25

I Saw a Miracle Upon the Water

J oron felt that they should have been jubilant. This had been *Tide Child*'s first successful action, as different from the shambles at Corfynhulme as it was possible to be. The boneship had cut through his opposition like a harpoon through a kivelly.

Yet, after the first shouts when the final flukeboat was ground under the hull of *Tide Child* had died away a strange silence followed. Maybe it was the screaming of the women and men in the water behind them as the longthresh went to work on their frail bodies, a reminder that they were not in their environment, that the sea welcomed no man and that the only woman it looked kindly upon was the Hag, who waited at the bottom for all those lost upon the waves. That *Tide Child*, strong as he seemed against the flukeboats, was simply a dot on the vast ocean that swelled beneath him. They were tolerated here. And they were here to die.

Or maybe it was because all had witnessed the power of the arakeesian – the flipper that had risen lazily out of the sea, propelling a boat up into the air and then smashing it apart without seeming effort or care. And now Meas drove them onward towards the beast, and the frailty of their ship against such a giant was as apparent as the frailty of flesh against the jaws of the longthresh in the reddening sea.

Every woman and man aboard watched the water, stared at the place where it was lightened by the vast body below. An area of water that looked to be as big as Bernshulme town, which rose and fell with its own rhythm, an area quite apart from, though still in harmony with, the ocean around it. The air smelled different – no longer of ozone, of the fresh, cold freedom of the sea. There was a heat to the air behind the arakeesian, but not an obvious furnace heat like that which burned down from Skearith's Eye. To Joron it felt like a blush, like he had stared into a fire for too long and when he walked away his skin still burned.

But it was not that which stole the moment from Joron, it was the form on the slate of the deck, looking like a pile of sticks covered in dirty white wingcloth: the gullaime. Why did it hurt him inside that this creature – which fascinated and scared him in equal measure – lay upon the deck? That its head was bent at a strange angle, that its legs were twisted and wrong-looking, that the few feathers on its head blew in a breeze not of the gullaime's making.

"Topboy," shouted Meas, "keep your eyes open for *Cruel Water* and *Snarltooth*, they should be done with their quarry soon enough. And I want to be the first to know if any other ship shows over the horizon."

As Joron stared at the gullaime he heard Meas approach him from behind.

"Why did you leave them so far behind, Shipwife?"

"Leave who, Deckkeeper?"

"The other ships," he said. "Do you not trust them?"

"I trust them, Deckkeeper." She took a pace nearer, and Dinyl joined them. His face was cut and blood darkened his coat. "Tell him why, Dinyl."

"This ship, this crew, they needed a victory, Joron."

"But we would have had one, a more sure one, with two more ships."

"Ey," said Meas. "But that victory would have been shared. This victory is theirs alone, and *Cruel Water* and *Snarltooth* got their share of the action too. Look." She pointed across the deck. "Look at them." And he saw how the crew mixed. Before, those from the old crew and the new had stood subtly apart, now they did not. Even Coughlin's men mixed with the deckchilder at the rail, staring forward at the water where the arakeesian swam. "Deckholder," she said more quietly, "how many did we lose?"

"Four," said Dinyl. "Four dead, eight hurt enough to go below."

"Not too bad," she said. "I thought the Hag would have called more, but she was generous today." Then she raised her voice. "You did well, my girls and boys, so well! And the Hag barely touched us. We'll send those she called down to her with all due ceremony – don't worry about that – but we have done well."

There was a moment of warmth among those on board, women and men turning towards each other, congratulating, sharing commiserations for lost friends. Then Coughlin very deliberately backed away from those nearest him, ignored by most, except Cwell and a small group of crew – ten, maybe less – who followed his example.

Meas continued: "But all we faced today was flukeboats, and we will face much worse, do not pretend otherwise. Once the Scattered Archipelago knows what swims through it, more boats, more ships, will come. We will be fighting our way from here to the Northstorm. When we don't fight, we will be alert." She seemed to grow a little, to stand taller. "In front of us" – she raised her voice – "is the future of the Hundred Isles, and we must keep the future alive to the Northstorm. Do you understand? If the future does not live that long we all die. Not everyone has the foresight you do, not all see the future as clearly." She took a step to the side so all on the slate could see the island of water that moved before them.

At that moment, as if rehearsed, the water swelled, rose, broke in a white froth as the arakeesian's rear flippers broke the water, spreading webs of skin each, as vast as the mainwings of *Tide Child*, catching the light of Skearith's Eye, throwing back the colour in a thousand rainbows before crashing back into the water. And even though the arakeesian had ten, or maybe fifteen shiplengths on them, the water rained on to the decks of *Tide Child*. "It blesses us," shouted Meas. "It knows we fly to protect it, and it acknowledges us in the only way it can, with the water that sustains it, and us! Let it know we are here, ey?"

A desultory cheer.

"Is that all you have?" she said. "We make history. *Tide Child's* name, your names, will be part of the Hundred Isles for ever more after this. Is that all you have?"

A louder cheer.

And Meas raised her voice almost to a scream. "Is that all you have?"

And this time the cheer was louder and longer, and she nodded.

"Good, now clean my decks. Truss the bows and set the wings. We fly the sea to make history – do not let me down!"

As they went back to work it seemed the mood lifted. But Joron did not feel it; he felt within a strange sadness. He knew this victory was barely that; bigger challenges and bigger ships would come, and for this small victory they had exhausted their single advantage: the gullaime who lay silent and still on the deck. It was odd how none touched it, none came near, none even looked at the windtalker even though it had made their victory possible. Joron leaned over it, the fishskin of his clothes creaking in time with the wings above him. The scent of it, desert and dry heat, was redolent of the feeling he got from the arakeesian that slid through the sea before *Tide Child*. But where the arakeesian was huge, undoubtedly alive, the same could not be said of the gullaime. There was nothing that said life in the windtalker, no movement, no sense of breath moving in and out of the creature's body, and if such things had a pulse Joron did not know how to find it.

"Take it below, Joron," said Meas quietly. She had approached across the deck without him hearing, and her words were meant only for him. "Take it below to its cabin, Joron. The crew may not look at it or talk of it, but they know it is special."

"It is d—"

She cut him off.

"Take it below. Take it to its cabin and tend to it, for it may be sore ill, but a beast that can call such winds as this one does will not die easily."

Joron wondered at this theatre. Surely the whole crew must know it was gone? But then he remembered where he was and what he was, and that his duty was to his Shipwife, and it was not to ask questions, it was to follow orders. He slipped his arms under the body of the gullaime – it felt like lifting air, like the gentle winds of the Eaststorm had been given form. The desert scent of the creature surrounded him. Its head lolled on its long neck. He found he could easily hold the body with one arm, so he used his other hand to place the gullaime's masked head over his shoulder and held it against him the way his father had carried him sleeping from their boat when he was a child.

As he passed through the underdeck the bonewrights rebuilt the ship around him. The courser's cabin, the gullaime's nest, the stateroom for the shipwife and the deckkeeper's cabin were all permanent, but the quarters for the deckholder, bonemaster, hatkeep, seakeep and deckmother were broken down for action. *Tide Child* was becoming less a ship of war with every moment.

Joron stepped around the industry with his burden and into the gullaime's cabin. It did not smell. He had always thought the scent was from the living quarters, that somehow it was imbued with the heat of the creature, but it was not. The smell of sand and heat came from the beast itself. Now it was gone. He laid the guillame in the nest it had constructed in one corner, near the bowpeek. When he put it down it sighed, and for a moment hope raised its head, but the beast made no other noise. Joron had tended corpses before and knew it was most likely he heard only the air leaving the body, the corpse sigh, the last exclamation made when a woman or man saw the Hag beckoning them into her domain.

"I'm sorry," he said, and he did not know why. He had not made it raise the wind, he had not forced it aboard *Tide Child*.

"Skearith's children are hard to kill, Caller." He turned. The old woman, Garriya, stood in the doorway.

"What?"

"Water it. Feed it. Keep it warm."

"It is dead," he said.

"Is it, Caller? Many would think so, but do you not feel the heat?"

How did she know? What did she know?

"Why do you say that?"

"You feel the heat. You do, don't you, Caller?"

"Why do you name me that?" he said. "Caller?"

She stepped back and the darkness of the underdeck swallowed her.

"You feel the heat," she said.

Joron walked to the door but there was no sign of the woman. Farys walked past, rolling a water barrel.

"Water, please, Farys," he said. She stopped and set the barrel flat, and he gave her his water bottle to fill from the spigot. He took it back, realising how thirsty he was once more, and drank a long swallow of the brackish water. It tasted brown, of dirt and land. He passed it back. "Fill it again, if you would."

"Ey, D'keeper."

When it was full he took it into the gullaime's nest, shut the door behind him and knelt by the creature. He took its head – so light – and tipped it back, opened the hooked, predatory beak with his thumb, hissing as he caught himself on one of the spines within. A bead of bright blood welled up. He dripped water polluted with his own blood into the gullaime's beak. Did he feel it swallow? Did something in its throat move? He didn't know. But he kept dripping the liquid in until he judged it would have had enough. Then he went to one of the bowls on the floor and took dried fish from it. Flaking it into small bits, he dropped them into the creature's beak, washing them down with more brackish water.

"Careful it does not choke. Rub its neck below the beak to make the food go down." He looked up. Now Meas stood in the door. Stepped in, boots tapping on the bone deck. He nodded, rubbed the creature's neck with his thumb, leaving smears of red on the pink skin, feeling nascent feathers as ridges beneath the flesh. "It lives then?" she said.

Joron shrugged.

"I give it water and food, but . . ." He left the sentence hanging.

Meas squatted by him.

"It may only be windsick."

"Windsick?"

"The godbird's spirit lets them control the weather, but they use it up. The godbird's spirit dwells in the windspires. It fills the gullaime when they visit — do not ask me how; that is for those who run the lamyards to know, not for decent folk — but this one had not visited a windspire in an age." She looked into Joron's eyes. "It hurts them, to be empty of the godbird. And if it hurts too much they can fall into a state where they seem to die. I have seen shipwives throw them overboard, thinking them deadweight, only to have the gullaime start screaming when the longthresh take them."

Joron dropped another flake of fish into the beak. Rubbed the throat. Poured the water.

"How do we tell the difference?"

"I do not know, Joron Twiner." She leaned in close. "But if anyone asks, we will say it is windsick. You will come down here twice a day to feed and water it — the crew must believe it lives."

"Why?"

She stared at him.

"To be shipwife, Joron, it is to juggle so much in the air. A crew, any crew, is held together by belief. They believe the shipwife knows best, so they follow me. They believe that the deckkeeper knows more than them, so they follow you."

"Even me?"

"Even you."

"Not all of them," said Joron quietly.

"Enough for now, and the number will grow."

"Will it?"

"Yes," she answered simply, looking into his eyes. "You did well today, and what they believe, well, that will be different for all of them, but most believe you will bring them through safe."

"And if they do not believe?"

"Mutiny, Joron, and you and I go over to feed the longthresh. It is harder on this ship because there will not be riches. The women and men aboard think they know why they fight, some because they want those they left behind to have their wages, most because they hope for freedom – to be off the deck of the black ship."

"That will not happen."

"And maybe they know that, somewhere deep down. In the end, do you know what women and men really fight for?"

"You said riches or freedom."

"That is what they think they fight for." Joron waited for her to finish her sentence while she waited for him to do the same. When he did not speak, she sighed. "If you saw someone attack Farys, would you stand back?"

"No."

"Why?"

"Because . . ." He realised he did not know. Not really. He thought hard before he spoke. "Because she would not stand back if I was attacked."

Meas nodded.

"Ey, that is it. Loyalty. That is what makes a ship work – ties of loyalty. To each other, to the ship. And every time we fight together, we are bound closer together. It is your nature, Joron, to like people and to be kind. Do not think I have not seen the leeway you give." He was about to interrupt but she held up a hand. "It works well for you. Every officer is different, but that is not why I speak here and now." Her stare unwavering. "Every woman and man, no matter what they think they fight for, or really fight for, needs one thing more. Hope, Joron Twiner, they need to hope. And when this gullaime flew us out of Bernshulme harbour by itself, having not been on land for months, oh, they may not have said anything. They may not have acted as if anything was different, but each one knew what I knew, that we have a creature of rare power aboard *Tide Child*, Joron. Our task is close to impossible, and they all know that. To take on eight flukeboats? That is nothing much. But bigger ships will come. I know it, you know it, the crew know it. They will have corpselights and they will have well trained crews. In that gullaime our crew see hope."

"But what if it is dead?" She stood, her clothes creaking, feathers catching the dim light.

"Then you will still come down here, still make a pretence of feeding it, and we will have to find some way to mask the smell for as long as we can." She turned and opened the door, pausing for a moment before she left. "And Joron, I meant what I said about your ways being good ones, but there are those who will mistake kindness for weakness and try to take advantage of you. Do not let them." With that she left, closing the door behind her, and he fed more dried fish to the gullaime, his bloody thumb rubbing back and forth on the rough skin of the windtalker's throat.

Later, he walked the slate, thinking on what she had said, considering it as he watched the great patch of flat sea that denoted the arakeesian before them. He knew there were those among the crew who did not jump as quickly to his orders as they should, and others, like Cwell and her followers, who openly resented him and, he was sure, meant him harm. But his way had been to breeze through it, and he thought it was working. But if Meas had decided to mention it, maybe he should look to how he worked.

Joron passed Chiciri. A big woman, she was kneeling on the deck talking to Sprackin, the former purseholder, and Destin, one of the wingwrights. He knew none of them were fond of him, and once he would have walked past them, but now he did not.

"If you have nothing do to," he said, "I believe Mevans is overseeing the restowing of the cargo hold. The shipwife was unhappy with the steering and wishes to try and get a little more speed out of *Tide Child* to ensure we can keep up with the arakeesian. You want to see the beast, I'm sure."

Chiciri stood first. The other two followed her and she pulled her shoulders back, making herself bigger, sticking her chest out.

"Very well, D'keeper," she said. "We'll just finish up here."

He heard the disrespect in her tone and wanted, more than anything, to just walk away. But he could not. To let them ignore his order and go on talking was to let go of his command.

"Now, Chiciri, if you will."

She took a step towards him. "But what if I won't?"

Then Chiciri was on the deck, knocked down by the heavy body of Solemn Muffaz hitting her. In his left hand he held a club, which he drew back to hit the prone woman. She raised a hand. Sprackin and Destin backed away, distancing themselves from their comrade.

"Now the deckkeeper," said Solemn Muffaz, "may be a man unused to the words of commoners such as you and I, Chiciri. And as such he may not have realised how disrespectful you just were." Black Orris, as if drawn by the confrontation, fluttered down to land on Solemn Muffaz's shoulder. "But I am a man of very poor upbringing, and I heard it sure as Black Orris says arse. And I am sure that, from now on, the deckkeeper will recognise when he is addressed in such a way as to make someone deserving of the cord."

Joron nodded. He managed not to glance over his shoulder

and look for Meas, who he was sure had steered this encounter as surely as she steered *Tide Child*.

"I will know it," he said, "and I will award the cord as deserved." He paused and glanced at Solemn Muffaz. Out of sight of the three before him, he held a hand by his thigh, showing four fingers. "In the morning, Chiciri," said Joron, "you will receive four strikes of the cord." Then he turned to Sprackin and Destin. "And you two will consider yourself lucky not to be joining her."

Solemn Muffaz smiled.

Black Orris opened his beak.

"Arse," said the bird.

26

To Sing a Song of Wind and Travel

The next morning the entire crew were called to the slate for the cording of Chiciri.

Solemn Muffaz brought the woman up from below and led her to the mainspine. There he tied her hands around it and bared her back. Meas read from the Bernlaw and pronounced the punishment: "Four lashes for insubordination." Her brow fierce, the eyes below cold, she let her gaze rove over the crew. "I would have it known," she said, "I think the deckkeeper overly lenient, for which Chiciri should thank him."

Joron knew she spoke to create a difference between them: a kinder side of the ship in Joron, a harsher one in her; but it still felt like she admonished him and his collar tightened around his neck. Or maybe that was because, from across the deck, standing with Coughlin's men, Cwell's beady eyes were locked on him.

"I could sort her." Whispered from behind him by Anzir.

"No," said Joron.

"It may not be a bad idea," said Dinyl, who stood by Joron.

"I will bring her round."

Dinyl shrugged, but conversation was cut short when Solemn Muffaz brought out the cord. It was not a thing a deckchild ever wished to see, a handle of polished varisk from which came two long, thin tails of braided birdleather. Along each tail were tied four knots. It could inflict terrible pain, even death, if used hard and long enough, and Joron was thankful that Solemn Muffaz only intended to deliver a lesson, not a sacrifice.

"Four strikes for the Hag, Shipwife," intoned Solemn Muffaz.

"For the Hag, four strikes, Deckmother," replied Meas.

Solemn Muffaz drew back his arm.

As he did, Joron heard Chiciri speak, her words loud enough for all to hear.

"I bet you will enjoy this, Muffaz, hitting a woman." And he saw Solemn Muffaz's arm falter, knew that Chiciri had wounded the deckmother, put him in an impossible position. For if he hit soft, all would think it was because Chiciri spoke the truth, and if he hit hard, all would think Chiciri spoke the truth.

Joron cursed inwardly, hating Solemn Muffaz for putting himself in this position.

He stepped forward.

"If I handed down this sentence, it is only right that I should carry out it," Joron said, though he felt his legs weaken at the thought. Solemn Muffaz turned, tears running down his face.

"No, D'keeper, it is the deckmother's duty. I carry it out with no joy. It is on the order of the deckkeeper and the ship-wife that I strike." With that he turned back, running the cords of the whip through one hand.

"Get on with it then, Deckmother," said Meas as Black Orris fluttered down to land on her shoulder.

Muffaz made the first strike. The cord cracked in the air and then cracked against Chiciri's back, leaving two bloody lines and making her hiss as she took in a breath, but she did not cry out. And she did not cry for the second or third or fourth, though when the last strike was made she slumped against the spine, unconscious, and had to be cut down and taken to the hagbower for her wounds to be treated.

After the cording Meas called Joron down to the great cabin, where she sat at her desk in its familiar place upon the bright white floor. From above came the sound of women and men cleaning the slate and working on the myriad tasks of a bone-ship, stowing shot, rolling hammocks and putting up the tables for breakfast.

"Joron," she said. The courser, Aelerin, stood behind Meas, whose desk was busy with charts. Behind them, through the windows of the cabin, *Tide Child*'s wake stretched out to show their passage through the grey sea. Beyond it he saw *Cruel Water*, the size of a toy, and far behind that ship, *Snarltooth*, not much more than a dot. Waves like knives cut the water, catching the sun, reflecting it back. "*Cruel Water* has relayed a message from *Snarltooth*," she said. "Ships rising on the horizon."

"Following us?"

"It appears so."

"Boneships?"

"Nothing so big, not yet. *Snarltooth* thought they may have seen something with three spines, but Shipwife Brekir relays she cannot be sure. All signs point to these being raiders, I think. A lot of flukeboats."

"Nothing that should bother us now the three ships are together."

"No," said Meas, "but come look at my chart." He took a step over. The chart showed a coast he did not know. On one side was the vast outline of Skearith's Spine. He saw a name but it was upside down and his reading was not good enough to decipher it.

"Arkannis Isle, two weeks away," said Aelerin.

"It is a problem and an opportunity," said Meas.

"How so?" Joron studied the map. The dark blue of a deep channel passed around the island and then between it and Skearith's Spine.

"As Kept Indyl Karrad said, raiders hold Arkannis. It is not big, and historically they have never been greedy."

"Greedy?"

"There are two towers, flimsy things, one on the Spine, one on Arkannis. They have gallowbows which cover the deepwater channel. The channel is one of the quickest routes northward, and the safest, as the current assists a ship's passage. The raiders use the towers to charge a toll."

"And this has been tolerated?"

"The towers are both too high up for shot to reach them from the channel. The tower on the Spine" — she touched the map with the point of the knife she held — "is practically impossible to assault. It is reached by a series of rope ladders."

"The tower on the island?" said Joron. Her knife point slid across the map.

"Again, not easy. The island is steep and heavily vegetated. As long as they do not ask too much in tolls and let fleet ships pass unmolested, it has been judged best to leave them to it."

"But you do not plan to leave them to it?"

She shook her head.

"No. The towers see a long way. They will see the arakeesian and us coming, and I cannot imagine they will let it pass. The gallowbows on the towers are huge, bigger than our great bows. They may be a real threat to the beast."

"So we must fight on land. Battle our way up this steep island," he said, and he could not keep the trepidation from his voice.

Meas nodded.

"Yes. We will take the tower on the island and use it to destroy the tower on the Spine. Its gallowbow has the range."

"You make it sound simple."

"It is."

"But if the island tower's bow can reach the spine tower, surely the reverse is true?"

Meas grinned at him. "No plan is perfect, Deckkeeper. But this plan has at least one plus."

"Which is?"

"Arkannis Isle has a windspire."

"So we assault the island while carrying an unconscious gullaime?"

"It does not weigh that much, Joron. How is the creature?"

"It does not move, does not breathe as far as I can tell. But it is not cold at least."

"All gullaime are cold," said Aelerin. "They are not like us."

"Ours is not cold."

"Maybe because it is ill," said the courser.

"No, it has never been cold."

"A cold or hot gullaime does not matter," said Meas. "What matters is getting it to the windspire and bringing those towers down, and doing it before the arakeesian comes in range." She tapped the chart. "The arakeesian is making a speed of about ten stones and does not seem to waver too much from that. The two-ribbers can make fifteen stones easily." She took a piece of parchment from a drawer in the desk and drew a long oval on the paper and behind it three crude ships. "This is us, behind the wakewyrm." She touched the oval with her bone knife. "We have about fourteen days before the arakeesian reaches Arkannis. We stay together for a week, then I will have *Cruel Water* and *Snarltooth* take up station in front of the wakewyrm." She drew two lines looping round the oval, placing them in front of it. "We will put up as many wings as *Tide Child* can bear with his damaged keel and make for Arkannis. If we take the direct route Aelerin has mapped out, we can arrive two days earlier than the sea dragon, which should be plenty of time for us to do what is needed."

"Are the two-ribbers to protect us if we fail?" said Aelerin. "I do not understand what they can do, if their weapons cannot hit the towers."

"They will protect the arakeesian — with their hulls, if need be."

"They will not last long," said Joron.

"No," said Meas, "they will not. One hit from those great bows would be enough, and the raiders have no reason to covet the jointweight of the ships if they think they can take the arakeesian itself. So they are more for show, and in case the raiders are foolish enough to send out boats."

"They do not deserve to be sacrificed," said Joron.

"No, they do not, not like this. That is why we must not fail." She glanced at Joron then turned to the courser. "Aelerin, I have already spoken to Dinyl. I will leave you and him to command *Tide Child*. Do not take him through the channel; take him around the island. In the week we have we will exercise the gallowbows and start sword drill. Coughlin and his men are . . ."

"Too dangerous to leave on board while Cwell plots," said Joron.

"Ey, they are. They will be coming to the island with me on the flukeboats. I will leave Cwell here but take some of her clique with us, so she will be too weak to cause any mischief." Aelerin nodded and their body seemed to relax a little under their robes. "And on the day we leave," said Meas, "we will pass the head of the wakewyrm." Something gleamed in her eye. "We could all die at Arkannis. Some will, and I would let them see what they fight for first, let them look it in the eye."

A shudder ran through Joron.

"Are you sure that's wise? You saw what it did to that flukeboat." He wrapped his arms around himself. "I have never seen such strength. It would make quick work of us."

Meas leaned forward over the desk, putting her head in her hands and pushing back her hair, the different-coloured strands mixing with the grey. When she took her hands away and sat back, they fell once more into the neat lines that Joron's wiry hair forever refused to follow.

"I have read much of arakeesians, and in all I have read, even when we had almost hunted the species to death, they only ever attacked ships when they or their fellows were attacked. So I think we will be safe, but even if we are not, I will still do it. I want to look it in the eye myself. I think it is worth risking death for, ey?"

And Joron did not reply, because he could not disagree. The idea of seeing the beast up close, of witnessing the flesh that clothed the bones that were so much a part of his everyday life was indeed exciting. He slid a finger inside the tight collar of his shirt, pulling it away from his skin. He was suddenly hot. The room felt stifling, the walls of bone closing in on him.

"You may go," she said, and he was glad of it. Glad of the way the air on the deck blew away the heat, the way the wind brought with it only the clean salt scent of the sea.

"Eight beakwyrms, D'keeper," said Farys with a grin as she made her way to the mainspine and her shift in the tops.

The first week passed quickly, too quickly for Joron. The weather remained kind and the Eaststorm smiled on them, driving the ships forward. Meas hosted the shipwives of *Cruel Water* and *Snarltooth* on board – Joron was shocked by the sudden improvement in the quality of the ship's food at these meetings – and told them of her belief the arakeesian would not move against them. Though no ship went too close, staying well out of the way of the creature's giant flippers: vague shapes as big as boneships beating beneath the sea, making their own currents which caused *Tide Child* to rock and shudder in a way unnatural to its hull, and made Bonemaster Coxward talk dark of pressures on the glue on the keel, which had never truly dried.

But life went on. In the mornings they worked the great bows and the smaller underdeck bows, though without shot and with old cord as Meas did not wish a stray shot to hit the keyshan. In the afternoons they did weapons practice. Coughlin, though unpleasant, knew his work, schooling them in how to fight on land. This was not the free-for-all of fighting on a ship. They learned to hold a shield wall, how to work together. And in between, the ship still needed caring for. Wings were raised and wings were furled; clothing was mended; decks were scrubbed; ropes were replaced, and the steady cycle of watches continued under the bright light of Skearith's Eye and the pale light of her Blind Eye. And though ships and boats were spotted rising on the horizon it seemed the Mother smiled on them and they were not engaged. The three black ships ate up the lengths and the hunths and the passages of the journey, and the head of the arakeesian drew slowly nearer.

Meas made Joron do extra practice with his curnow and also work with the straightsword, which, oddly, was curved, that she used until she pronounced him "passable". She tried to teach him what she said was the most useful curnow skill, the "quick unhook" – a method of removing his blade from his belt and swiping it up in one movement that would gut an opponent, though it seemed he could never quite get it right, more often tangling himself up or doing something that would have sliced open his own legs if the blade were real.

One day he had spat out, "I will never master this!" He expected angry words from Meas but she simply took the practice sword from him and held it in her hand.

"When you really need it, Deckkeeper, I am sure you will get it right." Then she gave back the practice blade. "But more practice will not hurt you."

And between his work and the extra weapons practice Joron had to find time to feed and water the gullaime. It showed no sign of life, no sign of breathing, no pulse. Nor did it excrete – for which Joron was thankful – but at the same time it did not corrupt. Part of him thought that maybe this was simply the way of gullaime – they were unnatural after all – but another saw reason for hope. He discovered a way of cradling the windtalker like a babe against his chest while he dripped water and food into its beak, and, day by day, the hot sand smell of it and the brittle feel of the bones beneath its skin became less upsetting for him, more normal.

He was not sure when he started speaking to it. He did not think it was a conscious act, but as he sat and stroked the gullaime's throat to make it swallow he began to tell it of his life. How he had been born Berncast because his mother died giving him life, and how the curse of that weakness had kept him in the fisher villages. How his father had held on to him so tightly when he was young that he felt he would always be safe. He told the gullaime how his mother was not weak, told it the stories his father had told him of her, of how his father's eyes shone when he spoke of her. He told it of the fisher boat, of his youth, of his father going without food so Joron could learn to read. All these things he told to the small, brittle body of the gullaime, and it never interrupted or replied or gave so much as a nod that it understood. But the talking helped Joron feel better, just as the passage of time and the ship through water helped the crew feel better, and as both man and crew learned to work together they felt more and more like fleet, like they were worthwhile.

It was Menday when they finally caught up with the head of the arakeesian. Meas had stopped bow drill, reckoning the teams worked well enough, though they still practised with weapons and shields. As *Tide Child* came up on the head of the sea dragon the officers stood on the rump, lesser officers on the foredeck, the deckchilder along the rail and along the spars. All gazed at the shape beneath the water.

How big was it?

Hard to tell. The size of the creature was such that Joron had no real way to measure it. Was it near the surface or way down?

What colour was it?

The blue of the water distorted everything. Beneath the surface all was shadowed, changed. It was not the world that Joron inhabited. In the same way that he could not leap into the sky, he could not dive down into the depths – until the day his sentence was carried out and he went to greet the Hag in her black abode at the bottom of the ocean.

He could only make out the vague shimmering movement of something beyond his experience. A great thick body perhaps narrowing to what he presumed must be a neck, then swelling again. Did something shine? The heat on his skin was almost unbearable, and it was not even noon. What he felt sure was the head narrowed and lengthened into a great beak-like mouth, but he could not guess at the size of it. The beak of the skull crowning *Tide Child* was not much thicker at its base than Joron's thigh, tapering to the thickness of his forearm at the end of the ram.

The wakewyrm was so much more.

"I would see it face to face if I could," said Meas quietly. "But maybe I will have to content myself with only seeing it in the deep."

"You could try ordering it to surface, Shipwife," said Mevans from his place behind her.

"I may be in control of everything on the deck, Mevans," she said, "but we look upon the high Bern of all the ocean, and I doubt she will listen to me."

Joron shared her wish. If he were to die on the island — which as each day passed he became more sure of — he would like to see an arakeesian first. Though the creature, of course, cared as much for his wishes as it did for Meas's. So he stood and stared and wished as it glided through the sea far, or near, below them.

"It rises." A voice from behind them — old, scratchy. They turned to find Garriya, as raggedy and worn as old rope.

"What are you doing on the rump?" said Meas.

"Bringing good tidings, I hope."

"Then do it from the deck," snapped Meas. "That is your place. And, besides, you cannot even see the beast from where you stand."

"A woman feels the sea, does she not, Meas Gilbryn?"

"Shipwife," snapped Meas, though her admonition was not as quick or as vicious as Joron had heard her be with others who trespassed upon her territory.

"But she does, doesn't she? Feels it. Knows what will happen before it does — a woman."

"Get off my deck," said Meas, "or I'll have you corded." The old woman nodded, backing away, but if she was worried about being whipped she showed no sign of it.

"Don't forget to feed your charge today, Joron Twiner," said Garriya.

"Deckkeeper."

"Ey, that too. Don't forget."

Rage was building within Meas, and all could feel it. Garriya trespassed, called officers by their given names and not their ranks, ignored the rules of the ship. But any eruption was forestalled by a call from the rail.

"Old Garriya has it right. The keyshan rises!" And all propriety was forgotten as everyone ran to the rails to greet a legend.

27

What Lies Beneath

It rose from far deeper than Joron had imagined, a great bone-white shape. Other, more familiar shapes moved above it. Long thin hissen flashed through the water like knives. Shoals of small galda fish frantically beat their tails to escape what must have seemed to them the suddenly approaching sea floor. Stinging ryulls, which wandered aimlessly on the currents, devouring whatever was unfortunate enough to come within reach of their arms, were pushed aside. Toothreaches pulsed forward, their long, clawed arms seeming to reach out and drag them through the water.

All these things happened and continued to happen as the arakeesian rose. And still it rose and it grew until the head, which they coursed along, roughly opposite, was almost as long as *Tide Child* and almost as wide.

"Hag's breath," said Dinyl, "it will smash us to shards. We should steer away."

Somewhere in the back of his mind Joron thought, *That should be my fear*, but he was not scared.

"No," said Meas. "We watch."

And still it rose, until Joron could look back along the beast's body and make out details: the bony plates along its back, rounded and covered with sharp barnacles like the ones that grew on the hulls of ships; its skin, bone-white apart from the black lines that ran from eight glowing points on the head, swelling and thickening until they disappeared behind the ship in long stripes down the body of the creature.

And still it rose.

And it rose.

And it rose.

And the ocean split above it, water rolling off it like layers of dead skin to reveal something new and beautiful and amazing. The heat of the creature burning Joron's face, and it felt as if his skin would be flayed off, revealing the white of his skull below.

But he did not draw back

And neither did any other.

As the head fully surfaced Joron realised that what he had seen as glowing spots on the keyshan's head were eyes. Two were huge, shaped like teardrops, with two smaller ones behind them. Another two small eyes above the beak and two right on top of the head. All the keyshan's small eyes were round, though to call them small was an injustice; they were as big and unblinking as plates.

A huge teardrop-shaped eye seemed to consider them as ship and arakeesian cut through the water together. Then a wave of colour flowed down the creature, white to dark purple to pink to white again. This was answered by a chorus of "Ohs" from the crew of *Tide Child*. Then the arakeesian opened its beak, the length of it filled with teeth as long as Joron's arm, and called, though for what it called Joron did not know. Its mate? A warning? A greeting? The noise was almost unbearable, so deep it shook the bones of the ship. Twisting through the sound were mid and high tones. It was like every instrument and song Joron had ever heard in his life played without thought to tune or timing.

And yet, while everyone on board covered their ears, Joron did not. He heard something in that noise. Heard some sense in it that was beyond his understanding. He felt a terrible melancholy. Then the creature's head rose clear of the water on a long, thin neck, sheets of water splashing down into the sea, Its head bent forward, on the back of its skull was a pair of huge, swept-back, many-branching horns. The arakeesian dipped its beak back into the sea, sending up waves of water, and made its call again. The sea vibrated, the ship as well, but when the call was filtered through the water there was a strange and beautiful music to the sound.

"It is loud," said Mevans, "I'll give it that."

"It is beautiful," said Joron.

"Ey, it is," said Dinyl from his place by him on the rail, and as he turned their hands touched.

Another shiver of colour ran down the creature, and Joron felt as if the ship and the arakeesian flew along the water in a bubble. There was an unnatural quiet between each hooting, singing call from the wakewyrm, a stillness, and though *Tide Child* ripped through the water it did not seem to disturb it; the rigging did not rattle or clink, the wings did not flap and clatter, the water did not hiss and gurgle along the hull. They simply existed in the same time and place as the arakeesian.

"We hunted these," said Joron more to himself than anything. "How could we do that? Why would we do that?"

"We needed them," said Dinyl. Joron moved his hand so they no longer touched.

The arakeesian shook its head, a movement that took place in slow motion, spraying water over the decks of *Tide Child*, and the movement continued all the way down its huge body, a complex wave of rainbow colours darting across its skin. From the back of its neck and down the keyshan's body huge flaps of bright red skin rose up on spines, audibly cracking into place.

"It has wings." Dinyl laughed and tapped Joron on the hand. "Look at it! They catch the wind." He leaned over the rail. "And it has folded its flippers against its body."

The wind around them strengthened – not markedly, not as

it did when it responded to the gullaime, but in a way that was not natural. The waves of a choppy, grey, cold sea now slapped against *Tide Child*'s hull, but around the keyshan it was calm.

"It controls the weather," said Meas quietly. "It flies across the sea just like we do."

The wakewyrm sounded again, breaking the spell.

Tide Child awoke, and all the noise and action normal on a boneship returned. "Back to work," shouted Meas "You would think you had never seen a keyshan before." There was laughter at that, the mood aboard bright now. "I'll have no slatelayers on my ship." She took her place by the spine. "To work with you."

"I must go water and feed the gullaime," said Joron.

"Do that," said Meas. "Then return here. I will hold station by the arakeesian for eight turns of the glass, then we make for Arkannis Isle."

Joron made his way down to the underdeck, dipping his head to avoid the overbones of the ship as he made his way to the gullaime's quarters. Outside the door he stopped. Lain by the door he found an assortment of oddments and he stooped to gather them. This had become normal. Though the crew never spoke of the gullaime, never asked how it was or acknowledged their interest in it, they knew it was special, and this was how they showed their regard – with gifts of carved bones, painted stones, strange shells and small objects. Most were of value only to those who had owned them, but they gave them freely and in doing so they made a quiet prayer to the Sea Hag for the windtalker's recovery.

Joron went inside. Before he fed the creature he added the presents to the growing collection in one corner of the cabin. Then, without quite knowing why, he opened the bowpeek, allowing air into the cabin, dropping the temperature but letting him see the giant head of the arakeesian. One glowing eye seemed to stare straight into the cabin, the heat coming off it beating against his face, making him look away.

Had the gullaime moved?

Joron was sure that when he came in it had been curled

into a ball, but now its head was pointing at the open hatch. He stared at it, waiting, expecting it to move again, for the beak to open and for it to rasp out his name.

Jo-ron Twi-ner.

But it did not. Nevertheless, when he sat to feed and water the windtalker he changed his position so that the gullaime remained looking out of the hatch while he poured water into its beak and forced dried fish down its gullet. All the time he waited for some subtle hint the creature lived. None came. Once he had fed the gullaime, he put it back into the nest of rags it had constructed before becoming windsick, arranging it so its head still pointed at the hatch where the huge eye of the arakeesian stared in. Then he set to his next task, weaving from oddments of rope he had scavenged around the ship a sort of basket he could wear on his back to carry the gullaime when they landed on Arkannis Isle.

There was a certain pleasure to this task. It was similar to weaving the nets he and his father had made and used when he was young. He had detested the job then, but now the subtle dance of the needle, down and round and up and under, let him drift away. *Up and around, Joron. The skeer chases the kively around the spine. Do it with love, and do it with care, for it is our livelihood.* For a moment he was no longer the deckkeeper of a ship of war, no longer a man condemned to death, no longer under threat. He did not think of the spikes and hooks that covered *Tide Child*'s hull, he did not think of curnows cutting into flesh and splashing out waves of red blood. He did not think of the fear within him when he fought and the other, deeper fear that others would recognise him as a coward. He did not shake and imagine the moment when a blade found his flesh and he added his own blood to the endless current that flowed between the Hundred Isles and the Gaunt Islands. He simply was. He simply existed in the moment and the heavy needle dragged the rope around and about as it created, from oddments and cast offs, the basket he saw in his mind. Through this, he was just a boy again, and he could imagine he might go up on deck and find his father at the oar, guiding him through life.

But then he was back in the cabin of a creature that he felt he could never understand, being stared at by something so immense he could barely comprehend it, on his way to kill or be killed on the orders of a man he hated. He glanced at the gullaime. The mask that should cover its blind eyes had slipped. Only a little, on the side nearest to him, exposing the roundel of grey feathers about the eye and the pink eyelid underneath with its long and thick lashes. Joron put down his rope basket and went over. It seemed wrong to leave the beast's eye uncovered when he knew from experience how fussy the creature was about having its mask interfered with. He had never before wondered why this was so. Maybe they regarded their empty eyes as sacred, or maybe as something shameful? Maybe they simply did not want others to see their disfigurement. He had seen blind people before but never wondered about the gullaime. Did they really put out their eyes at birth? Now he was close up it did not look like it; the eyelids did not appear to cover hollows. So was some other method used? Did he even want to know what was done to them?

He was not sure he did. He shuddered, and a thought invaded his mind, an old, almost forgotten memory.

An island ridge where the varisk and the gion had died back and left bare rock. A grey sky swirling with the Northstorm's anger. Skearith's Eye a weak silver disc. In silhouette on the ridge, a woman, stick in hand, leading a line of gullaime from the lamyards, their heads bowed, robes flapping in the wind as they shuffled along, the clinking of the chain that bound them showing as a black, bellying line between them, filling the air like a warning bell.

"Look away, son." His father's hand, rough and warm on his neck, turning his eyes away from the bound windtalkers, back to the sea, where the waves rose and fell and crashed against the harbour walls, keeping the ships prisoner in the harbour as surely as those gullaime were held by the rope.

Joron blinked. Shook his head to rid himself of the intensity of the memory. Was it wrong, this thing they did? The gullaime were a gift from the godbird to the Mother. They were part of life, their fate as much ordained as that of the Berncast.

But was it wrong?

What if it was wrong?

He reached out to straighten the mask.

The gullaime's eye flicked open, and Joron almost jumped backwards. Beneath its lid the eye was as white and hot as that of the arakeesian that cut through the water alongside *Tide Child*. Then, like a spiral on a spinning top, the pupil of the gullaime's eye appeared from its internal fire.

"You live!" said Joron, but his words were barely spoken. His heart beat within his breast like a call to action. Just as he was about to turn, to run to the deck and tell Meas that the gullaime had recovered, its beak fell open and its spike-like tongue lolled from its mouth.

"Shhhh."

Did it speak? Joron knelt nearer to it.

"Shh? Did you say ssh?" Did it nod? Did its head move the tiniest, smallest amount?

He could not be sure.

He sat back, stared at it.

He would say nothing.

He moved the gullaime a little, trying to make it as comfortable as possible. The pupil of the open eye spiralled shut and the lid closed, hiding its glow. Joron pulled the gaudily painted mask back into position. The nearer he got to the creature the more questions he felt he needed to ask.

"Deckkeeper!" The shout came from above. He left the cabin, trying to forget the gullaime and trying not to think about what might await him when they landed on Arkannis Isle.

28

An Island Excursion

The size of the Spine mountains made Arkannis look insignificant; they rose beyond seeing, steep sides vanishing into the clouds. Here and there flashes of bright colour marked where plants clung precariously to the rock. Birds, in multitude, swooped and darted, making homes on meagre ledges and in shallow holes and streaking the black rock with their guano. Even from so far away Joron could hear their calls over the ever-present hiss and jingle of *Tide Child* as the boneship made his way through the water.

Meas stood by him, staring though her nearglass.

"The island blocks my view of both its tower and the tower on the Spine," she said, sounding as if the island had planned this just to spite her.

The nearer they came to Arkannis the more it looked unpleasant to Joron. At the sea's edge a bright blue plant grew in abundance, a riot of waving branches. Above this were varisk vines, lurid pink and twisting up and up around the bruise-purple gion to nearly the height of *Tide Child*'s topspines. Higher up the jagged island earth had fallen away to expose the white rock beneath. The island looked like an ulcer: the blue of a bruise, angry purple and red flesh and dead white flesh within.

"Sickly, is it not?" said Meas.

"Ey, Shipwife."

"Wait till you get on it. Arkannis is said to stink like a rotten egg. A lot of the Spine islands do. And they have hot springs that will boil a woman or man alive if they fall in."

"It sounds delightful."

"I am sure it is." She closed the nearglass. "Now, look at the island. See how it rises and has two flat areas towards the top. You can just make out the higher one through the gion; the lower is behind it, over the ridge. That is where the tower is."

"Yes, Shipwife."

"The windspire is on the higher plain. You will take ten crew with you and get the gullaime to the windspire. Hopefully you will not be noticed. I will take twenty to assault the tower; that should be enough to deal with raiders. When you have delivered the gullaime to the windspire, bring your women and men to help me mop up."

"What if they find the gullaime, alone and defenceless?"

Meas extended the nearglass again, putting it back up to her eye.

"We shall have to hope they do not."

"Shipwife." She turned. Coxward stood on the deck, naked apart from his loincloth, dirty bandages and toolbelt, his meaty body nearly as pink as fresh varisk leaves. A diadem of sweat crowned his forehead and he looked grim, like a man with a growth that had become too large for him to ignore, presenting himself to the hagshand for its removal. Meas turned, collapsed her nearglass once more and placed it within her coat.

"I can help, Bonemaster?"

"I would speak to you in your cabin, Shipwife." He pulled his belly up with both hands, the way someone would ruffle up a shirt at the waist to make themselves look bigger.

"Very well," said Meas. "Joron, the rump is yours. Have the flukeboats made ready to take us to the island. You, I and

Coughlin will lead the assault; Dinyl will take *Tide Child* around the island to distract those ashore while we land."

With Meas gone Joron busied himself with getting the flukeboats ready, filling them with wyrmpikes, bows, arrows, curnows and shields. To the weapons he added a supply of water.

"D'keeper." He turned to find Farys before him, her scarred face pulled in to strange shapes by a smile. "Shipwife wants you, and she asks you bring the stonebound's leader."

"Coughlin?"

"Ey, that's the one – the big fellow. Wants you both in her cabin."

"Thank you, Farys."

Coughlin stood as he approached, bending his arms at the elbow, making himself bigger and flexing the muscles of his biceps and chest as if to show how much stronger he was than Joron.

"The shipwife wants us."

"For what?"

"Well" – Joron glanced towards where the island of pink and blue and white grew moment by moment – "as we are about to attack that island, I imagine it will be to do with that. It would not do to have you and your men running about without knowing your goal, ey?"

"No." Coughlin narrowed his eyes. "No, it would not. I will come."

Joron nodded to him. From the corner of his eye he caught Cwell watching as she braided together two ropes.

"Mind your head on the overbones," said Joron. "You are a tall man and not well fitted out for a ship." His words brought a chuckle from the deckchilder nearby, and Coughlin licked his lips as if he tasted the air to find out whether Joron mocked him or not. There was tension, but only for a moment, then Coughlin nodded.

"Lead on then. I would know what I take my men into on the land, for I know it is not your element."

Joron let that small jibe go and led Coughlin down into the gloomy underdeck, hoping the man would crack his head on an overbone despite his warning, but like many warriors he had a keen awareness of the world around him. Joron suspected, that, even without the wanelights, he would have found his way without injury. Something Joron was not sure was true of himself.

In Meas's cabin they once more entered a world of light. The desk sat in its ruts, Meas behind it and the bonemaster before it. On the desk was a hard round shiny brown thing about the size of a child's fist. Both Meas and the bonemaster stared at it.

"You wanted me?" said Coughlin abruptly.

"Ey, I did."

"To talk battle?"

"No," said Meas, her voice quiet, "not yet." Coughlin's wide brow wrinkled questioningly. "I will ask you a question, Coughlin. And I ask you to give me a truthful answer. I will hold nothing against you." He opened his mouth to speak but Meas held up her hand. "Wait. Just know, that before you say a word to me, I am shipwife. I know all that goes on within my ship."

"You spy on those you should trust," he said.

"Or those who I trust spy on those I cannot. It matters not. But I will ask you my question, so listen." She let a brief silence settle before carrying on. "Cwell, as I well know, is Cahanny's relation – niece, I believe." Coughlin nodded. "Has she asked you to get her off the ship?" Joron saw Coughlin's eye's widen, only momentarily, but enough to give him away. "I know she has," said Meas. "But I do not know where or when."

Coughlin glared at her, and Joron wondered if he would go for the eating knife at his belt, but then he shrugged.

"She did not ask. Cahanny told me I was to get her off the ship at the earliest chance."

"And now we have seen an arakeesian, maybe she is not so

eager to leave. Maybe there is a betrayal planned at Arkannis?" said Meas.

"She liked that idea but was more interested in leaving the ship. You should let her if it is what Cahanny wants," said Coughlin. He did not look worried or scared.

Joron wondered at how free he was with such information, and at the smile that crossed Meas's face.

"Do you know what that is, Coughlin?" said Meas, and prodded the brown thing on the desk with the tip of her knife. It spun a little and Joron recognised it. It was a set of three-lobed serrated jaws. They were shut now and no longer attached to a body, and Joron thanked the Hag for that.

"No doubt," said Coughlin, "it is some hagfilth from the depths that kills as soon as looks at you."

"Well," said Meas, and she sat back in her chair. "You are half right – the second half. It is not from the depths though. Deckkeeper, will you tell Coughlin what this is?" She tapped the object with her knife again.

"It is the mouth of a borebone," Joron said.

"So? Some ship thing," said Coughlin. "I do not see what this has to do with Cwell or me."

"It is a small borebone, that one," said Meas. "These jaws can grow as big your head, even yours, Coughlin. They live in ill-kept ships, eat through the bones of the hull, or the crew, if they come upon them unawares. They like the dark, see. Live in the bilges so they are seldom seen until it is too late, and suddenly your ship is sinking underneath you and the longthresh are gathering in the water to feast."

"So," said Coughlin, still plainly confused. "This is an old ship and ill cared for, a ship of the dead. But thank you for telling me it is unsafe. Cahanny wanted me to stay with the cargo once Cwell was off, but maybe we shall take the cargo and stay on the island." He smiled at Meas and, to Joron's surprise, she smiled back.

"Bonemaster," she said, "would you expect to find borebones on *Tide Child*?"

Coxward shook his head, the flesh of his jowls wobbling.

"No, Shipwife. I had him out the water, bilges emptied, whole thing checked well because I knew he would have to carry me back safe as well as your crew. There were no borebones aboard before we set sail."

"You must have suspected something was wrong if you were checking for them," said Coughlin.

"I was not expecting borebones," said Coxward, "but a good bonemaster checks the bilges, and because I know *Tide Child's* keel is not the best I have been diligent in those checks. One of my girls found this thing yesterday." He pointed at the jaws. "She was lucky − only lost a couple of toes to it before we killed it − but where there is one this size there will be more."

"So?" said Coughlin. Joron could feel his discomfort. Clearly, Meas had brought him here for a reason, and it was tied to the borebone jaws before them, and to Cwell, but Coughlin could not make the link any more than Joron could. "The fat man missed something when he went over your ship."

"I missed nothing," said Coxward, and there was a hardness in his voice that made Coughlin look again at the man, as if reassessing him.

"Tell me, Coughlin," said Meas. "What is your relationship with Cahanny like?"

Coughlin stared at her, a muscle twitching underneath his eye.

"We are both strong-willed men," he said.

"Would he remove you if he felt threatened?"

Coughlin shook his head, but Joron could see doubt on the man's face. Trying to understand what Meas was steering towards. Some doubt there, and worry.

"I have been with him a long time," he said. "Many of his men are as loyal to me as they are to him."

"So to move against you would split his organisation, ey?"

"Aye," said Coughlin. "So he would never do it."

"And he trusts you to smuggle arakeesian bone for him."

"What I do is of no—"

"I only ask because, if you do, that is the only bone on this ship that has not been checked for borebone eggs. And you are ordered to make sure Cahanny's niece is off the ship at the earliest opportunity. Off on dry land. Safe. Do you see the course I steer, Coughlin?"

"I . . ."

"Maybe your master could not move directly against you, but he would benefit, I imagine, if you vanished at sea."

"He . . ." Coughlin looked around the cabin – at the walls, the white floor, the heavy desk. Finally his eyes rested on the borebone jaws. "He would not."

"How many of those with you, Coughlin," asked Meas, "are loyal to you? And how many to Cahanny?"

"I only brought men loyal to me. Some of Cahanny's finest they are, and . . ." As his mouth formed the last words his voice died away. Then he roared, "Hag-twisted bastard! He has fit me up. I will kill him for this if it is true. And his Hag-cursed niece."

"We do not know it is true yet," said Meas.

"You would know these eggs if you saw them?"

"Oh ey," said Coxward.

"Come then, we shall open the boxes."

Coughlin led them through the ship and down into the hold where two of his men stood guard on the boxes.

"Away," barked Coughlin. "We let the shipwife see our cargo."

"But Cahanny said—"

"Hag take Cahanny! Open the box."

"Wait!" said Coxward. He vanished and returned with four bonehammers, flat on one side and viciously hooked on the other. "Best to be ready," he said, handing them out. "Just in case."

One of the men took a key from his belt, undid the lock on the box and then opened it, taking a step back in horror, not only at the smell – something damp and foetid and rotten – but at what he saw within. Coughlin did not move, his eyes widened as he stared at the contents of the box. Joron stepped forward. The inside of the top box was alive with borebones, small ones the size of his finger right up to ones the size of an arm, three-lobed jaws working as often on each other as the mess of brown and rotten bone that covered the bottom of the box. The slimy bodies were the same brown as the rotten bone, ribbed all the way along as they squirmed over each other in the sea of slime that oozed from pores along their length.

"Kill them," said Coxward and started to smash the creatures with the flat of his hammer. Coughlin did the same, and with each blow he spat, "Hag-bent! Berncast son!" punctuating the deaths of the creatures with his voice.

Like this they worked through the rest of Coughlin's boxes, and it did not escape Joron's notice that the box of hiylbolts had been hidden away. The last box was empty, the borebones having eaten through its bottom.

"He has killed me," said Coughlin. "The Hag-cursed man has killed me. And the rest of us. Well, I shall finish his niece off – I'll have that satisfaction at least." He turned away.

"No," said Meas. "We know the borebones are here now, so Coxward can deal with them. And Cwell may have her uses." Joron could not but feel a little disappointed that Meas intended to let Cwell live. "For now, Coughlin, enjoy her confusion when you refuse to speak to her, and her way off the ship is suddenly blocked."

"Ey," said Coxward. "While you help Meas take the island, I will put double teams on the pumps. Cwell will get more than her turn and it is fierce and hard work. By the time you get back we should have emptied the bilges and found any big ones. Then we can sweep for them each day. Once you have the island, find me lime rock and bring it aboard. We shall lime the bilges, and that will kill the rest of them and any eggs."

"I shall murder Cahanny for this," said Coughlin, "and I shall do it slowly."

"Well," said Meas, "first we must take an island and finish our mission."

"I can wait," said Coughlin. "Don't you worry about it. You have done me a service, Meas Gilbryn, and I do not forget such things." He paused, then added, "Shipwife." With that he beckoned to his men and returned to the deck, no doubt to tell the rest how they had been betrayed.

"I truly did not know borebones were such a danger to a ship," said Joron. "My father never feared them."

"Well," said Coxward, "the shipwife and I may have exaggerated the danger a little once we worked out how the beasts must have come aboard."

"So did Cahanny want him dead?"

Meas shrugged.

"Maybe. Or maybe he bought bad bones," she said. "Either serves my purpose."

"If he confronts Cahanny over this, or asks Cwell," said Joron, "he will know you lied to him about the danger."

Meas shrugged and gave him a small smile.

"I do not imagine Coughlin is the type to ask questions, Joron. I think he is a man of action."

"Why did you stop him killing Cwell?"

"Because then I would have had to kill him. I cannot have murder aboard. And besides, Cwell is clearly of value to Mulvan Cahanny. That may be of use to me at some point." With that she turned and headed back up the ladder to the underdeck, followed by Coxward, who could barely hold in his laughter.

On deck night had fallen and a wind had sprung up, stealing away the stink of the cargo hold from around Joron and replacing it with the salt tang of the sea. Behind *Tide Child* his two flukeboats followed obediently on their ropes, the larger one with its single wing furled and tied tightly to its spar on the spine. The smaller had its oars set out along the seats for the women and men who would crew it. Both boats bristled with weapons.

Gathered on the deck of *Tide Child* were the thirty Meas

had chosen for the mission: twenty crew plus ten of Coughlin's men. Coughlin stood at the head of his group, his face still dark with fury, and no doubt in his mind he turned over the betrayal he believed Cahanny had perpetrated on him. He was no longer bare-chested, but wore a jerkin of toughened birdleather sewn with metal strips, more to show wealth than for protection. Those with him were dressed similarly, while the deckchilder wore only their thin fishskin or woven and softened varisk, hardy and good for keeping out the cold, but no use for stopping a weapon. To Joron they looked like different beasts, the men of the rock dressed for land, where there was no fear of heavy clothing dragging you down to the Hag, the women and men of the sea more scared of the embrace of water than the thrust of the blade.

The flukeboats were brought up, Coughlin and his men to go in the larger one together with Meas and ten crew, the rest to go in the rowed boat. Joron scurried down to the underdeck, where he placed the inert body of the gullaime in the harness he had made and then struggled into it. Thankfully, when it was on he found it did not hinder his movements, and the weight of the gullaime was so slight he barely noticed it. When he returned to the deck Coughlin's men were still gingerly finding their way down the side of *Tide Child* in the dark and Meas paced impatiently up and down the deck. Joron understood why Coughlin's men should be so careful; the ship sides were a mass of spikes and hooks, and worse, one slip would put them in the water, where they would be lost to the depths or ground between the hulls of the ship and the boat.

His father's hand reaching from the water.

Joron's hands clenched so tightly he felt his nails bite into his palms.

"Good luck, Deckkeeper." He turned to find Dinyl, small, earnest Dinyl, holding out his hand.

He took it.

"Thank you, Deckholder. I may need it."

"Do your duty, and come back, Joron," he said with a smile.

"That is what we must do." He touched the black band around his arm. "It is what we all must do." He turned away, but not before Joron saw the pain on his face. *Poor Dinyl*. Joron had never really given much thought to him. He had been a man with a career in the fleet and been forced to give it up for Indyl Karrad. They had all lost much to ride *Tide Child*'s decks but maybe Dinyl had lost the most, and the most unfairly.

What if Dinyl did not return for them? Just ran with the ship? There were enough malcontents, and could Joron really blame the man?

"Deckkeeper!" He turned at Meas's bark, finding her and her boat ready to leave and his crew standing about waiting for him. "Now is not the time to stare at the sky and study Skearith's Bones! Get in the boat."

"Ey, Shipwife," he said and climbed over the rail.

When Joron's turn came to board the flukeboat he felt Anzir's steady hand at his elbow, guiding him down and to his seat in the darkness among the deckchilder: Farys, Old Briaret, Karring the swimmer, and others he could not quite make out in the darkness.

"You mind yourself, D'keeper," said Anzir. And this was echoed by the rest of the crew as they helped him along the boat to his place at the rump, kindly hands steadying, offering support.

Although a brisk, cool wind blew across the water, within the boat it was hot, a tense heat boiling off the bodies around him from the hag-knowledge, the knowing that some who sat upon the rough benches and took up the oars would never come back; their corpses would remain on Arkannis Isle for ever and their spirits would go to the Sea Hag. But this was their duty, this was where their shipwife took them.

They talked softly as they rowed, not complaining or worrying. But of the magic they felt at seeing the arakeesian, of how Meas was wise and would only lead them to where they must go. Among these criminals and cast-offs there was a powerful feeling that they were in the right. And these women and men were not just from Meas's old ship either; Joron had a mixed bunch around him. When they did not speak of Meas or the arakeesian they talked of the gullaime, which lay inert against Joron's back. They talked of it with pride too, of how it had helped them fight. And, well, if they were asked to help it shake off the windsickness, that was the least they could do, and if their deckkeeper needed help they would do what they must. As they talked, Joron felt his body relax and imagined how his father would have felt had he been here, to see Joron at the head of these woman and men, to see his son leading these strong, loyal deckchilder.

And he knew that the warmth he felt on the boat came from within, and not from tension, not at all.

"Do our duty indeed," he said to himself, echoing Dinyl's words.

"D'keeper?" said Farys.

"'Tis nothing." He stood. "Pull hard on those oars, my girls and boys." He whispered into the night. "Row us to the island. Meas has a wing on her boat, but let us see if we can beat her there anyway."

From behind they heard the rustle of cloth as *Tide Child* unfurled his wings and then the crack of wind filling them as the boneship began to move away. Dinyl had lit the lights on the rump and, with luck, any watcher would think the ship was leaving.

Before them Joron could just could make out the dull shape of the first flukeboat, its wing still furled and its presence more clearly marked by the rhythmic splashing of oars into water. Without the bulk of *Tide Child* to shelter them, the cold onshore breeze bit deeper, and Joron wrapped his fishskin coat more closely about his body.

The oars beat the water and the two boats moved towards the shadow of the island. The nearer they came the more they heard the songs of the land – no doubt comforting to Coughlin's men of the rock on Meas's boat, but to Joron's ears the rush of water on sand and rock was a dangerous sound, one that conjured up thoughts of beaching, of smashed hulls and bodies thrown from the deck to drown or be ripped up by the long-thresh. Nor were the calls of the landbirds in the night welcoming to his crew: they sounded like the screams of the unworthy as the Hag tossed them into her bonefire deep beneath the sea. The chatter died away and the rowers put their backs into their work. Joron saw the whites of wide, fearful eyes among them. "I would suggest we sing," he said quietly, "but I fear Meas would have my guts for it when we landed." A few teeth in the darkness – smiles. "So let us row hard, and when we land we'll rest in the forest edge until Skearith looks down upon us. Then we will bring the gullaime to the windspire and take a tower for the wakewyrm. How many can ever say they saved a life as a great as a keyshan's, ey?" More teeth in the night. "So we will be remembered for ever. Now let us row, and if you wish to hum a shanty to yourselves, then I'll not hold it against you. Just do it quietly so I keep my skin." So they rowed, the flukeboat accompanied by the sound of eleven women and men humming quietly enough not to be heard, but loud enough to raise their spirits on the night before they went to fight and die.

Shortly they heard the hiss of the first boat grounding on shingle, and Joron leaned on his steering oar, bringing his boat in next to the larger one and feeling pride within at the fleet way his crew raised their oars in unison as they came in. The moment the boat stopped, his deckchilder were over the side, splashing into the water and dragging the boat up the beach towards cover at the edge of the gion jungle. He followed them, experiencing the odd feeling of the land moving beneath his feet that always came upon him when he went from sea to land.

"Hag's tits!" A pained exclamation from further up the beach, though even that was relatively quiet.

"Quiet! What is that noise?" Meas's voice.

"Stingplates, all over the beach, Shipwife." The whispered reply.

"Are you poisoned?" Meas again.

"Nay, Shipwife. Just a single sting."

"Careful down the beach." Meas whispered.

Those pulling Joron's boat up the shingle slowed.

"Look to your feet," he said. Looking down he saw, as his eyes adjusted to the meagre light of Skearith's Blind Eye, that his foot was by a stingplate. The circular, gelid body was full of air that, when stepped on, would be pushed out into its ten stinging arms, sending them up and out to inject venom into the leg of whatever stood on it. These were only the flowers of the stingplate, the plant lived beneath the beach. A full sting was enough to kill an adult human, they may stagger on a little before collapsing, but not far. Then the stingplate would send tendrils up through the sand or shingle to digest the flesh. Fortunately, a single sting would not kill, though it was still painful. "Two of you go ahead with wyrm-pikes," said Joron. "Puncture any plates between us and the jungle edge."

"Ey, D'keeper," came the quiet reply, and they made their way more carefully up the beach, dragging the boat with them.

At the forest's edge Meas and her group already had the mast of their boat down and were hiding the hull under a mass of dead foliage.

"Do we attack tonight?" said Joron to Meas. She stared into the forest, and as if in challenge a chorus of calls and songs and growls came back.

"No," she said. "The gion forest this far south is no place to be at night. Howlers, loppers, fellscram and tunir all haunt it."

"And they sleep in the day?"

"No, but we have more chance of seeing them at least." In the darkness he could not tell whether she joked or not.

"What of the gullaime? It needs the windspire."

"If it has survived this long, Twiner, I am sure it will make it through one more night." Meas pointed towards where the crews were covering the boats. "Leave it with them. I will have the crews get what sleep they can. You and I will walk further round the headland, see if we can get a better look at the tower."

"What about the tide?"

"There is no tide down here. I do not know why, but it is one worry less for us. Just the wildlife and stingplates to look out for."

"A pleasant evening walk then."

"Ey," said Meas, "but one on which we will take Anzir and Narza just in case."

They set off along the beach, leaving instructions to those behind to set no fires but get what rest they could. Anzir and Narza walked in front of Meas and Joron, occasionally stabbing at the ground to puncture stingplates.

"Should we not walk at the edge of the forest, Shipwife?" said Joron.

"Why?"

"So we are not seen."

"Possibly, though if those on the tower are at all alert they will have seen us come in, and if they are not then I do not think they will be watching this beach too closely. And it is best to keep away from the forest this late too, even with Narza and Anzir to guard us."

"Is it so dangerous?"

"Yes," she said. "It is the tunir that worry me most."

"I have never heard or seen——"

Meas touched his arm, pointed down the beach and in a loud whisper said. "Narza, Anzir, stay still." Joron peered into the night.

The beach stretched away, grey against the black of the sea and the ever-shifting line where waves washed against the shore. The forest of gion, so bright and colourful in the day, was a drab monochrome. Joron found himself thinking how the beach was a strange place, neither land nor sea, an in between where it was easy to believe the legions of the Hag may emerge from the water to do her dark bidding. Above the island, partly obscured by the jagged soaring black peaks of Skearith's Spine, Skearith's Bones shone, smears of colour across the night sky, as lonely and cold as they were beautiful.

Then he saw why they had stopped, and a fear unlike any other, a deep primal fear, settled below his stomach. He did not know what he looked at, only that it was wrong and that no other creature he had seen – on sea or land – had made him feel this way. It was as if a piece of the night had detached itself from the sky and landed on the beach. What it did there Joron could not make out, nor could he tell how far it was from them or quite how big it was. It moved, only ever so slightly, but in a way he found utterly disquieting.

"What is it?"

"That, Joron, is a tunir. For years none were seen, but they have returned, and quite recently by all accounts. I have tangled with them before. It is best we stay quiet and hope it moves on."

Narza was drawing back the arm which held her wyrmpike as if readying to throw. "Narza!" Meas's voice, though quiet, was imperative. Narza froze. "I will need your skills on the morran, so do not waste your life on something that will likely kill us all if we attract it. And if it comes this way you will need that wyrmpike." Narza's arm slowly fell, though she kept the pike couched, pointing forward.

The tunir lifted itself from the beach, its lumpy body elongating, and from the mass of wet looking black fur stretched out three legs. Joron could make out no eyes or ears or mouth, and the way the legs moved was wrong, like the tunir had no bones or joints. The creature moved away up the beach, its legs rising and falling with an unnatural speed and rhythm that made the gorge rise in Joron's throat.

"I have never seen the like," he whispered.

"Now you know why we stay out of the forest at night."

"And right glad of that I am, Shipwife."

They continued along the beach without further incident, avoiding or spearing stingplates, and when they saw, or smelled, the corpses of beasts poisoned by the flowers they gave them a wide berth, reckoning they would not want to meet whatever fed on them at this hour.

Further on, a small river ran out of the jungle to spread its watery fingers over the shingle, and the air became full of tiny flies with painful — and unavoidable — bites. When Joron complained about them Meas told him to be thankful; the flies probably kept away the tunir.

At the end of the beach Meas raised her nearglass to scan the headland above them, adjusting the focus with deft fingers. Eventually she swore, passed Joron the glass and pointed towards the dark mass of Skearith's Spine.

"You'll find our island's tower on this line," she said. "Look for the glow of the fires against it and tell me what you see."

He lifted the nearglass to his eye. The world jumped towards him. At first he saw nothing but blurred darkness. Then he found himself staring into Skearith's Blind Eye and almost lost himself in its milky beauty, the way the Eye's scars created shapes, the illusion of valleys and mountains far above in the sky. He brought the field of view down, finding land and moving along it until he saw the subtle orange glow of fire. It took him time to make out what he saw, but eventually his mind put it together: a squat, square tower of mud bricks, at least three storeys marked by faintly glowing windows. Shadows moved against the walls, like figures of giants, as the women and men guarding the tower passed in front of the fires around it.

"Did you not say it was a flimsy tower, Shipwife?" he said, bringing down the nearglass and handing it back.

"It was," she said, "but it is three years since I have been this way and it seems Arkannis Isle's raiders have been busy. It will be harder to assault than I thought. When we return to the boats we will need to dismast the larger flukeboat; we'll need the rope from the rigging. And I think we will need all the women and men we have to take that place." She stared out to sea. "It is a pity we cannot contact Tide Child and bring ashore some bows. A couple of the underdeck bows would put enough holes in those walls to get us in." She placed the nearglass in her coat. "But we shall have to make do with what the Hag has given us."

"We should ask Coughlin," said Joron. "He may be a gangster but I watched him drill the crew. He has been seaguard at some point, I am sure of it."

"Ey. He may have an idea of how best to proceed."

"Or he may think it too difficult and refuse to help."

Meas shook her head. "Not now – while he thinks he has a score to settle with Cahanny and I remain his best way of doing that. Besides . . ." She let the word die away.

"Besides?"

"Have you seen him since he knew he would be leading his men to fight on land?"

"I have seen he wears armour."

"I do not talk of how he looks, Joron; I talk of how he is. I think he wants to fight. I think something in him wants to prove himself to me."

"Let us hope he does not want to stick a knife in your back."

Meas laughed.

"Narza," she said, "what happens to those who try and stick a knife in my back?"

For the first time since Joron had met her Narza raised her head so her face was not hidden by the curtain of dark hair. Her eyes were almost completely black.

"Those who try to betray the shipwife die," she said simply.

And as Joron met her gaze, he did not doubt for one second that what she said was true.

It's to the Northstorm we've got to go,
Chase keyshans through the ice and snow.

Half the crew to Hag have flown —
Go down, you vein flowers, go down.
And it's mighty draughty around Northstorm —
Go down, you vein flowers, go down.
Oh, make all my cuts and misery known —
Go down, you vein flowers, go down.

My Berncast mother she wrote to me,
My darling girl come home from sea.

Half the crew to Hag have flown —
Go down, you vein flowers, go down.
And it's mighty draughty around Northstorm —
Go down, you vein flowers, go down.
Oh, make all my cuts and misery known —
Go down. you vein flowers, go down.

Oh it's one more pull and that will do,
For we're the childer to kick her through.

Traditional rowing song

29

Onwards and Upwards

In the morning Joron strapped the inert body of the gullaime to his back and gathered his crew. Anzir stood by him, Farys to her side with Karring and Old Briaret. He had ten. Meas had changed her mind at the last minute about who she would send, and Hasrin was with him. Joron did not like it it, but no matter how the ex-deckkeeper might sneer under her breath at him he knew he would have no real trouble from her, as the rest of his band were loyal to Meas.

Meas had gone ahead with Coughlin. There had been talk, back on *Tide Child*, of splitting Coughlin's men between them, but now she had seen the tower Meas had decided to take them all. Meas and Joron were both sure Coughlin had once been seaguard, and as such would have knowledge of siegecraft – not that Meas was completely ignorant of such things, but she was not foolish enough to turn away expertise when it was on hand.

Joron peered into the thick forest, and the thought that the tunir may be somewhere in there made him shudder.

"How do we find the windspire, D'keeper?" said Farys. How indeed? Joron did not know the island, had no maps of it, and this was the time of year when the colourful forest was at its peak, growing so fast he imagined he could hear roots squirming through the soil.

"Meas said it is on the highest point of the island, so we will head upwards, and the Mother will guide us, I am sure."

"Arse!" Black Orris fluttered down, landing on Farys's shoulder and dipping his head twice. Beady black eyes considered Joron, eyes that reminded him of Narza. Then the bird dipped its head once more and began to preen the feathers of its wings.

"Was the bird not with Mevans?"

"Black Orris has brought us his luck, D'keeper," said Farys. Around her heads nodded, women and men looked a little brighter. "Maybe the Maiden's bird will guide us, though she's as like to trick as to triumph, ey?"

"Indeed, Farys." Joron stretched his shoulders, getting the ropes of the gullaime's harness comfortable. "Who among you knows the land well?" None answered, and Joron almost kicked himself. He may as well have accused them of being stonebound – no deckchild would admit to that. "Are there those here who Meas trusts to hunt when her ship needs food?" A man, Cruist, stood forward. His left ear was misshapen, almost non-existent.

"Meas sometimes sends me. My father was a hunter, though I am not like him; I am of the sea."

"I do not doubt it, Cruist," said Joron. "I have seen you fly up the rigging like a bird." The man nodded, a small smile spreading across his face. A woman from *Tide Child*'s original crew, Ganrid, stepped forward. Behind her was her brother, a small, stooped man called Folis who Joron had never heard speak. Ganrid, Joron was sure, could have been one of the Bern, but her brother was judged imperfect and that had tainted her. Or maybe she chose not to leave him – Joron had never thought to ask.

"Sometimes, when my brother and I were unable to find a ship, we have made our money hunting."

"Good," said Joron. "Then you, your brother and Cruist will go ahead and alert us to any danger." For a moment he had an image of the creature he and Meas had seen on the beach last night, and it was all he could do to keep speaking. "Meas says there are many dangers on these isles, so keep yourself alert. The rest of us will follow. Farys, take two and watch our rear. I want nothing coming upon us unaware.The rest of you, string your bows and have your curnows ready."

"Ey, D'keeper," came the replies.

And so they moved into the forest. Violently purple leaves as big as shipwings fought for the light of Skearith's Eye, and it filtered through them, hitting the pink leaves of the varisk lower in the canopy so they were covered in an ever-changing patchwork of pink, blue and purple light, as if bruises crawled across their flesh. Curnows rose and fell, cutting back the foliage to make a path − a path that swiftly closed behind them. From the front, they were warned of other plants: hurss, with poisonous spines, hierthrews, which, if disturbed, catapulted out barbed spines that were almost impossible to remove from the flesh and would then fester and sour, sending the afflicted mad with poison and pain. Add to this biting flies and small but fierce Gorrus birds, likely to dive out of their burrows and slash with clawed feet, and it was a slower and harder climb than Joron would have liked. Sometimes they had to take detours around impenetrable thickets, and once some trick of the light had Joron thinking he saw the black, light-absorbing shape of a tunir above them in the gion, but it was only a hole in the canopy. Still, it took a moment for the beating of his heart to slow and he paused. He felt overwhelmed, paralysed. Where to go? What to order? What if he got them lost? What if they went in circles?

Then Black Orris took to the air in a whirr of wing and feather, distracting Joron from his burgeoning panic. He breathed out, following Black Orris with his eyes. In the fleshy gloom of the forest he saw a bow. Saw a nocked arrow. Saw a hand draw back a bowstring . . .

And then he was shouting.

"Down! Get down!" throwing himself face first into the litter of broken vegetation. The arrow streaked out of the under-growth. Others came, singing through the air, clattering against gion and varisk, and at least one found a target – Joron well knew the sound of flesh being punctured now. A short scream followed, then there was roaring, and women and men running towards them. They were barely dressed, skin painted in the same blues, pinks and purples as the vegetation, faces stretched by fury, clubs and curnows held high. A man threw himself at Joron, bringing down a curnow. Joron, face down on the ground, could do nothing but roll. To avoid crushing the gullaime on his back he was only able to roll on to his side, and in doing so trapped his own curnow beneath himself.

He thought of the quick-release move Meas had taught him.

"When you really need the skill, Deckkeeper, I am sure you will get it right."

But that was no use now.

I have let you down, Shipwife, he thought. *What a way to die.*

The curnow was intercepted by Anzir, who snapped out her small shield, smashing the blade to the side, and thrust with her own sword, driving the blade into the attacker's chest. A woman came at Anzir from behind. Farys leaped on her, a small bone dagger in her hand which she drove into the woman's neck. Joron pulled himself to his feet. All around him there was struggling, fighting, screaming, shouting. He pulled one of the primed crossbows from where it hung on his jacket, shot an attacker in the back, reloaded it and shot another in the head. He unhooked his blade. It felt like he walked through a terrible dream. A man came at him – naked, painted, furious – and as he swung his curnow, the muscle memory of all those long hours on deck took over. He dodged to the side and took a step back, and the curnow whistled past his shoulder. Joron slashed sideways, letting the weighted end of his blade pull it round, and it bit deep into his opponent's side. For a moment the man looked surprised, then he fell to the ground, holding the gaping wound and screaming for the Mother to help him.

Then they were alone again -- their attackers had melted back into the forest, leaving five of their dead. Only one of Joron's party was down: the man hit by the arrow, Ganrid's brother, Folis. Joron went to where his sither knelt over him. The arrow had punctured his arm, and he had also taken a blow to the chest. Air bubbled through blood. Ganrid held her brother's hand tightly, speaking soothing words to him.

She turned to Joron.

"He fought well, D'keeper, even with the arrow in him," she said quietly. Joron knelt. Folis did not appear frightened or in pain, but his eyes looked very far away, and he surely heard the Hag's call. Joron took his other hand, and Folis's face took on a puzzled look.

"D'keeper," he said, a breath of air leaving him.

"Your sither is right: you fought well." Joron was not sure whether Folis heard him or not. "I will make sure the shipwife knows how well you fought."

Folis's face contorted into a smile, and then he coughed, groaned as if he were being branded, and the life left his eyes.

"Thank you, D'keeper," said Ganrid and wiped tears from her eyes. "He looked up to the shipwife, was proud to serve Lucky Meas. He will go to the Hag in peace now."

"We must carry on, Ganrid," he said. "Your brother is no doubt already warm at her fire."

"Ey," she said, "but there'll be more of the Hag-cursed out there." She pointed into the forest. "I doubt they'll attack head on again though. It'll be arrows from the bushes the rest of the way."

Joron scanned the plants around them but could see nothing other than gion and varisk, entwined around each other and creaking as they grew.

"Farys," he said, "get up a gion. See if you can make out how far we have to go. Anzir, they'll have to lie in wait; they'd make too much noise following us. I want you up front. You're a fighter and you're more likely to recognise an ambush than the rest of us." Anzir nodded. "Keep behind your shields as best you can. We'll stop cutting the gion too as it makes too much noise; we'll just have to push our way through. Ganrid and Cruist, stay up front with Anzir and deal with anything too vicious, but if it's just stings and scrapes from the plants we'll go through them, ey?"

"Ey, D'keeper," came the reply.

They waited while Farys climbed and when she shinned down from the gion stalk she pointed landward of Joron.

"Highest peak is that way. No more than an hour's walk, I'd say."

"Good, then we should get under way. If any of you lose sight of the rest of us, make a call like Black Orris, and I don't mean shout, 'Arse.'" Laughter and Joron's crew formed up around him.

"I do not need protecting," he said. "I am here for my share of the danger, just like you all."

"Kind to say, D'keeper," said Jilf, the oldest man in the crew, one-eyed and with only one tooth. "But we need your brains, see, and we need the gullaime safe. Right – proper true that is."

"Of course," said Joron, who had almost forgotten the creature on his back it was so light.

They pushed on through the jungle. Occasionally Anzir would stop them and listen. Twice she asked Joron to order flights of arrows put into the undergrowth, and the second volley was rewarded with a scream of pain. Farys's one hour turned into two as they had to make regular stops to regroup or climb the gion and check they headed in the right direction.

Joron wondered how Meas was doing at the tower. A voice in his head said she might be dead and he would be in charge, and wouldn't it be fine to get back what she had taken from him? But he did not feel any real joy at the idea. Oh, he may be more able now, but another part of him, a larger part, hated himself for wishing death on Meas, and more, he knew they needed her, the ship, the keyshan, the whole crew. And so, what had started as thoughts of how her death may benefit him became worry about what may happen if he did not hurry. If she needed him and he was not there. He became impatient, annoyed at every stop for water, at every delay to find a missing deckchild or climb the gion.

And yet he knew all this must be done.

"You wish for action, D'keeper," said Farys. "Me too. It is not rightly done this sneaking about, right it ain't at all."

He was about to tell her not to be foolish, that he didn't wish for action at all. Every time he had been into action he had been terrified beyond what he thought possible. But as he opened his mouth to speak he realised that at some level he did wish it, which was strange. It was not the fighting or the killing or the fury that he wanted, but the breaking of this constant tension he had not been truly aware of until now. With every step through the forest he became more sure an arrow was trained on him, more sure Anzir would miss something and they would walk into an ambush. More sure he would let Meas down.

"You are right, Farys," he said. "I do indeed wish for something to happen."

"It will, D'keeper. Don't you fret none, it will."

And of course it did.

They continued through the forest, making the best speed they could, twisted off course by thickets so dense they could not push through, until eventually they saw more blue sky above them than purple gion. The shorter varisk started to take over, pink leaves shining like open wounds. Anzir held up her hand and beckoned to Joron. When he crouched by her she pushed aside a tangle of vines and pointed.

For the first time in his life, he saw a windspire up close. He had expected it to be like the spine of a ship, a towering, slowly tapering spike that rose from the ground as if it had pierced the land from below, but it was no such thing. It was not white, for a start, but the colour of old and neglected bone, a pale yellowy white. It was also far, far larger than he had imagined. On Bernshulme only the Bern and the lamyard keepers could approach the windspire, and to get to it you must pass through the lamyards. No sane woman or man put themselves among so many gullaime.

So he only knew stories of the windspire, and those stories did it no justice. It rose, maybe ten times the size of a woman, from a thick base which tapered up to a rounded point, but it did not rise straight, it curved outwards so the tip hung four or five paces out from the curcular base. Neither was it solid. It looked more like the bone knife Farys carried, though what looked like carving on the windspire could not be the work of anything human, Joron felt sure of that. It was too intricate and strange and, somehow, wrong, otherwordly. It did not satisfy his sense of symmetry, though it pleased his eye in other ways: the detail, the repetition, the spirals and twisting lines that ran up and around it. In many places it was pierced, so varisk could be glimpsed through it. In other places the decoration was so subtle he only saw the lines because they were slightly darker than the rest of the spire. Nothing grew around it, but the large circle of bare ground which surrounded it did not look artificially cleared. It seemed the windspire required space, and the jungle respected that need.

And it sang.

It was not a loud song, and if they had not stopped in utter silence Joron may never have noticed it. But the windspire definitely had a song, a slow keening sound as beautiful and intricate as any bird's. For a moment Joron was lost as he looked upon the thing, felt its subtle heat on his face.

"Twelve," said Anzir quietly, and Joron tore his eyes from the windspire and back to what she talked of: the women and men in the clearing.

"I see only seven," he whispered.

"Five archers hide around the edges, one in the gion over there." She pointed up and Joron saw the figure crouched on a stalk. "Two are over there to landward and two more to seaward."

"How did they know we were coming here?" said Joron, more to himself than to Anzir.

Nevertheless she answered.

"I do not think there is much else on this isle we could be interested in." She did not look at him, only stared into the clearing. "And, no disrespect meant, Deckkeeper, but you have a gullaime on your back, which may be a clue." Was there a flash of humour there? He was unsure as she spoke almost in a monotone.

"Do you have any ideas for us to take this place, Anzir?"

"Were I in charge, I would have a bow trained on the one in the tree and send some round to take out those in the bushes as quietly as possible."

"Can it be done silently?" said Joron.

Anzir dug a finger into the dirt.

"Possibly not," she said. "I could, but the rest, they are not trained in death the way I am." They watched a moment longer, and then Joron tugged on Anzir's arm, pulling her back to where the rest waited.

"Farys," he said, "Anzir will show you where two raiders hide in the forest. Take who you wish and circle round behind them. Anzir will do the same. Hasrin." He barely believed he was about to make his next request of this woman, who was friends with Cwell and had once been a deckkeeper. "You were once deckkeeper." He took a crossbow from where it hung on his jacket. "You will know the use of this."

She nodded, looking at him as if he prepared some trap for her, but took the crossbow.

"I was ranked the best shot in the fleet, once," she said.

"Well" – he held out four bolts – "there is a man in the gion to the landward side of the windspire. You are to shoot him down." Hasrin narrowed her eyes at him, then nodded and took the bolts. "The rest of you, string your bows and be ready to shoot those in the clearing at my signal."

"What will the signal be?" said Farys.

"When I say 'hello'."

"D'keeper," said Anzir, "if any of us fails or Hasrin misses the fellow in the gion, you will be dead."

"That would be unfortunate," said Joron, "so I am ordering no one to fail or miss." Grim smiles met his words. "Now I shall count to two hundred. That should give everyone time to get in place and for me to remove the gullaime from my back."

It seemed to Joron, as he lay the gullaime beneath a vine and crouched in the undergrowth at the edge of the clearing, that his count of two hundred took an impossibly long time. It was not a comfortable time either as the same questions his little crew had asked him: *What if they miss? What if they fail?* spun round and round in his head and try as he might he could not put those thoughts in harbour, safe away from worry. Another joined them as he counted down – *Why did I choose Hasrin?* – and the possibility of death and how close he stood to it became more real. *Hasrin was once a deckkeeper, and nothing is more accurate than a crossbow.* He put one hand on a varisk vine, grasping the sinewy stem as hard as he could to still his shaking. *What if she does not shoot? What if she misses on purpose?*

At the moment he reached one hundred and ninety he muttered to himself, "Mother watch over your son." Then he stood and walked until he was among the thick foliage at the edge of the clearing.

"I am looking for the windspire," he said, and no one was more surprised than Joron that his voice did not waver or break. Then he took two steps forward out of the thick varisk. "Am I in the right place?"

Silence.

As if every woman and man and creature of the forest stopped what they were doing to look at this fellow who had stepped out and asked so politely where he was of those who would kill him. And though it was only a moment, the smallest sliver of time, barely a few grains of sand through a glass, it was long enough for Joron to think many things.

I should not have chosen Hasrin.

I should have had a better plan.

I will die here, foolishly, and my father will turn from me at the bonefire.

"Hello?" he said.

The arrows flew.

A bolt flew into the tall gion, and a body fell like ungainly fruit. From either side of the clearing came grunts and rustling as his crew attacked the hidden archers. Arrows cut into the seven in the clearing. Three fell, one was wounded. The three who remained ran at Joron, who found himself frozen, riveted to the spot as they came at him, weapons raised.

More arrows, and it was done. No one ever near enough to Joron to spit on him, never mind cut him, and the air which he had been holding in his lungs was once more moving in and out of his chest. Anzir strode across the clearing. Blood spattered her clothes, and he wondered if she would call him on his cowardice.

"That was brave," she said.

"Brave?"

"To stand unmoving and give the archers a second shot while your enemy ran at you. Few have the tits on them for that."

"Ey," replied Joron and wondered if she mocked him — if so he could not tell. "Well, it was not pleasant and I would rather not do it again. Now, let us get the gullaime to the spire." Anzir nodded and they fetched the creature — so light in Joron's arms. Anzir led the way back to the spire, the curnow in her hand dripping blood with every step. Joron found himself transfixed by the blood, having to shake his head to clear it of the sight.

Nearer to the spire, its song was louder. Joron knelt with the gullaime in his arms, not knowing what to do. *Surely the windtalker could feel the spire now?* He not only heard the song with his ears but felt it vibrate through his whole body. It was like he was a rope and the windspire was the wind howling past, making his body sing against his wishes when he was not ready for song. He expected something from the gullaime but did not know what. Some response. *Would it raise its head and sing back to the spire?* But the creature only lay limp in his arms.

"I think the gullaime must be touching it, D'keeper." Farys had joined them at the windspire. "That was what old Garriya told me."

"She knew what we did here?"

Farys shook her head.

"No, she just talks to me sometimes. Tells me stories, the sort a mother would, if I'd ever had one. In one story she said a gullaime has to touch the spire."

"There is a something like a cave here," said Anzir, "at the bottom of the spire."

Joron stood and carried the gullaime around to where there was an opening in the base of the spire. Here the song was even stronger, so loud it caused Joron pain, a jangling of his nerves. And he knew then, though he did not know how, that the gullaime must be placed inside if it was to wake. He knew this the same way he knew he was the only one who could do this. The crew may leave gifts for the gullaime, venerate it in their own way even, but they would not touch it, so this was his task. And even if some other had come forward, offered to take his burden, Joron would not have given it up to them. So despite the pain-growing-to-agony that being so near the spire brought him, he forced himself forward, crouched down to place the gullaime in the opening. To go into the noise was like dragging himself forward into a gale. Every movement required an almost inhuman effort, but the moment the gullaime touched the floor of the cave, the sounds and the pain stopped.

Everything stopped.

Joron sat before the spire.

Bathed in light and then plunged into darkness. The forest, his crew, the island – all were gone. He hung between Skearith's Bones, a thousand shining lights spread out around him.

He heard a single call – like that of a maidenbird – and the world came back fast at him, a riotous blur of colour and sound.

"Does it wake?" Farys said.

Joron blinked. Once. Twice.

He stared at the gullaime, hoping for some sign, but apart from the noise ceasing nothing had changed: the creature appeared as dead as it ever had. Though it was not, he was sure of that.

"How long will it take, D'keeper?"

"I do not know, Farys." He took a deep breath. "But I do know I am glad that noise has stopped."

"Noise?" She looked puzzled.

He did not know what to say. Had they not heard it? So in the way of officers everywhere who did not want to explain themselves, he changed the subject:

"Meas will need us at the tower."

"My old shipwife," said Ganrid from behind him, "told us you should never leave a gullaime. Said they run if you do. Get themselves in trouble, or killed."

"Well, Meas is not your old shipwife, and our gullaime is like no other." Joron looked up at Skearith's Eye, which was well over the halfway point of the sky. "We will leave it here. No one will hurt a gullaime, and if we are successful at the tower we can pick it up on our way back."

"And if we are not successful, D'keeper?" said Ganrid.

"Then no one will care."

30

The Two Towers

The forest had no wish to yield to the women and men pushing through it. It had no interest in their quick lives or the events that they considered so important that they had to hack and slash their way through. The gion and varisk forest, with all its attendant flora and fauna was to all intents and purposes eternal, and if it had any consciousness at all, the mission of Joron and his crew would not have concerned it.

For Joron Twiner, there was little but concern. Skearith's Eye was now slipping down the blue of the sky, and with every degree the deckkeeper felt the sand in the glass running out. When they came across breaks in the forest canopy he looked to the east, looking for the white smoke that Meas had told him to expect when the tower was taken. But no smoke came, and it worried him. If they had failed and she was dead, he would command *Tide Child*, but for how long? How long before the crew overthrew him and turned the ship into a raider? Would Joron have the courage to die rather than acquiesce to such a thing? He doubted it, and what would his father think of that? Would he turn his back on him when Joron approached the Hag's bonefire? Something sank within him, and the sweat on his brow was no longer from just the heat.

No, she must live. She had given him something, woken something within him. He did not understand it, but felt it was right. Felt himself becoming someone new, someone better. And he did not feel she was finished, that he was finished.

And had she not said she would never die on land? He could believe that. Most likely she waited for Joron to bring up his remaining crew to assault the tower. He needed to hurry. He needed to make sure he did not let her down.

"More thorns, D'keeper," said Old Briaret, her face drawn into a long frown. "Hierthrews. They will cut us to pieces if we try and go through."

"Then we go round," said Joron, raising his voice. "Anzir, we go round."

And so it went, hacking and slashing. Stopping to listen when Anzir thought something may be lurking in the forest. Whether human or animal, all Joron knew was that he would rather fight any number of women and men than the terrible black tunir he had seen on the beach.

He found himself cutting through the jungle by Farys. She was bleeding from a wound to her arm, and he could see that every time she swung her curnow it caused her pain.

"Where are you from, Farys?" He asked, more to distract her from her pain than out of real interest.

"Fallhulme, D'keeper," she said. "Old island. Used to be where they dumped keyshan hearts, and ain't a woman or man ever been born there that were Bern."

"Few of us are Bern or Kept," he said,

"My mother died bringing me to life, otherwise I were perfect before." She pointed at her burned face and then looked away as if ashamed. And Joron wished he had not started the conversation as he had no wish to hurt her, and little understanding of how to make someone feel better.

"My mother died too," he said, wanting her to feel less awkward.

"Really?"

"Ey. My father raised me as a fisher."

"My father died when I were not old. And my uncle sold me to a fleet recruiter." Joron did not answer. He had only intended to distract her, but now she seemed intent on telling him her life story, and he was not sure he wanted to know. "Went to a ship called *Keyshanheart*. The boneglue caught one night, and I were trapped in the hold. I got out, many didn't. Though most thought I would die in the hagbower – from the fire, see?"

"But you did not." He tried to make his voice light. Tried not to think about being trapped in a burning boneship.

"Oft wished I had, D'keeper," she said, her voice cracking, and turned her face from him.

"Well, if it helps any, Farys, I am very glad you did not," he said.

She turned back, eyes wet, streaks cut in the sweat on her face by tears.

"Thank you, D'keeper." And he thought maybe he should ask how she came to be on the black ship, but then did not because he knew it may be heard as an order. Such things were a deckchild's secret, to give or not as they wished.

"Come on," said Joron, raising his voice so all could hear. "Meas has not taken the tower yet as I see no smoke. If we do not hurry we will miss out, and who knows what riches these raiders hide?" Predatory grins greeted that, though Joron had to tighten his hand around the hilt of his blade to stop it shaking at the thought of action. When he closed his eyes he saw the raiders from the clearing running towards him, felt the terrible, bone-numbing fear that had rooted him to the spot.

Odd that despite his fear of pain and death he could still lead his crew towards it – through the thorns and past the vines, looking in vain for the smoke, occasionally sending someone up the gion to spy out the land ahead. His arm ached from slashing with the curnow and his legs ached from clambering over roots and fallen vegetation. His mind ached from staying alert to any threat that may emerge from the forest.

And still, when the cry came from above — "I see the tower!" — it felt like too soon.

All action slowed. No longer did they cut through the forest making little attempt to stay quiet; now they crept forward, Anzir still at their head. Joron checked that everyone wore the black armband that marked them as the dead.

Near the edge of the forest, where the smell of the regular fires used to keep the area clear around the tower was strong, Joron heard a voice.

At first it was faint, little more than another noise among the thousands of the forest, filtered as it was through bird calls and the buzzing of insects and the hiss of wind and the creak of growing gion and varisk stalks. Then he began to pick out the name "Meas" being repeated time and again like a mantra. Even nearer the tower, and he could make out the tone, mocking; a man was mocking Meas, and something about the voice was familiar.

". . . the great Meas Gilbryn, the feted shipwife! Lucky Meas! Not so lucky now, are you?" Who was that? "You break your crew on my tower like a wave breaks on the rocks. Come, all of you, you owe her nothing. Cut off her head and bring it to me, and I will let you into my tower. I will let you share in my coming riches!"

So the raiders who held the tower had seen the keyshan. They knew what approached, and it was more imperative than ever the tower be taken.

"Farys", said Joron, "get up that gion. See if you can spot the arakeesian and its escorts, or any sign of the shipwife."

"Ey, D'keeper." She scurried up the gion, feet finding purchase on its thick rubbery stalk.

While she climbed, Joron quietly made his way to the edge of the clearing, where already the violent pink of varisk roots was edging out into the blackened scrub before the tower. He pushed aside a fan-shaped gion leaf and stared at the tower. Not big, not really. A three-storey square tower of mud brick, it would have fallen quickly to a good-sized gallowbow, Joron was sure. But he may as well have wished for Skearith to come howling from the sky and lay an egg on top of the tower. To a force without a gallowbow, the tower was well-nigh impregnable, and the proof of that was lying on the burned ground: two bodies, pierced with arrows and twisted in death.

The man on top of the tower talked on. Joron squinted, trying to make him out. Occasionally he would catch a glimpse of his head as it moved along the battlements.

"Bring me her head, oh girls and boys. Now we're not on the ship, we are are a free troop. We make our own rules, and I welcome girls just as much as boys now. I'll turn no one down and . . ."

Kanvey. It was Kanvey atop the tower.

Kanvey, who had run rather than fight at *Tide Child*'s ill-fated first battle. How he had come to this place Joron had no idea, but he suspected the violent hand of the Hag at work, offering vengeance to the aggrieved. But who did the Hag offer blood to? Meas, for Kanvey's betrayal, or Kanvey, to finish what he had not managed at Corfynhulme with his spear?

"D'keeper." He turned to find Farys at his shoulder.

"Ey, Farys. What did you see?"

"I see the keyshan coming up the channel, cannot be more than forty turns away."

"That is little time to take a tower."

"Also I see *Snarltooth* and *Cruel Water*, but they do not front the beast."

"What do you mean?"

"*Snarltooth* lags behind and *Cruel Water* sails by the keyshan's neck."

"That is not how to stop gallowbow bolts."

"Was my thinking too, D'keeper. Are we betrayed?"

"I do not know. Did you see any sign of the shipwife?"

"Not of her, no, but the man on the tower is Kanvey." At the mention of his name Joron was sure he heard "Traitor!" whispered somewhere behind him.

"Ey. I recognised the voice."

"Good he's here," said Old Briaret. "Be a pleasure to force my blade into his body. He's stuck something of himself in others enough times without their say."

"I am sure you'll get a chance," said Joron. "You have more, Farys?"

"Ey." She pointed to seaward, towards a huge gion which rose above all the rest, giant heart-shaped purple leaves sprouting off to each side. At the very top one had broken off. "That is a better place to see the tower and clearing."

"We make our way there then," he said. "Come."

From where they squatted hidden in the forest, they circled the tower, keeping to the cover of the vegetation, and all the time Kanvey continued to harangue Meas. To offer her crew wild prizes and riches in exchange for her death.

"I wish he would shut up," said Old Briaret. "Never met a man in my life I wanted to shut up more than Kanvey, and it don't seem he's changed any."

Anzir held up her hand and they stopped. For a moment there was only the noise of Kanvey shouting and the wind through the forest. Joron caught a whiff of sea on the breeze and realised how much he missed that scent; the earthy smell of the forest was no comfort to him like the salt tang of the sea.

Narza appeared.

One moment she was not there and then she was. She did not look at them, keeping her face hidden beneath her black hair. In her hands she held her bone knives, carved and yellowed. Then she stood aside and waved them forward into a small clearing that had been neatly walled with woven thickets of thorns.

"Joron," said Meas. She sat in the middle of the clearing, surrounded by Coughlin, her seaguard and the crew she had brought with her. There was a new cut on her cheek sewn together with black thread. The feathers in her hair were askew. "I am glad you are here. We do not have much time to take the tower. Where is the gullaime?"

"We left it at the windspire," he said. Had he done the

wrong thing? Hurriedly he added, "It showed no sign of waking when we got it there, and I thought it best to come straight to you. None would hurt a gullaime."

"You were right to come," said Meas. She looked tired. "I will not lie. I had hoped you would bring the windtalker and it would help us take the tower. But clearly that is not to be."

"So what now?"

"We must take it another way."

Joron nodded.

"Farys here," he said, "has seen the arakeesian approaching. Says it is forty turns or less away."

"Then we do not have much time to finish this."

"She also says that our escorts do not escort."

"Oh?" said Meas. Suddenly all her attention was on him. Joron felt his cheeks burn and the world seemed a little quieter.

"*Snarltooth* hangs back, while *Cruel Water* flies near the head of the beast."

Meas nodded.

"So he decided to do it himself," she said quietly.

"Do what?"

"Shipwife Arrin and I spoke of what we should do if the towers were not destroyed. It was decided a ship would loose its bolts at the arakeesian, see if it could make the beast dive."

"It will destroy whichever ship does that," said Joron, unable to hide his shock. "We saw its power when the flukeboats attacked it."

"Ey," said Meas sadly. "I bade him command Brekir do it. Her ship being out of view that night bothered me, Joron. Still does."

"You think she lied?"

"A broken spar, Joron, is not reason to fall so far behind. Though it could simply have been poor shipwifery. However, it seems either Arrin does not trust her to do it, or he did not think it right for him to order another to their death."

"I did not think a Gau—" He was about to say "Gaunt Islander", give the whole thing away, but Meas interrupted.

"Sometimes you do not think at all, Joron," she barked, and he remembered the secrets he held. "Arrin knows what we are about and thinks it worth dying for. But I would rather he lived." She touched the cut on her face, winced. "Coughlin here has another plan." She pointed over her shoulder at the warrior. "Tell him, Coughlin." The man came forward, and Joron could not help thinking he seemed less resentful of Meas. He had fought with her twice now, and Joron was learning how such things could tie people together.

"Deckkeeper," he said stiffly. "That tower is built to withstand a siege."

"I can see that," said Joron.

"Aye, well, you cannot withstand a siege without water. I visited the old tower here, and there was a well, fed from caves beneath it."

"Coughlin says," said Meas, "that islands like this, made of the white stone, are riddled with caves. So we believe there may be a way in. That the caves will allow access to the tower's well."

"Believe or know?" said Joron. "They could have walled up access to the well when they rebuilt the tower."

Coughlin stared at the floor.

"They could."

"There will be a heavy price to pay if we assault the walls, Joron," said Meas, "and what Coughlin says makes sense. You only fortify a place if you think you can hold it, and to hold a place you need drinking water."

"So Coughlin will try and find these caves?"

The big man shook his head.

"They are generally not big, these caves. Too tight a squeeze for me."

"That and I want him up here," said Meas. "You are slim, Joron." A coldness within him. He knew what her next words would be. "You will lead the attack through the caves. Take Farys – she is small. Take Old Briaret too and also Namd, Karring and Narza." She raised her voice as she said each name and they came to join him.

"Six of us to take a tower; it is not many." And he was no great warrior.

"They will not expect an attack from below. Six will be enough." She glanced at the tower. "I will give you ten turns, and then we must attack anyway if we are to stand a chance of stopping them loosing on the wakewyrm. And an assault will keep their attention on us – give you a better chance."

"And if there is no way in for us, six will not be missed from your attack."

"In essence," said Meas. Then she leaned forward, and spoke quietly, putting a hand on his arm. "You will have five crew loyal to Tide Child's second in command with you, Joron. Someone who knows our purpose must always command the ship, do you understand?" Then she drew back again and pointed at the tower. "You need only open and hold the front gate long enough for us to get in, that is all." She smiled at him. "Narza will take you down the cliffs. Coughlin has shown her the way. Let her take the lead. She has done this type of work before and has an instinct for it. A good commander uses what knowledge they have available."

Joron nodded.

"Very well," he said. And as he started to move away Meas held out her arm, clasped his hand tightly in the deckwive's grip. "Good luck, Joron Twiner."

"And to you, Shipwife." He turned. "Narza," he said, "I am not a fool to ignore my shipwife's advice. You shall lead."

Narza nodded then led them into the forest and through the gion. It was not far to where the cliff fell dramatically away, and Joron could stare down at the white birds circling as the sea crashed against the rocks below. Narza pointed at a steep, narrow path leading down the cliff.

"We go down there," said Joron, managing not to make it sound like the question it was.

Narza nodded again and led them on, walking along the path like she was out for a morning stroll on deck. Farys followed her, similarly nonchalant, and behind her came old

Briaret, Namd and Karring, all deckchilder well used to heights and similarly unconcerned. For Joron it was different. The varisk spars of a ship he could depend on, but this path? It was little more than one foot's width wide and in places had crumbled away. Every time a foot fell on the path a little mud and white stone fell. Joron found himself wishing he was not last in the line. Every footfall eroded the path that little bit more. Each time Joron placed his boot down he expected the path to vanish beneath, to cast him into the yawing chasm below, smash his body on the rocks. For the marrow of his broken bones to become food for the wheeling seabirds that cried sadly as they flew in circles below.

"D'keeper?" He blinked twice. Namd was staring at him. The man was heavily bearded to hide the fact he had a cleft palate. Joron had noticed he rarely spoke.

"You seemed lost, D'keeper."

"Just thinking about how to approach this, Namd, that is all."

The man nodded, seemed satisfied, and Joron continued to inch his way along the path. Further down it widened slightly, doubling back under itself, and when Joron looked up he saw that all that held it in place was a tangle of roots. He felt a greying of his cheeks at that, and decided not to think of what supported the path below his feet; instead he whispered a prayer to the Mother to keep him safe. At the front Narza was cutting back bright vegetation, scannng the the cliff face, shaking her head and moving on. Eventually she found something and cut away more vegetation, then swore, sucking her finger where a thorn had caught it. Her head vanished into the wall of the cliff and when it came out her dark hair was greyed with the webs of insects. She pointed with her bone knife and beckoned Joron. He inched his way past the others and saw that the hole she had found was not much bigger than his own head.

"We go in there?"

Narza shook her head, then pointed at her ear. Joron leaned

in close to the hole, wary of whatever had made the webs that were caught in Narza's hair; in his experience there was little in the Hundred Isles that did not bite or sting. But when he placed his head inside the hole there was only a blessed coolness and a darkness so complete that it was easy to believe the world outside had stopped existing.

Then he became aware of the smell of water, but not seawater. Still water, earthy water – water that made his nose feel uncomfortable, made him want to recoil as if this was not a place he should go.

But he did not recoil.

He listened.

The first sound was the sea, the slow beat of the sea on the rocks, the back and forth of waves gradually eating away the base of the cliff. Then, barely perceptibly, he thought he heard the song of the windspire. A lament in a language he had no vocabulary for, meaning passed to him as a feeling. Above that he heard the murmur of voices, here and gone, and with those voices came a breath of wind. He turned his head, feeling the breeze on his cheek: a coldness on the seaward side of his face, louder voices, a coldness on the landward side, quieter voices. The breeze moved in time with the sea. He removed his head from the hole, squinting at the sudden brightness.

"Voices," he said. "They come and go with the waves so these caves are open to the sea somewhere." He examined the hole. Some of the the scree around it was loose, but they could not make the hole a lot bigger without bringing the hillside down around them. Still, he thought he could get through.

"Won't fit in there," said Old Briaret, holding out her hand in front of her ample chest. "The Maiden may have made me barren but she were more than generous in other ways."

Joron dithered. Leave Old Briaret, whose strength they may need, or see if they could find a larger hole?

A wave against the rock.

A rock against the wave.

"We go on, Narza, fifty steps, and if we do not find a better way in then we will have to return here and leave Old Briaret behind." The dark woman nodded and went on, studying the cliff wall as she did.

The path narrowed again, making them all press themselves against the cliff face, then as they rounded a corner it widened once more. Joron was so busy concentrating on where he placed his feet, it took him a moment to realise everyone but Narza had stopped and was staring out across the sea.

Joron could not help but join them.

The sky was blue, blue as dreams and as unreachable. Thin lines of cloud scudded across it. Below was the ocean, green and grey and cut with lines of white. To their landward side the sky and sea were divided by the black towers of Skearith's Spine, reaching up to impossible heights, their tops crested with snow and it looked like clouds nested there, resting before journeying across the Archipelago. Through the centre of this vista ran Arkannis Channel, and in the centre of the channel swam the arakeesian.

Vast.

Able to compare it to the pair of two-ribbers, Joron got his first true idea of the creature's scale. It took his breath away. It was like an island had come alive. The huge red wingfins on its back were raised, catching the wind and pushing the beast on inexorably. He tried to calculate how long they had before it came within range of the towers' gallowbows but could not. Not long enough, he knew that. The creature's branched horns stuck out of the water, marking its head. As if sensing his gaze, the arakeesian blew a plume of water out of the hole between its horns, and it reached up for the sky before vanishing into a cloud of droplets to be whisked away by the wind. The beast's flippers were held against its huge curving sides, and the long tail swept lazily up and down through the sea. From this distance *Cruel Water* looked about the size of Joron's hand, and *Snarltooth*, which sailed at the rear of the arakeesian, looked no bigger than his littlest finger.

"It is difficult, D'keeper," said Farys, "to understand how something so huge can even be alive."

"Ey, Farys, you are right. But it is and we must keep it so."

"It is a good thing we do, I think, D'keeper," she said and then bowed her head as if worried she had said too much and hurried off after Narza.

"It is," said Joron quietly with one last look at the beast. "I believe it is."

When he reached Narza she had found another hole and was busily pulling away vines. This was larger and would allow even Old Briaret to squeeze through.

"This looks good," said Joron. "Narza, you lead."

Narza nodded and produced a wanelight from her belt with a little container of oil. She filled the light and then lit it with a sparker. Joron wished he had thought ahead and brought his own light but Narza was prepared for forgetful deckkeepers and produced three more. Then they squirmed and squeezed into the darkness.

To enter the cave was to enter another world, one as alien to Joron as being underwater. So dark. Sound no longer behaved as it should. The voices Joron had heard were louder here, but he could not tell from which direction they came. The glistening walls of the cave threw sound around, turned it into a mush that hissed in his ears. The cave enclosed him, pushed him inside himself and at the same time pushed him physically down, forcing Joron and his small crew to continue on all fours. He did not hold a wanelight, and the meagre glow from those in front was as often as not blocked out by Old Briaret or Karring, and in those moments it was easy to believe he was utterly alone, the only sounds those of clothes scraping against rock. The only sensation the feel of loose shingle and slippery mud as it squeezed between his fingers. Everything here was alien to him, from the darkness to the way the decreasing space eventually forced him to move like a creature without arms and legs, wriggling along on his stomach. Progress was slow, and he felt the weight of the rock above, crushing him. Panic fluttered in his breast. To be stuck here was to die. To die alone in the dark.

His heart beating.

His breath rasping.

The air in his ears whispering.

The blood in his veins hissing.

Behind all this the ever-changing melody of the windspire, that strange, sad chorus, and it felt to Joron that the organs of his body had become part of it, that his body's struggle through the arteries of the island was a counterpoint to the melody of the spire far above. And though he did not know why, that song helped him. Had it not been with him, he was sure he would have been overwhelmed by the darkness. He was a man of the sea, and the weight of the island above him would have broken his mind, or worse, entombed him. But the song was like a guide: it pulled him on, cleared his mind of worry.

Then he felt less weight, more space.

The air around him was no longer cold and close but wider and moving.

The wanelights gilded his little group with golden highlights – hints of body, leg and head, breast and chest. Narza stood, then Namd, then Farys and Old Briaret, then Karring, then him. They were in a cave, a true cave, almost high enough for them to stand up. Two passages led from it. No one spoke – not, Joron thought, because they were afraid of being heard, but because this dark place did not invite speech.

Then he heard voices from somewhere ahead. Narza cocked her head, and the way the wanelight haloed her hair changed. She pointed to the seaward tunnel. Touched a finger to her lips. They followed her silently down the passage, the voices becoming louder, light growing before them.

Two people, two men.

They stood with their backs to the passage, a rope dangling in front of them. Joron could smell clean, fresh water.

Narza glanced over her shoulder – *did he see her black eyes?*

Were they lighter in the dark? — and motioned to them to stay where they were. Then she simply walked towards the two men, not attempting to hide or to slow or to mask her footsteps. If anything she speeded up as she approached. Joron had seen many fights, many deaths — nothing was as common as violence in the Hundred Isles — but he had never seen anything like Narza. Never seen anyone who committed so fully, as if they knew no fear.

By the time she reached the men, Narza was running. She threw herself at the back of one, knocking him to the ground with her shoulder and using his bulk to stop her forward motion. As the other man turned towards her, surprised, shocked, uncomprehending, Narza's bone knife slashed across his throat. He staggered back, never having drawn his curnow or made a sound, vainly trying to halt the flow of blood from his neck. Narza, still moving, let herself fall. It was a lazy movement. The man she had knocked down was pushing himself up. She fell on to him, elbow angled to dig in just below his ribs. Joron heard the air as it was knocked from his body by her weight. She rolled off him and came to her knees in one movement, then drove the bone dagger down into the man's skull.

It took her more effort to remove the blade from the man's head than it had for her to kill them, and Joron wondered if he found her more frightening than the journey through the caves.

Narza sheathed her knives. Far above in the roof of the cave was a circle of light — the cellar of the tower. The rope fell from it into a small spring surrounded by a woven wall of dried varisk vines. She grabbed the rope, pulled a bucket from the spring and took a long drink. Then threw it back into the well before yanking away the wall of vines and pulling on the rope until it was taut. Then she looked at Joron.

"Well," he said, "the arakeesian comes, and the longer we wait the more danger Meas will be in. Best we go up quick. And, Narza, best you go first." He pointed towards the two corpses. "It seems you are well suited for such work."

Did she smile then? Maybe, fleetingly, before she took hold of the rope, swung on to it, waving her leg to give herself a little swing which she used to to twist the rope around her thigh. Then she started to climb. Not wanting to appear cowardly, though he could not be unaware of the quick beat of his heart at the thought of the tower full of raiders above them, Joron grabbed the rope and did the same. Farys followed him with Karring, Old Briaret and Namd behind.

Up they went towards the circle of light in the ceiling. It looked very far away, but it also grew very quickly. Nearing the top, Narza freed her leg from the rope and climbed the last few lengths using just her hands, one of her bone knives clutched between her teeth. Joron took his cue from her and pulled his own knife, biting down on it and thanking the Hag as he had been sure his teeth were about to start chattering from fear. He glanced down – so far to fall. Farys, below him, also held a knife in her mouth. Her eyes gleamed, and the meagre light gave her burned face an inhuman look.

Narza vanished over the rim of the hole and Joron paused. Heard no sounds coming from above, though that did not mean there was no one there. Narza had proved how silently she could kill. Then he was at the hole, pulling himself up more slowly than Narza, keeping one leg entwined in the rope in case he should slip. Swinging himself from the rope to the lip of the floor, pulling himself over.

A cellar just as Coughlin had said. No one here. Boxes of food lined the walls. Joron could smell the slightly rank smell of dried fish that the damp had got into. Farys appeared, then Namd, Old Briaret and Karring. There was no door to the room; only a ladder which led up to a trapdoor.

"Narza," he said and pointed at the trapdoor. Now he felt his fear differently: no longer paralysing, instead it filled him with energy.

What had been terror at what was to come was subsumed by an inevitability that had not been there in the caves. There was no going back now. He could have found excuses up until this point. Not now. They were committed. Now they would fight and die or fight and live.

"Are you ready, my girls and boys?" he said.

They nodded, and he was amazed that they seemed to feel no fear, though maybe they did. Maybe they wondered that he felt no fear for his voice did not waver, and his mouth was bent into a grin that he did not understand, that he knew was a mask.

"Then we will show no mercy. We have no friends in the tower above us. We have only one task, to open the doors and keep them open." Narza was already at the trapdoor. "Kanvey is up there," he said quietly, but making sure he was heard. "He betrayed us, rowed away at Corfynhulme and left us to die. Threw a spear at the shipwife. Let us show him what happens to those who betray *Tide Child*, ey?"

A chorus of "Eys" and he was on the ladder behind Narza. Ready. Scared. Breath coming quickly.

"Open it," he said. "Open it now."

And she did.

31

Those Who Leave Us Will Return

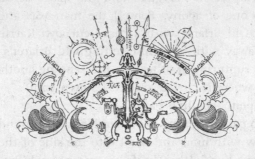

Narza's feet vanished above Joron. He followed closely. Where the tower basement had been full of the same damp as the caves, above the air was close and hot, trapped within the tower, mud bricks baking under the scrutiny of Skearith's Eye and turning the room into an oven. It was not a particularly big room, maybe twenty paces to each wall. To seaward was a staircase, to landward the doors. Joron barely had time to count the people in it – not many, ten, maybe? – before they were fighting.

Narza had fallen on them, her bone knives out, rising and falling, her teeth bared. She killed in utter silence. A group of raiders were standing at a table, shocked, apparently unable to understand where this sudden terror had come from. Joron pulled the curnow from the hook on his belt, fumbled the movement Meas had tried to teach him – *Don't give yourself time to think* – ran at them, bringing the blade down on the woman nearest him. It cut into her collarbone. She slumped to the floor, staring at Joron as if to ask, "Why did you do this to me?"

Then he was fighting. There was no great skill to it – there was not with a curnow. He slashed about himself with it as the remaining raiders drew their weapons.

Out of the corner of his eye Joron saw Farys raise her club. "Farys!" he shouted. "Ignore them! Get the doors open!" She ran for the doors as a man came at Joron. He held a hammer, but before he could bring it down Old Briaret was at him, her short wyrmpike in his guts, and the man's scream of fury turned to one of agony. Behind the man was another, who lunged at Old Briaret with a rusty curnow. Karring slapped the blow away with his hand, letting Old Briaret's spear dart out again, rupturing another gut and sending another body to the floor, where it curled around its own pain.

"It is open!" shouted Farys.

A sharp pain in Joron's shoulder. He swung round, bringing his curnow with him, and it bit into the side of the man who had just cut him with a knife. It was not a killing blow, so Narza finished him, thrusting one of her knives into his ear.

"Back!" shouted Joron. "We must hold the door." Five raiders remained but they were wary, hanging back while one shouted up the stairs for help. "Namd, with me!" shouted Joron. "The table!" The two ran forward. Three defenders ran to meet them, but two shied away when the one in the lead was felled by a hammer thrown by Karring. Joron and Namd grabbed the table. Dragging it over to the doors when more women and men came streaming down the stairs. Among them was Kanvey. Much larger than the rest, he swayed rather than walked down the stairs.

"Bows!" Kanvey shouted. "Get some bows and bring them down! And anyone that comes through the door behind them!"

Joron glanced behind him, looking out through the doorway. Against the colourful riot of the forest he could see Meas leading her crew in a sprint across the clearing, dodging from side to side to avoid the arrows coming from the top of the tower.

"We need the bows up top," shouted a voice from above.

"Nay," Kanvey shouted back as Joron and Namd wrestled the heavy varisk table up in front of them like a shield. "They'll get in now, but so we must kill them down here." For the first time Kanvey looked at the women and men crouched before the open door to the tower. "Joron Twiner," he said. He seemed in good spirits. "Well, I confess I did not expect to see you again, and definitely not still wearing the onetail." Raiders with bows began to take positions on the stairs around Kanvey. "Try not to kill Twiner," he said. "He has a dainty turn of leg. I would have some fun with him."

The first arrows came in. A hail of them, biting into the table. Namd let out a yelp and swore: "Hag's tits." An arrow had passed through the flesh of his bicep. Without word or pause Narza leaned forward, grabbed the shaft of the arrow in both hands and snapped the feathered end off. Before Namd could even cry out, she had pulled the arrow out. Namd let out a low, angry moan, bent over and lost in his own pain for a moment, then he straightened as much as he could in the shelter of the table.

"I'll pay some stonebound back for that, I will."

Joron heard bodies hit the door and Meas poked her head through the doorway, low down. Another round of arrows bit into the table.

"Good of you to arrange a little shelter, Deckkeeper."

"Ey, but how we get from here to those stairs I do not know."

"Well we must; the keyshan approaches. Give me a moment." Her head vanished and then reappeared. "I do believe I gave you a couple of crossbows?"

He stared at her for a second, then felt his eyes widen.

"Ey, you did."

He pulled at the crossbows attached to his jacket as Meas passed through another with some bolts and a couple of bows with arrows. "See if you can make them duck so we can get in without taking an arrow," she said.

Joron primed his crossbows and after the next volley of arrows looked over the edge of the table, searching in vain for Kanvey, but he must have retreated from danger and joined the rest of his women and men further up the tower, so he loosed his bolt at the scrum on the stairs. He did not hit anyone, nor did he expect to, but from the shouts the bolt provoked it was clear their adversaries had not expected anyone to shoot back.

"Bring oil!" went up the shout from the raiders. "Bring oil! We'll burn them out."

"That's not good, D'keeper," said Farys. For the first time he heard an edge of panic in her voice. "I do not want to burn again."

"You will not," said Joron with more authority than he felt. And he would do all he could to stop that happening. "Meas will have us up those stairs before they get the chance."

Meas's head appeared again.

"Make way," she said. "Get ready with your bows. Coughlin and Anzir are coming through. Namd, be ready. We will move quickly, and they will need your strength. When I shut this door, loose at the stairs."

Before Joron could ask what was planned, Meas vanished and the door shut. Joron stood and shot his crossbows, and at the same time Farys, Old Briaret and Namd stood and loosed arrows. They had no time to aim, and those on the stairs were in little danger, but the volley made them duck. At the same time Coughlin and Anzir slipped through the door and crawled to each end of the table.

"Grab the middle of the table, Namd," said Coughlin. He wriggled his upper body to get the shield on his back into a more comfortable position. "When I say go, we lift the table and go forward. Ready?"

"Forward?" said Joron.

"Ey!" said Anzir "We must take the tower or lose the keyshan, and Meas will not have that." Then Namd and Joron realised what they were about: they intended to use the table as a movable shield to attack the stairs.

"Be ready," Joron said quietly to Farys, Briaret and Karring. "When they move forward it should surprise those on the stairs enough for us to get in an aimed shot." His heart beat so hard inside his chest he though it would explode. "Make that shot count."

Coughlin glanced across at Anzir and Namd, gave them a nod.

"Go," he shouted loudly enough to be heard by Meas on the other side of the door. "For the keyshan!" With a grunt they lifted the heavy table and ran forward.

Joron stayed where he was, along with Farys, Karring and Old Briaret. He saw the faces of the raiders on the stairs stretch into surprise. They looked like hard women and men used to fighting. Joron extended his arm, picked a target. Took a second to make sure his man was lined up. His target drew back on his bow. Joron loosed his bolt, aiming at an eye, taking the man in the chest. As he shot he saw two women struggling down the stairs with a pot of oil. Beside him he saw Farys alter her aim and loose her arrow at one of the women, hitting her in the neck. She fell, the oil spilling from the pot onto the stairs and all those below her.

Through the doorway streamed the rest of *Tide Child*'s crew, screaming at the tops of their voices and brandishing their weapons. Those with bows loosed at the defenders on the stairs. Arrows came back. Two of Coughlin's men fell, and one of *Tide Child*'s crew dropped with an arrow in her forehead. The rest ran on, screaming.

The raiders' arrows stopped as those covered in oil realised what soaked their clothes. Oil dripped down the stairs, pooling at the bottom. At the top of the stairs a women with a burning torch appeared. A defender glanced up, realised why she was there and with a shout of "No!" made a grab for the torch. The woman, either unaware or not caring why the man wished to stop her, tried to brush him off. The two struggled. She tried to draw her knife; the man grabbed her hand, and his foot slipped on the oil-covered stairs. Both fell, tumbling among their slick and glistening fellows, and with a great bark of air being consumed the crowd of raiders went up in a screaming inferno.

"Back!" shouted Meas, though she had no need to worry about her crew as Coughlin, Anzir and the rest were retreating rapidly. The women and men who had been defending the stairs screamed as they burned. The air filled with the smell of singing hair and roasting flesh. "Use your bows!" shouted Meas. "I'll not have them suffer." Arrows flew, and soon there were none left alive on the stairs, but the flames still burned and the stink of charring flesh filled the room. "Open both doors," said Meas. "That is lamp oil. It burns fierce and quick, and I would have it burn itself out. But it will steal the air from a room as it does. I'll not have Kanvey come down to find us passed out and easy pickings; we have a job to do here." The doors were thrown open, and the flames leaped up but found nothing more to burn than already blackened bodies, and soon there was only smoke and stink in the room.

When the smoke had cleared Meas called her crew together. "Joron," she said, "choose a few to guard the doors in case anyone hides in the forest and tries to come at our rear." With that she started up the stairs, stepping over charred corpses. "Come, my girls and boys! Up the tower and there'll be a fair few less of them to meet us. Come on." She lifted her sword. "For the keyshan!" And the crew of *Tide Child* echoed her, shouting "For the keyshan!" as they trampled bodies beneath their feet.

In the sudden quiet, he heard sobbing.

Farys had retreated to a corner of the room and was curled up on herself, as if she could hide from the world.

"It is the fire," said Old Briaret. "She still remembers when it tried to take her. She cannot forget." Joron knelt down by her. Farys was lost but he understood why. That same fear which overtook her lived within him every time he thought of his body, of its weakness and of the things that could be done to it.

"Farys," he said softly. She looked up, her eyes red, clear mucus running from her nose. Was it shame that crossed her scarred face?

He did not know what to do.

"I am sorry, Deckkeeper. I hid." Words creeping out through her tears. "'Tis the cord for cowardice, or death, I know that."

"I see no coward, Farys. The shipwife needs me up in the tower, but I must leave some here to guard, so that would be you, Namd, Karring and Old Briaret." Farys stared at him. "I will leave you in charge."

"Me?" she said. "But I have—"

"—proved yourself," he said. "More than enough. I saw you decide to take down the women who held the oil despite knowing what that meant."

"I just—"

"—saved many of *Tide Child*'s crew, Farys, that is what you did."

"They burned," she said, and her eyes glazed over.

Joron raised his voice.

"Does anyone have a problem with me leaving Farys in charge?" He looked over his shoulder.

Namd shook his head, Karring nodded and Old Briaret smiled at him, showing him her sparsely toothed gums.

"No better deckchild to serve, D'keeper," she said.

"Than it is decided," said Joron and put out a hand for Farys. She blinked, looked at him. Nodded. Then she took his hand and he pulled her to her feet. "If anyone gets past you and up those stairs, I'll have you all corded."

"Ey, D'keeper," said Farys. "There'll be no need for that."

"No," said Joron, "I do not believe there will. Karring, you come with me."

"Ey, D'keeper," said Karring.

With that Joron turned and ran up the stairs after Meas and the rest of the crew, through the wisps of smoke that threaded the air with the smell of roasting flesh.

On the first floor he found a few bodies – nobody he recognised. The sounds of fighting came from above and he rushed up to the second floor. What he found puzzled him at first, for though speed was of the essence Meas and *Tide Child*'s crew were holding back, standing at the top of the stairs screaming encouragement. Then he understood: this sort of fighting was the true domain of Coughlin and his men – they were trained for it. He could see their backs at the next set of stairs, and then the raiders must have broken and they were gone up to the top of the tower.

"Shipwife Meas!" came Coughlin's voice.

"Joron," she said, "with me." She pulled one of the crossbows from her coat and they ascended.

On the top of the tower Kanvey and ten of his raiders remained. They were corralled by Coughlin and his men, all armed with shield and sword, into one corner of the tower, away from the big gallowbow. Narza ran to the bow, looked it over and then kicked it, hard, twice and pulled the cord from it, showing it to Meas.

"Hag's arse," said Meas. "They have cut the cord rather than allow us to use it."

"Why do we need it?" said Joron.

Meas pointed across the strait to the other tower.

"To take down that, before they take down us."

"What do we do with them?" said Coughlin, pointing at the women and men around Kanvey. "There is little fight in 'em now."

Meas looked over the little group.

"I need cord for this gallowbow," she shouted. "I have little time. I imagine the other tower already suspects this one is taken. Anyone who tells me where there is launching cord may join my crew and live."

"There is none," said a tall woman with blood dripping down her face from a cut to her head. "That was our last."

"There is the old cord," said a small man holding a wyrmpike in a hand with only three fingers, "in the red barrel on the second floor. But there is not much tension left in it."

"Mevans," said Meas, "get that cord. You two" – she pointed at the man and woman – "over here. When Mevans returns you will help him string the gallowbow." Meas strode to the edge of the tower and, taking the nearglass from her coat, stared down the channel. "Hag's breath." She said it so quietly only Joron heard her. "They are near now." Then she swung the nearglass round to inspect the other tower. It did not look like much to Joron, just a flimsy construction of gion and varisk, but it must have been stronger than it looked to mount a bow like the one in front of them. Mevans reappeared with a length of bowcord and together with the two raiders began to string the great bow as Meas watched the other tower through her nearglass.

"Down!" screamed Meas, and all hit the floor of the tower. It felt as if every brick of the tower jumped, making a noise like a club hitting a head, but so much louder. The air filled with choking dust.

"What happened?" Joron raised his head, spitting out thick air.

"The other tower," said Meas. "They loosed a wingbolt at us." She stood. "Everyone down the stairs . . ." she began and then her voice tailed off. Half of the top of the tower was gone, as was their route of escape. Kanvey, along with what remained of his raiders, had vanished. Where they had stood was a void. The wingbolt had destroyed the corner of the building where the raiders had been, the stairs and part of the floor below. Coughlin stood with his men on the edge of the void, looking dumbfounded. "Mevans!" shouted Meas. "Get that bow strung now!"

"Almost done, Shipwife," he shouted. And if he was at all disturbed by the destruction of the tower he did not show it. "But the fellow was right. There's little tension left in it. I doubt we'll—"

"I will hear no doubts!" she shouted, then looked through her nearglass. "They are getting ready to loose again but they are not fleet," she said. "We are. So we will be ready before they launch again."

"Ey, Shipwife," said Mevans as he threaded the bow. "Well, spin it then," he shouted to the two ex-raiders standing by the bow. "And someone bring me a wingbolt!" Coughlin stumbled over, holding one of the heavy stone bolts, which must have weighed nearly as much as he did.

"Anzir," he said, "help me load this. I have no wish to be swept off the tower like those other poor fools."

"Not yet," said Mevans. "We are not full wound yet." He watched the two raiders as they spun the winch, and if he was worried about another bolt hitting the tower Joron could not tell, though he could feel the tension rising among those who stood around him.

Meas continued to stare through her nearglass.

"Are we ready yet?" she said. "For they almost are."

"Nearly, Shipwife."

Meas did not look at him, only continued to stare through her nearglass.

"Down!" Meas shouted again and they hit the floor once more. The building shook, but this time not as violently. Joron was one of the first to his feet, to find Meas already up and leaning over the parapet staring at the ground. "That one hit the base of the tower. There are cracks in the wall but we still stand. It will not take much more though – it seems raiders are shoddy builders. Come on, Mevans, spin that bow, Hag curse you."

"Load!" shouted Mevans, stepping back, and Coughlin and Anzir hurried forward, placing the bolt into the bow.

Meas ran across to stand behind it.

"Mevans, two points to seaward if you would," said Meas. Those atop the tower, covered in dust, aware that death could come at any moment, held their breath as Meas, calm as it was possible to be, lined up her shot. "Raise its beak a touch, Mevans . . . Another point to seaward." She stared a moment longer until those on the tower were wound as tight as any firing cord. Joron knew the bowteam on the other tower would be spinning their own bow, getting ready to loose again. "That's it, Mevans. Loose! Loose it!"

Mevans pulled the cord, jumping back as the bow sang its violent song and the wingbolt skidded along the shaft and out into the air. The deckchilder on the tower roared as if their shout could give the bolt extra force and help it on its way.

Their roar was swiftly stilled.

The bolt was not going to reach its target. Mevans had been right: the cord had little fury left in it. The wingbolt glided out from the tower, losing height all the while, and by the time it was a third of the way across the strait was already well below the height of the tower on the other side. They watched forlornly as the bolt splashed into the sea barely halfway across the channel.

No one spoke.

Joron felt that the Hag was a step away from claiming them all. There was little they could do to stop the other tower launching. In the silence he could hear the tower below him creaking and moaning like a boneship caught in a storm. Joron was sure it would not take another hit.

"What are you standing about for?" shouted Meas. "Spin that bow up, Mevans, and cinch the cord as far as it will go. I care not if we risk it snapping."

"They will loose again soon," said a voice from behind them.

"And they may well miss," snapped Meas. She put the near-glass to her eye. "Spin it!" And the process started again, a little area of furious activity around the bow while everyone else could only stand and watch, trapped on top of the tower and with nothing to do but wait for the inevitable shot from across the strait. "Skearith's Broken and fiery heart!" Meas said. "They mock us."

"What?" said Joron.

"They are about to loose," she said, "and they are waving at us. Any who wish to lie down to meet the bolt may. But I will stand here and meet it head on." She gazed across the sea, and if a look could kill then the tower across from them would have been stricken. She raised her nearglass. "Here it comes."

It seemed a bad day to die. The air was so clear, the sky so blue and the sea so clean and cold. But this was the way of the Archipelago: this was how the Maiden liked to trick, how the Mother taught hard lessons and how the Hag loved to mock. They had fought so hard, done so much, but it meant nothing. A breeze caressed the back of Joron's neck. He heard the cry of a bird.

The wind brought the faint shouts of triumphant women and men and the cough of the other tower's gallowbow as it launched.

He heard the bird cry again – this time louder – and it seemed like time atop the tower slowed.

Black Oris landed on Joron's shoulder. Joron turned to look at the bird.

And there, climbing over the edge of the parapet behind him, was the gullaime windtalker. It hopped across the broken roof on to the great bow and from there on to the one of the crenellations of the tower. All watched in silence, some confused by its sudden appearance, some shocked, some pleased. It snapped its beak at the air. At the same time it flapped its robed wing across the front of its body, as if batting away some troublesome insect.

Joron heard the whistle of the incoming bolt, and Black Orris flew from his shoulder.

Did he imagine it, or gestured did he actually see the bolt swerve? See it caught in a gust of wind. See it tumbling and spinning though the air until it landed in the clearing below the tower, throwing up a great splash of earth and carving a huge divot. The gullaime turned its head – but not its body – to face Meas.

"They miss," it said. "Don't you miss, ship woman."

"Load the bow," she shouted. Coughlin and Anzir were there. Mevans had already spun it back and then the bolt was in. "Loose!" And all those on the tower rushed to the parapet to watch the bolt.

It fell. Just like the first bolt.

The gullaime let out a furious screech and threw both its wings forward. From far below and to seaward its call was answered by the deeper, multi-toned shout of the approaching arakeesian. Joron's ears hurt, and he thought he heard the song of the windpsire, loud and triumphant and beautiful as it twisted in and out of the call of the gullaime and the call of the keyshan. Then the windtalker raised its wingclaws above its head, wind howled around the tower and out to sea. It lifted the falling bolt, raising it higher and higher higher on invisible currents, far above the height the bow could have taken it to. Then the gullaime let out another screech, one full of fury, and once more it was answered by the sea dragon far below. Then the windtalker brought its wingclaws down.

The bolt dropped like a stone. The impact of the wingbolt on the opposite tower was so powerful it seemed to explode. The bolt smashed through the platform, the scaffolding and the floor below, sending varisk and bodies flying through the air, cascading down the cliff face to splash into the uncaring sea below.

Silence.

The gullaime turned, hopped down from its perch, walked across the tower and jumped up on to the opposite parapet. It glanced towards the missing corner where the stairs should have been and shook itself.

"How you get down, Joron Twiner?" it said. Then it climbed head first down the outside of the tower. From out of the sky came Black Orris, landing on Joron's shoulder once more.

"Arse," said Black Orris.

Bird take an oar.
Godbird lights the way.
Maiden take an oar.
Trick for the Maiden.
Mother take an oar.
Duty for the Mother.
Women take an oar.
Honour for the Bern.
Men take an oar.
Coin for the Kept.
Pull for the Hag.
The Hag takes all.

Traditional rowers' chant

32

Sooner Not Start Than See a Job Half Done

Ropes, that was how they got down. Farys and the others Joron had left at the base of the tower had survived the bombardment and found ropes to throw up. Once everyone was down, Meas ordered the tower to be burned. As they left the island in the flukeboats Joron looked back to see the fire do its work and watched the tower as it crumbled into the sea, sending up great plumes of water as *Cruel Water* and the arakeesian passed.

The gullaime rode on Joron's flukeboat, perched on the prow like a particularly ugly figurehead. It did not speak, only stared forward. The rowers looked tired, and Joron knew how they felt. His muscles ached, he stank of fire, and when he closed his eyes he would see one of the many moments when he had come close to losing his life: The first strike of the wingbolt, one moment, Kanvey and his raiders the next, the fires of life extinguished in the blink of an eye.

He looked at Farys, who led the rowing, calling out the stroke using an old song, and though tiredeness was writ in her every movement she found time to smile at Joron.

"We did a good job, D'keeper?"

"Ey," he replied, straightening where he sat on the rump of the boat, "and I am rightly proud of you all." Heads went down in the boat, as if it was difficult for them to hear his praise, but he felt they were pleased by it. He sat back and let them row, aware, in a way he never had been before, that his rank created some impenetrable barrier between him and those who were under him. He would, *must*, rely on them, be prepared to put his life in their hands, but he would never get to call them his friends. He would always be apart from them and they from him. Some of those in the boat had been with him when he had called himself shipwife and would once have laughed at the thought of following any command from his mouth. They should still see him as a fool, but they did not. Meas had wrought some strange magic, and he had been reborn through her.

The flukeboats met up with *Snarltooth*, which followed the tail of the sea dragon. The two-ribber's shipwife, Brekir, ordered the boats to be taken in tow, so the deckchilder put up their oars and got some longed-for rest.

They passed between the cliffs of Arkannis Channel, black to seaward, white to landward, and Joron stared up at the smouldering wreck of the tower and quietly asked the Sea Hag to look after those who had fallen there. He was awed by the mountains of Skearith's Spine, from their base, where waves crashed and foamed against the rock to the almost-lost-in-the-clouds splashes of snow on the summits. His crew saw no wonder there, they demonstrated one of the great skills of the true deckchild – the ability to sleep anywhere, and the fluke-boat was pulled through the sea to a chorus of snores.

Later, and safely back on board *Tide Child*, Meas congratulated him and poured him a cup of akkals, the harsh spirit beloved by the rich on Bernshulme. It had been a long time since Joron had touched alcohol, and though the warmth of it in his gullet was welcome it brought back unpleasant memories of the man he had been, hiding in the derelict flensing yards and trying to drink himself to death. He did not ask for another glass, though neither did Meas offer.

"We have done well," she said eventually, "though without the gullaime we would have been lost."

"Never question the Maiden's gift," said Joron, the alcohol having loosened his tongue a little.

"No, never do that. And I do not." She picked up her cup, put it down. "It was a hard fight, but from now onwards hard fights will be our lives."

"It will?" said Joron. And he wished he had asked for another cup of akkals. His mouth was dry and his body longed for alcohol, but he shut the desire away.

"Ey," she said, placing her hands on the surface of her desk. "We have passed the capital line now; the weather will only be getting colder."

"But the nearer we get to the Northstorm, the emptier the sea will be. There are fewer islands so that should benefit us."

"Maybe," said Meas, then stood and walked to the door. "Have Aelerin and Dinyl brought to me," she shouted. Joron heard the call echo through the ship, and a minute later the courser walked into the cabin, closely followed by the deck-holder.

"You wanted us, Shipwife?" said Dinyl.

"Ey." Meas pulled a chart from a drawer and spread it on the desk. "Courser, show Joron and Dinyl where we think the arakeesian will go and where we should worry."

"Yes, Shipwife." They leaned over the desk, putting a slim finger on a blue line that snaked up the map. As they moved their finger along, Joron saw the distance eaten away, saw the days and weeks passing with each small movement. "Here," they said, "the wind sings me about a week's journey. We can expect to find the first touches of the Northstorm. I do not think gales and such, but the wind will not be as kind to us. It is also here that there is a thinning of the ocean, not so you can see, but underneath and it will force our course. If we were hunted by Hundred Isles ships, this would be where to pick us up."

"So they may have a fleet waiting for us?" said Joron.

Dinyl shook his head.

"They should not have. Kept Karrad and his allies in the Gaunt Islands are stirring up more trouble to keep the fleet busy and drawn towards the Southstorm. They may know about the arakeesian by now, but neither side will want to stop watching the other."

"That is true," said Meas, "and any ship would be hard pressed to catch us without killing his gullaime. Our real danger is from anyone who already knows what we are about and hunts us for it."

"I thought none knew," said Joron.

"A secret cannot be kept for ever," Meas said quietly. "*Hag's Hunter* went north before we did."

"Ships are sent north all the time," said Dinyl. "That does not mean—"

"And *Tide Child* was searched the night before we left."

"For Cahanny's cargo," said Dinyl.

"You think it was that?" Meas raised an eyebrow. "Do not forget what else we should have had on board when they came looking."

"You mean the bolts to poison the arakeesian," said Joron.

"I am glad you are not asleep, Joron," said Meas.

"Karrad would not betray us," said Dinyl more forcefully. "He understands duty, as do I."

"He had a you put on a black ship," said Joron.

"For duty," said Dinyl. "To end the trade in bones."

"You think that?" said Joron. "Are you sure you had not simply displeased him? For that is why I am here."

"Kept Karrad would not—"

"Karrad had me condemned for killing his son in a duel."

"I am sure it was not that simple. I heard that—"

"It was a fair duel," said Joron, heat rising to his face, "and legal by all the Hag's laws."

"In court, it was said the boy was drugged," said Dinyl.

Joron stood, his chair screeching on the white deck.

"He was drunk!" he shouted.

Dinyl stood as well.

"Stop!" said Meas. "What is past is past and Karrad's reasons do not matter. And besides, Dinyl is right: Karrad would not betray us in this. Peace matters to him, but at the same time little goes on in the Hundred Isles without my mother hearing whispers."

"You think the Thirteenbern knows what we are about?"

Meas tapped the desk with her bone knife, then shook her head.

"No. If she knew, the entire fleet would have been on us from the moment we set out. But the search — sending *Hag's Hunter* north . . . Since we set off I have wondered if she suspects something and guards her rear. We will have to watch our horizons closely." She looked up. "Carry on, Aelerin."

"Thank you, Shipwife," said the courser. "Up here, after we touch the Northstorm, we keep on until here" — they tapped the map — "where the only deep water is on the Gaunt Islanders' side, so we must cross the Spine."

"Here is where we will have trouble," said Meas. "There are towers. They are little more than watchtowers and do not have great bows, but they will alert any ships in the area."

"And how many will that be?"

"Minimum? I imagine two, maybe three two-ribbers, but it would not surprise me if there was something bigger in the area. The Gaunt Islanders are not fools." She tapped the gap in Skearith's Spine with her knife. "Make no mistake about it, we will be in a fight about here."

"Further up we will pass back through the Spine to Hundred Isles waters." Aelerin moved their hand, and again Joron had the dizzying sensation of flying at speed over the water. "More watchtowers here," said the courser.

"I am less worried about those," said Meas. "The cold north is rarely patrolled now. The ice is too dangerous and ships too precious to risk on its spines." The courser nodded. "Thank you, Aelerin, you may leave us now." They waited until the courser was out of the cabin.

It was Dinyl who broke the silence:

"A long journey."

Joron ignored him.

"So, when we reach here, Shipwife" — he touched the map — "all we need do is pass through the icefields and kill the arakeesian."

She smiled at him. "You make it sound simple, Joron."

"Killing the arakeesian should be," said Dinyl. "Indyl Karrad has supplied the weapon for that. One poisoned bolt in the eye of the beast and it is done." Quiet fell upon the cabin. "That is what you want, right?" said Dinyl. "An end to the risk the dragon's bones pose?"

"Of course," said Meas. "Dinyl, if you would go to the hold and check the condition of the cold weather clothes."

Dinyl hesitated, and Joron saw something akin to pain cross his face at the dismissal, then he he nodded and left.

Meas gave him time to get below before she stood and went over to the great window to gaze out at the arakeesian. *Tide Child* flew the sea slightly in front of the creature's head, and it appeared as if Skearith's Eye, low in the sky, was held between the branches of its horns. Below the horns the keyshan's many eyes burned, and Joron felt once more he could hear the song of the windspires on the wind.

"We should not forget," said Meas quietly, "that Indyl Karrad no doubt has his own agenda, and Dinyl is his agent. At the least he is here to spy on us. Karrad wants what he wants, but why? And I doubt he told me everything." She turned from the arakeesian. "Well, I have said all I need to. We have a ship to run, Twiner, and you do not appear to be doing that, so I suggest you get on with whatever duties you have."

Joron left her cabin and went next door to his. He had been back on board *Tide Child* two days and had not seen the gullaime since it hopped off the flukeboat and vanished into its cabin. It was not that he avoided it, simply that he had been too tired from the fighting on the island and then too busy working the ship. But he was not scared of the windtalker now; in fact, he wanted to talk to it, to find out about the sound he kept hearing, the constant song. So he would call on the gullaime now. He opened his door to find Dinyl waiting for him in the gloom of the underdeck.

"Joron."

"You should address me as Deckkeeper, Deckholder."

"Of course." He took a step back. "My apologies, Deckkeeper." He looked at the floor. Dinyl was a smaller man than Joron, though better built, stronger. "What I said in the great cabin, about the duel. I . . ."

"As Meas said, such things are the past." Joron did not look him in the eye, only made to go around him, but Dinyl put a hand on his arm, stopped him.

"Yes, they are. But what I said was not in the past, it was said today. It will be like a cold breeze between us if it is not addressed."

"Well, it is best to have some distance between ranks in the fleet," said Joron, as fleetlike as he could. "I am told this is how it is." Again he tried to step around Dinyl.

"Deckkeeper," Dinyl said, his words soft, "I am trying my utmost to apologise."

Joron stopped. Let out a breath.

"I did not drug Rion Karrad," he said. "I went to that duel fully expecting it to be my last day under Skearith's Eye and to spend that night at the Hag's fire."

"I should never have said what I did in the Shipwife's cabin, Deckkeeper," said Dinyl. "They were Indyl Karrad's words coming from my mouth, not mine."

"I did not see him in the cabin, Deckholder. Now, if you will let me past I have work to do."

"I was Karrad's man for so long that it became second nature to me, to voice his opinion. I should have thought before I let the wind from my mouth." Dinyl took off his no-tail hat and scratched at his hair; he wore it short, unlike most men of the Hundred Isles. "I knew Rion," he said. "Karrad said you had drugged his son, and I heard it so often as he convinced others of it that I even came to believe it myself."

"You speak like you knew he was not drugged." Dinyl looked away. Something dark rose within Joron and he stepped nearer to the deckholder. "You did know," said Joron, incredulous. "How?"

"I was his second that day, hanging back in the shadows behind the rest. We were all drunk."

"You were there? You were his friend?" There had been a glimmer between them, a ship friendship growing, even. And now?

"Not his friend," said Dinyl, he looked miserable. "Never that. His father appointed me his son's minder though I was not that to Rion. I was the butt of his jokes, his punchbag on occasion, servant on others. That morning he drank. I tried to convince him not to but he would not listen. He did not fear a fisher's boy. 'I could kill him drunk and blindfolded, Dinyl.'" He looked away again. "I felt like cheering when you killed him."

"But you never told the truth of the matter? You could have saved me from the black ship." Joron wanted to spit. "You could have told them it was a fair fight."

"I was frightened. I thought Karrad would never forgive me for not stopping his son drinking, so I pretended I was not with him that morning, and when the story got about that he had been drugged, it seemed like I was off the hook."

"Why tell me this, Dinyl? Why now?"

Dinyl took a breath. Let it out. Shrugged and stared at the overbones.

"I am alone on this ship, Deckkeeper. Trusted by none. You are the nearest I have had to a friend and yet even that small friendship I do not deserve."

An inkling awoke within Joron.

"Is that why Karrad sent you on here, to join the condemned?"

"Of course. He is the Thirteenbern's spymaster. He knew all along that I had let his son drink the day of the duel. He only waited for a time when his vengeance could also be useful to him. But now you know that, you know I am no more favoured than you and am just as committed to our cause as any other. Meas need not send me away, and I will do my duty. I can only regain Karrad's favour by doing my duty. And I am fleet through and through – duty is my all. Karrad told me it was my duty to support him, he served the fleet. He paid for my education." Joron did not think he had ever seen a man look as miserable, or as trapped. "What could I do?"

For a moment Joron thought of striking Dinyl. Of how good it would feel for his fist to meet this man's flesh. Here, in front of him, was someone he could blame for his fate, for the fact he was one of the condemned. He clenched his fists. Felt his muscles tense, and then a stray thought passed through his mind. Of the cabin boy, Gavith. Of how Meas had said that if the boy did not come with them the Kept would kill him simply because he was inconvenient to them. Could Joron doubt for one moment that, even if he had walked away from the death of Rion Karrad, if the Bern had said it was a just death, that he would have lived for long?

Of course not.

One night someone would have found him, started an argument in a tavern or slipped a knife between his ribs on the docks.

He let his muscles relax a little. Unclenched his fists.

"It is brave of you to tell me all this, Dinyl," he said.

"I had offended you anyway, Deckkeeper. And you, all I had for a friend."

Joron let out a sigh.

Had he not thought to himself only days ago how he was a better man for meeting Meas – how he was born anew? Could he really hate Dinyl for his part in putting him on this path?

"Call me Joron. At least when no one is in hearing so Meas cannot pull us up on it. What is it she says? That we leave all we were behind when we join the black ship?" He put out his hand. "Let us leave what we were behind."

Dinyl looked at the hand as if it were something completely alien to him. Then a wide smile crossed his face and he took it.

"We can be friends again?"

"Ey, friends. We may not live long, so let us not be lonely while we still draw breath."

"No," said Dinyl, and his hand was warm in Joron's.

"Well, now I must see to the gullaime, and you must see to cold-weather clothes, unless you want Meas to order you corded."

"Yes, Deckkeeper," he said, and grinned at Joron as he let go of his hand.

Joron watched him walk away and felt a little lighter of step himself.

He crossed the underdeck and knocked on the gullaime's door.

"Come, Joron Twiner," it squawked, and he passed into its sanctum.

The room had changed much since the first time he had been here. It was still messy to Joron's eye, but he felt like there was some sense of order to it now. And the smell – that smell of heated sand and parched desert land, the lifelessness he associated with the heartgrounds: where in days past the huge and glowing hearts of the keyshan were dragged, and all around them sickened and died, where still nothing grew today – it was not gone from the gullaime's quarters, but transmuted. The cabin still smelled of heat, but not a dead heat, a clean heat. Heat like a summer morning, when the sea lapped against the sand and the wind was kind and you knew the nets you cast that day would come back full. A heat full of promise.

The gullaime itself looked different. It had feathers now, not just little white spines. The feathers had no colour, looking more like short wiry hair on the creature's face. The cloak it wore had changed as well: it was no longer dirty, and the tears had been sewn up more carefully. And they had a shared secret. The reason Joron felt like he was being scrutinised whenever the gullaime turned its masked head towards him was because he was: he knew the windtalker was not blind like the rest of its kind. He had seen the shining eyes behind the mask, eyes that should not be there.

The gullaime opened its beak, showing the cave of spines within, and his name crept from its mouth as two definite, separate syllables: "Jor-on" – the first stressed and said slowly, the second bitten off.

"I came to thank you," he said.

"Thank gullaime? No one thanks gullaime."

"Well, Meas said this ship would run differently, and if you had not come to us at the tower we would be dead. You did not have to do that. You could have escaped."

"Go where, Joron Twiner? Go where?"

"I do not—."

"Joron Twiner saved gullaime."

"I did?"

"In the windsick gave blood, gave time. Saved gullaime." Suddenly it was standing, although not fully. It shuffled forward at half its normal height, body swaying from side to side. "Know why you weep," it said. "Heard all. Gullaime lost much too." A shock. He had told it his secret thoughts thinking it dead, or at least asleep, but it had heard.

After the shock, curiosity.

"What did you lose?"

"Nestlings. Nest father. Nest mother. All gone."

"I am sorry," said Joron.

The gullaime snapped its beak at the air, almost but not quite in his direction.

"Why?"

"Well, I am—"

"Gullaime die, yes? Is what gullaime for. Gullaime speed ships so humans may kill. Gullaime die to do this. Humans die when gullaime do this. All is death and death and death." It snapped at the air again and settled back into its nest.

"But the Gaunt Islanders—"

"Kill guallaime too. Blind gullaime too."

"But you are not blind," said Joron, glad to escape the discomfort the gullaime's words made him feel about the world he lived in. The world he was part of.

"No," it said and raised the mask a little so he could see those magnificent, bright eyes. "First gullaime to witness sea sither in more years than human can dream." It rearranged some of the torn material which made its nest, apparently finding some comfort in this. "First," it said quietly.

"How?" said Joron.

"With eyes," said the gullaime. It put its head down, rooted through the objects on the floor with its beak as if suddenly bored with Joron.

"I did not mean that; I meant how did you keep your eyes?"

It stopped utterly still then lifted its head to stare through its mask at Joron.

"Two eggs rare in gullaime," it said. "Nest father escape lamyard. Hid second egg, buried it in warm near spire. Hatched into dirt. Born fighting. Fighting to breathe. Fighting to surface. Born singing the great song." It made a sound like a gentle cough, something ineffably sad. "Nest sibling went to train, be blinded. Gullaime stayed hidden. Pretended to be sibling when needed."

"And no one noticed?"

"All gullaime alike to human, yes?" It did not give Joron time to answer, hurrying on with its tale, mouth open, words emerging. "Nest father sent to sea. Never came back. Nest sibling not strong, not strong. Get windsick. Die. This gullaime take place on training."

"What of your mother?"

"Mothers not stay." It said this offhandedly. "Gullaime train. Learn lots. Train and train. The weak die. Say nest mother weak. Say nest father weak. Say nest sibling weak." It clacked the air twice again. "Gullaime show them who weak."

"How?"

"Drop rock on bothy."

"What?"

"Drop rock on bothy. Kill trainers."

"And that is why they sent you to the black ship?"

The gullaime let out a deafening squawk. "No! Not know, not know. Think accident. Say accident. All gullaime gathered, expected sad torturers die." It settled down on the nest.

"Then how did you end up on *Tide Child*?"

"Rude," it said, and drew the word out like the long sigh of a wave retreating down a beach.

"You were rude?"

"Rude like Black Orris rude. Shipwife not liking rude gullaime. Not loving it. Send it away."

"And you let them send you away? I have seen what you can do."

"Wanted escape. Wanted escape and help all gullaime. But cages and drugs and windsick on fleet ship."

"You are not windsick now. You could wreck us, escape."

The gullaime stood in that upsetting way it had of simply seeming to levitate from sitting to standing. It stalked across the small cabin to stare out of the bowpeek. Outside the arakeesian glided through the sea, its eyes burning. Joron's mind filled with the the song of the winds and the sea.

"Gullaime with the sea sither," it said quietly. "This is where gullaime is. This is where gullaime should be." Then it settled down to watch the arakeesian, and Joron had the feeling that he was intruding upon some form of communion. He did not feel threatened by it, only fascinated, but at the same time he did not want to spoil the strange and delicately balanced friendship he seemed to have established with the windtalker. So, very quietly, he left the cabin, his questions about the song forgotten.

33

The Drum Beats Out and All the Deckchilder Answer

A rhythm to the day.

Wake, eat, work, watch, eat, watch, eat, work, eat, sleep, wake, work . . . and a keyshan off the seaward side.

Days passed into weeks, and the weather passed from the gentle hands and warm breezes of the Eaststorm into the cold anger of the Northstorm. The three ships built up another rhythm, a martial rhythm: working the bows in the morning, arms practice in the afternoon and every Menday the three shipwives met on *Tide Child*.

Meas's crew became more and more familiar with their ship, knew its ways, and now when the shipwife thought that they should tie down a mainwing or loosen a forewing she would find her crew already there, waiting for her order. In the way of a good ship, no one on *Tide Child* was ever idle; far gone were the days of lounging on the slate, and if someone tried, their fellows would pick them up on it. The gallowbow crews became increasingly proud of their skill, and scrimshaw work started to appear on the weapons, carvings telling of *Tide Child's* victories so far, few as they were.

Wake, eat, work, watch, eat, watch, eat, work, eat, sleep, wake, work . . . and a keyshan off the seaward side.

It felt to Joron as if, with every turn of the sandglass, the air dropped a degree, and for every day of travel they made, more cold-weather clothes were broken out. Deckchilder moved across decks which now rose and fell with the waves far further than before, but all aboard, even Coughlin's men, had their sea legs now and had reached the point where the thought of land, sturdy and unmoving beneath their feet, had become quite alien to them. Meas had shortened the watches. No one stayed in the tops for longer than twenty turns of the glass, as the shipwife knew how hard it was to be up there when the north wind plucked at their skin and tried to freeze the water in their eyes.

They saw few ships as they ran before the Northstorm's capricious gusts. Sometimes there were wings on the horizon but none were true boneships; all were merchanters, lumpen brownbones – ill-made ships cobbled together from old keyshan bones that no other wanted. Ships that forced their way through the sea taking cargoes hither and thither, ships of no threat to *Tide Child*, his flotilla or the arakeesian.

Wake, eat, work, watch, eat, watch, eat, work, eat, sleep, wake, work . . . and a keyshan off the seaward side.

Flukeboats too, were seen, sometimes in great fleets of as many as fifty, hunting sunfish, said the sagest old hands, as it was the time of year when those great and gentle creatures rose to the surface. Meas had them watched nonetheless, but if any of them caught sight of *Tide Child* and his escort, three ships of war that flew no flags for them to recognise, they steered well away, and so it was that they continued, alone, in their course along Skearith's Spine.

Hastin, who was once a deckkeeper, seemed changed by the trust Joron had put in her on Arkannis. She slowly left the poisonous orbit of Cwell and gravitated towards Solemn Muffaz and Gavith, where they stood on the midships. When they approached settlements Meas had either *Cruel Water* or *Snarltooth* fly by them first with Gaunt Islander flags flying, as though they searched for children to take back to their islands beyond the Spine. Up here, past the capital line, nothing was more certain to keep men and women in port and behind their defences than a Gaunt Islander ship of war cruising past. So, though their work was hard and the way was damp and becoming increasingly cold and uncomfortable, it was peaceful enough. Life became a routine. The cold, the exercise of the bows, the practice with bow and weapons, even the sight of the arakeesian as it swam along by them, massive, tireless and awe-inspiring, even that eventually simply became part of their world and something hardly remarked upon.

Wake, eat, work, watch, eat, watch, eat, work, eat, sleep, wake, work . . . and a keyshan off the seaward side.

One day *Cruel Water* left their small convoy. Joron had got used to thinking of them as a triumvirate, and to look out and see only one set of extra wings, black against the grey and swelling sea, he found oddly troubling. Meas said nothing about the missing ship, so Joron presumed the disappearance of *Cruel Water* was part of some plan she had chosen not to share, though another part of him worried she did not speak of it because she had not planned it, could not stand that a ship had deserted her. He knew the crew had noticed too, that they whispered of it, but he could not talk to them about it.

Although he grew in confidence, seemingly every day and with every order he gave Joron was more conscious of how the increasing respect of the crew for him was also a growing wall between them. Even those he considered close to him — Farys, Karring and Old Briaret — now saw him more as an officer than as a man, as a person. It saddened him that he could not be both, but he knew it had to be so.

The weather became colder.

The rhythm continued.

Wake, eat, work, watch, eat, watch, eat, work, eat, sleep, wake, work . . . and a keyshan off the seaward side.

A change to the rhythm came abruptly with the return of

Cruel Water. Meas called Joron and had him set the blue lights burning in the tops of the spines.

"You call the other shipwives?" he said. "But it is not Menday."

"I ask you to obey, Deckkeeper," snapped Meas, "not provide commentary." She stalked away and he set to doing as he was told, knowing that he had indeed been told. Three turns of the glass later he saw the faint glow of the lights in the beaks of approaching flukeboats as they rowed over to *Tide Child*. He could also smell the scent of a fine fish being roasted for a grand dinner and above that the sweeter scent of a boiled pudding. He wondered what had caused Meas to make this sort of gesture.

"Bad news for us, I imagine," said Dinyl, wrapping his stinker coat more tightly around his shoulders as he came to stand by Joron.

"What?"

"If she's having cook use up some of the last of our sweetsap for a pudding then it must be bad news. Treat them with good food, then they will be less bitter when you give them bad news, that was what Karrad always said."

"It is not bad news, not unexpected bad news anyhow," said Joron. "Only that we make the turn for the Gaunt Islands tomorrow. No doubt *Cruel Water* has been spying out the route."

"She tells you that but does not share it with me." Dinyl looked away, at the roiling sea.

"I do not think that was intentional."

"So you think, but I am not invited to the shipwives' dinner."

"Because she trusts you to run the ship."

Dinyl stood a little nearer, gazed into his face.

"Do you trust me, Joron," he said, "or are we no more than shipfriends?"

"Of course I trust you," he said, But though he knew Dinyl's warmth, his friendship and trusted him himself, somewhere within, he was not as sure the shipwife felt the same, and he could not meet Dinyl's eye. "But someone must command the ship while she gets the other shipwives ready."

"Ready for what?"

"To fight their own people of course. We have only fought raiders up until now. It is a different thing to kill your own women and men, or so I imagine."

"Surely a death is a death?" said Dinyl.

"To the blade that causes it maybe," said Joron, "but I reckon it is a fair difference to the mind which holds that blade."

Dinyl stared at him, and it seemed to Joron that the deckholder wished for something from him, but he did not know what.

"You are a deeper thinker than I expected," said Dinyl.

"I may not know as much as I think, Dinyl. The shipwife may only wish for Arrin to share his information while it is fresh in his mind. A lot of what we do next will depend on what *Cruel Water* has found out."

"If that is where he has been."

"Where else would he be?"

"I do not know," said Dinyl, "but neither do you, as she shares so little." He seemed to shrink down into his stinker, and Joron could not lose the idea Dinyl was hiding himself within it, moving away from him and the ship in some way. "Karrad shared almost everything with me."

"She is not Karrad," said Joron.

A few turns of the glass later, after the shipwives had been whistled on board, greeted by a far tidier and fleet-like crew than Joron had ever seen *Tide Child* put up before, Joron was asked down to the great cabin to join the meal. He took a seat next to Meas and placed his one-tail hat on the back of his seat, following the example of the other deckkeepers, sturdy Oswire next to one-legged Arrin – who sported a cut on his face – and Mozzan, a man with skin as dark as his own whose hair was woven into long thick snakes, beside Brekir – her deckkeeper as cheerful as she was morose.

"So, now we have a full table," said Mozzan, "does this mean we can eat?"

"Ey," said Meas. "Mevans! Bring through the first course." The hatkeep appeared at the door, holding it open for two crew, Chalin and Fornir, to bring in a huge plate on which was a roasted jawfish surrounded by root vegetables. The fish was as long and thick as a man's leg, curled on the plate so that its fanned tail propped open a fearsome mouth full of backward-facing spiny teeth. As tradition dictated, the officers were served only one side of the fish, the other side having been removed to treat the crew, and the fish had been arranged to hide the bare ribs. Before they started on the fish, Farys appeared with a steaming bowl of pounded varisk pulp, flavoured with dried berries.

"What a feast," said Arrin. "I do not think I have had jawfish since before I took on my black ship."

"I fear Shipwife Meas seeks to treat us with food in an attempt to make whatever task she has for us less bitter," said Brekir, staring at the opaque eyes of the fish on the plate. A crueller soul than Joron might have suggested that Brekir and the fish bore a distinct resemblance to each other.

"Ah, Shipwife," said Mozzan, "grim work is the lot of the dead, so we should enjoy what life we can."

"If you say so, Deckkeeper," she said with little enthusiasm.

Meas stood, lifted her cup, and Mevans appeared with a bottle of akkals and filled it, going around the table seaward side to landward.

When he came to Joron he covered his cup. "Only water for me, Mevans," he said. "It will be my watch after the meal." Mevans gave him a smile, nodded and moved on.

"We have seen action," said Meas, "and we have acquitted ourselves well. You both serve your ships well and have no need to prove this to me. I bring you food in the name of the Maiden, the Mother and the Sea Hag. Enjoy what is provided and be thankful the sea has not taken us."

She sat, and as she did everyone at the table raised their cups and gave the traditional reply.

"Be thankful for this, for the Sea Hag waits for all!"

The jawfish was portioned up and plated, and the pounded varisk served with it. Joron, used to hard gion bread and dried-fish stew, thought he had never tasted food so fine. Then came a soup made of the last of the ship's kivellys. They had stopped laying eggs a week ago and sealed their fate. Drink flowed and stories were told, jokes made, and by the time the glutinous steamed pudding was served, even morose Brekir was smiling, on occasion. When Mevans cleared away the plates and served a tisane to aid digestion, it would have been easy to forget that, just as much as the lowest woman or man on the ship, they were all women and men condemned to die.

Joron was talking to Mozzan, finding out how he braided his hair. It seemed a good way of keeping it out of his face; unlike Joron's wiry mop which was always escaping. Mozzan was giving a very detailed description of how to do it, all big gestures and smiles, when Meas interrupted.

"So," said Meas, "we have eaten, we have drunk and now we approach the quiet wake of the meal. Shipwife Arrin, tell us how your trip to Keyshanhulme Sound went." Mevans appeared and cleared away the last of the plates. And with them went the atmosphere of joviality and gentleness. The shipwives and deckkeepers were now all business, for this was important, this was the information they lived and died by. This was the business of war.

"We left you, and the north wind was kind, for once, almost as if it wished to hurry us to trouble. My contact was to meet us at Kwiln Howe – do you know it?"

"Meas is of the Hundred Isles," said Oswire. "Of course she does not, unless she has raided it." Oswire turned to Meas. "Have you?"

"No," said Meas, ignoring Oswire's tone. "I have rarely been this far north. Mevans, ask Aelerin to join us with their charts, if you would?"

"Ey, shipwife."

"But you did raid," said Oswire.

"Yes, I did," said Meas. "As did you, as did Brekir."

"Enough, Oswire," said Arrin. "What is past is past. We fight to end such things."

"So we do," said Oswire, and swirled the drink in her cup before taking a sip. "So we do."

They waited in silence until the courser appeared, rolled charts in their hands.

"Aelerin, the chart covering the area around Keyshanhulme Sound, if you would."

"Ey, Shipwife," said the courser and unrolled a chart on the table. Joron looked upon his world the way Skearith must have once stared down on it from the sky.

"Well," said Arrin, "I see your courser has marked out where we shall follow our charge through the deep-water channels. Not being so restricted we took a more direct route." He traced a line with a finger, passing through Keyshanhulme Sound, then dancing between islands on the other side until he stopped at one among many – nothing special, just an island like any other.

"The towers on Keyshanhulme are still there?" asked Meas.

"Ey," said Arrin, "but they do not have the range to cover the channel. As long as we keep to the centre they have little real chance of hitting us."

"Were there ships moored there?"

"A few flukeboats, nothing to worry about. One came out to meet us on our way back and was friendly enough. I said I would be returning later on, coming back through with a flotilla."

"You think we may be able to pass through without arousing suspicion?" asked Meas.

Arrin shook his head and his stripes of command fell into his eyes. He pushed the multicoloured hair out of his face. "Unlikely. The Gaunt Islands have no four-rib ships of the dead. We may get away with it. News travels slowly and they may think *Tide Child* newly taken, but even so, I suspect the fact we accompany an arakeesian will draw more than a little curiosity." He smiled and Meas let out a quiet laugh.

"I thought as much," said Meas.

"As did I," echoed Brekir, her voice barely raised above a miserable whisper.

"Carry on with your story, Arrin," said Meas. "I presume it involves a fight?" She pointed at the cut on his face.

Arrin grinned.

"Oh indeed," he said. "We arrived at Kwiln Howe. I expected my contact to meet us on the beach as we were not exactly inconspicuous and she knows what we are about, but it was not so. In fact, there was no one on the beach, which I thought true strange. Kwiln Howe is not often visited as the north side of the island is a heartground, and you know how suspicious women and men are about passing near the dead places. Usually any visitor to the island is gladly received."

"But not this time," said Brekir. "So runs our luck."

"It could have gone better, ey," said Arrin. "Anyway, I made my way to the village. They are all bent or twisted in some way. Berncast, you would say."

"You should have sent Oswire," said Mozzan. "The Hag cursed her with an eternally surly face – she would have fitted right in."

"I could pull off one of your arms, Mozzan," said Oswire, "and then who would fit right in?"

Mozzan laughed, though Joron was not sure Oswire was being humorous.

"Ey, that I would, Oswire, that I would."

"Carry on, please, Shipwife Arrin," said Meas. Though she did not say this was a rebuke to the two deckkeepers, the thought of it was a current running through her words.

"The villagers were having some type of festival. Spirits were definitely high, and they had raised a scaffold for a hanging. On the scaffold stood my contact. She was not in as high spirits as the rest of her people."

"They had found out about her? That she is for our peace?"

Arrin shook his head.

"No, it was local trouble of some sort. Something about a marriage contract that had been broken or not adhered to correctly, and they believed this had brought down the wrath of the Hag in the form of disease on the village. Why this worried them, I do not know; they all fall to keyshan's rot before they reach any great age on Kwiln Howe."

"And?" said Meas.

Joron realised he was enjoying the story. Arrin was a good tale teller.

"I explained that I needed to speak to the woman on the scaffold, and the headwoman and I had a disagreement." He pointed at the cut on his face. "As you can see."

"Did you lose anyone?"

"No, thankfully. They could not stand up to my deckchilder, but sadly I no longer have a spy on Kwiln Howe, though I at least have one more crew member."

"I hope the information was worth it."

"I think so," said Arrin. He passed Meas a piece of parchment with symbols scrawled on it. "She had this for you. I do not know the code so cannot tell you what it says. And she had other information for me which I will give you now. There is a patrol running up and down the Gaunt side of the sound." He traced a circle on the map with his finger. "This is the route they take. A pair of two-ribbers and a four-ribber."

"So we are equally matched with them," said Meas.

"Well, maybe not," said Arrin. "Coming back we saw them, beautiful ships with light purple wings, the colour of twilight. The four-ribber has four corpselights, each two-ribber has two, and they are all the blue of firstlight, so we know they are well maintained ships with no damage."

"Ours are hardly falling apart," said Meas.

"They still have the advantage," said Brekir, staring at the table. "No doubt they are straight out of dock, newly fitted out, no weed on their bones to slow them. And the deckchilder always think a ship with the lights of life has an advantage over a dead ship."

"Unfortunate, but it cannot be helped," said Meas. "Do they have gullaime?"

"I only saw them from a distance but the four-ribber, I think it is the *Wavebreaker*, was going against the wind so it, at least, must have gullaime aboard."

"Hopefully it wears them out and they will be windsick by the time we arrive," said Brekir.

"No," said Arrin. "This island here" – he touched a point on the map right in the middle of the circular course the ships were sailing – "has a windspire. Probably why they are happy to use the gullaime so carelessly."

"Blasted hearts," said Meas. "Aelerin," she said, "if we come through the sound and head immediately north, can we outrun the Gaunt Islander ships?" Aelerin leaned over the chart, and Joron thought he could hear the courser's gentle voice as they worked the complicated mathematics of wind and current through in their head.

"No, Shipwife. I do not think that is the song the winds sing me," said the courser. "The deep-water channel twists, and we will often have the storm against us, so it will slow us if we must follow the arakeesian. The Gaunt Islander ships can cut between the islands and use their gullaime and the prevailing winds to catch us."

"Why not just leave the keyshan?" said Oswire. "Run ahead and wait for where it rejoins. We have seen what it can do to a boat; I do not think a boneship would fare any better."

Meas nodded slowly, more to herself than any other, but Joron knew she was thinking of the poisoned bolts in the hold. If Indyl Karrad had found some, there was no guaranteeing that the Gaunt Islanders did not have them too. It was unlikely, Joron was sure of that, but also not a chance he thought Meas could take.

"What if they have—" he began, and Meas's head came up, her eyes locked with his, and he realised that she must not have shared everything with her fellow shipwives. He had been about to give up more than she wished. "—more ships somewhere?" he said.

Meas's glare turned to a nod.

"My deckkeeper is right. No, we cannot let them near the keyshan."

"So," said Brekir, "we stay with the arakeesian and get ready to fight a running battle. It will not go well as they have the advantage in first lighted ships and gullaime. They can wear us down from a distance — all they must do is match us shot for shot. And if they know the keyshan routes, they can lay in wait to ambush us where they wish."

"They will do that too," said Arrin. "I knew *Wavebreaker's* shipwife — she was a friend, once."

Meas leaned forward and put a hand on Arrin's arm.

"It is hard to fight your own. Especially when you were close once."

Arrin nodded.

"We waste our time and our lives," said Oswire. "The beast is stronger than any ships."

"I think the decision is made, Deckkeeper," said Arrin. The look on his face was one of acceptance. "What we do, it is for a higher cause, ey?"

"It is." Meas leaned back in her chair. "Mevans, could you ask the gullaime to come through. Ask it politely."

"You bring a windtalker into the shipwife's cabin?" said Oswire. "That is not the way things are—"

"We find new ways, Deckkeeper," said Meas. She stressed Oswire's rank, and something burned in the Gaunt Islander's eyes that Joron did not much like.

The gullaime, when it appeared, came in slow and hesitantly, pausing part way through each step with its foot raised, then it made a snapping motion with its beak as if catching something from the air, before finally rounding the table much more quickly, so it stood by Joron.

"Joron Twiner," it croaked. Joron noticed that all those around the table, Meas and Aelerin excepted, had moved slightly further away from him and the windtalker.

"Gullaime," said Meas, "thank you for coming to us." The gullaime made a clicking sound in response. Meas drew the circular course of the Gaunt Islanders' ships on the map. "Conventional tactics tell us when confronted by an equal force to hang back and fight a war of attrition or avoid combat completely."

"Avoiding is best," said Brekir.

"Arrin," said Meas, "you said you knew the shipwife of the *Wavebreaker*. Is she good?"

"Yes," said Arrin. "Not spectacular, but competent."

"Were I her," said Meas, "I would stay at range and try to slow us while sending off one of my two-ribbers to gather every flukeboat possible. Then they could ambush us with as much force as they could muster, the boneships covering the flukeboats so they can board us."

"That would work," said Arrin. "There are troops at the towers, and on several of the islands around there are villages and towns that will send women and men if called."

"Then we must attack the boneships as soon as we leave the sound."

"It will be carnage," said Brekir. "We have been at sea for months; they will be fresh to the fight and fully crewed. They will likely destroy us if we go broadside to broadside."

"Then we will not do that."

"What do you mean, Meas?" said Arrin.

"They will travel with the two-ribbers line astern behind the big ship. We will do the same. When they see us approach they will think we mean to go broadside to broadside."

"That is how ships such as ours fight," said Brekir, "filthy as the work is. Side on side until one ship can no longer shoot back or burns."

"But we will not fight that way," said Meas. "Gullaime." The windtalker's head snapped round. "Can you give us enough wind for all three ships? I want to fly between the rump of the four-ribber and the beak of the first two-ribber."

"Can do that," said the gullaime.

"No windtalker is that strong," said Oswire.

"Kindly," said Meas, "do not tell me what my crew are, or are not, capable of. If the gullaime says it can do this, then it can."

Oswire glared at her, and an uncomfortable silence fell like drizzle in the cabin.

"We will still be under their bolts, though," said Arrin.

"And to go head on like that, every shot they loose will rake the entire length of our ships, it will be carnage, Meas, truly. Think about this. We generally spend half a fight trying to manoeuvre into position to loose down the length of an enemy ship. You speak of offering them this advantage for free."

Meas ignored him.

"Gullaime, on Arkannis Isle you deflected an incoming bolt from the other tower. Can you do that again?"

The gullaime made a noise like a door slowly opening.

"Yes and no. Yes and no."

"You can or you can't, beast," said Oswire.

It was as if a fire was lit behind Meas's eyes. "You will be quiet on my ship!" she shouted. "You are a deckkeeper, so know your place. You will respect my rank, my knowledge and my rules and stay silent when I speak to my crew." Oswire opened her mouth as if to reply but a look from Arrin had her think better of it. "Gullaime, please explain what you mean by 'Yes and no'."

"So near. Less time. Wingbolts bigger, easier. Big arrows less easy, cannot stop."

Meas nodded.

"Very well." She placed her knife on the table. "If I could borrow your knives, please?" Bone knives were passed to Meas so she had six, and she placed them on the table in two parallel lines. "This is them." She ran her finger down one line of ships. "This is us." She pointed to the other line. "We start as if we fight in the traditional manner, broadsides on. We will stay just out of range, then we will perform a sharp turn." She moved the knives representing her ships so they now made the stem of a T intersecting the other line behind the first ship. "The gullaime will provide all speed and what cover it can for us. *Tide Child* has the most gallowbows so we will do everything we can to take down *Wavebreaker* and the first two-ribber. We are the biggest ship so we will soak up as much shot as possible. Maybe it will tire out their bowteams." She bared her teeth in a humourless smile.

"You will pay a high price," said Brekir.

"Someone must." She glanced up at Brekir and Joron found himself thinking, *You do not trust her, do you, Meas?* Then Meas returned to the knives. "Arrin, you will follow *Tide Child*, and hopefully take fewer bolts for our work. The real danger to you is from their last ship." She took the knife that represented the last Gaunt Islands ship. "When we attack, *Wavebreaker* the next two-ribber will slow. If the shipwife of the last ship has anything about them they will come around their fellows to bring their broadside to bear."

"By bringing up the rear," said Brekir, "when you and *Cruel Water* break though, I could find myself trapped by that third ship and surrounded."

"I will bring *Tide Child* about as quickly as possible, Brekir," said Meas. "Gullaime, can you protect *Snarltooth*?"

"Not and give wind to steer big ship," croaked the windtalker. "Too far. Must choose." It pointed at the third ship. "Hard. Hard to see."

"You are blind, bird," said Oswire.

Meas let that slide.

"Blind, not blind. Feel the bolt in the air. Hard when air disturbed by many wings. Hard."

"You are right, Brekir," said Meas. "Whoever brings up the rear will be hard pressed if we cannot do significant damage to *Wavebreaker* and his consort," she said quietly.

"I will do it then," said Arrin.

Brekir stood. "No, Arrin. You flew with the arakeesian, were ready to put bolts in it to drive it down, knowing it would be the death of you. Now it is my turn."

"But I knew Meas would come through at Arkannis, Brekir."

"No, you hoped she would. *Snarltooth* will bring up the rear, and I will hope Meas comes through also." She turned to the gullaime. "Windtalker, my ship and my crew will thank you for whatever help you can provide, but if it is our day to meet the Hag, then so be it." By her Mozzan nodded, his smile undimmed.

"Will help," said the gullaime, "but . . ."

"But?" said Meas.

"Feather," it said, and pointed with its wingclaw at Meas's head.

She reached up, touched one of the black feathers braided into her hair.

"That is your price?" said Meas.

"Not price," said the Gullaime softly. "Will help. But . . ." It snapped at the air, a gentle movement, as if it searched for the right words in the air of the great cabin. "Gullaime like feather."

Meas continued to stare at the windtalker, then nodded. She picked up the knife she had used to represent *Tide Child* from the table and cut away the end of one of her braids with the feather attached.

"For you," she said, and held it out.

"Part of you, for me?"

"You are part of this ship, Gullaime," she said, "so you are part of me also."

The windtalker nodded its head and extended its long neck, the feathers growing on its head refracting the light in rainbows across the curve of its skull, then it opened its beak and very gently took the braid and the feather as if they were great treasure and tucked them inside its robe.

"Right." said Meas. "We should get ready. We will make full speed for Keyshanhulme Sound."

Meas and Joron escorted their guests back up to the slate of the maindeck, and it was clear to the crew of *Tide Child* that something had been decided. The crew had grown together and could read the mood of their officers. Meas stood by the rail as Brekir, Mozzan, Oswire and Arrin climbed down to their flukeboats. As Arrin walked past her he paused, leaned in and said something. Joron saw Meas nod. When Arrin's flukeboat was gone Meas ordered *Tide Child*'s wings to be spread and then came to stand by Joron.

"The parchment Arrin delivered – there was a coded message from Indyl Karrad."

"What did he say?"

"He reminded me of my duty. That I must kill the arakeesian. And he also said that *Hag's Hunter*, with my sither as shipwife, patrols the north. They are looking for the wakewyrm."

"So they know?"

"It seems so." She crumpled up the note and threw into the sea.

To the north, Skearith's Eye dipped below the horizon, and it was as if it bled into the sky, spreading a violent pink across the clouds, edging them with fiery yellow and molten silver. A sea mist was coming in, and it spread Skearith's colours further through the sky, made the air still, smothering the sounds of the ship. Heavy air, they called it.

"It is like we spread our wings to fly into a furnace," said Joron.

"Ey," she said. "Fire in the sky, water beneath us. Smiths use fire and water to set their weapons."

"What did Arrin say to you before he left, Shipwife?"

"He apologised for Oswire's behaviour in my cabin. Asked me to make allowances for her interruptions. Said she is new to the black ships and from an old family. It is hard for her."

"It is going to be hard for us all," said Joron as Skearith's Eye continued to blaze glorious colour across the horizon.

"It is," said Meas. "So let us fly fast, let tonight's fire and water set this weapon, for when we meet *Hag's Hunter*, Twiner – and we shall – we will need to be sharp and we will need to be keen." A smile moved across Meas's face like a bird caught by the wind: there one moment before suddenly falling away. The expression that replaced that fleeting smile Joron could not read. Then she walked back up to the rump to take her customary place by the spine.

Joron gazed after her and he realised what her expression had been in that moment she thought of *Hag's Hunter* and her sister waiting in the north.

It had been a look of satisfaction.

34

The Flight to the Death

They called the Northstorm the warstorm because those who lived on land thought it brought nothing but anger and death. The women and men of the sea knew different. The Northstorm was like war because it was unpredictable: it could be calm for weeks on end. It would lull you into a false sense of security before loosing its fury. And like war, the storm's fury, when unleashed, was terrible and deadly.

But, the Northstorm could be surprisingly gentle, and it was with gentle winds and shallow waves that the Northstorm flew *Tide Child*, *Cruel Water* and *Snarltooth* towards war, towards killing, towards wreckage and death. And whether it would be their own or another's they did not know. But one of the Maiden's greatest gifts, or greatest tricks, was to gift women and men the belief in the moment, of their own immortality. Without that belief then the likelihood of pain, the possibility that the next day they would sit at the Sea Hag's bonefire, well, who would ever go to war then? But each and every deckchild had the ability and the instinct to believe, quite wholeheartedly, that the worst would not happen to them.

Or so Joron thought, and he cursed them for it. Cursed their songs which grief still left him unable to sing, cursed the jaunty way they walked the decks as if action were something to be longed for. Cursed the way they talked of how they'd "show the Gaunt Islanders a thing or two" and cursed himself for not being able to see anything but his own coming demise.

Joron had the late watch that night, wrapped in a thick stinker coat and watching Skearith's Bones as they made their slow progression across the sky. He could find no peace. Every time he closed his eyes he heard the song of the windspire and saw the wingshot hit the tower. One moment women and men stood there, the next they were gone. Never mind that they had been the enemy. A single step forward and he would have joined those who had died at the tower. As surely as the bones in the night would change so these thoughts dogged him.

Tomorrow we will fight.

Tomorrow I may die.

Sleep had eluded him for days, but when it did come, it was not the coming action that he dreamed of, it was of being under the water, and not of drowning, not of fear. In his dreams he became something terrible, something sure of its terribleness, he had imagined that such a feeling would bring him peace but it did not because he knew this surety was misplaced. As he sheared through the water, glorying in his vast displacement, in the way that all creatures ran before him, he was haunted by the knowledge that he was not invulnerable, that there was a threat he did not know or understand but was no less real for that. And this dream, in the way of all dreams, faded into something nebulous and barely remembered by the time Joron slid from his hammock to take up his watches. All he had left of it was a creeping sense that he had missed something important but did not know what it was.

He stood on the deck of *Tide Child* as Skearith's Eye rose and the black basalt of Skearith's Spine gave up its secrets to the coming light: wheeling birds, vines and plants grimly clinging to the rock, tiny beaches where the midtide creatures came ashore to lay their eggs. While the spine revealed itself,

Tide Child hid his identity. A Gaunt Islander flag flew at the topspine in its savage glory, circles of silver and black.

"You think the flag will fool them?" said Dinyl as he approached.

Joron wished he would keep his voice down a little.

"If you spoke a little louder, Dinyl, I think the whole crew would hear you questioning the shipwife's orders."

Dinyl scratched his head, pushing fingers up under his no-tail hat to pull them through greasy brown hair.

"I only ask a question, is all."

"And it is a question you should not ask of Twiner." They turned to find Meas striding up the deck. "You should ask it of me and ask it in the privacy of the great cabin." Where Joron was tired and Dinyl looked resentful, Meas looked like she had slept the sleep of the just and been visited by the peace of the Mother. "But on this occasion it is a question I do not mind you asking and do not mind the crew hearing my answer."

Around them heads were raised – not obviously; nobody pausing in the myriad small or large or easy or complex tasks that kept a boneship running. But heads were angled, hair was tucked behind ears, hammers were put aside for quieter tools so that the shipwife's words could be heard.

"The flag will not fool them, not for long. Once someone who knows the ships of the Gaunt Islands well is consulted they will know they do not have a four-ribber. But they will wonder if this ship has been taken. So they will pause, they will wonder, and maybe they will let us pass through without checking or sending out a flukeboat to look at us."

"Maybe," said Dinyl.

"Oh, I know it is unlikely." Meas grabbed a rope and climbed on to the rail, staring out at Skearith's Spine and the birds wheeling and squabbling around its base. Then she turned to face the deck and raised her voice. "But it is worth a try, and the longer we have before the ships out there know of us" – she pointed through Skearith's Spine – "the better." She waited while her words sank in, then took a breath. "There is more I must tell you, and now is the time. I have not been truthful with you, and I must be that now. A shipwife does not have to explain herself, ever, but I choose to. I did not know all of you when I came aboard. Did not know what a fine crew you would turn out to be. Or if you would follow, if you would be loyal, if you would understand duty. But I do now. And I trust you to trust me. So stop what you do, my deckchilder, and listen."

They did. All around work stopped. Old crew and new crew and Coughlin's men and even those few that still followed Cwell gathered before the rail. The shipwife watched them gather, let them gabble excitedly and waited for them to settle, before she spoke again.

"Both *Cruel Water* and *Snarltooth* are Gaunt Islander ships." A sharp intake of breath at that, but Meas carried on. "They chose to join us, to protect the wakewyrm with us. So they may be able to pass us off as their prize, but they may not."

Cwell stepped forward, her face bent with scorn. She spat on the deck.

"You make us into traitors."

Meas jumped down from the rail to stand in the centre of the ship's deck.

"Have I made you into traitors?" She walked around Cwell, meeting the eyes of every woman and man but her. "Or have I made you into real deckchilder, into real crew? Into women and men with a bit of pride? Into fleet!" Her voice rose. "You saw *Cruel Water*," she said to Farys. "Saw him with his gallowbows pointed down, ready to loose on the arakeesian to keep it safe, even though they knew it was certain death for them." She walked across to Barlay. "Those ships will fight with us because they see what we see." She pointed to the wakewyrm. "They see the keyshan! They understand the keyshan! They know its bones bring war and killing for ever. And you" – she picked out Karring this time – "you have four children back in Bernshulme, children you see fit to kill others to protect.

The Hundred Isles, the Gaunt Islands — if either takes the arakeesian, we will fight for ever."

"That is what we do," said Cwell. "We fight the Gaunt Islanders." She turned to look into the faces of the crew. Joron could not read them. They looked uncomfortable, that was true, but were they uncomfortable with what Meas said or that Cwell challenged her? Cwell walked up to Meas, standing tall before the shipwife. "Fighting Gaunt Islanders is what we do."

"It need not to be," said Meas. "The wakewyrm is the last arakeesian. In the far north, where the water is too deep and dangerous to recover the body, we are to kill the beast." There was more shock at that than at the mention of working with Gaunt Islanders. "We carry the right weapon, an old and fabled weapon. One shot is all we need and then we let the corpse sink. The wakewyrm is the last one, the wars will stop."

Cwell took a step closer to Meas.

"If it is the last, we should take it for the Hundred Isles. The advantage would let us wipe out the Gaunt Islands."

"It does not work that way," said Meas. "Ships are taken and bone can be smuggled. No. The beast dies — it is the only way."

"I may be a murderer," said Cwell, and she turned to the crew, "but she is a traitor! A traitor!"

Would they turn on Meas? Joron could not tell. Maybe either the death of the keyshan or working with the Gaunt Islanders would have been accepted. But both? Was that too much? There were whispers. Tools were picked up from the deck as if to use as weapons. Was the fight lost before it had even started?

Barlay stepped forward, and as it was rare she chose to speak all action stopped. All talk stopped.

"Gaunt Islanders took my boy," she said. "Took him to sacrifice for their ships. He were not even whole — born with half a leg he were. I wanted him to be a shoemaker on Hoppity Street." She smiled then, a pleasant memory blowing across her face. It quickly passed and the storm followed. "They probably fed his blood to their ships, I reckon, maybe even those ones out there, that we head towards."

"See, Shipwife?" Cwell turned Meas rank into a sneer. "And you want us to be friends with these people." She turned her back on Meas. "This woman who calls herself Shipwife, she has lied to us. She has made us into betrayers. All know you get off a ship of the dead by doing some great deed. This could be our great deed, women and men of *Tide Child*. We can work together." She pointed at the deck, her hand shivering with anger. "We can remove a traitor from the slate of this ship. We can bring home the body of an arakeesian to the Thirteenbern. We will get rid of our black bands and become rich!"

"You have mistook me, Cwell," said Barlay. "What the ship-wife says is if there are no more arakeesians, there are no more bones. And if there are no bones there will be no more great ships. Varisk is too brittle, Gion is too soft for the big ships, and all know if it ain't got keyshan bone in it, then the Hag will take it. That is what the shipwife says — says women and men will not be able to raid or war. Says there will be no more children taken." She turned back to Meas. "That is right, is it not, Shipwife? I am right?" Her face was screwed up as if she fought, as hard as she may fight any physical opponent, to see past the world she knew into the possibility of another one.

"You are right, Barlay," said Meas. "That is what I dream of. That is why I stand on this deck with you. And I do not think I have ever heard any put it better than you."

"You do not stand with us," said Cwell. "You call yourself Shipwife, and put yourself above us. We are just Berncast to you. We are the twisted and the weak, and good only to serve."

"I lead, that is right enough," said Meas, "and I enforce discipline, for a ship will not work without it. But I stand among you, not above you. And is Joron Twiner good only to serve? His mother died bringing him to the world. They call him Berncast, say he is only a fisher's boy."

"Fine words," said Cwell, "yet you wear boots and we go barefoot. What do you say, Barlay?"

Barlay glanced at her, then her head turned to Meas. Her gaze travelled down the shipwife's body to her shoes. Then to her own bare feet. She stood stock still apart from her head, which moved slightly, nodding to herself. Then she lashed out, her fist catching Cwell on the chin and knocking her unconscious. She stared at the body of Cwell.

"You can't climb rigging with boots on, fool," Barlay said to the unconscious body before her. "If the shipwife dreams of a world where children are not taken and raids are not made, then I say" – she looked to her left and her right – "that is a world worth fighting for, no matter who we must fight or who with. But more than that – Farys, Mevans, Old Briaret, Karring, Solemn Muffaz, Anzir, and I can name many more – we have learned to trust the shipwife, ey?"

"Ey." This from well over half the crew and almost together. Meas nodded.

"Very well. And I am right proud to have you with me, Barlay." She turned on the spot. "Proud of the whole crew. But I know I ask a lot, and I will not force any of you to follow me through Keyshanhulme Sound. Any that do not wish to come may take a flukeboat. Do it now." She waited, but none came forward. "Very well. Then we must get ready to fight. The arakeesian swimming below us will no doubt be the cause of some uncomfortable questions from the Gaunt Islanders on watch, so be ready when we enter Keyshanhulme Sound. I want most of you in the underdeck. We must look like a ship manned by a prize crew, not a ship of war. If, and when, the time comes to fight I will call you. Do not worry – none will miss out." She smiled. "Apart from Cwell, as she will be locked in the brig. Solemn Muffaz, if you could see to that."

Laughter at that, and a strange sense, not of joy, but of rightness. That this was the way the crew believed things should be, that Meas would tell them what to do and she would tell them right, that she would call upon them if needed and in return they expected she would take care of them. That she had thought to fly the Gaunt Islands flag, that she would think how to attack and to defend and do her best to keep them safe. At some point this crew of the violent and the lost had decided that Meas could be trusted, and if she kept her side of the bargain then they would keep theirs. It was an odd thing, thought Joron, to find a purpose in such a dark place as a black ship.

He leaned over the rail and stared at the huge body gliding through the water below. This creature from legend was what bound them together, and Meas had used it to create a crew unlike any other in the Hundred Isles.

Had she known when she found him?

That he was born Berncast?

That she could use that when the time came?

Did she plan so far ahead?

And if so, where was his resentment? Where was his promise to take the two-tailed hat from her? Joron took a deep breath of sea air, fresh with the scent of the mountains they flew past. He laughed quietly to himself. His promise had been left a hundred thousand shiplengths behind, along with the bottles of drink and a version of himself he no longer wanted to think about.

He turned from the keyshan, saddened that it must die.

"Sound in view!" The call came from above.

"All below except bowteams one to five," shouted Meas. "We will work the ship. Mainwings only on the spines." Women and men climbed the rigging, brought in the unwanted wings, and *Tide Child* slowed. As if sensing it was part of the convoy, the arakeesian slowed too, letting the ships pull ahead.

Joron watched as the gap in Skearith's Spine came into view, the mountains appearing to move as *Tide Child* approached, those nearer sliding away to reveal the sound. He could just make out ropes tied across the cliff faces to provide handholds for those using the paths that wound their way up to the watchtowers. Both were old and had been repeatedly patched with gion and varisk for so long it had ossified, making them look like giant stone plants reaching out of the basalt into the sky. He could see people moving on top of the further one, little more than dots. As he watched, *Cruel Water*, under full wing, came past *Tide Child* to take up station at the front of the convoy, and intercept any boats coming out to investigate them. As if in answer, two flukeboats left the jetty below the further tower and headed towards the centre of the sound. Both were big enough to mount two gallowbows, one to each side, and they were bristling with armed men and women.

"Farys," said Meas as the girl walked past with a coil of rope.

"Ey, Shipwife?"

"Go below, have the landward underdeck bows untrussed, strung and ready to loose. Those boats are better armed than I would like, and *Cruel Water* may need some assistance." She pulled out her nearglass and put it to her eye. "Slow *Tide Child* by three rocks, Joron," she said. "I would have us look like we are preparing for inspection."

One of the approaching boats slowed to let its officers board *Cruel Water* while the second turned toward *Tide Child*.

"What is happening on *Cruel Water*?" asked Joron.

Meas lowered her nearglass. "Oswire speaks with the Gaunt Islanders."

"Why not Arrin?"

"I expect he takes a calculated risk. By not appearing himself he makes it appear that this is not important to him. The man who has gone aboard is probably insulted; the conversation they are having is exceedingly animated." She glanced at the approaching flukeboat. "Have them spin the bows of the underdeck, Joron, load them and be ready to open the bowpeeks. But have them do it quietly." She lifted her nearglass once more. "I don't like this."

"Ey, Shipwife." Movement caught his eye. "More flukeboats are leaving the towers, Shipwife."

As he headed to the underdeck hatch to pass on her orders, Meas turned her nearglass to the second pair of boats.

"Hag's teeth." Joron rejoined her on the rump, and she directed her nearglass back to *Cruel Water*. "One or two is fine, but the sound is too narrow for us to manoeuvre without coming under the bows of the towers. Fighting three boats full of crew while being shot at by the towers is something I could do without before facing three boneships."

The first flukeboat approaching *Tide Child* was commanded by an officer wearing a one-tail hat just like Joron's, and the two gallowbows on his boat – more a small ship, if not one fit for the open sea – were both loaded with wingshot. Bowsells stood behind them with burning torches.

"They load their wingshot with hagspit, Shipwife," murmured Joron.

She shook her head.

"I see it. Do nothing except look confident and pleased to see them."

Joron's heart beat fast, his breathing becoming shallower.

"I fear I look neither confident nor pleased," he said as Dinyl came to join them.

"You look rather sick actually, Joron," he said.

"Thank you, Dinyl."

Meas watched the deck of *Cruel Water*.

"Come on, Oswire," she said under her breath. "Convince them we are their ships."

The flukeboats kept on coming towards *Tide Child*.

"How is your Gaunt Islander accent, Joron?" said Dinyl.

The oars of the flukeboat beat, pushing it nearer.

"Poor," said Joron.

"You joke," said Meas, watching the boats approach, "but we may have to try it out."

The Gaunt Islander officer on *Cruel Water* appeared on the rump of the boneship. He shouted something and waved at the flukeboat approaching *Tide Child*, which hoisted oars and glided to a stop. The officer on the flukeboat gave Meas, Joron and Dinyl a salute, and the boat turned, making for the jetty. Joron felt he could breathe again.

"Well," said Meas, "I had thought Oswire surly, but she must be charming enough when duty requires it."

"And now we have only the three Gaunt Islands boneships to fight," said Dinyl. "Little more than a walk up the Serpent Road." He smiled at Joron, who did not share his bravado.

"Full wings!" shouted Meas, and women and men scurried up the spines. Joron watched the wings fall, felt *Tide Child* pull away. "When this is over I shall owe Oswire a drink of some sort," said Meas absent-mindedly as she watched *Cruel Water* drop his wings, catch the wind and start a slow turn to bring himself round into line behind *Tide Child*. "Deckholder, have the underdeck gallowbows trussed. Twiner, get us on our way before they catch sight of the keyshan and have some awkward questions for us."

"Shipwife," said Joron, "could we not use the same trick on the boneships? Pretend to be Gaunt Islanders?"

"I doubt it," she said.

"Why?"

Meas pointed at the towers. Thick white smoke was pouring from them and figures ran towards the jetty. The flukeboats were turning, though Joron doubted they could catch them now the boneships were under full wing.

"Because now they have seen the wakewyrm."

35

Three Ships Rising, Ho!

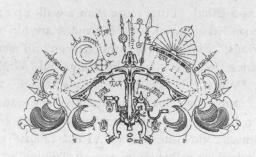

They flew for a day, the winds brisk but cold, pushing them forward and plucking at their skin with icy fingers. In idle moments the crew gathered in small groups, standing close and sharing warmth until Meas saw them, shouting that it was work that would keep them warm not gossip. Then they would hop to whatever tasks were nearest. Where once Joron had avoided the underdeck, finding it stifling, now he found excuses to go there for the shelter it provided from the constant freezing wind that made his ears ache. Even there it was cold and the wind, like vermin, found its way into everything. For every gap that was stopped it found two or three more places to squeeze through and chill the skin.

They flew another day.

Tasks previously avoided, manning the pumps or moving cargo, physically taxing work, became more popular for the warmth they gave. Meals were no longer served cold; everything, from the bowls of gluey fossy pet they broke their fast on to the hard bread to the watered anhir was heated, and extra rations of drink were always coming up in steaming buckets, until Meas put a stop to it, claiming her crew spent "more time pissing over the side than working". Joron found excuses to be in the small galley and watched sadly as their supplies of varisk charcoal dwindled.

They flew another day.

The waves grew, not into the truly dangerous, vertiginous waves that would topple a ship, not yet, but Joron had no doubt the Northstorm would bring them eventually, that it held them in reserve, waiting for *Tide Child* to displease the Hag. For now the waves rolled like gentle hills, lifting the ship towards the sky before lowering it into the valleys between each wave and the next. It was a soporific motion, as if the sea cradled *Tide Child* and its consorts. Below them the arakeesian remained unaffected, gliding through the depths with its backwings down, sometimes surfacing to reveal its glistening skin. Then the waves washed over it once more, and in their wash Joron could see it was not skin at all but tightly packed feathers, ruffled by the water the same way Black Orris's feathers were ruffled by the winds that drove *Tide Child* onward.

"Ship rising!" came from the tops and Joron returned the call.

"Say again, Topboy!"

"Three ships rising to landward!"

Words like icewater, shocking a crew become drowsy with the ponderous motion of the waves.

"Deckmaster! Deckholder!" shouted Meas as she grabbed a rope and started up the rigging. "Clear the ship for action! They may be a way off but it will do us good to blow the dust from these slatelayers!" Then she was lost among the black wings of *Tide Child*'s spines.

"You heard her!" Joron shouted. "Ring the bells, bang the drum! Get these slatelayers running!"

Solemn Muffaz nodded to Gavith, who ran to the bell on the rail at the fore of the rump of the ship.

"Clear the ship!" shouted Solemn Muffaz. "Clear the ship for action or feel the cord against your backs, you sluggard slatelayers. You sunfish-slow lot."

And like kwiln on a beach, disturbed by a sankrey's shadow,

they moved. Running hither and thither. Joron had seen this same action at the start of the journey, when none knew what they must do. But *Tide Child* was a different ship now. What he saw was not the chaos it seemed. Women and men knew their places on the ship, knew their jobs, knew what had to be done. Coxward and his bonewrights could be heard below collapsing the underdeck officers' cabins. Gavith ran below to drag the hagshand's chest of saws and knives down into the lowdeck in the bilges where the hagbower was, and where those cut or broken in action would be further cut and broken in hope of life. Dinyl would be watching as Farys, bowsell of the underdeck, had her crews secure the hammocks against the hull, check the bowpeeks, make sure they could be opened, and ensure that the bows, each lovingly named and carved, could be trussed and untrussed as easy as each woman and man could put on their clothes on waking.

Joron walked to the rump rail to look out over the ocean behind *Tide Child*, the sheer size of the rolling wave they climbed tilting the ship crazily, making him feel like a skeer, staring down as the crew of *Cruel Water* behind them worked their ship in a similar frenzy. No doubt *Snarltooth*, climbing the wave behind, did the same, and he hoped Meas was wrong about Brekir. Joron had seen the shadow of distrust on his shipwife's face. He turned from the rail to see Meas jump the last few lengths of the spine to the deck. She looked around at the bustle on the deck and said nothing – as good as any word of approval – then came over to Joron.

"Three ships, just as was reported to Arrin. A four-ribber, though I think it is a newer one, so smaller than *Tide Child*, and a pair of two-ribbers in escort."

"And corpselights?"

"They all fly them, but the two-ribbers are on their lastlights and the four-ribber also, but for one light which is on second light."

"So their condition may not be as good as was reported, and we may have an advantage in size."

"Yes," said Meas. "We are matched at least, I reckon. And if they are surprised by our tactics we will get in a full side of shot, do plenty of damage with our first loosing, and put those lights out. That will hurt their morale."

"We will take shot coming at them. From at least two of the ships."

"We will," said Meas, and she held herself straighter. A stray gust of wind picked up the tails of her hat and blew them about, twisting them around one another and just as quickly untwisting them. "We will have to bear it. It is my plan and we are built stronger than *Cruel Water* and *Snarltooth*, so it is rightly our burden." She looked out to sea, over the bustling deck of her ship. "Have a team with ropes ready to fix any broken rigging. And bring up twisters and wingshot for the gallowbows. First pass we'll do our best to take down their wings and spines. A ship can't fight without wings to fly it with."

"And if they do the same to us?" Dinyl came to stand by them.

"We shall come in at an angle to them; it is a hard thing to judge, hitting a spine, even harder from an angle. Then we will be loosing straight along the decks of the ships to either side of us and, trust me, to be loosed into from behind does fearful damage. Whatever pain is doled out to us on the way in will be paid back tenfold." Dinyl nodded his head. "But, you should know, Deckholder, it is not done to invite the Hag's misfortune before a battle. So I'd thank you to throw some paint at the base of a spine and clear the air."

"Of course, Shipwife," he said, then walked to the pot at the base of the rumpspine, dipped his hand in and splattered blue paint on the bottom of the spine. "For the Hag, may we not see her soon," he whispered.

"How long till we intercept them, Shipwife?" said Joron.

She shrugged and looked up into the wings as they cracked and shuddered in the wind.

"Steer us four points on the for'ard shadow, Barlay," she

said, then turned to Joron as the ship heeled over and the great boom came across the deck to collect wind from a different angle. "If the wind holds and they decide to come to the bow? A couple of hours. If it doesn't or they choose to run, then more."

"Do you think they have seen us?"

She nodded. "Ey. The course they fly. I suspect they have run parallel to us for a while, just over the horizon where we could not see."

"That sounds like they knew we were coming, Shipwife."

"The smoke from the towers at Keyshanhulme Sound will have warned them," said Meas. "But now, at this time and place, whether they knew or not makes little difference. They will be very sure we are coming soon enough."

"Shall I bring up the gullaime?" Once again Joron looked up into the wings, the whistling mass of ropes, cloth and spars that swayed above.

"No, this wind suits us," she said. "We shall come in as though we intend to go side on side and then turn sharply, as I said. I do not think the speed advantage the gullaime could give us is worth risking it falling to an unlucky shot. We will bring it up as we turn to engage, have it guide in the wing-bolts, and if we can crack one of *Wavebreaker*'s spines then the battle is half won."

Tide Child's crew then had an hour of quiet with little to do but fret, and many a deckchild spattered paint at the base of the mainspine. By the time the three ships of the enemy were in plain sight of all, little black showed through the patterns of red and blue paint left in hope of the Hag's protection.

"*Wavebreaker*'s a big one," Joron heard Karring say to Old Briaret.

"Ey, big enough, but not as big as us."

"He 'as corpselights too."

"Ey, but we have Lucky Meas, ain't it. So I reckon they is already part with the Hag."

Joron smiled and walked on along the deck.

His shoes no longer hurt his feet.

It was strange to him that they sailed so serenely, that the weather was so undramatic and clear, that there was no sense of panic in the crew around him when inside he was screaming as he watched the enemy ships get larger and larger.

There is my death, he thought. *There is surely my death.*

He could make out the gallowbows on the three white ships, see they were all strung and ready, see the corpselights dancing around the spines, see the purple wings flap and change shape, inflate and deflate as small course corrections emptied and then filled them with wind. On the *Wavebreaker* he watched a woman or man – he could not tell from this distance, but someone much like him – staring out across the sea at *Tide Child. Soon I will try to kill you*, he thought, *and you me, but if we met in an inn maybe we would be friend*s. His familiarity with the shipwives of *Cruel Water* and *Snarltooth* had robbed him of any belief the Gaunt Islanders were the monsters of childhood tales – it seemed odd that he had ever believed such a thing.

He smiled to himself. *When this is done I shall get Mozzan to tie my hair like his.*

He found himself standing before the mainspine and crouched, dipped his hand into the paint pot and spattered paint on the deck, bright red against the black. *Soon there will be more red*, he thought, *but it will not be paint*. He straightened and peered across at the enemy ship, trying to find his double but failing. There was some activity around their centre gallowbow. He was sure he heard the sound of it launch, saw the figure at the trigger stand back as if to watch the shot, and then, five or so lengths from *Tide Child*, a plume of water shot up as a wingbolt crashed into the ever-shifting sea.

Laughter on *Tide Child*'s deck. An easing of tension.

Meas stood at the rumpdeck rail.

"Barlay," she shouted, "ease us a little closer, make us a little more tempting." She grinned at her deckchilder. "Let them insult the Hag by firing at her domain when they stand no chance of hitting us." More laughter. "And let the Hag know . . ." She turned, dipped her hand in the blue paint and spattered some on the deck. Then she drew a blue line across her face. "Let her know I come. Lucky Meas is here, and she should know that when we loose our bolts, my girls and my boys, we shall not miss. The time of blood and pain comes, but it shall be their blood ey?"

A rousing shout of, "Ey!" and Joron noticed Hasrin, the ex-deckkeeper, was one of the first to raise her voice.

"And their pain, ey?"

A louder, stronger shout of, "Ey!"

"Then stand to your posts, listen to Joron, listen to Dinyl and listen to Solemn Muffaz. Listen to your bowsells and most of all listen to me. We do this for each other, and we look to *Tide Child* and the Hag to watch over us." She paused. Sand dropped through the glass as she stared at her crew, gathered on the slate. The sea flew by. "Are you ready, my women and my men? Are you ready? For I am ready."

"We are ready, Shipwife!" The shout came from Solemn Muffaz, at the back of the crowd.

In answer the whole deck raised their voices: "We are ready, Shipwife. We are ready!"

"Then, to war!"

And they ran to it.

Ran to their gallowbows, ran to the rigging, ran to their places on the deck and ran to take up curnow and wyrmpike and bow. Each and every one radiated a fierce joy, and Joron knew that joy, had felt it. And he hoped he would feel it again because now, in this quiet moment while they bore down in their enemy, he felt only terror.

A hand on his shoulder.

He turned to find Meas by him.

"Hold fast, Joron," she said quietly. "Try and know what they know."

"What is it they know?" It felt like he gasped the words.

"That where we head is unavoidable. Soon as run towards it as run away. Sooner get it over with."

"Is that how you think?"

"I try not to think. The hard bit comes soon. We – you and I and Dinyl – must stand on the rump and look unconcerned while those ships loose at us. I know it is not easy. But I saw something in you that day on the beach, and you have not let me down." She looked into his face. "You will not let me down. And you know by now that I know my business. Trust in that. Trust in me." He gave her a nod, a small smile. "Now, stay busy. A busy deckchild has no time for fear." And she moved on, as did he, scouring the decks for work to do as *Tide Child* carried them towards action. The fear was not gone, but her words had hardened something in him, and he would stand, he knew that.

He would stand because there was nowhere to run to.

He would stand because she had asked him to.

A second projectile was launched at them. Came nearer but still fell short.

Meas kept *Tide Child* on a course converging with the Gaunt Islanders, level with the leading four-ribber.

"They'll hit us soon," said Solemn Muffaz from where he stood before the rump, "if they can shoot straight."

Another bolt, again into the sea. Joron returned to the rump to stand with Meas and Dinyl.

"Should we untruss the bows, Shipwife?" said Dinyl.

"Not yet, Deckholder. Wait until we are truly under shot. It will give the deckchilder something to do."

Meas shouted for *Tide Child* to straighten his course.

A fourth bolt. Again only the sea was hurt, and the sea healed quicker than any woman or man.

"Poor shooting that," said Solemn Muffaz. "I'd cord that bowsell if they were mine."

"Time soon enough for you to judge our own bowsells, Muffaz," said Joron. To his amazement his voice neither wavered nor broke. He could have been discussing the weather or his shoes for all the care he showed.

"Aye, so right that is, D'keeper. Hag knows, they spend more time cuddling up to them bows than working 'em, and if I find them slack I'll be cording 'em for sure."

"You can keep your cords off me, Mother," said Karring as he passed. "For my bow will wreak a terrible toll or it ain't named Vile Billy."

"Vile Billy, is it?" said Solemn Muffaz. "You'll be first for the cord, Karring, mark me." But Joron heard the humour in the man's voice and Karring walked away smiling.

They were struck low on the hull, and the ship rang with the impact. It took all Joron had not to duck, to hide from flying bone splinters and shards of bolt, but he did not. He managed to freeze like he had felt nothing, heard nothing. And no splinters came flying for the bolt had hit too far down.

"About time they started shooting straight," said Meas.

"Ey, Shipwife," said Muffaz. "But 'tis wasted shot at this range."

"It will raise their morale a little," said Dinyl.

"And ours," said Meas, raising her voice. "See, my girls and boys, they shoot, they even hit on occasion, and yet they cannot damage *Tide Child*'s hull. He stands as strong as any wall. What need have we of corpselights when our ship is so stout?" There was a general murmur of agreement that made Joron smile, until another bolt rattled against the hull. Meas turned, watching the three ships opposite them. "I think we should act now," she said to herself then shouted. "Full wings!"

And the unacknowledged tension was broken. Women and men raced to obey, pulling themselves up the rigging and letting down the last of the wings. The flying rigs were put out, extra wings that stuck out from the side of the ship, and Joron felt *Tide Child* leap forward. Behind them *Cruel Water* and *Snarltooth* followed suit, though not putting up quite as much wingcloth as *Tide Child*; the smaller ships were lighter and faster, and needed to do less to keep up.

Meas watched as they gained on the ships opposite them.

"Coxward," she shouted, and the bonemaster came running.
"Ey. Shipwife?"

"I want to do a hard turn. Will the keel take it?"

Coxward licked his lips and scratched at a sore on his arm.

"I don't rightly know. *Tide Child* is a strong ship but we set off too early from Bernshulme. Is it not a little late to be asking?"

"Yes or no, Bonemaster."

"'Tis not so easy. Depends on the currents. If we could pull him out and I could look at the keel, I could tell you." Another bolt splashed into the ocean to seaward of *Tide Child*.

"We are rather occupied just now, Bonemaster. Hauling the ship out of the water is a little impractical."

"Anything I say would be a guess," he said.

"Your guess is worth any other's certain knowledge."

He scratched at a sore on his neck.

"Yes, then. That is my guess, but if you do it now you will not get to do it later. The keel will not take it."

Meas nodded.

"Well, I'll not save for later what will serve me today." She walked forward. "Bring in the flying rigs. I want all spare women and men ready to run for the landward rail when we come about. Barlay and Solemn Muffaz, I'll want all your strength at the steering oar." Crew scuttled across the spars to bring in the rigs, and *Tide Child*, moving at a speed so ferocious that Joron saw the beakwyrms now spun through the water at *Tide Child*'s side, unable to match him as he drew ahead of the enemy ships to seaward of them.

"They are not as fast as us, Shipwife!" shouted Dinyl.

"Few are, Deckholder," said Meas, "few are." She glared across at the enemy ships. "Barlay, angle us in towards them. Let them think we are getting ready to come in for a broadside. Bowsells! To your bows!"

"Shall we untruss to loose at them?" said Joron.

"No," said Meas, putting her nearglass to her eye. "We shall not waste ammunition, but they watch us as surely as we watch them, so let us put on the show they expect to see and they will not think far past that." She folded the nearglass. "Complacency is the enemy of every officer, Joron. Keep that in mind when you see how we surprise them."

With a whistle like a man hailing a friend, though its intent was never so amicable, a bolt cut through the air over the rump of the ship, punching through a taut wing with a sound like a hand on a drum.

"Well," said Meas as she took a step forward to stand between Joron and Dinyl, "it seems their bowsells have finally got their eye in." As she placed the nearglass within her coat, Joron noticed her hand shook slightly, and there was a thin sheen of sweat on her top lip despite the cold of the day. Meas took a deep breath, seemed to steady as the ship rocked then shouted, "It begins now, my girls and boys! Now our real work starts! So stand firm!"

As they angled towards *Wavebreaker* and its consorts, Joron watched the corpselights dancing above the Gaunt Islands ships, four in all – one the blue of firstlight, three the yellow of lastlight – bobbing and weaving in the topspines. Deckchilder crowded the spars and formed little knots around the bows. He knew that sand would have been scattered across their decks to provide grip and absorb blood, just like on *Tide Child*. Knew that deckchilder would be dipping their hands into red or blue pots of paint at the base of the mainspines and spattering paint there to ask the Hag's favour. Some would be scared and pretending they were not; some would be filled with joy at the thought of battle; some would be trying to find jobs belowdeck where it was safer, and all would be dreading being taken down to the hagbower, where the hagshand waited to do what they could for those wounded in battle.

He saw the *Wavebreaker*'s bows launch, the action of the bone arms, their sound stolen by the wind. Bolts flew towards *Tide Child*. One hit the hull with a solid boom, the others hurtled through his rigging, doing little damage, and flew on.

Another volley of bolts, again causing little damage, and it seemed to Joron that *Tide Child* was still. Oh, the ship moved, almost skipping across the waves, but all aboard were unmoving, waiting, dreading, knowing.

"Stand steady," shouted Meas. Across from them, the quickly growing *Wavebreaker* opened his underdeck bowpeeks. "Now he shows his teeth, ey?" said Meas to Dinyl.

"Bravado," said Dinyl, "Underdeck bows cannot hit us yet."

"No, they cannot." Then she added more quietly: "I would have you two move around the ship a little. Let the crew know we go among them, that we do not stand here aloof." Joron and Dinyl nodded and set off down the ship, as if strolling on a pleasant day. Another round of bolts hit *Tide Child*. Most were high, but the crew around ducked instinctively, as they heard the whistle of approaching bolts. It took all Joron had not to do the same. He locked his sweaty hands behind his back, holding the fingers of his one hand so hard with the other that they throbbed for want of blood.

"I reckon about five loosings per three-quarter-turn of the glass, Joron," said Dinyl. "Passable, if not extraordinary. Is that how you count it?

"How do you stay so calm?" said Joron quietly.

"What do you mean?"

"Just letting them loose at us, having to wait?"

Dinyl gave him a small smile.

"I have no other choice, and neither do you. Nor them." He nodded at the crew. "Experience helps. Knowledge too – the reality is there's little chance of a bolt killing you, not at this range. Sweeping the deck bow to stern? A bolt is a fearsome thing then, but right now we have little to fear." More bolts hit, and Dinyl glanced over at the enemy ships. "Three more volleys, Joron," he said, and there was a waver in his voice that spoke of suppressed fear. "Three more rounds of bolts, and we will be near enough for them to load wingshot and cutters. That's when it really starts, that's when you know you're in a fight, that's when you find out if you will break."

He laughed quietly. "So don't break now, Joron. If you must break then at least wait until they really mean it." He clapped Joron on the shoulder and leaned in close. "When she tells the crew to lie down, stay on your feet but stand behind the spine as it will provide some cover. We do our duty, ey?"

Joron nodded, and Dinyl walked on down the deck, sand crunching beneath his feet as he made his way to the beak, exchanging words with deckchilder as he passed.

Another round of bolts.

Tension building like a wound bow arm.

Another round of bolts.

The sea sliding by, the air filled with the spume of *Tide Child*'s passing.

Another round of bolts.

The wind plucking at Joron's coat.

"Lie down!" The shout came from the rump, and all around Joron crew hit the slate. He took a step back, so the mainspine, as thick as any two women and men, hid the enemy ships from him. He heard the wingshot come in, making a very different sound to bolts, a hollow howl, and the noise when they hit was deafening. Rocks smashed through rigging and spars, crashed into the hull. A rain of broken varisk fell from above.

When Joron looked up he expected the whole spine to have been shattered, but it still stood. Ropes fluttered in the wind; the corner of one wing had been torn loose, and the end of a spar smashed, but deckchilder were already lashing on varisk, retying ropes, hanging as if weightless from *Tide Child*'s rigging. He heard sobbing and turned. A wingshot had hit the landward rail and smashed it into splinters. Two of the team for bow six lay dead, the third sobbing and holding his gut, from which a splinter of bone protruded.

"Get him to the hagbower," shouted Meas. One of the crew Joron had thought dead picked himself up and shook his head. "They did not kill you, Vedin?" shouted the shipwife.

"Nay, Shipwife," he said, "though Cassit is done for." As

he finished speaking two deckchilder joined him at the bow. The dead woman was thrown overboard and the wounded man taken below for the hagshand to ease him into death, for his was a wound there was no recovery from.

"Hold, my boys and girls, hold," said Meas. As she walked up the deck, another round of wingshot came ululating in. Joron felt his insides clench as the projectiles crashed through the rigging. There was a scream and a body fell from above, smashing into the deck along with a spar. "One more round," shouted Meas. "One more round from them, my lovelies, and then we shall untruss our bows and avenge ourselves. We'll show them what a real ship of war can do. We'll pay them back a thousandfold for this."

But it was not one more round, it was three, and each time Meas had them hold fast. Strode the decks past the screaming wounded. Shouted orders as if she were invulnerable while crew died around her. Then – and Joron did not know how she judged it, how she knew they could take no more, what made her decide – the time came. She sprinted up to the rump of the ship, shouted, "Up! Up, you slatelayers! 'Ware the heavy boom. Barlay, Solemn Muffaz, put your backs into the steering oar. The rest of you to the landward rail." She stood proud on the rump while Joron and Dinyl ran to throw themselves against the landward rail of *Tide Child* with the rest. "Now!" shouted Meas, "now!"

And *Tide Child* came about.

The huge boom attached to the central wing came over as the beak of the ship turned towards the three Gaunt Islander boneships. The deck started to tilt, the rail Joron stood against rising into the air so he had to push his legs out to keep his feet. The sand on the deck slid, sticking where blood moistened the slate. Joron was forced to peddle his legs to find grip and stay in position as the turn became steeper and steeper. His arms hurt where they were locked about the rail and he knew now why Meas had been worried about the keel. As *Tide Child* turned, the stress on the keel would be immense. Further along, deck crew attached to ropes tied to the spines were standing on the rail and leaning over the side to stop *Tide Child* capsizing as he came about. If the keel went now, Joron knew it was over, that they were food for the longthresh that dogged *Tide Child*'s wake.

All this and the ship was only a third through its turn.

"To the rail!" shouted Meas, somehow, miraculously, still standing in the centre of the rump, one hand braced against the rearspine, one leg bent to keep her body upright. "More deckchilder to the rail!" she screamed, and more crew boiled up from the underdeck. Joron had never before understood why, when they cleared for action, ropes were laid across the deck, but now he did. The crew had to climb up the deck to get to the rail. The slope of the ship was so extreme he found himself almost looking down on *Wavebreaker* and his consorts. He could see the Gaunt Islander officers pointing, unbelieving at Meas's manoeuvre, and *Wavebreaker*'s great bows being loaded with wingshot.

"Brace," shouted Meas. "Any deckchild leaves the rail, and I will feed them to the longthresh myself. This will hurt, my girls and boys, but we will exact a heavy price in return, I promise you that." And Joron understood why their bows remained tied, imagined the untrussed bow's great shafts, swinging from side to side, adding to the danger.

Only two of *Wavebreaker*'s bows could be brought to bear on *Tide Child*, but their teams did not intend to waste an opportunity like this. *Tide Child* was almost deck on to them and an unmissable target. The deck officer opposite Joron was shouting, arm raised. It fell. The wingbolts smashed into the centre and beak of *Tide Child*'s deck, and the sound was like being in the centre of a thundercloud. The shot splintered on impact, sending shards of stone flying. Spidery cracks appeared in the deck; pieces of slate sheered away and fell, smashing through the seaward rail. Wingshot splintered on impact, sending shards of stone as well as the slate of the deck flying. Screams, bodies falling from the landward rail as stone shards pierced them. Women and men bouncing off spines and spars before they hit the sea. Something buzzed past Joron, and he felt a sharp pain in his cheek. Warm blood flowing.

Then they were round.

Tide Child righting himself. Shot still incoming, but the big ship was moving fast and the shot was poorly aimed. For some reason – surprise, inexperience, Joron could not know – *Wavebreaker*'s bows were targeting the black ship's hull when they should have continued trying to take down his rigging. Joron glanced behind him and spotted Deckkeeper Oswire on the beak of *Cruel Water*. *Tide Child* had done his job and attracted most of the Gaunt Islanders' shot; the two-ribber behind them had hardly been touched.

"To your bows!" screamed Meas. Bowteams ran to their stations. "Knot!" Ropes were loosed from bows. "Now lift!" Shafts were pulled up, locking over gimbals. "And string!" Cords were run through bows and cinched tight.

"Ready, Shipwife!" ran up and down the deck from the bowsells.

"Then spin!" she shouted. "For'ard Bows, get me some shot on those ships. I'll not have them loose at me without answer. I'll not have *Tide Child* unavenged!" Meas sounded furious, but each and every woman and man on the bows was grinning at her words. Another volley of wingshot came in, making *Tide Child* shudder in the water as the for'ard bowteams spun their bows. "Cutters, load cutters! Bring his rigging down!"

Dinyl stopped a woman and man bringing up wingbolts.

"Hag's piss, do you have gills for ears? She wants cutters, not wingbolts. No, stack 'em at the rail. Go on, run!"

"Load!" called the for'ard bowsells, and the loaders went to work.

"Dinyl," Joron grabbed him. "Why do they not fire cutters at our rigging?"

"Joron," said Dinyl, "I would suggest questioning the enemy's tactical mistakes is a discussion for after the battle. Should you not be with your teams?"

"Ey, I should." He was breathing fast, exulting at being alive, at the sheer audaciousness of the move Meas had pulled off and that he had been part of it. Joron ran forward. The teams on bow one, Poisonous Hostir and bow two, Maiden's Trick, had already loaded cutters – two sharpened stones joined with chain made of hardened varisk. They would spin through the air, cutting rope and flesh, smashing spar and bone and rigging.

Tide Child raced at the enemy, aiming for the gap between *Wavebreaker* and the two-ribber immediately following him. *Not much of a gap.* Joron turned away. *Concentrate on your bowteams. Hitting the gap is Meas's job.* He thought he could loose a round, maybe two, from each pair of bows. No longer did he stand behind the bows, now he commanded the bowdeck while Meas steered *Tide Child* towards the swiftly moving ships.

"Bowsells! Aim!" The shout that came from his mouth did not sound like his own voice; it was harsher, louder. "Loose when you have a target. Bring down their rigging!"

"Loose!" shouted Anzir from bow one.

"Loose!" shouted Old Briaret from bow two.

And the sound, the terrible sound, the warmoan of taut cords, the crack of launching bows.

"Spin!" shouted Joron. "Spin the bow like your life depends on it, for it surely does."

"Ready!" shouted the bowsells of bows three and four at almost exactly the same time.

"Loose as we come by!" shouted Joron.

Shot was still coming at *Tide Child*, but with the bows to command – the frantic loading, spinning and aiming – Joron barely noticed the bolts flying through the air, the ring of stone on bone, the crash of rigging being torn away, the screams of the maimed. He glanced behind him at *Cruel Water*. Arrin had not loosed yet. The Gaunt Islands ships were in range, but he must be waiting to make sure of his target. Joron turned back to see the effect of his bowteams' first shots just as one and two launched again. He shouted to his third pair to make ready. No change in *Wavebreaker*'s corpselights yet, though Joron saw spars and rigging fall. He knew from *Tide Child* that big boneships could take a pounding — keyshan bone was tough. But the two-ribber to seaward — he could see his name now, *Sunfish Rising* — was a wreck. His rigging had been cut by their first shot and that had brought down the entire top half of the ship's mainspine. This in turn had dragged down the other spines, and the deck was awash with wings and rigging. Only one light remained, that a sickly yellow. Crew worked frantically with axes to cut away the wreckage. The ship had almost stopped, forcing the final ship in the enemy line to alter course.

Nearer and nearer and nearer came the gap. And already it felt like they had scored a major victory.

We can win this, thought Joron. *We will win this*.

"Not long now!" shouted Meas. "Oh we'll cause some pretty chaos when we're between them." She ran to the top of the underdeck stairs and shouted down, "Drop the bowpeeks!" then turned. "Dinyl, get down there with Farys and get those bows ready!" Something in Joron quailed at the thought of the damage about to come to *Sunfish Rising*. The underdeck bows were not as big but were far more numerous. Ten to each side. Meas turned from the stairs. Glanced behind *Tide Child*.

Joron saw a look cross her face that he did not understand. It was not panic, not quite.

Not fear, not quite.

It was hate, and fury.

He turned.

On *Cruel Water* something was being pulled up into the rigging, something that fought and struggled as it rose. For a moment, Joron could not fathom what was happening. Everything in motion: *Tide Child*, *Wavebreaker*, *Sunfish Rising*, *Cruel Water* and *Snarltooth*. All coming together in anger and violence.

Arrin, he thought. *It is Arrin*. And it was a strange thought.

As if all action ceased around him while he considered this odd occurence.

That is Shipwife Arrin being hung from his own rigging.

He could not for the life of him understand why that would be happening.

Then on the deck of *Cruel Water* he saw Arrin's deckkeeper pointing at *Tide Child*. Oswire. Screaming at the crew. Wearing a two-tailed hat. And *Cruel Water* came about, her gallowbows armed and ready and aimed at *Tide Child*.

"We are betrayed," he said, more to himself than to those about him. He nearly shouted it, but managed to hold the words in. Meas had not said a word, and she did little for no reason.

So close and broadside on to *Tide Child*, *Cruel Water*'s eight gallowbows may not be great bows like *Tide Child*'s, but they would cause carnage. The stern of a boneship was his weakest point with the thinnest bone and the fragile glass of the state rooms at the rump. And Joron knew why Meas said nothing. Because there was nothing to be said. To shout betrayal would only distract her bowteams, and she would rather keep them loosing, keep them working, keep them unaware that they had already lost. But she did not turn away from what was coming. Death. She knew it. Joron knew it. *Cruel Water* would deliver a crippling blow. And here, with three Gaunt Islands ships to fight, that was the same as death.

Time slowed. Oswire raised her hand, a smile on her face. Strangely, Joron found he did not hate her. Maybe she saw this as her way back to the deck of a boneship. Maybe she believed it was her duty.

And it was too late for hate.

He fancied that bow four on *Cruel Water* was the one that would do for him. He could see it, Focus on it. Then he saw nothing else, heard nothing else, just focused on that team of women and men as they finalised the aim of the bow. He got ready for his body to be smashed by the projectile.

But he had reckoned without *Snarltooth*.

He took for granted that the two ships would work together. Had Meas? Had she simply presumed, like him, that what was true for one was true for all? So had she also not watched *Snarltooth* as Oswire betrayed both Meas and her own shipwife. Had she simply thought her mistrust for Shipwife Brekir was playing out, and that she would come about and turn *Snarltooth* to landward as *Cruel Water* turned to seaward, ready to add its weight of stone and finish *Tide Child*.

But Brekir did no such thing.

Did not turn *Snarltooth*.

Did not slow her ship.

She drove it into *Cruel Water*.

The impact of *Snarltooth*'s spiked beak threw Oswire to the deck, threw gallowbow teams over the side and heeled *Cruel Water* over at an angle that rained women and men from the rigging into the sea. It filled the air with screeching and grinding almost as loud as the arakeesian's call.

Sense and sensation came back to Joron. His first thought was that Brekir had been taken by surprise by *Cruel Water*'s abrupt manoeuvre; she had not struck him as a particularly competent shipwife.

He was soon disabused of that idea.

Snarltooth's crew, led by the furiously snarling Brekir and Deckkeeper Mozzan, were streaming from the beak of their ship on to the decks of *Cruel Water*, showing no quarter and cutting down all they came across.

Meas ran back up to the rump of *Tide Child*.

"Ignore the traitors! Brekir will deal with them. Load the gallowbows with wingshot. Get the gullaime up here!"

But it had already emerged from the underdeck and was in its place at the centre of the deck as if it had anticipated Meas's order. Its wings were wrapped around its body, masked head darting from side to side as it took in the carnage.

"Death, Joron Twiner!" it squawked. "It is all death!"

Then *Tide Child* was behind *Wavebreaker* almost in a position where his bows could be brought to bear on the fragile rump of the Gaunt Islands four-ribber. *Sunfish Rising* was stricken and starting to come round so it was side on to *Tide Child*, its gallowbows still tangled in rigging.

Meas smiled.

"Gullaime," she shouted, "slow our progress!"

This a mighty roar, almost a scream, and for that second she had everyone's attention. Joron's ears hurt as the wind changed direction, blew back. *Tide Child* shuddered as he was slowed in the water.

Lucky Meas Gilbryn, shipwife of *Tide Child*, smiled as her bows came to bear.

"Those ships." She pointed to either side with her drawn blade. "Kill them."

The great bows spoke, and above the low moan of their cords loosing could be heard the higher-pitched sound of the underdeck bows loosing. No longer was Meas concentrating on the rigging of the enemy. The first broadside was all wing-shot. *Tide Child*'s shot swept the decks of *Wavebreaker* and *Sunfish Rising*, doing so much damage that with one volley the remaining corpselights on both ships flickered and went out.

Arrows started to pepper the decks of *Tide Child*, loosed by archers in the spines of *Wavebreaker*. One hit Meas in the shoulder but was almost spent, and she pulled it from the fishskin of her coat and threw it aside without breaking stride. "Coughlin!" she shouted and pointed at *Wavebreaker*'s spines. "Deal with those archers!" He nodded and sent some men with bows up into the rigging.

Behind them the fighting on *Cruel Water* was furious, and *Wavebreaker*, unable to launch at *Tide Child*, was loosing its fury on the two tangled ships, though under the constant bombardment of *Tide Child*'s bows the loosing was sporadic. But despite its tattered and smashed rigging, *Wavebreaker* was starting to pull away.

"Bring hagspit!" shouted Meas. "Fire the stones. Don't let that ship escape!" Joron had dreaded the order while knowing it would come. Fire on a boneship was a thing to be feared.

Though bone itself did not burn easily, boneglue caught quickly. Belowdeck the barrels of oil were tapped and the oil brought up to pour into the shot.

A huge crash from seaward, and Joron turned. The third Gaunt Islands ship had smashed side on into *Sunfish Rising* – now to all intents and purposes a dead ship, with blood running in bright streaks from his bowpeeks down the white bone. The impact pushed *Sunfish Rising* into *Tide Child*, and the bigger ship groaned.

"Clever," said Meas to Joron as she rushed up to the rail to look over the side. "Using the stricken ship as a shield. Coughlin!" she screamed, her voice hoarse. "Prepare to repel boarders. Get everyone who can fight up here with a curnow or wyrmpike! Protect the seaward gallowbows until *Wavebreaker* is burning!"

Below women and men from both Gaunt Islands ships prepared to board *Tide Child* as the ship beyond *Sunfish Rising* loosed at *Tide Child* with frightening accuracy, smashing his number two bow and sending its team sprawling. Grappling hooks came over the side. From behind him Joron heard the rush of the first fired wingshot being launched from *Tide Child* and the squawk of the gullaime as it guided it home. He glanced round, saw the shot hit *Wavebreaker*'s wings, spilling burning oil down wingcloth.

A sheet of flame across the ship.

"Hag save you all," he said and turned away. He unhooked his curnow and pulled a primed crossbow from his jacket as the first of the boarders climbed the rail. He could hear fighting below as Gaunt Islanders tried to get in through the bowpeeks. He ran to the stairs. "Hag's sake, you fools, close the those bowpeeks!" He turned. Found a Gaunt Islander coming at him. Shot the man in the neck with his crossbow. Behind him came another, curnow raised. Joron swept his own curnow up as hard as he could. There was no skill in it, only desperation. He smashed away the man's blade, at the last moment realising his attacker also had a knife and he had left himself open.

Anzir nearly took the man's head off with a rope axe as she ran to Joron's side.

Joron turned, saw the gullaime standing alone as the two-ribber's deckkeeper ran towards it. No fool, she recognised the danger it posed and intended to end it with her slim blade. Meas lifted a crossbow to shoot the deckkeeper down but had to turn to defend herself from an attacking deckchild. The gullaime stood, stock still in the face of the advancing threat and Joron thought it must be paralysed with fear. He could not reach it, was too far away. He was only able to watch helplessly as the officer launched herself at the gullaime. The blade came around in a slash but the windtalker slid beneath her blade, riptide quick. One of its long thin legs flashed out; a curved claw cut through the woman's throat, and she fell to the deck, her blood lost in the dark sand on the slate.

All was chaos.

Coughlin had formed a shield wall before gallowbows three and five to protect the teams as they continued to pour fired shot into *Wavebreaker*, while the fight on *Cruel Water*, between crews who until only an hour ago had been on the same side, was even more fierce and furious.

Then noise.

The loudest thing Joron had ever heard.

He turned, and not only him. Everyone turned. The fighting paused. Fire must have got into *Wavebreaker*'s oil store, and the resulting explosion had blown out the centre of the ship. Black smoke billowed into the sky, and bone, spars and pieces of burning wing rained down. *Wavebreaker* immediately began to list, to scream as the remaining bone of its hull was stressed beyond bearing. The whole ship tilted slowly to landward, the air filling with the awful stink of burning bone.

Then Joron was fighting again – no time to watch – Anzir slowly guiding him back towards the comparative safety of Coughlin's shieldwall. Fallen spars and ropes everywhere, knots of women and men struggling to kill each other, threats from all angles. Dodge. Block. Thrust. Kill. He was cut – once, twice, three times. Thirsty. Wounds to arm and leg and face, Anzir the same, and had it not been for her he would have died many times over. He saw Old Briaret, dead on the deck, staring up into the rigging. No surprise escape from death this time, her chest hewn open. He saw the gullaime, spinning and twisting, using claws and beak as weapons. Far more dangerous than he had ever thought something so slight and brittle could be.

And Meas, alone on the rump with the shipwife of the two-ribber, fighting sword on sword. Where all else was chaos and brutish and hard and stinking and bloody, they were elegant. Slim silver swords, lithe bodies, arm and knee bent at just the correct angle. It could have been a duel on a field over a pretty Kept.

Were they both smiling?

The tails of their hats jumped as they danced forward and back. Lunge and feint. Block and twist. Then Meas had her, a lunge that went through her opponent's defence, took her in the chest, pierced a lung. Fatal, but not quick. The stricken shipwife fell to her knees, dropped her sword, and with one fluid movement Meas swept her blade across the other shipwife's throat, ending her suffering.

And with that it was over.

Some fought on, died. Most did not. Meas offered quarter, and those who accepted were coralled into a corner of the deck to await their fate.

Joron turned to look at *Cruel Water* behind them. Brekir stood on the rail and she raised her bloody sword to Meas in salute. Meas nodded and did the same, and it did not escape Joron that this was the first time he had ever seen Brekir look truly happy.

From the underdeck came Dinyl, hat missing, hair slick with blood.

"We won?" He seemed surprised.

"Ey," said Joron. "It seems we did."

36

The Pain of the Victors
Is No Pain At All

It is said in fleet circles that any victory you walk away from is a good one. Joron doubted Meas Gilbryn would agree, although the mood on on the slate was a jubilant one, and Joron, on his way to the great cabin, had heard the women and men of *Tide Child* singing Meas's praises:

"Four ships against two, and she brings us all in safe. No other shipwife could do such a thing."

"Ey, that is right enough, and one of those four a traitor as well, a no-good backstabber. But Meas didn't fall for it. Saw it coming the whole time, I reckon."

"Ey, we are lucky to have her, ey?"

"I'll throw paint to that."

No doubt such conversations continued above him now; the ship certainly sounded like a happy one, and a busy one. Hammering and sawing filled the air as *Tide Child* was cut away from *Sunfish Rising*. The two-ribber was not only entangled in *Tide Child*'s rigging, but the burrs and hooks of its hull had been smashed into the black ship when the other Gaunt Islands ship – smaller than *Sunfish Rising* and named *Sea Louse* – had used it for cover. Now the crew of the black ship worked to disentangle all three ships. Similar work was taking place on *Snarltooth*, though there was more to do as the damage to Brekir's ship was even worse than that to *Tide Child*.

But *Tide Child* was sorely damaged. Coxward said that the keel had not held as well as he had hoped through the turn, though how he could tell Joron had no idea. Not that he doubted the man.

The crews of *Tide Child* and *Snarltooth* were busy cannibalising the *Sunfish* and *Cruel Water* for parts and spares and shot. But every report that came in from Coxward or Solemn Muffaz or the seakeep told Meas that the damage to *Tide Child* was far greater than she had feared. He was holed in many places, some below the waterline, and the grind of the pumps ran counterpoint to the rasp of saws and the beat of hammers, and still the ship took on water. There was no replacing the smashed maindeck gallowbow, as only *Wavebreaker* had carried great bows, and that ship was gone, marked only by a growing pool of flotsam and the occasional bubble breaking the surface as it escaped the sunken hull. Gallowbow six had also taken a hit. Although not enough to destroy it, the bow would never loose again.

But the damage to *Tide Child* was minor compared to the that suffered by *Snarltooth*. Ramming *Cruel Water* at full speed had crippled the smaller ship. Its entire front was smashed in, the beak broken, and Brekir's bonemaster reckoned they had cracked the spine of the ship too. He could fly, but barely, and would need to be nursed back to a dry dock.

So it was a dismal little council that met in *Tide Child*'s great cabin. The only ray of light was that, miraculously, Shipwife Arrin had survived Oswire's treachery.

"I was sure the Hag had come for me," he said, his voice little more than a whisper, the burn of the rope a livid red ring on his neck. Mevans served him heated anhir to soothe his pain. "But it seems she is not done with me yet. When Brekir ran her ship into *Cruel Water* and he heeled over, I was able to grab the mainspine and climb up far enough to loosen the rope."

"I will never, in all the days left to me," said Brekir, "forget Oswire's face when she turned to find you with a sword at her back."

"Did you smile then, Brekir," said Arrin, "or did the rope damage my eyes?"

"Me?" said the dour shipwife. "Smile? You must be drunk, Shipwife Arrin. No more anhir for you." They laughed. And Meas laughed. And Joron laughed, and it was an infectious thing. Even Meas's hatkeep, Mevans, who was generally a silent and serious presence when officers gathered, had to turn away to hide his amusement.

But the laughter did not last, and as it died away Meas spoke, her face stony.

"We have some serious decisions to make, Shipwives. I fear we may have won the battle but lost the war."

"Ey," said Brekir, and her face returned to its usual state of sad repose. "*Cruel Water* cannot be saved; I broke him utterly." She glanced at Arrin. "I know you loved that ship, Arrin, and you have my apology."

"I love my life more," said Arrin. "You have no need to apologise."

"It is not that we lost a ship," said Meas "I am confident that when we have it free, *Sea Louse* will be able to take *Cruel Water*'s place." She glanced at Arrin. "It is a newer ship – not as well made, right enough, but it mounts bows and flys the sea. That brings us to our real problem."

"Crew," said Arrin.

"Ey," said Meas. "The price of our victory was high. All those on *Cruel Water* who sided with Oswire are dead."

"There is no fiercer fighting than between those who feel betrayed," said Brekir. "This morning they called those who betrayed them friend. It is a bitter meal to be served."

"Ey," said Arrin, staring at the table. "Though I do not mourn their passing. Those who sided with Oswire were murderous; they killed everyone they did not trust. This debacle, Meas, it is on me." He looked up, coughing. "I was *Cruel Water*'s shipwife; I should have known what Oswire planned. I knew her before the black ships but did not realise the depth of her resentment."

"You served with her how many years before the ship of the dead?"

"Eight."

"Eight years of keeping each other alive; it is a hard wall to see past, I reckon."

"True," said Brekir. "But it is done now, and we must move on. The Hag has no pity for a deckchild who cries about yesterday."

"Ey," said Meas. "Paint that on a doorway. So, down to it. Every moment we delay, the wakewyrm draws away from us. Stay here too long and we will not be able to catch it. None remain of *Cruel Water*'s crew but Arrin. Brekir, how many of yours live?"

"I did not lose many in the fighting on *Cruel Water*, ten or twenty at most. We had the numbers and they were in shock from the ramming. But as soon as *Wavebreaker*'s shipwife saw we were taking the day, she swept the decks with his bows. It was good loosing too – I would be dead if not for Mozzan."

"How is he?" said Joron.

"He is in the hagbower." She put a hand on the table, spreading out her fingers. "He will not leave it."

"I am sorry," said Meas. "He was a good deckkeeper."

"Ey," said Brekir. "But all in all I have lost nearly half my crew."

"And *Tide Child*," said Joron, "has lost a third. Twenty are in the hagbower and will never leave. Another ten or so are unlikely to be up and about any time soon."

"We have enough crew to fly *Tide Child*," said Meas, "but not enough to fight him, and *Hag's Hunter* waits in the far north."

"Then there are the prisoners," said Arrin.

"Ey," said Meas. "Then there are the prisoners."

"We could . . ." said Brekir. She took a deep breath, did not look the other shipwives in the eye. "We could load the prisoners on to *Snarltooth*, put my crew on *Sea Louse* and sink *Snarltooth*."

There was quiet while her words settled. After a while, Meas shook her head.

"No. It is one thing to kill in battle, but that is murder, plain and simple, and I will not countenance it."

"I am glad you said that," said Arrin.

"As am I," said Brekir. "But—"

"—someone had to suggest it so we could know we were of a mind not to do it," finished Meas. "I know that. But it is in situations like this that we decide who we are." She let silence settle in the cabin. "And I am glad of the people we are, the people that sit around this table." She let the silence settle. Then changed the subject. "Joron, if you would call Aelerin . . ."

Joron dipped out of the great cabin and returned with the courser.

"Shipwife?" said the courser gently.

"You have a course for me, Aelerin?"

"Ey, Shipwife." They handed over a chart and Meas spread it across the table. "I could only plan for the weather how it usually is, but the winds do not whisper a great blow to me – I hear no near anger from the Northstorm."

"That is good to know, Courser," said Meas. She turned to Brekir. "Cassin Island. It is a long way, but Aelerin has set a course that should avoid any fleet ships and follows only gentle currents."

"That is the opposite way to the arakeesian," said Joron. "What is there that is so important?"

Meas glanced up.

"There are many others who feel as we do around this table, Joron – did I not tell you that? And we have been stockpiling equipment and what ships we could. *Sea Louse* is a welcome addition and *Snarltooth* will be fixed, but, more important, *Sea Louse* and *Sunfish Rising* had two gullaime each aboard, and they survived. If we, at some point in the future, must fight, we will need gullaime. They are worth more than ships in their way."

"So we abandon the arakeesian to *Hag's Hunter*?"

Meas shook her head.

"No, we do not. Brekir, you will transfer your flag to *Sea Louse*. We'll put the prisoners on *Snarltooth* and you can tow him to Cassin Island. I will need thirty crew. I appreciate that will leave you short-handed and you will have to deal with the prisoners but—"

"—if the prisoners wish to keep *Snarltooth* afloat they will be too busy pumping to cause trouble. But I cannot order my crew to their deaths with you, Meas," she said. "I have never been that type of shipwife, even though they are already dead, I suppose."

"Very well. I will take as many volunteers as will come to my deck. All my wounded I will send to you. Many can still work, so you should not be too short-handed if some choose to leave you."

"Meas," said Arrin, "*Tide Child* is in no state to fight a ship like *Hag's Hunter*. Even fully crewed and fresh from the docks, it would be too much to ask."

"I have a duty, Arrin," said Meas. "I have made a promise." She tapped the table with her finger. "And, after all, I am shipwife on a ship of the dead. We both know what that means."

"Let me be the first volunteer. You take *Sea Louse* and then find another ship. Your expertise is invaluable to what we do. Please, let me take *Tide Child* north."

Meas shook her head and reached across the table, grasping Arrin's hand. "*Snarltooth* will be fixed for Brekir, and *Sea Louse* will need a good shipwife; those who believe in us will need a good shipwife." She smiled, "And do not doubt me, Arrin." She let go of his hand and sat back. "Kyrie is my sither and was my deckkeeper before she was shipwife on *Hunter*. I know how she thinks; I know how she fights. I have advantages you do not."

Arrin glanced at her then shrugged.

"If any can beat her, then it is you."

"Ey, that is true," said Brekir.

"Then let us get to work. Every moment spent talking here the wakewyrm makes into distance between us."

Many turns of the glass later *Tide Child* left *Snarltooth* and *Sea Louse* behind him in the gathering dark, the two ships illuminated by the burning hulks of *Cruel Water* and *Sunfish Rising*. Something ached in Joron. Not because he was watching a jointweight of bone that would have made every woman and man on board *Tide Child* and *Snarltooth* rich beyond imagining go to the bottom of the sea, but because he was leaving behind people he had come to like, and though he knew Meas had spoken bravely, he also knew it was a mask. Brekir and Arrin had known it too. *Tide Child* was no match for *Hag's Hunter*.

"We should throw the bolts overboard," said Joron as he stood with Dinyl on the rump.

"Bolts?" said Dinyl.

"For killing the keyshan. If *Hag's Hunter* takes us and finds them, the keyshan is theirs. And all we have done will be for naught."

"We have a duty, Joron," he said. "We can lead *Hunter* a pretty chase, lose it among the storm isles, then do what we must when *Hunter* is behind us."

"Look to our ship, Dinyl," he said. "You think it is possible we will lose *Hunter*?"

"To be fleet is not to do what is possible, it is to do what you must." Then he walked away, wrapping his thick coat about himself against the cold.

"Joron Twiner." He turned to find the gullaime. It was like a different beast now. Still thin, still delicate-looking, but the feathers on its head were glorious – black in the night, but in the daylight blue and gold and red.

"I am sorry they took your people away," he said, nodding towards the ships slowly vanishing into the glow of bonefire behind them.

"Not sorry," it said. "They will live." Then it made a sound, a repeated *yarking*, bobbing its head up and down. Joron thought it was going to vomit for a moment before realising it was laughing.

"You don't think we will?"

"Who knows? You know? Meas know? No one knows."

"All this," said Joron, "to save us from ourselves, and yet we do not even want to be saved."

The gullaime stopped moving, became utterly still, and Joron thought he heard the echoes of the windspire song carried on the wind.

"Sea sither knows you protect it, Joron Twiner. Sea sither knows much."

"Can you speak to it?"

"Speak?" It did it again: *Yark, yark yark.* "Not speak. Not talk. We are small, quick. It is big, slow."

"Can you make the keyshan understand? Tell it to hide from *Hag's Hunter*? To join us later?"

"You hide from insect?"

"No."

"Hide from a million insect?"

"Yes."

"This" – it tapped the smashed rail of *Tide Child* – "make you a million insect. But sea sither not understand that."

"Can you make it understand?"

The gullaime fixed him with its painted mask.

"Gullaime think fast. Like you. It is slow." And then it turned on the spot and vanished into the underdeck.

"I think that was a no," said Dinyl from where he was tying rope across a break in the rail so none fell overboard.

"Ey," said Joron. And in his mind he heard the song of the windspire.

37

The Hag's Word Is Never a Good Word

They sailed for three days before they sighted the arakeesian. Three hard days where the weather changed and Aelerin was forced to chart a stormfoul course, the wind never in the right place and the courser hearing no hint in the windsong that it would change. So *Tide Child* tacked seaward and tacked landward, chasing the wakewyrm through a series of zigzags, and each time they came about Coxward would disappear into the bilges of the ship, knee deep in stinking water, listening to the bone and hearing the creaks and sighs and cracks of the ship as surely as any other heard the words of the lover they clung to in the darkness in hope of warmth. Each time the ship turned he came up to the slate, soaked and filthy, his face more drawn, his sores looking rawer, and he could give Meas no good news.

But still they flew on.

The weather became colder and wetter. Rain became a constant, sometimes thin – little more than a wetness in the air – at other times a deluge, rain so thick you could not see your hand before your face. There were not enough stinker coats or cold-weather clothes on board so when the watches above deck came below clothes had to be exchanged, leaving those below shivering together in little groups, or huddling under thin blankets in their hammocks. All was misery. Gone from the islands they passed were the cheery colours of the warm months; no bright purple gion or pink varisk grew this far north. Instead the islands were covered in grey, low, densely growing plants that shuddered in the wind, making it appear as if the islands moved gently from side to side.

It felt both unreal and unsettling.

However, the crew held up well. Whereas Meas, Joron and Dinyl knew how little the chances of the battered and broken *Tide Child* were against *Hag's Hunter,* the crew seemed oblivious. Their victory over the Gaunt Islanders had sealed Meas's reputation with them. They did not see any way they could lose with Lucky Meas on the rump, they talked away the size of *Hag's Hunter* and callled him slow as a seaslug. Said Lucky Meas would run rings around her sither.

Joron wished he could share their confidence

But he could not.

There were small pleasures. The gullaime had taken to walking on deck, often accompanied by a squawking and swearing Black Orris, and though neither of them was of any help they shared an intense curiosity in the workings of the ship. The crew, who had first been scared, then awed, by the windtalker, had accepted and finally welcomed its presence. It became quite normal for Joron to pass the gullaime, mask fixed on some deckchilder as they explained some arcane part of the ship's working or routines. Twice Joron asked Meas if they should not use the gullaime to gain speed and stop the constant tacking. The first time Meas patiently explained they would need everything the gullaime had to stand a chance against *Hag's Hunter*. The second time he was, less patiently, informed that he had no place questioning her on the deck of her ship.

His friendship with Dinyl continued, though their conversations always ended up at the same place. The end. The coming battle with *Hag's Hunter*, and Dinyl refused to humour Joron's doubts; he would talk only of the duty of a fleet officer. So when they spent time together, they read books on navigation or studied maps of the Scattered Archipelago, because there was nothing else to be said and no comfort to be had.

So it went on for Joron, day after miserable grey day.

The day they saw the red wings of the arakeesian was a particularly taxing one for Joron. It was good to see the beast – he felt a strange kinship for it, a fondness – even though if they did manage to protect it from *Hag's Hunter* – and he was sceptical they could – it would be only to kill it later. He felt it deserved more, should be more than simply a pawn in Archipelago politics. It had a majesty about it that nothing he had ever seen before possessed – more power and beauty than even a five-ribber under full wing.

But as Dinyl so often said, Joron had a duty. And Meas had a duty and a dream, a dream of a land without war, and Joron did not imagine for one moment that she would sell that out for some romantic notion of an animal's nobility.

As Joron thought of the wakewyrm, *Tide Child* tacked, the great boom swinging over the deck and the ship creaking alarmingly as his keel complained, changing their course to catch the wind but losing ground on the arakeesian, which vanished from his line of sight as if it had never been.

"And soon we, or another, will undo you, and your kind will be gone from the world for ever," he said to himself and to the grey water before him.

"Where do you think it came from, D'keeper?"

Joron turned, annoyed at himself at being heard musing on things he should keep to himself. But it was only Mevans, idly tidying a coil of rope.

"Outside the storms, I imagine, Hatkeep."

"How do we know there are not more of them out there? It's a lot bigger than the skull on *Tide Child*'s beak."

"It is," he said, staring out into the grey, looking for the creature.

"Only, by my reckoning, I think that makes it older. Cos it's bigger, see."

Joron nodded.

"If it is the last, it must be tremendously lonely, Mevans, do you think?"

"Ey," he said, "if it is." He finished tidying his rope and walked away, leaving Joron at the rail.

The next day they caught up to the arakeesian proper, and the wind moved around behind *Tide Child* so the constant, wearying tacking finally stopped. The convoy of animal and humans followed the deep-water channel towards where they would pass through Skearith's Spine on their journey back to the Hundred Isles.

Joron's dreams, which for days had been of his father's death, constantly replaying that moment when the boneship *Mother's Wish* had ground his father to mulch between his hull and their little flukeboat, changed that night. He dreamed once more of being something vast and eternal, gliding through the depths of the sea surrounded by water and strange, sad songs, and in those moments he found a calm entirely lacking from his waking hours.

They flew on through days grey with clouds, grey with damp air, grey within his mind.

In the third week they turned for Skearith's Spine and Namwen's Pass.

A fog blanketed them as they entered the pass, clouds falling from the great plates of black rock on either side to sit upon the ocean, masking *Tide Child's* course as completely as time masked the future. Joron moved from job to job wrapped in freezing opaque air, the familiar sounds of the ship around him muffled and ghostly. In the evening he stood upon the rump with Dinyl peering forward, wary of reefs, listening to Seakeep Fogle as she cast the weight with a steady rhythm.

"Cast!" the shout. Then a splash, the sound held close to the beak by the enfolding mist. Fogle's voice counting out the seconds as the rope ran through her hand until it hit bottom – or not. Namwen's Pass was deep in the centre and shallow at the sides, but Meas had ordered them to avoid the deep channel as that was where wakewyrm swam, and she did not know how it would react if they ran into it. So they had to make their way carefully through the shallows. They could not afford the damaged *Tide Child* to even nudge the sea floor, so they edged forward with all but the topwings furled, listening to the calls from the front. "No bottom, no measure. No bottom, no measure. Fifty lengths and sand and shale. Forty lengths and sand and shale." And as Fogle called out the depths, Dinyl directed Barlay at the steering oar.

Meas trusted them to do this. She was up in the topspines, hoping for a break in the cloud. Hoping not to see *Hag's Hunter*.

"Were I his shipwife," she had said to Joron earlier, "I would sit at the exit to Namwen's Pass and wait for us. Our only real advantage is manoeuvrability and speed, and in our state we don't have as much of either as I would like, though they cannot know that. But if they can catch us leaving the pass we have nowhere to go but through them. My sither could simply sit and pepper us with wingshot." There was no emotion on Meas's face at the thought of fighting her sibling. "They have enough weight to finish us in two or three rounds."

"So we are finished?"

"I do not think so. My sither has many admirable qualities but patience is not one of them. It caused more than a little friction between us. I think it more likely she will patrol and rely on the watchtowers putting up a signal when we come through. We are tied to the arakeesian, so if *Hag's Hunter* has maps of the old migration routes she does not have to worry about losing us."

So they edged forward, and Meas watched for the ship that could end them. Fogle called out the depths, and Dinyl called out directions, and Barlay steered the ship, and Joron shivered and itched inside his stinker coat. When he had looked, the skin at the tops of his arms was red and raw, another little misery to add to the many that went with life on a fleet ship.

This was not the life his father had told him stories of: the dashing work of the fleet, a life of honour and good cheer.

He heard boots on slate and a moment later Meas appeared from the mist, hair and hat dewed by damp air.

"What news, Shipwife?"

"Fair news and foul, Deckkeeper."

"Well," said Dinyl, "best furnish us with fair, the better to stand the foul."

"It was ever thus," said Meas as she came to stand by the two men. "Well, fair is that my thoughts on Kyrie's personality were correct. She had no patience for sitting and waiting, so I am sure she now patrols the northern oceans."

"This is good, is it not?" said Dinyl.

Meas made a clicking sound, twisting up one side of her face as if to say, "All is not as it seems."

"In a way, it is, ey, but I fear *Hag's Hunter* is near. I had hoped this mist would let us pass undetected but we are seen. The landward watchtower sends up a plume of smoke that was not there three turns ago, so we must presume *Hag's Hunter* is close enough to see the signal."

"If it can see the smoke for this mist," said Joron.

"The fog lies low. It is clear above the mainwing, and *Hunter* is taller than us." She shrugged. "It will see the smoke."

"Are the towers likely to fire on us?" said Joron.

Dinyl smiled, as did Meas, though with little humour.

"'Tower' is a rather generous description of them," said Meas. "If the arakeesians truly returned, maybe there would be towers here again, but for now they are little more than huts. We need not fear much more than them spitting on us."

Black Orris landed on Meas's shoulder.

"Hag's arse," said Black Orris.

And at that that moment they broke from Namwen's Pass, the mist chose to stay hugging the land and *Tide Child* emerged from the vapour like a ghost, dragging curls of thick air with him only to shed them as the wind picked up. Free of the mist, the air was crystal, cold and cutting and clear, the sky as blue as the best dyes, the visibility good for tenths in every direction.

"Pleasant," said Meas, taking out her nearglass and raising it to her eye, "but not the weather I would have wished for. These are poor conditions for hiding." Before them the arakeesian ploughed on, the great red wings on its back raised. It brought its beak from the water, letting out its call, something painfully loud but also joyous, as if it celebrated seeing Skearith's Eye. Within the sound Joron heard so many beautiful and complex melodies that it moved him to tears, and he turned from those around him to wipe the moisture from his eye.

"Well," said Dinyl, "if anyone within a hunth of this passage was in doubt we are here, that doubt is dispelled now."

They flew on for four days without sign of another ship, and had they not been running towards a battle Joron believed they could not win, it would have been pleasant. Had *Tide Child* not creaked and groaned through damage, or been tied to the path of the arakeesian he was sure they would have flown like never before. They had perfect winds, flat seas. Far to the north the dark line of the Northstorm, occasionally illuminated by flashes of lightning, rumbled and grumbled, but it made no move to loose its anger on them.

"Ship rising to the east!"

The call came on the fifth day, and Meas was up the spine as quick as Black Orris could take to the air. When she returned she was grim-faced and serious.

"It is the *Hunter*, coming towards us with all wings set." She glanced over the side at the arakeesian. "If only it did not choose to swim in such a leisurely fashion." Then she looked to the Northstorm, so very far away. "Call the courser for me, Joron."

Joron sent the call on to Solemn Muffaz who passed it to the underdeck.

Aelerin appeared and made their way to the rump.

"Ey, Shipwife?"

"The Northstorm," said Meas. "What chance its anger will be raised? What songs do you hear it sing? Will we get storms and rough seas any time soon?" Aelerin took a moment, then their cowl shook as they shook the head hidden beneath it.

"It grumbles and moans, but its ire is not raised yet. Another two weeks and we would be into storm season, but this weather we have now will continue, Shipwife. I am sad to bring you foul news."

"It is not your fault," said Meas, "and to be truthful, I am not sure how *Tide Child* would manage were we to be chased through a storm. *Hag's Hunter* could barrel though with his weight, our damage may well steal any speed I would hope to win."

"If only we had something they wanted," said Dinyl. "We could lead them away."

For a moment Dinyl must have thought Joron was about to strike him, so singular was his focus on him. Then Joron smiled.

"Women of the Sea, Dinyl! We do have something they want."

"We do?" said Dinyl.

"Ey. If we presume *Hunter* is waiting for the arakeesian, then it will need the weapons to hunt it, the hiylbolts. And remember *Tide Child* was searched before we left?"

"That seems a lifetime ago," said Dinyl.

"They must have been looking for the bolts. That means *Hunter* must take us or it cannot hunt."

A smile spread across Dinyl's face, then he looked beyond Joron to where Meas stood, and the smile fell away.

Joron turned. "Do you not agree, Shipwife?"

She shrugged.

"A decent thought, Deckholder," she said. "One I have had myself."

"You do not think they searched us for the hiylbolts?"

"Oh, no doubt they did," she said. "But remember, Karrad told us he tracked them down from old papers but found none where the papers said? In the end he found a forgotten store in a forgotten and ruined room?"

"I remember," said Joron.

"Do you also remember what my sither said on Bernshulme docks?"

"She crowed over her new command – I remember that."

"It seems we both go a-hunting . . . Let us see who brings

home the prize.' That is what she said. I thought she spoke of Gaunt Islands ships at the time. But now she is here, waiting for us."

"You think she spoke of the keyshan?" said Dinyl.

"Ey, I do," said Meas. "And I think the reason Karrad did not find his bolts where he expected was because my mother already had them."

"You cannot know . . ." began Joron.

Meas raised a hand.

"My mother is a very clever woman. If she had really needed what was in our hold she would simply have had us stopped and searched at the harbour mouth when she knew it far more likely all our cargo would be aboard."

"Why let us go?" said Dinyl.

"To bring the keyshan safely here, where *Hunter* waited?" said Joron.

Meas nodded.

"Then we are lost," said Dinyl. "We have no bait with which to lead *Hunter* away, and we stand little chance in a fight."

"No," said Joron. "That is not the case." Meas turned to him, raising an eyebrow. "You said your sither was impatient and impulsive?" Meas nodded. "Well, we do have something she wants, Shipwife, we have you. She was all too keen to tell you she was better than you at the dock. Surely she will want to prove that at sea."

Meas stared at him. The ship creaked and groaned and complained.

"Barlay!" shouted Meas. "Steer us three points to landward off the keyshan's course." Then she walked to the mainspine and shouted up into the tops, "Watch *Hunter* as if it brought you food and you were starving. I would know if it changes course to pursue us."

"Ey, Shipwife," floated down from above.

"Gullaime!" shouted Meas. The creature sidled over from where it had been inspecting the broken gallowbow.

"Meas?" it said.

"Bring me wind, bring it strong. I want that ship to think we are running away."

"We leave sea sither?"

"If the ship chases us, then yes. We will draw it away."

The gullaime nodded and went to the rail then started cawing and screeching at the water.

"What is it doing, Joron?" said Dinyl.

"Gullaime," asked Joron. "What do you do?"

"Tell the sea sither we go. But for it."

"Even though it cannot hear, as it is slow and we are quick?"

The gullaime *yarked* its odd laugh.

"Even though," it said, then took up its place before the mainspine and became still. The pressure rose and the wind swirled around *Tide Child*.

"Unfurl the mainwings," shouted Meas. "Stop slatelaying, lazy deckchilder. Let's find us some speed!"

Up the spines ran the crew, and the great black sails fell from the spars to catch the wind as Barlay leaned into the steering oar. *Tide Child* came about, groaning and creaking as the boom crossed the deck.

Coxward cursed and vanished below, to listen to the ship but Joron did not need to go to the bilges, ear against the hull, to know something was wrong; the sounds as *Tide Child* heeled over were too loud, too off key, as if the ship were an ancient complaining as they were forced to move from a comfortable seat.

If Meas worried she gave nothing away. She strode to the bottom of the mainspine to stand next to the gullaime, who was lost in its own world, bringing the wind that powered *Tide Child* forward. The chest beneath its robes rose and fell as the pressure in Joron's ears ebbed and flowed, making the sound of the sea around him pulse like waves on a shore. When Meas was happy with *Tide Child*'s course, she had Barlay straighten the ship, and the creaking and moaning from the ship's bones stopped.

Meas returned to the rump and stood by Joron.

"Now we will see if you were right, Deckkeeper," she said. "Aelerin!"

"Shipwife."

"If *Hag's Hunter* follows us, in the state we are in I do not think we can outrun them and *Tide Child* will not take any hard manoeuvres, so I need something else. Get to the charts and find me shallow water where *Hunter* cannot follow." Meas waited for Aelerin to vanish towards the great cabin, where the charts were kept, but they did not. "Well?" said Meas.

"Forgive me, Shipwife, but I reckoned on you wanting that or somewhere to hide. The islands here in the north are not kind to us in that way. The water is deep, the Islands low, not tall enough to hide us from *Hag's Hunter*."

Meas nodded, her eyes unfocused as she thought.

"Very well. And no sign of a storm. What chance of mist do you hear sung?"

"The Northstorm is brisk now as it runs up to the time of tempers. It sings only a slow gaining of anger in the winds."

Meas nodded.

"So, no mist, nowhere to hide and nowhere to play clever tricks."

"What do we do?" said Dinyl.

"We string them along," said Meas, "for as long as we can."

"But our mission," said Dinyl. "The keyshan must die in the Northstorm, and—"

"Quiet yourself, Deckholder," she hissed.

Dinyl stared at Meas, and Joron saw suspicion return to his face.

"You do remember our mission?" he said quietly.

"Do not think to remind me of what I do or do not remember," said Meas through gritted teeth. "Ask such questions in front of the crew again and I will break you to the deck, do you understand?"

Dinyl bowed his head, took a step back.

"Of course, Shipwife," he said.

They flew on, the ship skimming across the waves, and after ten turns of the glass the call came from above.

"It follows! *Hag's Hunter* follows!"

Meas walked to the far rear of the ship and raised her nearglass.

"It is already larger in the glass than I would like. Kyrie must be showing her gullaime no mercy."

"How long?" said Joron. He had no need to give any further detail.

Meas gazed through her nearglass, taking her time. The sea rose and fell without care.

"Not long enough, Deckkeeper. Not long enough. Go below, Joron, find the crate with the hiylbolts and make sure they are readily accessible. And put three wingbolts in the crate with them. If it comes to it, the crate goes over the side. We will not give Kyrie more ammunition."

Joron glanced around, making sure no crew were near.

"Why not just do it anyway? Now."

"Because Dinyl was right: we have our duty, and I have not given up all hope. I am a better shipwife than my sither. We may yet carry the day." She raised her nearglass again. "You have work to do, Joron," she said, and he knew himself dismissed.

It was hard work in the hold, damp and stuffy and stinking, but the crate of hiylbolts was eventually found. As he was struggling to drag the box up the stairs, he found himself face to face with the gullaime.

"Joron Twiner," it said.

"You are not needed on deck?"

"Wind shifted," it said. Then it sniffed twice. "Smell death, Joron Twiner."

"This is why *Hag's Hunter* chases us, and not the arakeesian." He nodded at the box. "It is bait."

The gullaime took a step closer.

"Not lie, Joron Twiner," it said, then touched its open beak with a wingclaw and Joron was enveloped in the smell of hot sand. "Tasted your blood."

A sudden shift, a scent of rain on the air, a knowledge of the currents moving around the ship that was not his, all experienced with senses he did not possess, and then he was looking at his own face. Dark skin, wiry hair escaping the one-tailed hat that clung tightly to his skull, and the lie was there on his face as bright as paint splattered on a doorway. Then he was back, staring into the painted eyes of the gullaime's mask.

"It is not my decision," he said.

"Is hers?"

"Yes." And he felt the gullaime deserved an explanation. "She wants to save lives."

"Many lives need saved," it said, then shuffled past him him and down the narrow stairs before turning at the bottom. "Gullaime live too." It vanished into the gloom, but its voice came sailing back, though not its voice as he had known it, not the harsh croak he was used to, something different and sweeter, something he felt sure only he could hear:

"You know the song, but you would lose it for ever."

And he did know the song. The song had been growing in his mind since he had touched the windspire on Arkannis Island, but he did not know what it meant or what it was for − or if it was for anything at all.

"Joron!" The call came from above and he returned to his shipwife. A brisk wind filled the wings of *Tide Child*, pushing him over the water at a speed that, if not breathtaking, was impressive.

It was not enough.

Behind them, *Hag's Hunter* loomed. How long had be been in the hold? Ten, twenty turns of the glass? When he held up his hand and looked back, the topspines of *Hag's Hunter* stuck up above his fingers.

"Impressive, is he not?" said Meas.

"Yes," he replied. Because it was true. Blue corpselights burned above the ship, bone-white hull smashing through the sea, sending up great clouds of spume. Vast wings caught the wind, a tower of white cloud above the ship.

On the rump Coxward stood by Meas.

"We cannot outrun it, Shipwife," he said. "*Tide Child*'s bones simply will not take much more." Joron glanced up into the sky. Skearith's Eye was well down in its journey to the horizon. "The *Hunter* will not catch us before night though," the bonemaster added. "*Tide Child* does what he can."

"Will they attack at night?" said Joron.

Meas nodded.

"If Kyrie wants me, and to get back to the keyshan before it makes the high northern currents, then she must."

"So we run on?"

Meas closed up her nearglass.

"No, Joron. We are tired, and as Coxward says, the ship is tired also — we have flown across the entire Archipelago and we will only get more tired. If I thought we could run, I would run. But Kyrie will catch us." Meas placed the nearglass inside her coat. "For as long as I have know her, Kyrie has desired our mother's favour more than any other thing, and here she sees her chance to win it. She will show no quarter." There was an alarming groan, and Meas put her hand on the spine, as if to comfort the ship. "*Tide Child* has served us well, and I had hoped to lead the *Hunter* on for longer. But it seems we do not have that luxury." She glanced at Coxward, who bowed his head as if shamed at his inability to do more for the ship. "To have any chance, I fear we must turn and fight, Joron. While we still can."

"Do we have a chance?"

She put a hand on her sword hilt.

"There is always hope. We attack while it is still light so that when we go at it the bowsells can aim for *Hunter*'s stern, where the steering oar engages the tiller. Damage that enough it will—"

"We have to get past the *Hunter*'s bows first, Shipwife," said Dinyl. "And it has three decks of them."

"Bother me not with details." She stared at the larger ship a moment longer before turning to Dinyl and Joron. "We are a ship of the dead. Sentence has been given: we only wait for it to be carried out." She turned from them. "Now, I have told you I intend us to go into action. Why are my decks not being cleared?"

38

The Hag Opens Her Arms, and Deckchilder Sink into Them

Joron walked the slate. He wore his best, and only, fleet jacket – fishskin of dark blue, Mevans had re-dyed his hair so streaks of bright blue now ran through the black and he had braided his hair the way Mozzan of *Snarltooth* had shown him. Mevans had re-dyed Meas's hair too and colourful streaks ran through the grey.

Tide Child turned in a vast circle, nursing his cracked keel and damaged hull. The gullaime squatted in the centre of the deck, bringing the winds, gentle and sweet, that turned the ship and filled his wings – the currents the windtalker brought barely made Joron's ears ache. As soon as they started their turn *Hag's Hunter* had turned also, keeping his beak on them, a pointing finger kept on his intended prey.

Joron did not know quite why he had chosen his best clothes to die in; it just seemed right.

The ship was cleared for action and pristine, shot and bolt stacked on the cracked slate of the deck, teams standing to attention by their bows. All those not working were lined up on deck, neatly arrayed, dressed in their best, and Joron noticed that each and every one of them had a blue tint to their clothes, just like Meas, just like him. He passed Farys, her burned face twisted into a smile, and gave her a nod. Gavith stood by her. It felt odd to see Farys without Old Briaret, but that would not matter soon. He passed down the lines, a word here and there: the odd admonishment for a poorly turned-out bit of clothing or a mark not fully excised from the deck, but they were small things, said jokingly.

He realised as he passed, as he studied their faces – scarred, dirty, deformed but above all familiar – that he had undersold these women and men from the start. He had thought them simple, accepting Meas as an almost magical being who would guide them through danger. He had heard them speak as such, but now, as he moved among them, he realised how wrong he had been. The old hands, the steady deckchilder, those who had roved the sea, drifted along its currents – they knew the truth. It was not unheard of for a four-ribber to take down a five. Not impossible by any means. And had the ship not been so damaged, had they not been so brittle, had they not been so undercrewed, then no doubt every woman and man among them would have backed Meas to win.

But the ship was brittle and damaged.

The ship was undercrewed.

The stories he had heard from his father, that buoyant sense of self-belief that only a fleet ship knew, he understood them now. They were not real. They were just tales spun by old hands to steady those below them: to stop any wavering, to calm fears, to make the inevitable feel unlikely, to conjure hope from nothing. But in the older faces he saw the truth. They knew they went to their deaths, that *Tide Child* flew towards an inexorable fate. That deep below the sea the Hag opened her arms ready to welcome them. And each and every one of them, each woman and man, had accepted that. They did not wail or cry or shake. Where Joron had to put his hands behind his back, clasp them together to make sure he did not give away his fear, there was an easy jocularity among the crew – a smile for him, for the deckchilder around them. They were content. Sentence had been pronounced, and now it would be carried out.

"My crew, my fancy crew." The words came from the rump, and Joron turned to see Meas. Dinyl stood to landward of her, Narza behind her, and while she surveyed her crew and they looked back at her, seeming to stand a little taller as they did, he joined her. Anzir came to stand behind him and when Joron stood by Meas his hands no longer threatened to shake. The images of his body being ripped apart, pierced with bone or burned alive faded from his mind, and he found he understood how the crew did it.

Here, at this moment, he also accepted his fate. Not because he wanted to die, but because he knew there was no other option. Dinyl had talked of duty; his father had talked of duty, and now he knew he would do his. So he stood and he listened to his shipwife speak.

"I will not lie to any woman or man among you," said Meas. "It looks bleak for us." She let those words settle in. Chains in the rigging chimed, the wind whistled through the ropes and the wings cracked. "But I have been in bleak situations before, and walked away. For I am Lucky Meas, I am the witch of Keelhulme Sounding, and you are my crew. Now, my girls and my boys, I have flown bigger ships, and I have flown far more prestigious ships and I have flown newer ships." She paused again, taking her time, letting her words sink in. "When I came aboard this ship, you were nothing. Rabble. Drunks. Fools."

"Some still are!" A shout from the back, and there was laughter, but Meas did not join in.

"Calm those words!" she shouted. "For you are not those things. You are a crew now! And you are my crew. And as there is no better shipwife in the Scattered Archipelago than I, than Lucky Meas Gilbryn" – her voice was as serious, harsh and rising like the clouds of the Northstorm – "Then I say, there is no better crew than that which fly with me! And that great ship out there!" She pointed at Hag's Hunter. "It outmatches us, most would say. And they would be right." She looked up and down the rows of crew. "But only in size and bows. And you" – her gaze focused on Farys, roved across the crew – "and I and Dinyl and Joron, we will take that ship on, unafraid. They sent us to kill a keyshan," she shouted, "and maybe we will not manage that, but they also sent us to stop anyone else taking that keyshan. They sent us to make our families, our children and the children of so many others safer. If I die doing that, then that is enough for me! Is it enough for you?"

"Ey," said Barlay. "It is enough for me."

"And the rest?" said Meas.

"Ey." Ones and twos from the deck.

Then Mevans' shouted.

"Is that the best we can do? I say ey! We all say ey! 'Tis a great thing to do, to save the future! Ey?"

A pause. Then Farys stepped forward.

"I say ey!"

Then the cabin boy, Gavith.

"And I say ey!"

Then Karring, the swimmer.

"'Tis ey from me."

And Solemn Muffaz.

"I say ey!"

Then the whole crew were shouting, and it was deafening. "Ey! Ey! Ey!" And then from somewhere in the dense crowd on the slate came another shout: "For Lucky Meas!" And that was taken up, repeated, chanted until Meas had to quieten them, and did Joron see a glistening in her eye? Or did he fool himself?

"We will do our best to beat that ship," she shouted, pointing once again at *Hag's Hunter* as it made its serene way forward, seeming to glide across the sea, eight bright corpselights in tow. "But above all we shall stop it taking the keyshan and prolonging the war that eats our people's lives. To do that, we must destroy his tiller, and to do *that*, we must cross *Hunter's* gallowbows. I shall not pretend that it will not be fearsome. I shall not pretend that all will walk away. The Hag will take her due today. But when we have taken out his tiller *Hunter*'s size will mean nothing. We shall leave that ship in no state to chase the keyshan. I would rather the beast escaped than provide its bones for more war, and I shall consider my life well spent if that is all I do." Silence. "Now," she said, and lifted her sword, raised her voice. "Untruss my bows! Let us go to war!"

There should have been a cheer then, but there was not; for a moment there was only a heavy silence as what Meas had said sank in – that this was truly to be the day they died. Then a shout came from the crowd, the voice of Garriya, the woman Mevans had insisted be brought aboard as lucky, a small and unkempt presence among the deckchilder.

"Sing for us, Joron Twiner," she said. "Sing us to our grim work."

Joron had not sung since his father had died, but after a moment's faltering hesitation the words came. He opened his mouth and he sang a song his father had sung to him as a child. But the tune was not the one his father had used. Oh it was similar, but subtly changed, familiar and yet not familiar. He sang the song of the windspire, the song he heard when he dreamed of moving, free and vast, beneath the ocean.

> I'll not deny the Hag my love,
> Let us fly to her in pride.
> I'll not deny the Hag my love,
> For duty have I died.
>
> I've always loved the sea, my love,
> So deep and blue and true.
> I've always loved the sea, my love,
> As much as I loved you.

And when he had finished the first chorus, after they had got used to the strangeness of the tune, the crew joined with the familiar words of the deckchild's lament.

I'll not deny the Maiden love,
I'll play her games and sport.
I'll not deny the Maiden love,
I'll die as I was taught.

I've always loved the sea, my love,
So deep and blue and true.
I've always loved the sea, my love,
As much as I loved you.

The gullaime joined them, calling out a counterpoint, a harmony beyond the ability of any human, singing many notes at a time and changing the song, bending it, twisting it.

I'll not deny the Mother love,
She birthed me into life.
I'll not deny the Mother love,
So to honour her I'll die.

I've always loved the sea, my love,
So deep and blue and true.
I've always loved the sea, my love,
As much as I loved you.

I'll not deny the Hag my love,
Let us fly to her in pride.
I'll not deny the Hag my love,
For duty have I died.

As the last bars of the song died away, Joron could feel a change. He did not know if anyone felt as he did, but from the way they looked to one another there was definitely some awareness that a difference had come upon them. A sudden energy. As if the ship shivered. And there was some hope, some possibility that they were not completely lost, that they may stand a chance.

Meas glanced at Joron and spoke quietly.

"A good choice of song, Joron. It has lifted our spirits." Then she raised her voice. "Well! What do you stand around for? To the bows! Set the wings! Have the flukeboats put overboard. Bring up the hagspit and we'll fire the bolts we send at them. Get yourselves moving! I do not allow slate-layers on my deck!" And all was life and action.

Joron put a hand on the rail. It felt as if the whole ship vibrated, but not from the many feet that ran across the decks and up the spines. This was something else. He turned to find Garriya standing behind him.

"What just happened?

She smiled her toothless smile at him.

"You gave us a chance," she said. "Now I should get to the hagbower before the hagshand kills anyone."

"But there is no one down there yet."

"Do not underestimate his incompetence."

Behind her the gullaime cackled.

"Death, Joron Twiner. Death is coming."

"Enough of that." Meas's voice cut across the deck. "Gullaime, come to me. You too, Joron."

As Joron crossed the deck he watched the profile of *Hag's Hunter* change as he came around, angling to make a pass at *Tide Child*, side on side. When he looked back, the gullaime was before Meas in a posture that, had it been human, he would have taken as subservient, but something about the gullaime made it only appear curious. It was crouched down before her, head angled up to look at her as she spoke. "Can you speed us past the *Hunter* and call up enough wind to throw off their shot at the same time?"

The windtalker let out a harsh croak. Black Orris came fluttering down from the rigging to land on Meas's shoulder. The windtalker angled its head towards *Hag's Hunter*.

"Twelve of the nest ride that ship." Then it called again, opening its beak and making a swallowing motion as the noise rose into the air. "They will fight me. I will fight them. Speed or shot, Meas Gilbryn. Speed or shot. Speed easier." It let out a throaty croak."Think less. Keep strength longer."

Meas stared at the enemy ship, at the great gallowbows on its maindeck, at the the two decks below, bowpeeks raised to reveal smaller but still fearsome bows. It appeared to Joron that she stared past it and into the future, into the moment the bows loosed and the shot flew and her crew were dying around her. Her landward foot tapped on the slate.

"Which would you choose, Joron?"

He tried to imagine twenty-seven gallowbows sending their deadly cargo across the sea. Gullaime guiding them home. The devastation, the maiming, the pain.

"You know *Hunter*'s shipwife," he said. "How fast will they loose their bows?"

A pause before she answered, and she did so with a touch of pride.

"Fast enough."

"Then speed," he replied. "She chases us out of pride, to best you. She won't want to do it with fired wingbolts, not with us so outclassed. So we are safe from burning, I reckon. I imagine she'll want to be able to feel like it was a fair fight. We just have to hope the spines survive what she sends at us, then we can loose for their tiller and hope to cripple them."

Meas nodded.

"Dinyl?"

"It is a Hag's deal," he muttered. "I would say the opposite of Joron: protect the spines from shot at all costs, even if it leaves the gullaime dried out on the deck. Without spines we have nothing." She nodded at that too.

"A Hag's deal indeed," she said, "but I think speed, in this instance, is the better choice of two bad ones."

"Do we lie flat," said Dinyl, "and take our punishment?"

Again Meas stared into the future, seeing the carnage and what she hoped to get from it.

Joron touched the birdfoot on a string that hung around his neck, the one his father had given him for luck. *I shall see you at the bonefire soon*, he thought. *And I have missed you so much.*

"No, we stand," she said. "I don't want Kyrie to guess what we are about, so we must answer them shot for shot. To see their bright blue corpselights dim a little will give the crew some cheer." She raised her voice. "You hear me? We'll not simply let him rake us! Spin the bows! Load the shot. Gullaime, fill our wings with wind!"

Sudden activity, every body on the ship moving. Coughlin's men climbing up into the rigging with their bows, though Joron doubted the ships would pass near enough for them to be of use.

And *Hag's Hunter* came on. Beautiful and implacable.

"Load our wingbolts for fire," shouted Meas. "We'll gain nothing here from mercy." Hagspit was measured. Torches passed around.

Joron's ears hurt as the gullaime brought the wind to them, and *Tide Child* leaped forward, a great wave kicking up from the front and a great groan coming from his hull. Joron hurried to stand by the mainspine, Dinyl going on to the forward spine and Meas remaining by the rumpspine.

And *Hag's Hunter* came on. Parallel to them now but passing in the opposite direction, his decks full of women and men.

"Spin the bows!" shouted Joron.

And the calls came down the maindeck: "Bow spun, D'keeper." And the calls came from the underdeck: "Bow spun, D'keeper."

"Load the bows!" shouted Joron.

And the biggest, the heaviest of the stone wingbolts were placed on the shafts. And the calls came down the maindeck: "Bow loaded, D'keeper." And the calls came from the underdeck: "Bow loaded, D'keeper."

"Put fire to 'em if you have it!" shouted Joron.

And on the maindeck hagspit oil was carefully poured and torches applied. Flames flickered above the bows. And the calls came down the maindeck: "Bow fired, D'keeper."

"Aim!" shouted Joron.

The heads of the bows came round to track the mass of *Hag's Hunter*.

Hunter's bows came round to track *Tide Child*.

And the calls came down the maindeck: "Bow aimed, D'keeper." And the calls came from the underdeck: "Bow aimed, D'keeper."

The moan of wind passing over tensioned cord filled the air.

It felt, to Joron like the whole ship, in unison, breathed in. Held that breath. Enjoyed the moment, the smell of the sea, the wind on their faces. He wished it could last for ever.

"Loose!" He did not need to shout it, did not need to scream it out as every ear on the ship was turned to him, awaiting that word. And on that word the bows released. And as *Tide Child*'s bows loosed so did *Hag's Hunter*'s, as if the two ships were somehow tied together, and the moment, the second of stillness, was torn apart with such violence as Joron had never known.

The whole ship felt as though it was punched a length backwards. Spars and rigging torn away; the hull rang with impacts, and the air full of the whistle of flying debris. A half-second of shocked silence. Then the screaming of the wounded and dying, the crash of falling rigging and wings. Joron ducked, covering his head as a mass of ropes and spars fell around him.

"Spin the bows!" His voice, coming out of his mouth, loud, almost without volition. Wounded being dragged away from the bows. Dead going overboard. Crew filling empty spaces. Blood, dark in the sand.

"Bow spun, D'keeper." Was that one answering or all of them? No matter. A body hit the deck by him, an arm ripped away by shot. A face screamed.

"Load the bows!" Women and men moving. Hauling the great stones up. The wind still blowing. The gullaime standing just down from him. Gavith running past, scattering more sand on the slate. Someone sobbing.

"Can you control the wind from belowdeck, Gullaime?"

The mask turned to him.

"Yes, yes."

"Then do it. Stay safe. We need the wind."

"Bows loaded, D'keeper!"

How was he thinking?

How was he thinking when that huge ship was slowly sliding past them, not two hundred spans away, readying to loose again? One round of shot had wreaked such havoc on *Tide Child* like he could not believe. How was he thinking? And yet he was.

"Aim the bows!"

Were they keeping up with *Hag's Hunter*? Were his bowteams as fast as those on the fleet ship opposite them?

"Bows aimed, D'keeper!"

"Then lo—"

Bolts incoming. The *thruuum*, the howling through the air, the smashing of rock into bone. Something plucked at his leg, knocked him to the deck. A massive spar came down. landing on the second gallowbow, flattened the women and men around it, cracked the slate, creating runnels which blood flowed along. Branching streams of red reaching out for him. The air full of dust as a mainwing came down. A shroud of black material covering him.

Pushing against it, fighting off the sudden darkness.

"Loose!" Shouting into a void. "Loose the bows for the Mother's sake!" Could they even hear him? "Loose! Loose!" *Light!* He saw light! Crawling from under the variskcloth. *Oh, Mother's mercy!* Only one bow left working on the deck, the others either smashed or swinging free. But there, standing at its aiming point, was Meas. The bow launched, the underdeck bows launched. Bolts sailed through the air. A corpselight above *Hag's Hunter* flickered yellow and vanished as *Tide Child's* bolts smashed through sails and spars.

Trying to stand, his legs betraying him.

Shouting.

His voice hoarse.

Throat burning.

"Spin! Spin the bows, Hag take you." And women and men running to do it. But so few. So very few.

Time. Time trickling by. The grains in the glass. The blood on the sand on the shattered slate deck.

Before the reply, before the expected shout of, "Bows spun, D'keeper!" Meas screaming.

"Down! Get down!"

Then he is on the deck, face in the grit, teeth clenched as the shot comes. No duty to concentrate on. Trying not to scream in terror and horror. The noise of it. The unbelievable noise as bolts tear into *Tide Child*. Sounds of such violence he can barely believe he lives through them. When it stops he rolls on to his back. Clouds around the ship. Hag's mercy, are they hidden by mist? No, not clouds, not mist. Dust. Clearing slowly. Drifting away from *Tide Child* in a light breeze. Showing him the mainspine. Cracks running hither and thither around it.

A dull groan.

A sharp, high crack.

A terrible moan from *Tide Child* as the mainspine starts to lean. A pause as the rigging holds it. For a moment it is still. Then a hundred whipcracks as the topweave gives way. Ropes like knives snapping through the tops. Cutting through whatever, whoever, they touch.

The whole lot comes down.

Mainspine first, dragging the rumpspine with it, and the weight of the two together snaps off the top third of the for'ard spine. The tangle of ropes, spars, tackle and raggedy wings all coming down. A great plume of water as it hits the sea, slewing over *Tide Child's* deck, in a wave, washing over Joron, washing back tinged with red. The drag of broken wings in the water brings *Tide Child* to a halt and pulls the deck over to rest at a giddy angle.

Meas, shouting.

"Axes! Cut the spines free before they drag us over!" Joron sees her. Staring round her ruined ship. Watching as crew – one, two, three – try to drag themselves up. Joron tries and his legs give way beneath him. He sees her, sees her look around. Sees the momentary look of utter despair. Then she stands on the remains of the shattered landward rail and pulls her two-tailed hat off. Waving it in the air, her hair flying free in the breeze. "We are done!" she shouts. "We are done!" She throws the hat into the sea so the crew of *Hag's Hunter* can see her surrender.

They wait.

They wait.

More women and men appear on the deck. In ones and twos. In threes and fours. Limping, bloodied, dust covered.

And they wait.

Wait to see if the *Hunter* accepts.

Wait to see if the three decks of bows will loose again.

Wait as the huge ship slows.

Have they even touched him? All this death and destruction and have they even really touched him? But then Joron sees the corpselights, only seven now, and four of those faded to lastlight. Sees *Hag's Hunter*'s pristine white wings full of holes. Rigging that hangs loose from his spars and blood that runs bright red down the side of the ship, is smeared along his side.

He tried to get to Meas, and found his right leg worked but his left would barely support him. Not broken though, bruised maybe, painful. He found a piece of spar to lean his weight on and joined her at the rail. It was so quiet. Faces on the other ship staring at them.

"Why stop, Shipwife?" he said. "We are a ship of the dead, we are here to die."

"For a reason, Joron." Her voice was harsh and he wished he had some water for her. "We die for a reason. The spines are gone and we cannot fight. The underdeck is a wreck. Look over the side if you doubt me." He did not. "Now we try and buy time for the wakewyrm to get as far away as it can. That is the most we can do."

"You fought well, Meas, my sither." The call from the other ship sounded oddly unreal, distorted by distance and the movement of the waves between the two craft. *Hunter's* shipwife stood on her rail, a speaking cone at her mouth to amplify her voice. "You have nothing to be ashamed of. You never stood a chance really, not on that wreck. Not against me. It would be good to give Mother your account of my victory. Let all hear how I bested you and I will let your crew live."

Meas did not reply. Only stayed there, staring at the other ship.

"She lies of course," said Meas quietly. "She always did lie."

"Come, Meas," Kyrie shouted.

"You are to call me Shipwife!" Meas shouted across the sea. "You have not earned the familiarity of my name. A child could have beaten us with a ship like yours. So you will call me Shipwife. And if you wish to ignore my rank and tell our mother you truly bested me, then bring your blade over here and earn the right to do so."

The sound of the sea against the hull. The gurgle of water moving within the stricken ship.

"Admit you are beaten by a better shipwife, Meas," Kyrie shouted. "I'll not let you goad me into some last-ditch fight for glory. I have my bows loaded. I have my bows aimed. I will smash your ship to shards and your story will end here and none will ever know of this brave last stand. I shall tell Mother the great Lucky Meas ran her ship aground on a reef and died."

Joron saw Meas take a deep breath. Then she whispered:

"Get below, Joron. You may yet survive." She turned from him and shouted, "I'll give you nothing. So loose your bows, coward!"

"Very well. I had no wish to . . ." Kyrie's words died away. The deckchilder arrayed along the rail of *Hag's Hunter* were pointing towards *Tide Child*.

Why?

Joron did not understand. Then a shout went up from *Hag's Hunter*. A roar.

"Keyshan!" The word was drawn out, elongated in a mixture of wonder, elation and terror. "Keyshan rising!"

Joron turned. A mountain of frothing water rose behind them, taller than Shipshulme Island, and from it came the Keyshan, mouth open – a cave of teeth – white eyes burning, skin undulating with a million colours. It called; the noise so loud it made *Tide Child* shake. At the moment he thought they must be dashed to pieces by it, the sea-dragon dived and *Tide Child* was lifted by a massive smooth hill of liquid, which pushed him up and towards the sky. Then Joron was running to the rail, despite the pain in his leg. Staring over the side as the huge body of the wakewyrm passed below them, pale skin blueing as it dived. He saw the shadows of flippers come out, beat twice, and the shape of its body changed.

Rising.

Keyshan rising.

White eyes burning in the depths.

Hearing the song, the song, the song.

So loud. Huge mouth opening.

Ship rising!

The *Hag's Hunter* rising.

Rising from the sea. Clasped about his middle the mouth of the wakewyrm *Tide Child* had shepherded across the oceans of the Scattered Archipelago.

The beast

Massive.

Awe in form of flesh.

Women and men no doubt screamed as the *Hag's Hunter* was thrust from the water, the Hunter's hull below the waterline bright green with weed. Held in jaws longer as the massive ship. The keyshan rose, and rose, its body growing and thickening as more and more of it was propelled from the water by its tail. To Joron it seemed impossible that something so huge could rise so far. He watched deckchilder fall screaming from the ship, and then, at the height of the keyshan's breach, it closed those huge jaws. Its teeth, each as big as a tall man, grinding through the hull of *Hag's Hunter*. Joron imagined the horror and panic in the underdeck of the ship as its bones closed in on them, crushing them. Then the wakewyrm let itself fall sideways into the sea, smashing *Hag's Hunter* into the water. Breaking it in two. An immense wave surged out from the site of the keyshan's impact, swamping *Tide Child*, and if not for Meas screaming awed deckchilder to the pumps Joron had no doubt they would have sunk under the weight of the freezing liquid. And all was action as the water soaked him to the skin.

Washed him clean of battle.

"Joron Twiner." He turned. The gullaime stood by him, resplendent in its feathers. "We sang, Joron Twiner," it said. "We sang. And it heard."

And as if in answer, the keyshan sounded, that impossibly loud sound filling Joron with fear and awe and beauty.

For he was alive.

It was good to be alive.

39

A Really Needed Skill

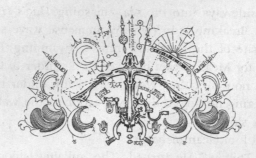

*T*ide Child lay in the water while her women and men —
those who still survived or were not, like fearsome Narza
and loyal Anzir, lying wounded in the hagbower — worked on
his bones to try and make him seaworthy. Holes were patched
under the watchful eye of Bonemaster Coxward. The wingwrights reported one full and two half-height spines could be
rigged from what they had recovered — enough to get them
moving at least. And as they worked, the keyshan lay by them,
unmoving, huge, its eyes blazing from the water.

Joron was in the hold, sorting out what must be kept and
what could be thrown overboard to lighten the ship, when he
heard a noise that — though not alien — should not be heard
at this moment when all worked simply to keep *Tide Child*
afloat. More, it was a noise that sent fear through him. The
grind of moving handles, the complaining of bone arms as
they were drawn back, the shiver of a tight cord.

Someone was spinning their last remaining great bow.

He ran.

Up through the ship. Jumping over wreckage, chunks of
bone strewn across the dark underdeck. Bits of body. Blood
making his footing treacherous. *What now?* What attacked

now? This was unfair. They had nothing left. They were done. Finished. Spent. Had given their all.

Up a ladder, his curnow thudding against his thigh. Past smashed bowpeeks and bows. Women and men watching his flight and then, as if drawn by it, following him. Emerging into the bright, cold day above. Feeling the heat of the arakeesian to seaward on his face. At the same time hearing Meas's voice. Loud. Furious.

"What goes on here?"

Dinyl was standing by the last remaining gallowbow with two deckchilder and the crate of poisonous hiylbolts.

"We have a duty," he said, "to end the keyshan, end the killing."

"To be carried out in the far north" — she stamped over to him — "and at my order. Not here. Not at your order."

But Dinyl stood his ground.

"We cannot get to the far north," he said. "If the arakeesian chooses to swim, we cannot keep up with it. Not with the ship how it is. All can see that."

"If it dies here," said Meas, "we simply provide a corpse to be picked over, and all can see that too."

"Who will find it here? Who will see it here? We are as far north as we will ever get," said Dinyl, "and we have a duty."

"Not kill sea sither." The gullaime had appeared from below-deck. It made no move to approach Meas, Dinyl and Joron, only stood by the hatch to the underdeck amid a mass of tangled rope and broken spar, occasionally clacking its hooked beak shut. "Not kill sea sither," it said again.

"It is the last," said Dinyl. He looked around, found the whole crew watching him. "Do you not understand? This is what have fought for. When it is gone, there will be no more boneships built." His eyes were wide, and Joron knew in that moment that Dinyl felt the terror of battle just as keenly as he did, maybe more so. "No more dead children." He turned to the gullaime. "No more blinded gullaime. No more battles like the one we have been through."

"Not kill sea sither," it said again.

"It is the last!" shouted Dinyl. "The bow is loaded. We can end it all. Go back, report this place to Kept Indyl Karrad. He will have the corpse towed away. This will be the end of war."

But for his voice the only sound was the lapping of the sea against the ship and the grind of the pumps.

"Not last," said the gullaime.

"What?" Meas stepped forward, standing within an arm's length of Dinyl and Joron. "What do you mean it is not the last?"

"More come," said the gullaime. "Sea sither is first only."

Joron glanced to seaward. The great head of the arakeesian lay in the water, one burning eye regarding them as if it were unconcerned with its own mortality.

"If that is true," said Dinyl, "then it is even more important it dies. Indyl Karrad can use the bones. Sell them. We can use the money to forge alliances." He locked eyes with Meas. "We can still change our world."

"What do you think, Joron?" Meas said.

And Joron, to his own surprise, found he did not hesitate.

"It saved us," he replied. "We needed it and it came. It seems a poor way to repay it, to put a bolt through its eye."

"No!" The word from Dinyl's mouth was a howl, his expression one of utter misery. "Joron, it is our duty!" Then, more quietly: "We were given a duty."

"To be fleet is about more than duty, Dinyl," said Meas. "It is about honour and it is about loyalty."

"I am loyal!" he shouted. "And I have honour. I remember my promise." He turned to the deckchild at the bow. "You, loose the bolt!"

Joron felt himself flinch, waited for the low *thruum* of the bow launching, but nothing happened. The deckchild at the trigger only stared at Dinyl.

"I obey the shipwife," she said. "I do as she orders."

Dinyl looked at her. Nodded to himself.

"Very well," he said and produced a small crossbow from behind his back. He raised it and pointed it at Meas's temple.

"Give the order, Shipwife."

"Mutiny, is it, Dinyl?"

"No." He looked miserable, sounded it. "I have no wish to remove you from command. You are the greatest shipwife I have ever served. I only ask that you give the order. Only ask you to do your duty."

"I believe my duty has changed. Somehow, that keyshan came when we needed it. Maybe death is not the answer."

"Please, Shipwife," said Dinyl. "Give the order."

"Put down the crossbow, Dinyl, and we will forget this happened." She turned so she stared at him over the weapon. "Do as I ask."

"I have done everything that has been asked of me." Was that a tear in his eye? "I have given up everything, taken on the black armband when it was asked of me. Lost my family because it was asked of me. Become a disgrace because it was asked of me. If I do not deliver what Karrad wishes, I will never remove the armband, never get back what I was. Shipwife Meas, I have no wish to kill you, but I will. All I ask is that you do what you were ordered to do when we set out."

"I told you at the beginning, Dinyl, once you wear the black band there is no taking it off."

"You make us into traitors," said Dinyl.

"She is no traitor," said Joron, taking a step closer.

"No traitor?" shouted Dinyl. "Why do you think she is here? Joron, you can convince her, please, for our friendship. Tell her to give the order."

"I will not, Dinyl." Meas smiled at Dinyl over the weapon he held in her face.

"I will kill you if I have to, Shipwife. Give the order to launch."

"No."

"Then" – his voice shook – "I am sorry for what I must do."

Joron's hand went to the curnow at his hip. Unhooking it, he brought the blade up in a fluid, skilful movement that cut cleanly through Dinyl's wrist. The crossbow bolt flew harmlessly over the side, and Dinyl staggered back, grasping his bleeding arm, his eyes wide with pain. Meas moved, and Joron saw the flash of the rockfist wrapped around her knuckles as it cracked into Dinyl's temple, knocking him to the slate, unconscious.

"Get him to the hagbower," she said, staring down at him. Two deckchilder stooped to gather him up. "Make sure his arm is seen to." She turned to Joron. "See, I told you. When you really needed the skill you would get it right."

He Joron tried to smile but could not for he knew had as much as killed a man he come to hold dear.

"It is kinder to let him die today from blood loss," he said quietly, "than to save him to be thrown to the longthresh later for mutiny."

Meas shook her head.

"Dinyl did what duty demanded of him, and I can respect that. I can not even say he may not have been right. He is a good officer and I will keep him, if he survives." She turned to the deckchild at the bow. "Those hiylbolts," she said, "they are simply weight we do not need. Put them over the side."

She watched the weapons go over the rail, and as if this was some agreed signal, the wakewyrm raised its head and opened its beak, letting out its deafening call, and Joron heard the beautiful spinning song within it. Then it began to move.

Tide Child rocked as the sea was disturbed by the beat of the keyshan's flippers. They watched it swim away, its huge body building up speed on the surface until it lowered its head and dived, massive tail rising from the sea and waving as if in farewell before disappearing into the depths.

"So," said Joron to the air, "it is over." He felt more than heard the gullaime come to stand by him. The heat of its body. The hint of a song in its voice.

"No, Joron Twiner," it said. "Now it begins."

The story will continue in book two of the Tide Child trilogy.

Appendix: Ranks in the Fleet and the Hundred Isles

Bern The ruling class of the Hundred Isles consisting of women who have birthed children well-formed and unmarred.

Berncast Second-class Citizens of the Hundred Isles. Those who are born malformed or whose mothers die in childbirth proving their blood "weak".

Bonemaster In charge of the upkeep of the ship's hull and spines.

Bonewright Specialist crew member who answers to the bonemaster.

Bowsell Head of a gallowbow team. A bowsell of the deck is in charge of all the gallowbows on each deck of a boneship.

Courser Ship's navigator and holder of the charts. Although all officers are expected to be able to navigate, the sect of coursers are specialists. They are believed to be able to dream the coming weather and hear the songs of the storms.

Deckholder Third officer, generally known as the d'older. Larger ships may have up to four deckholders, who are known as the first d'older (most senior), the second d'older, and so on.

Deckkeeper Second to the shipwife and speaks with their authority. Larger ships may have up to three deckkeepers, who are traditionally known as the d'keeper (most senior), the keepsall and the decksall.

Deckchild A crew member who has proved themselves capable of all the minor tasks required in the running of a boneship.

Deckchilder A generic term for the entire crew of a ship below the rank of whoever is using it.

Deckmother In charge of discipline aboard a boneship. A traditionally unpopular rank.

Gullaime Also called windtalker and weathermage. An avian race of magicians able to control the winds and as such invaluable to the running of a boneship.

Hagshand The ship's surgeon, who works in the hagbower. Few who go under the knife of the hagshand survive.

Hatkeep Steward to the shipwife. A post often given to a deckchild who has proved particularly loyal or clever.

Kept The chosen men of the Bern.

Oarturner In charge of steering the ship.

Purseholder In charge of the ship's funds, weapons and food supplies.

Seakeep A seasoned deckchild with thorough knowledge of a boneship and how it should be run. The seakeep is expected to run the ship if there are no officers on deck and often acts as a go-between should the crew wish to communicate something to the shipwife.

Shipmother Commander of the fleet. There are five shipmothers. The ruler of the Hundred Isles is the most senior and has four deputies. These are named for the Northstorm, the Eaststorm, the Southstorm and the Weststorm. Shipmother of the North, Shipmother of the East, etc.

Shipwife Master and commander of a ship. The shipwife's word is law aboard their ship. To disobey is punishable by anything up to being sent to a black ship or death, depending on the shipwife's whim.

Stonebound The lowest rank on a ship. Used as an insult or as a quick way of denoting that someone does not really understand how the ship works or is not fleet.

Topboy The lookouts posted at the top of a ship's spines.

Wingmaster In charge of the wings and rigging of a boneship.

Wingwright Specialist crew member who answers to the wingmaster.

Afterword and Acknowledgements

I get lost in the sea. It's one of the things that I find endlessly fascinating, hypnotic even. Never still, always changing, so many colours and shapes. It's also a huge part of our civilisation: so much of history and pre-history begins with the sea. So much of history and pre-history is lost beneath it.

I think fantasy is often about journeys, beginnings and ends and new starts, and here we are, you and I, at the end of a new start. I hope you've enjoyed your time with Joron, Meas and her crew. I probably, first of all, owe an apology to anyone who understands the tremendously complicated business of sailing a tall ship. One of my great loves is the literature of the sea, from *Moby Dick* through C. S. Forester to Patrick O'Brian, but on writing *The Bone Ships* it quickly became obvious that I had a choice between meeting a deadline and fully understanding ships (or understanding them at all – they are fiendishly complicated). So if you've read this and got annoyed with how very fast and loose I have played with sailing and navigation, mea culpa, it got sacrificed in pursuit of the story, but I hope my deep and abiding love of the sea comes through.

Books are never created in a vacuum and I wouldn't be doing this without my lovely agent, Ed Wilson, and I wouldn't be making much sense without my brilliant editor, Jenni Hill, who does her best to nudge me onto the right course, even when I might not want to be nudged. And of course, you probably wouldn't be reading this without my excellent publicist Nazia who does a great job of getting what I do out there and generally harassing me on the internet. Orbit and everyone there have been brilliant to write with and I am hugely glad I get to do it all over again with these books.

And of course, my family are massively important. Without them around me, the distraction provided by my son, support of my wife and maybe even the occasional bites from the cat, I doubt I would be doing this.

I also owe a debt of thanks to Paul Walsh who helped me out with distances, travel and my early maps; any errors (ha, any! Should say all) are my own. And my early version readers for this book, Dr Richard Clegg, Fiona Pollard, Matt Broom and Mike Everest Evans, your mixture of cheerleading and nit-picking helps me more than you will ever know. There's also a whole host of book bloggers, reviewers and BookTubers who have supported the Wounded Kingdom books, and I can't name you all for fear of forgetting someone (because we all know I would) but each and every one of you know who you are and that you have my thanks. Then there's the various people running cons, events and podcasts who have been kind enough to have me along to talk nonsense, as well as *Starburst!* and *SFX* magazine who have been hugely supportive. Also Phil Lunt, Helen Armfield and everyone else at the British Fantasy Society and the wonderful booksellers at Waterstones. You are all wonderful people and you all make me very happy.

Oh, and then there's authors. Often terrible people such as Jason Arnopp (author Xtra), or Scott K. Andrewerson (I'll get it right one day, Scott), Gavin Smith and his big green coat, Tade (don't call me Tayd) Thompson, Nicholas, the great award stealer, Eames and Sir Edward Cox who all do their best to stop me working. But largely wonderful people like Adrian Tchaikovsky, Anna Stephens, Pete Mclean, Adrian Selby, Mark Stay, Catriona Ward, James Barclay, Jeanette Ng, Gemma Todd, David Hutchinson, Ed McDonald, Jenn Williams, Tasha Suri (and Carly), Stephen Aryan, Robin Hobb (and family), Mike Brooks, Tim Pratt, Justina Robson, Gareth Hanrahan, Lucy Hounsom, Stark Holborn, Stephen Erickson, Kim Stanley

Robinson, Micah Yongo, Bradley Beaulieu and oh my I have met so many and you have all been so forebearing and my memory is so very bad. To the person(s) reading this and thinking, "Oh, but you forgot me!" nudge me and I'll put you in the next one.

I absolutely must mention Tom Parker, whose drawings have helped shape this book and its world (as well as the Wounded Kingdom before it) and they grace the chapter headings (more in the next books) and his wonderful map is in the front. As well as Hannah Wood who designed the beautiful cover that no doubt caught your eye.

Lastly, music. I always write with music and apart from my mainstays (the Afghan Whigs, Fields of the Nephilim and 16 Horsepower/Wovenhand) I've been listening to a lot of Cult of Luna and Myrkur while writing this as it seemed to match the mood. Editing has mostly been accompanied by The Last Internationale.

And, of course, I must thank you. For reading what I write, telling people about it, leaving reviews. All these things help us keep doing what we do. I hope you've enjoyed Joron's journey of discovery and that you'll follow him, Meas, the gullaime, *Tide Child* and his crew for the rest of their voyages and further exploration of the world of the Scattered Archipelago.

We will see so much.

We may break your heart.

RJ
Leeds, February 2019

extras

www.orbitbooks.net

about the author

RJ Barker lives in Leeds with his wife, son and a collection of questionable taxidermy, odd art, scary music and more books than they have room for. He grew up reading whatever he could get his hands on, and has always been "that one with the book in his pocket". Having played in a rock band before deciding he was a rubbish musician, RJ returned to his first love, fiction, to find he is rather better at that. As well as his debut epic fantasy novel, *Age of Assassins*, RJ has written short stories and historical scripts which have been performed across the country. He has the sort of flowing locks any cavalier would be proud of.

Find out more about RJ Barker and other Orbit authors by registering for the free monthly newsletter at www.orbitbooks.net.

if you enjoyed
THE BONE SHIPS

look out for

JADE CITY

by

Fonda Lee

TWO CRIME FAMILIES,
ONE SOURCE OF POWER: JADE.

Jade is the lifeblood of the city of Janloon — a stone that enhances a warrior's natural strength and speed. Jade is mined, traded, stolen and killed for, controlled by the ruthless No Peak and Mountain families.

When a modern drug emerges that allows anyone — even foreigners — to wield jade, simmering tension between the two families erupts into open violence. The outcome of this clan war will determine the fate of all in the families, from their grandest patriarch to even the lowliest runner on the streets.

Jade City is an epic tale of blood, family, honour and of those who live and die by ancient laws in a changing world.

CHAPTER 1

The Twice Lucky

The two would-be jade thieves sweated in the kitchen of the Twice Lucky restaurant. The windows were open in the dining room, and the onset of evening brought a breeze off the waterfront to cool the diners, but in the kitchen, there were only the two ceiling fans that had been spinning all day to little effect. Summer had barely begun and already the city of Janloon was like a spent lover—sticky and fragrant.

Bero and Sampa were sixteen years old, and after three weeks of planning, they had decided that tonight would change their lives. Bero wore a waiter's dark pants and a white shirt that clung uncomfortably to his back. His sallow face and chapped lips were stiff from holding in his thoughts. He carried a tray of dirty drink glasses over to the kitchen sink and set it down, then wiped his hands on a dish towel and leaned toward his co-conspirator, who was rinsing dishes with the spray hose before stacking them in the drying racks.

'He's alone now.' Bero kept his voice low.

Sampa glanced up. He was an Abukei teenager—copper-skinned with thick, wiry hair and slightly pudgy cheeks that gave him a faintly cherubic appearance. He blinked rapidly, then turned back to the sink. 'I get off my shift in five minutes.'

'We gotta do it now, keke,' said Bero. 'Hand it over.'

Sampa dried a hand on the front of his shirt and pulled a

small paper envelope from his pocket. He slipped it quickly into Bero's palm. Bero tucked his hand under his apron, picked up his empty tray, and walked out of the kitchen.

At the bar, he asked the bartender for rum with chili and lime on the rocks—Shon Judonrhu's preferred drink. Bero carried the drink away, then put down his tray and bent over an empty table by the wall, his back to the dining room floor. As he pretended to wipe down the table with his towel, he emptied the contents of the paper packet into the glass. They fizzed quickly and dissolved in the amber liquid.

He straightened and made his way over to the bar table in the corner. Shon Ju was still sitting by himself, his bulk squeezed onto a small chair. Earlier in the evening, Maik Kehn had been at the table as well, but to Bero's great relief, he'd left to rejoin his brother in a booth on the other side of the room. Bero set the glass down in front of Shon. 'On the house, Shon-jen.'

Shon took the drink, nodding sleepily without looking up. He was a regular at the Twice Lucky and drank heavily. The bald spot in the center of his head was pink under the dining room lights. Bero's eyes were drawn, irresistibly, farther down, to the three green studs in the man's left ear.

He walked away before he could be caught staring. It was ridiculous that such a corpulent, aging drunk was a Green Bone. True, Shon had only a little jade on him, but unimpressive as he was, sooner or later someone would take it, along with his life perhaps. *And why not me?* Bero thought. Why not, indeed. He might only be a dockworker's bastard who would never have a martial education at Wie Lon Temple School or Kaul Dushuron Academy, but at least he was Kekonese all the way through. He had guts and nerve; he had what it took to be somebody. Jade made you somebody.

He passed the Maik brothers sitting together in a booth with a third young man. Bero slowed a little, just to get a closer look at them. Maik Kehn and Maik Tar—now *they* were real Green Bones. Sinewy men, their fingers heavy with jade rings, fighting talon knives with jade-inlaid hilts strapped to their waists. They were dressed well: dark, collared shirts and tailored tan jackets, shiny black shoes, billed hats. The Maiks were well-known members of the No Peak clan, which controlled most of the neighborhoods on this side of the city. One of them glanced in Bero's direction.

Bero turned away quickly, busying himself with clearing dishes. The last thing he wanted was for the Maik brothers to pay any attention to him tonight. He resisted the urge to reach down to check the small-caliber pistol tucked in the pocket of his pants and concealed by his apron. Patience. After tonight, he wouldn't be in this waiter's uniform anymore. He wouldn't have to serve anyone anymore.

Back in the kitchen, Sampa had finished his shift for the evening and was signing out. He looked questioningly at Bero, who nodded that the deed was done. Sampa's small, white upper teeth popped into view and crushed down on his lower lip. 'You really think we can do this?' he whispered.

Bero brought his face near the other boy's. 'Stay cut, keke,' he hissed. 'We're already doing it. No turning back. You've got to do your part!'

'I know, keke, I know. I will.' Sampa gave him a hurt and sour look.

'Think of the money,' Bero suggested, and gave him a shove. 'Now get going.'

Sampa cast a final nervous glance backward, then pushed out the kitchen door. Bero glared after him, wishing for the hundredth time that he didn't need such a doughy and insipid partner. But there was no getting around it—only a full-blooded Abukei native, immune to jade, could palm a gem and walk out of a crowded restaurant without giving himself away.

It had taken some convincing to bring Sampa on board. Like many in his tribe, the boy gambled on the river, spending his weekends diving for jade runoff that escaped the mines far upstream. It was dangerous—when glutted with rainfall, the torrent carried away more than a few unfortunate divers, and even if you were lucky and found jade (Sampa had bragged that he'd once found a piece the size of a fist), you might get caught. Spend time in jail if you were lucky, time in the hospital if you weren't.

It was a loser's game, Bero had insisted to him. Why fish for raw jade just to sell it to the black market middlemen who carved it up and smuggled it off island, paying you only a fraction of what they sold it for later? A couple of clever, daring fellows like them—they could do better. If you were going to gamble for jade, Bero said, then gamble big. Aftermarket gems, cut and set—that was worth real money.

Bero returned to the dining room and busied himself clearing and setting tables, glancing at the clock every few minutes. He could ditch Sampa later, after he'd gotten what he needed.

'Shon Ju says there's been trouble in the Armpit,' said Maik Kehn, leaning in to speak discreetly under the blanket of background noise. 'A bunch of kids shaking down businesses.'

His younger brother, Maik Tar, reached across the table with his chopsticks to pluck at the plate of crispy squid balls. 'What kind of kids are we talking about?'

'Low-level Fingers. Young toughs with no more than a piece or two of jade.'

The third man at the table wore an uncharacteristically pensive frown. 'Even the littlest Fingers are clan soldiers. They take orders from their Fists, and Fists from their Horn.' The Armpit district had always been disputed territory, but directly threatening establishments affiliated with the No Peak clan was too bold to be the work of careless hoodlums. 'It smells like someone's pissing on us.'

The Maiks glanced at him, then at each other. 'What's going on, Hilo-jen?' asked Kehn. 'You seem out of sorts tonight.'

'Do I?' Kaul Hiloshudon leaned against the wall in the booth and turned his glass of rapidly warming beer, idly wiping off the condensation. 'Maybe it's the heat.'

Kehn motioned to one of the waiters to refill their drinks. The pallid teenager kept his eyes down as he served them. He glanced up at Hilo for a second but didn't seem to recognize him; few people who hadn't met Kaul Hiloshudon in person expected him to look as young as he did. The Horn of the No Peak clan, second only in authority to his elder brother, often went initially unnoticed in public. Sometimes this galled Hilo; sometimes he found it useful.

'Another strange thing,' said Kehn when the waiter had left. 'No one's seen or heard from Three-Fingered Gee.'

'How's it possible to lose track of Three-Fingered Gee?' Tar wondered. The black market jade carver was as recognizable for his girth as he was for his deformity.

'Maybe he got out of the business.'

Tar snickered. 'Only one way anyone gets out of the jade business.'

A voice spoke up near Hilo's ear. 'Kaul-jen, how are you this evening? Is everything to your satisfaction tonight?' Mr. Une had appeared beside their table and was smiling the anxious, solicitous smile he always reserved for them.

'It's all excellent, as usual,' Hilo said, arranging his face into the relaxed, lopsided smile that was his more typical expression.

The owner of the Twice Lucky clasped his kitchen-scarred hands together, nodding and smiling his humble thanks. Mr. Une was a man in his sixties, bald and well-padded, and a third-generation restaurateur. His grandfather had founded the venerable old establishment, and his father had kept it running all through the wartime years, and afterward. Like his predecessors, Mr. Une was a loyal Lantern Man in the No Peak clan. Every time Hilo was in, he came around personally to pay his respects. 'Please let me know if there is anything else I can have brought out to you,' he insisted.

When the reassured Mr. Une had departed, Hilo grew serious again. 'Ask around some more. Find out what happened to Gee.'

'Why do we care about Gee?' Kehn asked, not in an impertinent way, just curious. 'Good riddance to him. One less carver sneaking our jade out to weaklings and foreigners.'

'It bothers me, is all.' Hilo sat forward, helping himself to the last crispy squid ball. 'Nothing good's coming, when the dogs start disappearing from the streets.'

Bero's nerves were beginning to fray. Shon Ju had nearly drained his tainted drink. The drug was supposedly tasteless and odorless, but what if Shon, with the enhanced senses of a Green Bone, could detect it somehow? Or what if it didn't work as it should, and the man walked out, taking his jade out of Bero's grasp? What if Sampa lost his nerve after all? The spoon in Bero's hands trembled as he set it down on the table. *Stay cut, now. Be a man.*

A phonograph in the corner wheezed out a slow, romantic opera tune, barely audible through the unceasing chatter of people. Cigarette smoke and spicy food aromas hung languid over red tablecloths.

Shon Ju swayed hastily to his feet. He staggered toward the back of the restaurant and pushed through the door to the men's room.

Bero counted ten slow seconds in his head, then put the tray down and followed casually. As he slipped into the restroom, he slid his hand into his pocket and closed it around the grip of the tiny pistol. He shut and locked the door behind him and pressed against the far wall.

The sound of sustained retching issued from one of the stalls, and Bero nearly gagged on the nauseating odor of booze-soaked vomit. The toilet flushed, and the heaving noises ceased. There was a muffled thud, like the sound of something heavy hitting the tile floor, then a sickly silence. Bero took several steps forward. His heartbeat thundered in his ears. He raised the small gun to chest level.

The stall door was open. Shon Ju's large bulk was slumped inside, limbs sprawled. His chest rose and fell in soft, snuffling snores. A thin line of drool ran from the corner of his mouth.

A pair of grimy canvas shoes moved in the far stall, and Sampa stuck his head around the corner where he'd been lying in wait. His eyes grew round at the sight of the pistol, but he sidled over next to Bero and the two of them stared down at the unconscious man.

Holy shit, it worked.

'What're you waiting for?' Bero waved the small gun in Shon's direction. 'Go on! Get it!'

Sampa squeezed hesitantly through the half-open stall door. Shon Ju's head was leaning to the left, his jade-studded ear trapped against the wall of the toilet cubicle. With the screwed-up face of someone about to touch a live power line, the boy placed his hands on either side of Shon's head. He paused; the man didn't stir. Sampa turned the slack-jowled face to the other side. With shaking fingers, he pinched the first jade earring and worked the backing free.

'Here, use this.' Bero handed him the empty paper packet. Sampa dropped the jade stud into it and got to work removing the second earring. Bero's eyes danced between the jade, Shon Ju, the gun, Sampa, again the jade. He took a step forward and held the barrel of the pistol a few inches from the prone man's temple. It looked distressingly compact and ineffective—a commoner's weapon. No matter. Shon Ju wasn't going to be able to Steel or Deflect anything in his state. Sampa would palm the jade and walk out the back door with no one the wiser. Bero would finish his shift and meet up with Sampa afterward. No one would disturb old Shon Ju for hours; it wasn't the first time the man had passed out drunk in a restroom.

'Hurry it up,' Bero said.

Sampa had two of the jade stones off and was working on the third. His fingers dug around in the fold of the man's fleshy ear. 'I can't get this one off.'

'Pull it off, just pull it off!'

Sampa gave the last stubborn earring a swift yank. It tore free from the flesh that had grown around it. Shon Ju jerked. His eyes flew open.

'Oh shit,' said Sampa.

With an almighty howl, Shon's arms shot out, flailing around his head and knocking Bero's arm upward just as Bero pulled the trigger of the gun. The shot deafened all of them but went wide, punching into the plaster ceiling.

Sampa scrambled to get away, nearly tripping over Shon as he lunged for the stall door. Shon flung his arms around one of the boy's legs. His bloodshot eyes rolled in disorientation and rage. Sampa tumbled to the ground and put his hands out to break his fall; the paper packet jumped from his grasp and skittered across the tile floor between Bero's legs.

'Thieves!' Shon Ju's snarling mouth formed the word, but Bero did not hear it. His head was ringing from the gunshot, and everything was happening as if in a soundless chamber. He stared as the red-faced Green Bone dragged at the terrified Abukei boy like a grasping demon from a pit.

Bero bent, snatched the crumpled paper envelope, and ran for the door.

He forgot he'd locked it. For a second he pushed and pulled in stupid panic, before turning the bolt and pounding out of the room. The diners had heard the gunshot, and dozens of shocked faces were turned toward him. Bero had just enough presence of mind left to jam the gun into his pocket and point a finger back toward the restroom. 'There's a jade thief in there!' he shouted.

Then he ran across the dining room floor, weaving between tables, the two small stones digging through the paper and against the palm of his tightly fisted left hand. People leapt away from him. Faces blurred past. Bero knocked over a chair, fell, picked himself up again, and kept running.

His face was burning. A sudden surge of heat and energy unlike anything he had ever felt before ripped through him like an electric current. He reached the wide, curving staircase that led to the second floor, where diners were getting up and peering over the balcony railing to see what the commotion was. Bero rushed up the stairs, clearing the entire expanse in a few bounds, his feet barely touching the floor. A gasp ran through the crowd. Bero's surprise burst into ecstasy. He threw his head back to laugh. This must be Lightness.

A film had been lifted from his eyes and ears. The scrape of chair legs, the crash of a plate, the taste of the air on his tongue— everything was razor sharp. Someone reached out to grab him, but he was so slow, and Bero was so fast. He swerved with ease and leapt off the surface of a table, scattering dishes and eliciting screams. There was a sliding screen door ahead of him that led out onto the patio overlooking the harbor. Without thinking, without pausing, he crashed through the barrier like a charging bull. The wooden latticework shattered, and Bero stumbled through the body-sized hole he had made with a mad shout of exultation. He felt no pain at all, only a wild, fierce invincibility.

This was the power of jade.

The night air blasted him, tingling against his skin. Below, the expanse of gleaming water beckoned irresistibly. Waves of delicious heat seemed to be coursing through Bero's veins. The ocean looked so cool, so refreshing. It would feel so good. He flew toward the patio railing.

Hands clamped onto his shoulders and pulled him to a hard stop. Bero was yanked back as if he'd reached the end of a chain and spun around to face Maik Tar.